James Craig has worked as a journalist and consultant for more than thirty years. He lives in London w[...] Inspector Carlyle novels, *London Calling* [...] *Explain*; *Buckingham Palace Blues*; *The* [...] *rows*; *Shoot to Kill*; *Sins of the Fathers*; [...] *Violence* and *All Kinds of Dead* are also a[...]

For more information visit www.james-craig.co.uk, or follow him on Twitter: @byjamescraig

Praise for *London Calling*

'A cracking read.' BBC Radio 4

'Fast paced and very easy to get quickly lost in.' Lovereading.com

Praise for *Never Apologise, Never Explain*

'Pacy and entertaining.' *The Times*

'Engaging, fast paced . . . a satisfying modern British crime novel.' *Shots*

'*Never Apologise, Never Explain* is as close as you can get to the heartbeat of London. It may even cause palpitations when reading.' *It's A Crime! Reviews*

The Inspector Carlyle series

Novels

Short Stories

THE
CIRCUS

James Craig

CONSTABLE • LONDON

CONSTABLE

First published in Great Britain 2013 by C&R Crime,
an imprint of Constable & Robinson Ltd

Reprinted in 2017 by Constable

3 5 7 9 10 8 6 4

A CIP catalogue record for this book
is available from the British Library.

ISBN 978-1-4721-0037-5

Typeset by TW Typesetting, Plymouth, Devon

Printed and bound in Great Britain by Clays Ltd, St Ives plc

Papers used by Constable are from well-managed forests
and other responsible sources.

MIX
Paper from
responsible sources
FSC® C104740

Constable
is an imprint of
Little, Brown Book Group
Carmelite House
50 Victoria Embankment
London EC4Y 0DZ

An Hachette UK Company
www.hachette.co.uk

www.littlebrown.co.uk

ACKNOWLEDGEMENTS

This is the fourth John Carlyle novel and thanks for their help in getting it over the line go to: Polly James, Gillian McNeill, Paul Ridley, Michael Doggart, Luke Speed and Peter Lavery, as well as to Mary Dubberly and all the staff at Waterstone's in Covent Garden.

Particular mention has to go to Chris McVeigh and Beth McFarland at 451 for all their help in promoting John Carlyle online.

I will also take the liberty of doffing my cap to Richard Lewis, Simon Beckett, Ryszard Bublik, Michael Webster and William Baldwin-Charles for their enthusiasm and encouragement, without which this latest effort might well not have seen the light of day.

Of course, nothing would have come of any of this without the efforts of Krystyna Green, Rob Nichols, Martin Palmer, Emily Burns, Becca Allen, Joan Deitch and all of the team at Constable.

Above all, however, I have to thank Catherine and Cate who continue to put up with all of this when I should be doing other things. This book, like all the others, is for them.

Politics is the art of looking for trouble, finding it everywhere, diagnosing it incorrectly and applying the wrong remedies.

Groucho Marx

The closer you get, the more you smell the shit.

Adam Boulton

ONE

At least it wasn't raining.

Buttoning up his jacket against the evening chill, Duncan Brown fired up a Rothmans King Size and took a long hard drag that made his eyes water. Coughing, he stepped off the pavement, still holding in the smoke. Standing in the middle of the empty street, he pawed at the tarmac with the toe of his shoe before turning back to face the small theatre that he had just slipped out of in order to enjoy a crafty fag.

He smiled to himself: couldn't even wait for the interval! This was his second packet of the day. Wasn't he supposed to be giving up?

Finishing his cigarette, he flicked the stub towards the gutter and lit another one. The second smoke never tasted as good, but it was good enough. Inhaling, he scanned the poster for the show that his girlfriend had dragged him along to see. *A beguiling blend of puppetry, animation, music and live action ...* claimed the blurb.

Beguiling?

Uh-huh.

Flicking some ash on to the ground, Duncan blew a plume of smoke into the orange night sky. *Fucking puppets? How old was he to be watching a puppet show?* Gemma had said this show had been a hit at the Edinburgh Festival. 'Well,' he mumbled to himself, 'who gives a monkey's about that? This isn't the bloody provinces.' He glanced enviously towards the Grapes of Wrath on the corner of the street, seventy yards away. He could see the flickering TV screen hanging from the ceiling – they would doubtless be showing the Arsenal game. He wondered about heading over there, ordering a pint of London Pride and catching what was left of the second half. It was very tempting. On the other hand, Gemma would be more than pissed off if he did a runner now. Tonight was supposed to be their 'quality time' for the week, and therefore they were watching a one-man puppet show. What did *that* say about their relationship?

A loud collective groan from the pub was followed seconds later by an electronic chirp from his pocket. Grabbing his mobile, he opened the text message to confirm what he already knew: the Gunners had gone a goal down to some bunch of erstwhile no-hopers. They were playing at home, too. Finishing his second smoke, Duncan shook his head. At least he wasn't missing much. The mood at the Emirates had been ugly for some time and he could imagine the waves of frustration and bile rolling round the stadium as the team huffed and puffed to no great effect. Imagine paying a grand a season to watch that kind of crap. The manager's on borrowed time, Duncan thought, just like I am if I don't get back inside that bloody theatre sharpish.

Deleting the text, he felt the phone start vibrating while still in his hand. There was no number on the screen but he had a good idea who it was. He lifted the phone to his ear. 'Yeah?'

'Where are you?' The voice on the other end of the line sounded bored and annoyed at the same time.

'Out and about.' Duncan stepped back up on to the pavement to let a car slide past. 'What have you got?'

'We need to meet.' The source sounded like he was in a pub himself as, in the background, the commentary to the Arsenal game was clearly audible.

Duncan let out a heavy sigh. All this cloak-and-dagger bullshit was pissing him off, big time. In terms of actual column inches generated, it was proving to be a total waste of effort. 'Why?'

'There have been some developments,' the source went on.

'Like what?' he asked, not bothering to hide his growing exasperation.

'I can't talk over the phone. It has to be face to face.'

'Okay, okay.' Duncan scratched his head. He wasn't in the market for a story right now. Tomorrow was deadline day and he was sorted for Sunday's paper. It was officially the silly season for stories, and his interview with a newlywed who saw her husband devoured by a shark might even make the front page. '*I can still hear his screams in my sleep*,' she'd sobbed. The shark had never been caught. He thought about his byline under a 72-point HONEYMOON HORROR headline and smiled; it was the best piece he'd had for ages. 'How about early next week?'

'Nah, needs to be tonight.'

There was another groan from inside the pub.

'I'm busy.'

There was a pause. On the commentary, audible over the phone, he made out the phrases '*horror tackle*' and '*red card*'.

'It has to be tonight,' said the source finally, not raising his voice, thus leaving Duncan straining to hear over the background noise. 'The police have been forced to re-open their investigation into the newspaper.'

'Don't we know it,' said Duncan wearily. It had taken him the best part of two days to delete all his emails and shred every potentially incriminating scrap of paper. He seriously doubted that would be enough, if he came under close scrutiny, but it was a start.

'Some plod from Nottinghamshire is now in charge.' A sly chuckle.

'Why Nottinghamshire?'

'Why not? It was always going to be someone far removed from events in London. A fresh pair of eyes; an independent perspective. Apparently they don't have any phones worth hacking up there.'

'That doesn't surprise me.'

'Anyway, your name has come up.'

Duncan felt a spasm in his bowels. 'What?'

'They're on to you.'

Fuck, fuck, fuck . . . Duncan thought about how much he had come to hate his shitty job in the last few months.

'We need to get your story straight.'

'Yeah, yeah.' He glanced back towards the theatre; it must be time for the interval, surely. Gemma would kill him, but he would have to deal with that later. 'Do you know a pub called the Grapes of Wrath? It's on the corner of Harp Street and—'

'Too public.'

'For fuck's sake . . .'

There was a pause at the other end of the line. Then: 'Where are you right now?'

'Okay.' Duncan gave him the name of the street. 'I'm standing outside the Cockpit Arts Theatre.'

'Where's that?'

Duncan provided some perfunctory directions.

'Wait there. I won't be long.'

Standing with his back to the bar, the source watched the journalist end their call and light up another cigarette. You look stressed, he thought. Like a man not in any way in control of events.

Around him the pub was rapidly emptying as the game reached its final minutes. A couple of feet away, a trio of facsimile fans in replica shirts were moaning loudly about their team's various shortcomings. Their frustration and angst were clearly genuine. Why did grown men allow themselves to get so wound up about football? It wasn't as if they could actually do anything to influence the result. The whole thing was beyond him. Anyway, if winning was all that mattered they should support one of the financially doped teams, like Manchester City or Arsenal. Money had totally fucked the game. If you couldn't see that, you were a mug.

Finishing his Grey Goose vodka, he headed for the door, glancing up at the screen just in time to see Arsenal concede a

4

second goal. They were dead and buried now, and fans inside the stadium were streaming for the exits. Aside from the odd curse, the mood in the pub was suitably funereal. To add insult to injury, the television replays showed that the latest goal had been well offside. Some of the supporters at the bar gestured at the screen angrily; one of them started a chorus of the popular terrace lament 'The referee's a wanker', but he found no takers among his fellows and the words quickly died in his throat.

Trying not to smile, the man heading for the door shook his head; *life can be so unfair*.

As the game restarted, the fourth official signalled that there would be six minutes of added time – which, ironically, was longer than Duncan Brown had left on this earth.

TWO

No, no, no . . .

'For God's sake!' Marc Harrington tipped back his head and threw more of the white wine down his throat. After a week spent kowtowing to a bunch of unbelievably demanding Israeli clients, he had to come home to this? It just wasn't fair. Angrily, he banged the glass down on the granite worktop of the Boffi kitchen and glared at his wife. 'We spend seven million to buy a house on bloody Wellington Road and we end up stuck with the neighbours from hell.' As if on cue, the music next door ratcheted up another notch. It was now so loud that Marc imagined he could see the windows shaking. 'I told you we should have gone to Highgate, but oh no . . .'

Knowing better than to rise to the bait, Angela Harrington sipped nervously at her gin and tonic, making a face – too much tonic. They had only moved into the neighbourhood three weeks ago and already her dream home was turning into a nightmare.

'Instead we're stuck here with all these bloody chav parvenus.'

Thank you for pointing that out, Angela thought. She wanted to scream at her aggressive, know-it-all husband. Instead, she took another gulp of her overly diluted Blackwoods 60, hoping that the gin would start kicking in sooner rather than later. Maybe for the next one she would just dispense with the tonic altogether. Somewhat embarrassed, she glanced at the three-quarters-empty bottle. It had been purchased from Waitrose

6

only two days ago; not for nothing was gin known as 'mother's ruin'.

Pulling open the door of the wine cooler located in the middle of the triple fridge-freezer, Marc grabbed another bottle of Chevalier-Montrachet Grand Cru 2006. After violently removing the cork with his Legnoart Grand Cru Sommelier black acrylic corkscrew, he refilled his glass, spilling some of the £345-a-bottle wine over his lime-green Lacoste polo shirt as he did so. 'Bollocks!'

Despite everything, Angela felt a grin spreading across her lips. She quickly turned away before her husband noticed.

Taking another gulp, he gestured furiously in the direction of number 40, next door. 'That bloody boy of theirs will have been left on his own again.'

'He *is* sixteen,' Angela pointed out, her words barely audible over the rock music crashing across what the estate agent had called a 'Mediterranean-style secluded garden'.

'The parents have basically given up,' Harrington snorted.

Unlike you, Angela mused, as she clasped the remains of her G&T to her weary bosom.

'He's an idiot.' Madeleine Harrington, sixteen herself, appeared in the doorway in an AC-DC *Back in Black* T-shirt and grey jeans. Her father noted with some distaste that her platinum-blonde pixie hair had been given a red tinge since the last time he had seen her. 'Is there any wine for me?'

The music died away, before quickly building back up to another crescendo. 'Go and tell him to shut that crap off first,' her father snapped.

'It's 30 Seconds to Mars,' Madeleine said, slouching past her father and reaching into the dishwasher for a wine glass.

Her parents looked at each other blankly.

'That's the name of the band,' she explained, helping herself to some wine. '30 Seconds to Mars.' She sighed – this really was like talking to a pair of retards. 'American soft rock.'

'That little sod is thirty seconds from a good kicking,' her father grunted. By now he had the best part of a bottle and a half of Chevalier-Montrachet inside him and he could feel the alcoholic buzz feeding his fury.

'Whatever.' Madeleine took a mouthful, her expression suggesting she thought that the wine was okay but nothing special. 'Anyway, I'm not going over there. The randy little sod will try and jump me . . . again. He thinks that somehow I'm his girlfriend just because I let him come along to that party the other week. If he's not careful, Ben will give him a hammering.'

Mention of his only daughter's real boyfriend, a useless, lazy little twerp whose father was nothing more than a glorified car salesman – he sold Minis, for God's sake! – did nothing to improve Marc Harrington's mood. Another couple of gulps and his glass was nearly empty again.

'Anyway,' Madeleine grinned from behind her wine glass, 'right now he's probably in there playing with himself.'

Harrington almost choked on his wine. 'Too much information, Maddy,' he grunted.

'He's addicted to porn.' Madeleine flashed her parents the standard naughty-little-girl grin that had stood her in such good stead over the last decade or so.

That act is getting a bit tired, young lady, her father thought sourly. You're going to have to find something else.

'He made me watch some one time.'

Her father held up a hand. 'Enough!'

'Marc . . .' Angela shot her husband a look.

'Okay, okay.' Harrington took a final slug of the wine and placed his empty glass on the Calligaris Park dining table. 'I'll do it.' Like I have to do everything around here, he reflected. Pining for the quiet leafy streets of Highgate, he stormed towards the door.

THREE

Hovering on the kerbstone, Hannah Gillespie waited for a gap in the traffic. Standing at her shoulder, her friend Melanie Henderson was wittering on about some cute boy called Ricky that she'd met at the Westfield shopping centre the weekend before. Hannah was not really interested in boys; at least not since she'd got herself a man, a proper bloke.

Smiling at the thought, she clocked a couple of creeps sitting in the front of a silver Range Rover, shamelessly eyeing her up. Hannah knew exactly what they were thinking and felt the urge to gag. If her boyfriend were here, he'd give them both a good slap. They were old enough to be her dad – even older, probably. They were parked on a double yellow line, too; hopefully they would get a ticket.

Melanie gripped her arm. 'I'm sure he fancies me . . .'

'Uh-huh.' Hannah took a tentative step into the roadway, hoping that one of the passing cars would slow down to let them across. Time was pressing. She needed to get back to do her homework. Then she had plans.

Inspector John Carlyle sat in the passenger seat of an unmarked police car and watched the two girls struggling to cross the road in the face of an unrelenting stream of traffic. Catching the eye of the prettier of the pair, he saw a look of annoyance cross her face before she rudely gestured towards his car with the middle finger of her right hand. Ignoring her, he stared at his reflection

9

in the rear-view mirror. I look tired, he thought, rubbing his hand across the five o'clock shadow on his jaw. But it's more than that. Time is moving on, and it's certainly not waiting for me. The face that stared back at him contained the familiar quizzical plebeian features of yesteryear, but there was no denying the growing bags under the eyes and the suggestion of greater fleshiness under the chin. Middle age might be an increasingly amorphous concept, but there was no denying that he had reached it. His temples were now almost exclusively grey and there was even the first hint of a receding hairline. 'You're getting old, you old bastard,' he nearly said aloud. Then thought: Talking to yourself, too? Going fucking senile, sunshine.

Maybe not quite yet.

A break in the traffic allowed the two girls to reach the middle of the road.

'What do you call an exploding monkey?'

'Eh?' In the driver's seat, Sergeant Joe Szyszkowski turned to face his boss.

'It's a joke Alice told me,' Carlyle explained. 'She's been wandering round the house with a big fat joke book, picking out the ones that make her giggle.'

'Kids . . .' Joe shrugged. He was a family man himself – he had two, a boy and a girl, to Carlyle's one daughter.

'This one is her current favourite – at least it was as of last night.'

Joe nodded indulgently. With the best will in the world, other people's kids were just not that interesting.

Ignoring his sergeant's lack of enthusiasm, the inspector tried again. 'So, what *do* you call an exploding monkey?'

The girls finally made it to the pavement on the far side of the road and disappeared down another street. Releasing his seatbelt, Joe opened the car door. 'Dunno.'

'A baboom,' Carlyle cackled. 'Geddit? Ba-*boom*!'

Joe groaned as he eased himself out of his seat. 'Tell Alice from me, that's terrible,' he said.

'What d'ya mean?' the inspector protested. 'It's brilliant. A *baboom*! Outstanding. Best joke ever.'

'C'mon,' Joe said wearily. 'I should have been home more than an hour ago. Let's get this over with.'

FOUR

The Troubles. *The* Troubles ... was there ever a more boring subject in the world than Northern bloody Ireland? What the hell were these people fighting about? Like they were the only ones who ever had problems. With a sigh, Hannah Gillespie let her history textbook fall to the floor as she stretched out on the bed. As she did so, Emeli Sandé's 'Next to Me' started playing on the LG mobile on the bedside table. Grabbing her phone, Hannah opened the newly arrived message and grinned.

R u coming?

Any feeling of tiredness immediately evaporated as she typed her reply.

15 mins.

After carefully deleting the original text, Hannah jumped up from the bed. Pulling on her red Puffa jacket and Reebok trainers, she slipped out into the hall. Even with the door closed, she could hear the television in the living room. Her mum would be watching *EastEnders* with Emma, her older sister. Dad wasn't home from work yet. Heart pumping, Hannah realized it would be easy enough to leave the house without anyone noticing, but she was cuter than that. Pushing the living-room door open, she leaned against the frame. 'I'm just going out for a little while, Mum.'

Slumped on the sofa, Alison Gillespie did not look up from the couple of characters arguing on the screen.

'Going round to see Rosie for an hour,' Hannah explained.

Alison scratched her arm, eyes still glued to the television. 'Does Rosie's mum say that it's okay?'

'Of course.'

'Have you done your homework?'

'Ye-es.'

'Are you sure?'

'Sure. History. It was about the Northern Ireland Peace Process and the suspension of Stormont in 1972.'

Her mother made a kind of grunting noise that could conceivably be misconstrued as indicating that she had even the first clue about internment and the introduction of Direct Rule.

Emma shot her sister a look that said *You lying cow*, but said nothing.

Smirking, Hannah turned for the front door. 'See you later. Bye.'

'Make sure you're home by no later than nine-thirty,' her mum called after her. 'It's a school night, remember.'

FIVE

30 Seconds to Mars had moved on to 'The Fantasy' by the time Horatio Mosman flopped onto the cream Ligne Roset Togo sofa and switched on the Loewe Xelos LCD/LED HD 1080p Digital TV, flicking through the muted channels until he came to British Talent, his favourite porn channel *du jour*. For once, he had the place to himself. His parents, God bless them, had gone into Town to see something worthy at the National Theatre. Dad's firm was sponsoring a production of *South Pacific* at the National Theatre – on the South Bank – yawn! There was no way they were dragging him along to *that*. Meanwhile, his annoying siblings, sister Lizzie and brother Ignatius, were also out and about somewhere, being boring, no doubt.

All in all, this was a major result.

Sucking greedily on a bottle of ice-cold Carlsberg, Horatio loosened the belt on his Evisu jeans and settled in for a happy half hour with Debbie Armour, star of *Debbie Does Derby* and of similar shows set in various other sad little towns and cities around Britain that he knew he would never have the misfortune of having to visit. Wiping beer from his chin, he moved around on the sofa until he got himself comfortable. '*South Pacific*?' He snorted and belched. 'Hah!'

On the 40-inch screen, Debbie was enthusiastically but silently fellating an Asian man behind the counter of a fish-and-chip shop.

Mmm.

The thought of food made Horatio suddenly feel hungry. With his free hand, he reached for his mobile and pulled up the number of a local takeaway. Time to speed things up, he thought, as he listened to the phone ring.

'Forbush Pizza,' said a cheery female voice at the other end of the line. 'How can I help you?'

Having placed his order, Horatio attended to the urgent matter at hand. Then, reaching for the box of tissues on the coffee table, he became aware of movement behind him. *Shit!* Someone must have come home early. Leaning forward, he made a grab for his trousers, just as a noose was slipped round his neck, metal encased in plastic like a bicycle chain, pulling him backwards on to the sofa.

'Hey!' He tried to scream but it came out more like a grunt. For a moment, the boy flopped around like a dying fish, his hands not knowing whether to reach for his neck or for the jeans around his ankles.

This couldn't be happening.

The music was suddenly switched off and a gruff male voice barked, 'Sit still!'

'Ow!' No longer concerned about his nakedness, Horatio pawed at the makeshift necklace. 'You're hurting me,' he cried. 'Let go!'

The response from his assailant was to yank the noose tighter. 'Sit still and shut up.'

Embarrassedly aware of his own damp stickiness, Horatio finally did as he was told. Letting his hands fall to his sides, he glumly looked towards the screen as young Debbie expertly dodged the money shot which flew across the shop, ending up in a pail of freshly prepared batter. Urgh, Horatio could not help thinking. How gross is that? As Debbie turned to the camera and winked, he felt a twitch in his groin and glanced down. Despite his recent endeavours and the rather unexpected turn of events, the youngster was surprised to see that his erection remained essentially undiminished. Instinctively jerking forward, he felt the necklace cut into his throat. From somewhere deep in his brain he vaguely recalled reading something on the internet about people deliberately cutting off their air supply in order to heighten sexual pleasure; so maybe that was what he was experiencing.

Leaning back on the sofa, Horatio remained still for several moments. There was a slight loosening of the noose, whereupon he tried to move his head. For his trouble, he was given a swift smack.

'Don't look round.' The man spoke quietly but firmly. 'Do what you are told and you will be okay.' A gloved hand appeared from somewhere behind his head and pinned a small, clear plastic bag to the boy's Jack Wills striped Henley shirt. Horatio dropped his chin to his chest to peer at it. Inside was the image of a painting which looked like it had been torn from a catalogue or a textbook.

'What's that?'

'Don't worry about it.'

For a moment there was silence. Then Horatio heard a click by his left ear. At the edge of his field of vision, he saw a small red light begin blinking on the improvised collar. The man took Horatio's hand and brought it up to the collar so that he could feel the small device, about half the size of a cigarette packet, attached to one side.

'Just don't make any sudden movements.'

'Why not?' Horatio wanted his mum. He wanted to cry.

'Because now, sonny, now you're wearing a bomb.'

There was nothing Debbie could do to help him now. Clenching his buttocks tightly, Horatio watched his member belatedly start to droop. There was a noise from behind him that could have been disgust, could have been amusement. Through the open doorway, Horatio gazed forlornly at the front door, willing it to open and for his parents to walk into the hall. Where were they when he needed them? Watching a bloody musical!

Overwhelmed by confusion and self-pity, the boy found himself unable to speak.

'Maybe you should pull up your trousers.'

'Okay.' To his own ear, Horatio's voice sounded small and far away. With exaggerated caution, he did what he was told.

'Don't worry,' the voice chuckled. 'As long as you don't try anything silly, you won't set it off by accident.'

After buttoning his jeans, Horatio wiped his nose on the sleeve of his shirt. 'What do you want?'

'That's none of your business.'

'Not my business?' Horatio echoed, incredulous. Feeling a gentle hand on his shoulder, he kept his eyes straight ahead. Meanwhile, on the TV, Debbie was on to her next scene. He watched ruefully as she writhed in simulated ecstasy in front of a bald man with the over-developed torso of a steroid-abusing body-builder. The girl was certainly putting her own body and soul into it. For a moment, Horatio was again transfixed. Not for nothing, he mused, had she won Best Anal Performance at the recent British Adult Video Awards Ceremony.

'Switch it off,' the voice commanded.

Horatio picked up the remote control and switched off the TV. In an instant, Debbie, his last link with normal life, disappeared into a black void. He dropped the remote on the sofa. 'What do you want me to do?'

'Just sit still.'

Horatio started nodding, then thought better of that.

'When the police arrive, answer their questions clearly and simply.'

'Okay,' said Horatio, though not understanding. Sensing the man step away from the sofa, he lifted his left hand to touch the device on his neck. Tears were not far away. 'How long do I need to keep this on?' There was no reply. He was suddenly conscious of the accelerated beating of his heart. 'How long?' Horatio repeated.

'That depends,' the man said finally.

'On what?' The boy's eyes were welling up.

'On nothing that is in your power and control, so just sit tight. The police will help you. Just make sure they don't try and take off your collar.'

'No?' It sounded like a question.

'No. If they try to do that,' the man said slowly, 'then it will be . . . *kaboom*.'

SIX

'Osmund Caine.'

'Mm.' The inspector smiled as he savoured the pleasant burning feeling in the back of his throat. Having developed a taste for Irish whiskey in his twenties, he was a confirmed Jameson's man. But that didn't mean he couldn't enjoy a nice glass of single malt when it came his way. And at 50.8 per cent proof, the Bladnoch would certainly help to take the edge off what was sure to be an uncomfortable meeting.

Towering over him, Sir Michael Snowdon pointed at the figures on the canvas. 'It's called *Bathing Beach* and was painted in 1938.' The old man must have been well into his seventies but he still cut an imposing figure. Six foot two, with a shock of white hair and clear blue eyes, he wore a navy blazer with a spotted handkerchief sticking out of the breast pocket and grey slacks. His red and white striped shirt was open at the neck and there was a Patek Philippe Golden Ellipse on his left wrist. 'That was almost a decade before a French structural engineer called Louis Réard came up with the idea working on the American nuclear tests at Bikini Atoll.'

'I see.' Not knowing what else to say, Carlyle looked imploringly at his sergeant for some help. However, sitting in an oversized armchair, Joe Szyszkowski was too busy tucking into a large slice of Lady Snowdon's Victoria sponge cake to notice his cue. Looking like a stranger in her own drawing room, Veronica Snowdon herself hovered nervously at the window, waiting for her husband to dispense with the pleasantries and get down to the matter in hand.

'Caine was an interesting character,' Snowdon continued. 'He worked for the Military Police during the Second World War, then went into teaching.' He took a sip from his own glass, which he had filled far more sparingly than the inspector's. 'It's a nice addition to our small collection.'

'Yes.' Frowning, Carlyle watched Joe take another bite of his cake. Irritatingly, Victoria sponge was one of the few cakes he himself didn't like; the cream put him off.

'We only just got this painting recently, as it happens – at a GAC auction in St James's.'

'GAC?' Carlyle enquired. Unlike Lady Snowdon, he was in no hurry to get down to the matter in hand.

'The Government Art Collection,' Snowdon explained.

'I didn't know they had one,' the inspector mumbled, still not remotely interested.

Joe popped the last of the cake into his mouth and washed it down with a mouthful of Earl Grey tea. 'I read about that the other day,' he interjected cheerily. 'The whole collections's worth billions, apparently.'

'I'm not sure about that.' Snowdon signalled for the inspector to take a seat. 'Maybe low hundreds of millions, rather than billions.'

'Not that billions are worth much these days,' Carlyle shrugged, 'given the complete and utter mess we're now in.'

'At least we're all in it together,' Joe quipped, 'as our Prime Minister likes to say.'

'Yeah, right,' Carlyle muttered.

'Anyway,' said Snowdon briskly, 'that collection has always been a fairly mixed bag, it has to be said. Little more than bits and pieces which have been added over the years, here and there. It's most certainly not a collection in the sense of something put together by someone with an overarching vision, who has sought to create a coherent whole. And it contains few if any top-notch items. But it certainly is big. Having basically been ignored for decades, now they're selling bits of it to help pay off some of the national debt.'

'Good luck with that.' Bending his knees, the inspector slowly lowered himself on to the edge of a four-seater cream sofa. 'Maybe they can raise enough to bail out some small provincial building society that no one has ever heard of.'

'Every little helps,' Joe quipped, as he licked his fingers clean. *Manners!* Carlyle wanted to glower at him but couldn't summon up the energy. 'It's not like there's much point having a government art collection, anyway.'

Just another example of politicians taking the piss, in Carlyle's opinion. *Plus ça change.*

'You have to remember that art has long been seen as a useful tool of diplomacy.' Snowdon smiled. 'The collection was first set up in the 1890s, when MPs decided that it would be cheaper to hang paintings on the walls of British embassies around the globe rather than spend money redecorating them.'

'That's the great thing about our elected representatives,' Carlyle grumbled. 'Always focusing on the important stuff.'

'At its peak,' Snowdon continued, politely ignoring the plebeian boorishness of his guest, 'before they started selling things off, the collection contained around twenty thousand works located in embassies, consulates and official residencies in more than a hundred and thirty countries.'

'You know a lot about it.' Satisfied that his hands were now clean, Joe wiped a crumb from his mouth.

'I was a civil servant,' Snowdon reminded him.

'Of course,' Joe nodded.

'Michael was Permanent Secretary in the Foreign and Commonwealth Office,' Veronica Snowdon chipped in. Apparently resigned to the meandering nature of the conversation, she fluttered nervously across the inspector's field of vision and took a seat in the chair opposite Joe. In a grey, long-sleeved woollen dress and a brown cardigan, she looked smaller and more frail than he remembered.

That explains the gong, Carlyle thought. For services rendered. For all that he liked the man, the inspector was acutely conscious that Sir Michael Snowdon was a true pillar of the Establishment. By definition that meant he had to be handled most carefully.

'I had a very nice Gillian Carnegie on my office wall for several years,' Snowdon mused. 'It was amazing how it could lift the spirits.'

'Mm.' The inspector smiled weakly.

'I hear that the Prime Minister has even put a neon art installation in Downing Street,' Joe contributed. 'Apparently it helps brighten up the place.'

Carlyle stared into his whisky. That boy is just a wonderful repository of useless information, he thought. Not for the first time he was pleasantly surprised by Joe's ability to master small talk. It was not something he had ever been any good at himself.

'Ah, yes,' Snowdon replied, 'a red neon light saying something like *Grab the future*, or some such childish vacuousness. They put it in a hallway outside the Terracotta Room. It makes the place look like a nightclub, so I've heard.'

Joe smiled at his boss, who clearly didn't have a clue what they were talking about. 'It was a gift to the great British nation from the celebrated Peruvian artist and performer Yulissa Vasconzuelo.'

Carlyle stared at him blankly.

'She's famous for . . . something or other.'

'That certainly sounds like Edgar Carlton's cup of tea to me,' Carlyle sneered.

The inspector deferred to no one in his hostility towards the Prime Minister, a profound personal dislike derived from professional experience. Before getting the keys to the front door of 10 Downing Street, hobnobbing with Peruvian artists and changing the art on the walls, Carlton had stymied an investigation into a particularly sordid case involving rape and murder. The officer in charge had been one J. Carlyle.

Veronica Snowdon gave her husband a look that said *Get on with it*. 'Thank you for coming, Inspector,' she said as a cue.

'Yes,' said Snowdon, tipping a nod to Carlyle and Joe Szyszkowski in turn, 'we very much appreciate you both coming.' He took a nervous sip of his scotch before continuing, 'Especially given that this has never *really* been your concern.'

'It is our pleasure, sir,' said Carlyle gently, as he launched into a variation of the same speech that he had given several times before. 'We,' he gestured at Joe, 'knew your daughter and had great appreciation for her work. I was in touch with her, before she died. We will always be happy to do what we can.'

From behind his tumbler of whisky, Michael Snowdon nodded sadly. It was almost two years now since Rosanna Snowdon had been found with a broken neck at the bottom of the stairs in the communal entrance to her Fulham apartment building. Pretty, and coming from a rich family, the girl had already made a minor name for herself as a local television presenter, so the press had soon been all over it.

She had also been one of Carlyle's contacts.

Rosanna had fallen down the stairs. Tests showed that she had been drunk at the time, so it could have been an accident. At the same time, there was also evidence that she might have been pushed. The local police had come under immediate pressure to find a suspect and the name in the frame was Simon Lovell, a thirty-two year old with learning difficulties. Lovell was an obsessive fan and borderline stalker who regularly patrolled the pavement outside the presenter's flat. Rosanna had come to the inspector to ask for help in ending this harassment. For his part, Carlyle liked the girl well enough, even if her shameless ambition made him uncomfortable. Besides, she had helped him during the Edgar Carlton case and he owed her a favour or two. When she looked to cash in his IOU, he made all the right noises without actually investigating what could be done. Thus, after she took a dive down the stairs, it was a matter for the Fulham police and he was happy to leave it well alone.

Seemingly more distraught than anyone, Lovell was only too happy to confess to the killing. However, the trial was a fiasco. In the absence of any forensic evidence, everything rested on Lovell's statement. On the morning of the first day the judge was told that Lovell had a mental age of eight – gaining him the inevitable tabloid moniker of 'Simple Simon' – and hence a willingness to sign anything that was put in front of him. The case was thrown out before lunch on the first day.

After Lovell was released, there was nowhere for a moribund investigation to go. The coroner had ruled the death 'suspicious', so foul play had not been ruled out. Meanwhile, the case would remain in limbo unless or until a killer was identified and caught. Rosanna's parents were left in a legal and emotional no man's land that made the parent inside Carlyle shiver and the policeman inside him think, There but for the Grace of God.

On more than a couple of occasions, the inspector had wondered whether he could have done more at the time to help the young woman. While not exactly overcome by guilt, he was aware that he could have acted differently – or at least faster. Whenever this happened, he would quickly tell himself to stop brooding on something that was beyond his control. As Shakespeare said, *What's gone and what's past help should be past grief.*

Past grief? Try telling that to the parents of a dead girl. So here he was, drinking Sir Michael's whisky, while trying to sound vaguely supportive. Staring into the single malt, he tried to remember how many times now he had sat here saying nothing of any import.

Three? No . . . four.

This was his penance. The inspector genuinely hoped that these little get-togethers gave his hosts some comfort. Otherwise they were pointless.

SEVEN

'Spotted dick tonight. Jolly good.'

'Mm.' Prime Minister Edgar Carlton sat beneath the imposing portrait of Kitty Pakenham, a long-dead minor aristocrat, and sipped daintily from his oversized snifter. After almost four years as Prime Minister, enjoying a very large measure of Hennessy Paradis Impérial at Pakenham's had become an all-too necessary pre-dinner ritual. The cognac helped take the edge off the permanent sense of frustration and anxiety that came with the job.

The gentlemen's club in St James's provided a refuge from civil servants and colleagues alike. The Cabinet Secretary, Sir Gavin O'Dowd – known as GOD to the fawning scribes of the lobby – didn't like the fact that it had become an informal annexe to Number Ten, but that was tough. These days, the club was the nearest thing Edgar had to somewhere he could call home. Certainly it was one of the few places where he could find any peace. A wicked thought suddenly crossed his mind and he laughed out loud.

Christian Holyrod, the Mayor of London and Edgar's closest political friend and ally, looked up from the evening's menu. 'What's so funny?'

'I've just had a fantastic idea. Why don't we sack O'Dowd?'

Holyrod raised an eyebrow. 'From which job?'

Edgar frowned. 'Whatever do you mean?'

'Augie has three jobs,' Holyrod grinned, referring to O'Dowd by his middle name, which was Augustine.

'He does?' Edgar looked genuinely surprised.

'Yes,' Holyrod nodded sagely. 'As well as Cabinet Secretary, he's Permanent Secretary to the Cabinet Office and Head of the Civil Service.'

'Interesting.' Edgar thought about that for a moment. 'So what's the difference between them?'

Holyrod shrugged. 'Not a lot, as far as I can see. At the end of the day, it all comes down to the same thing.' Dropping the menu, he picked up his glass, half-filled with Balblair 1965, and took a careful sip.

'At the end of the day,' Edgar mused, 'he's just a posh fixer.'

The Mayor stared into his whisky. 'Quite.'

'And if we wanted to, could we sack him from all three jobs?'

'I suppose so.' Holyrod took a larger taste of his single malt and let it roll around his tongue. 'The question is – *why* would we want to? I thought he was doing quite a good job.'

'I suppose so – but we could replace him with a woman,' Edgar giggled, waving his glass in Kitty's direction. 'And then she couldn't get admitted here. Then there would be one place in this damn city where I could be left alone.'

'Good point,' Holyrod noted. The last bastion of civilized behaviour, Pakenham's had never allowed women through its doors, and with a bit of luck never would. 'Why not? It might be worth a try.'

Feeling his stomach rumble, Edgar glanced at the clock on the far wall. 'As it is, the bugger has insisted on coming over to brief me before dinner.'

'On what?'

'This phone-hacking business.' Edgar sighed. 'It's turning into a complete pain in the backside.'

'Yes.'

'Technology can be such a total bugger. It makes life so much harder in so many ways, and it's just impossible to keep up with it. I can remember the good old days when we didn't even have mobile phones.'

'Me too, just about,' Holyrod interjected, not wanting to sound too old school.

'Now,' Edgar continued, on a roll, 'it seems that everybody's got two or three of the damn things, and everybody's listening to everyone else's calls.'

'No one's safe,' Holyrod agreed sadly. 'Not even the royal family.'

'Who'd have thought that it could be so easy to hack into the wretched things? One of the interns explained it to me the other day. Apparently most people don't bother to change the factory-default PIN for their voicemail, so anyone can just ring up and check their messages.'

'Mm.' Holyrod hadn't even realized that he had a PIN. He would have to tell one of his PAs to get it changed asap. A cheeky thought popped into his head. 'So, has *your* phone been hacked?'

Edgar Carlton thought about that for a moment. 'Not as far as I know. But if anyone wants to listen in to my messages they're more than welcome. It's not like I ever receive anything interesting. It's normally just Anastasia complaining about the kids' latest transgressions or the fact that she's gone over her credit-card limit again.'

'Mm. That might be of interest to the tabloids.'

Edgar shot him a worried look. 'Which?'

'Either. Both.'

'I would have thought they would be far more interested in the call I got from Sophia recently,' Edgar remarked waspishly.

Holyrod held up a hand. 'I don't want to know.' Sophia Carlton-Holyrod, Edgar's half-sister, was technically still married to the Mayor. However, the pair had not lived together for years. Tired of her husband's flagrant infidelities, Sophia had decamped to a riad in Marrakesh with her bodyguard boyfriend. 'I hope you deleted the message.'

'You should sort that out,' Edgar admonished him.

'I'm not giving her any more money.'

'Whatever. It's your problem, not mine.' Edgar suddenly

remembered the original cause of his complaint. 'I've got to sort out this hacking mess.'

Finishing his whisky, the Mayor placed the empty glass carefully on the side table by his chair. 'How long?'

'Sorry?'

'How long,' Holyrod repeated slowly, 'do you have to wait for O'Dowd?'

'I don't know.' Finishing his drink, the PM pushed himself to his feet. 'He's late, so I'm going to have another drink.'

'Fine.' Holyrod jumped up too, and hastened towards the door. 'I'm starving. I'll see you in the dining room.'

Refilling his glass, Edgar caught sight of his image in a nearby mirror and winced. His magnificent hair now contained more than its fair share of grey; it was as if he had aged decades in the last few years. 'Chin up,' he mumbled to himself. 'You're not done yet. Win election number two and the rest will take care of itself.' The best part of ten years in Downing Street would be more than enough. Then it would be time for the memoirs, a few lucrative consultancies and the American lecture circuit.

A polite cough drew the PM from his reverie. He half-turned to find Sir Gavin O'Dowd standing behind him, with a couple of other advisers in tow. Hovering in the background was the reassuring figure of the Downing Street Security Chief, Trevor Miller.

'Sir Gavin,' Edgar smiled, resisting the temptation to call him Augie as Christian had done. Having recently returned from a fortnight's R&R at his villa in Tuscany, the civil servant looked tanned and relaxed, something that made his boss resent him even more.

'Prime Minister.' Putting his hands together, O'Dowd gave a small bow that Edgar found deeply irritating. For God's sake, he thought angrily, stand up straight, man. We're not Japanese.

'Thank you for coming over.' The PM then glanced at Miller,

who was in inscrutable mode. *Everybody's going bloody oriental on me*, Edgar despaired.

The others kept a discreet distance, waiting to see if they would be called into the conversation.

'No problem.' For a Knight of the British Empire, O'Dowd's choice of language was often rather common. Then, again, he was rather common. Born in Brixton, he had studied Economics at Warwick University – Warwick, for God's sake! Could one even find it on a map? – graduating with First Class Honours before joining the Treasury. There he rose quickly through the ranks, on his way to becoming Permanent Secretary. From Great George Street, it was only a short hop to Number Ten, where he had gone on to serve four different Prime Ministers in various roles.

Not for nothing was the bureaucrat known by the moniker 'GOD'. After his election victory Edgar Carlton had quickly realized that, to the extent that anyone was actually running the country, it was Sir Gavin O'Dowd.

It certainly wasn't Carlton himself.

Edgar raised the fresh snifter to his lips. 'Would you like a drink?'

O'Dowd lifted a hand. 'No, thank you.'

'Fine.' Edgar tried to remember if he'd ever seen a drop of alcohol pass the apparatchik's lips. In his book, a man who didn't drink was not to be trusted. Maybe he really should go ahead and sack the little bugger. Smiling at the thought, he let a mouthful of Hennessy trickle smoothly down his throat.

O'Dowd looked at him expectantly.

'You're late, and dinner is waiting,' Edgar said, and with some effort, stifled a yawn. 'I can give you ten minutes.'

A look of annoyance fleetingly crossed Sir Gavin's face, only to be immediately extinguished as the mandarin's mask slipped back into place. 'My apologies,' he said evenly. 'Let me just recap where I think we are.'

If you must, Edgar thought wearily. 'That would be most helpful.'

'Well . . .' Sir Gavin shot a look at Miller, who showed no signs of leaving them to it.

'Trevor is my Senior Security Adviser,' Edgar explained smoothly, 'and as such he needs to hear this.'

'Fine.' O'Dowd cleared his throat. 'So, stepping back for a minute, what do we know? What are the known knowns, as it were?'

Get on with it. Edgar impatiently tapped his foot on the rather threadbare carpet.

Taking a deep breath, O'Dowd ploughed on. 'It seems clear that the row over the involvement of the police in phone hacking undertaken by certain journalists is not going to go away.'

'We know that,' Miller grunted.

'More specifically, it has not been defused by our decision to set up the Meyer investigation.'

Our decision? Edgar wondered. It was your idea to pluck some provincial plod from obscurity and place him in charge of the biggest and most high-profile police internal investigation since the Corruption and Dishonesty Prevention Review Board in the 1990s. However, it was too late to quibble about that now. They were all in it together. 'That doesn't mean that creating a taskforce under Chief Inspector Meyer was not the right thing to do.'

'No.'

'It was important that Operation Redhead was set up so that people can perceive that we are taking this matter seriously.'

Perceive being the key word.

'Indeed,' O'Dowd smiled. 'But it is going to be a slow burn. And don't forget, Operation Redhead comes *after* Operation Tulisa and Operation Elf. It's not the first time we've tried to sort this thing out.'

'What he's trying to say,' Miller interrupted, 'is that they need to get on with it. There have been less than two dozen arrests so far. People want to see more action. The FBI are even saying that they will step in if we drop the ball again.'

'Jesus!' Edgar exclaimed, coughing as a mouthful of cognac went down the wrong way. 'We don't want that.'

'No, we don't,' O'Dowd agreed. 'But, by the same token, we have to follow due process. Meyer has to proceed with care. He cannot afford to do anything that might prejudice any potential future criminal investigation.'

'Why do you think we put him in charge in the first place?' Miller grumbled. 'We don't want any of this getting to court – on either side of the Atlantic.'

'Due process,' O'Dowd repeated.

'In the meantime,' Miller went on, 'we ourselves are getting nowhere, the Americans are threatening to stick their oar in, and the expenses keep racking up.'

Edgar made a face. 'How much is all this costing?'

'The bill for Operation Redhead is already more than four and a half million pounds,' O'Dowd said, 'including almost a million spent on overtime. The current run rate is more than three hundred and fifty thousand pounds a month.'

'So?' The last thing the PM wanted was a lecture on finances. It was only the little people who had to worry about money.

A pained expression appeared on O'Dowd's face. 'Well,' he said gently, 'it will have to come out of *someone*'s budget.'

'Pfff . . .' Edgar made a gesture as if he was swatting a wasp away from in front of his face. 'The Commissioner will have to raid one of the MPS's slush funds.'

'Slush funds?' Now the civil servant looked offended.

'Or whatever,' Edgar huffed. If that fellow Chester Forsyth-Walker, head of the Metropolitan Police, doesn't have some cash stashed away for a rainy day, he thought, then more fool him. 'Just make sure that it gets dealt with.'

'Of course.' O'Dowd paused. 'Then there's one other thing that you have to bear in mind . . .'

Edgar sighed theatrically. That was the big problem with his job: there was always *one more thing*. 'Which is?'

'Which is the potential for Chief Inspector Meyer himself to become something of a liability.'

'What?' Edgar gripped his snifter so tightly that his knuckles went white. He looked at Miller. 'I thought you told me he was the most boring provincial plod you could find.'

Miller shrugged. 'Apparently there is a relationship with a Community Liaison Officer that we didn't know about.'

'Neither did his wife,' O'Dowd added. 'And there are dalliances with a couple of civilians to consider too.'

'Women?' Edgar asked, as a whole range of possible scenarios began whizzing through his mind.

'Yes,' Miller nodded. 'Nothing exotic, I'm glad to say.'

'Well,' Edgar said, 'I suppose that's something, at least.'

'The boy likes playing away.' Miller grinned. 'Seems he just can't keep it in his trousers.'

'That's one of the risks when you pluck this kind of person from obscurity,' O'Dowd said, 'and they go straight under the glare of the media spotlight. There's always something to be dug up – skeletons in the cupboard and all that. You never know for sure if they can survive the scrutiny.'

'Mm.' Despite the news about Meyer, the cognac was beginning to make Edgar feel a little mellow. 'Should I sack him, do you think?'

'I would try and avoid that, if possible,' O'Dowd replied. 'It would undermine the legitimacy of the whole process at a very early stage.'

'And we wouldn't want to do that, would we?' Edgar's stomach had started rumbling again and he was distracted by the thought of tucking into a hearty plate of spotted dick.

'No, we wouldn't.'

'Anyway,' Miller interjected, 'we've checked out every Chief Constable in England and Wales, and none of them come without baggage of some description. So a bit of extra-curricular shagging is manageable.'

Don't I know it. Edgar struggled to stifle a smile. 'So – where does that leave us,' he wondered if he sounded ever so slightly drunk, 'in terms of the, ah, underlying issue?'

'In the absence of anything else,' O'Dowd told him, 'the phone-hacking issue is still dominating the news agenda.'

'Maybe we should do something about that,' Edgar said.

'Such as?'

'I don't know.' This time Edgar Carlton did allow himself the merest grin. 'Maybe we could go and bomb Syria or something.'

'Anyway,' O'Dowd continued, politely ignoring the infantile suggestion from his boss, 'questions about press regulation, media ownership, the police, and relationships between politicians and journalists are not likely to go away. We all know where we are on this.'

'After years of rumours,' Miller chipped in, 'the *Sunday Witness* newspaper has, as you know, finally admitted intercepting voicemail messages of prominent people to find stories. Zenger Corporation, the parent company, says this was the action of a few rogue members of staff who have since left the paper.'

'As you would expect,' said O'Dowd.

'As you would expect,' Miller agreed. 'They claim that the problem has been dealt with, so there is no longer any hacking taking place.'

'Meanwhile, the MPS has launched a series of investigations over the last few years. None of them have added up to much. That's why we have to stick with Operation Redhead.'

'Bloody Met,' Edgar hissed. 'They should have sorted this out years ago.' *In other words, before I became Prime Minister.*

'Decisive action is now required,' O'Dowd persisted.

'Isn't that what I've been saying?' Edgar snapped.

'There's decisive and there's *decisive*. Sir Chester might have to go, even though it was not on his watch.'

'The Commissioner!' Edgar exclaimed. That was a bit close to home. Forsyth-Walker was a self-proclaimed 'copper from the old school' who, after an undistinguished career in the provinces, had been appointed to the top job in the Met by Christian Holyrod, in his capacity as Mayor of London. Edgar didn't like the thought of such a senior figure having to fall on his sword. It gave people ideas.

On the other hand, if it stopped the scandal from reaching Downing Street, it was a price well worth paying.

The Cabinet Secretary inspected his beautifully polished shoes. 'I wouldn't rule anything out.'

'Not with Horsegate still rumbling on,' Miller said.

'Tsk.' Edgar angrily waved away the mention of the latest pseudo-scandal.

'Mr Miller is right.' O'Dowd smiled sadly.

'This is nonsense,' Edgar said testily. 'I am the Prime Minister, for goodness sake – the Prime Minister! How many times do I have to say this? I am *not* going to get into a conversation about whether or not I went riding on a nag called George Canning . . .'

With some difficulty, Trevor Miller stifled a guffaw.

'. . . or any other horse, for that matter.' He jabbed an angry finger in the direction of O'Dowd. 'How was I supposed to know that the Metropolitan Police were lending out their spare horses to Sonia Claesens and her bloody boyfriend?'

You idiot, Miller thought. These people are toxic. What the hell were you doing, going riding with them in the first place? 'Look on the bright side,' he said aloud. 'It saved our four-legged friend from the knacker's yard, at least for a while.'

For a moment, it looked as if the PM might explode in the face of such rank impertinence. Trying to calm the situation, O'Dowd held up a hand.

'These things happen,' he said. 'With the benefit of hindsight, was it wise that you went riding on a police horse with your close friends, the head of Zenger Corporation's media division and her toyboy? Probably not. However, now we have to look forward, not back, so it is best if we don't fixate on it.'

'I don't even know if that was the actual bloody animal I sat on,' Edgar whined.

'Such details don't matter. The point is, as Mr Miller has shown, this trifling incident will, for the moment at least, keep you tied to the wider problem.' O'Dowd spread his arms. 'Which means we have to be seen to be treating the wider problem with the utmost seriousness. Which in turn means that, if the Commissioner's position becomes untenable, you cannot flinch from making sure that the right decision is made. And made quickly.'

Which means I will have to lean on Christian to sack him, Edgar thought morosely. What's that going to cost me?

'Not that we are prejudging the issue,' O'Dowd flashed one of his most insincere smiles, 'in any way, shape or form.'

'Of course not,' Miller agreed.

'Glad to hear it.' Edgar took another sip of Hennessy to calm his nerves.

'It all depends on how diligent he proves to have been in terms of dealing with . . . perceived abuses among the rank and file of the MPS.' O'Dowd pushed back his shoulders and clasped his hands in front of his chest. This was the standard undertaker's pose that he liked to adopt when doling out bad news to politicians and other naughty children. 'But I'm afraid, Prime Minister, we can rule nothing out at this stage. The horse George Canning is, of course, a distraction but it is also symptomatic of how this has now become really quite a serious matter.'

'I know all this,' Edgar groaned. 'The question remains: how is the issue going to be resolved? How do we make it go away?'

O'Dowd ignored the PM's gripe. 'In the short term,' he said evenly, 'I fear that it isn't. So far, the police have a list of a thousand possible targets.'

'Targets?'

'Targets of the media – people who we think may have had their phones hacked by rogue journalists.'

'The current number is fifteen hundred,' Miller interjected, 'and it's growing all the time.'

'Quite,' O'Dowd nodded. 'The point is that it will take years to check out all the potential cases.' *Years, as in long after the next election.* 'Meanwhile the victims will troop through the courts looking for compensation.'

'Almost all these cases are celebrities, footballers and politicians,' Miller continued. 'Not groups likely to gain much public sympathy.'

'No,' O'Dowd agreed. 'Far more worrying are the allegations that police officers have been selling people's phone details to journalists.'

Not as worrying as the risk of us having to forfeit the very generous donations that Zenger has made over the years to Party funds, Edgar thought. Not to mention the Zenger cash we need to fight the next election. 'So, what should we do?'

O'Dowd raised his gaze to the heavens, as if the PM's question was a bolt from the blue. 'That,' he said finally, 'is something that you are going to have to consider very carefully in due course. For the moment, we have to wait and see how things pan out.'

Wait and see, thought Edgar morosely. In other words, the standard civil-service line when they don't have a clue.

'Now, let me leave you to your meal.'

Edgar gave a curt nod and watched the Head of the Civil Service solemnly make his way to the door. 'Bloody fence-sitter,' he grumbled into his almost empty snifter. 'Never gives you a straight answer.'

'I think he wanted an invite to dinner,' Miller grinned. He was feeling hungry himself, but was more of a Big Mac man. Steamed suet pudding was just not his thing.

'I'm definitely going to sack him,' Edgar mumbled. 'Give his jobs, all of them, to some bright young filly with a double-first from Oxford, great teeth and a monster rack.' There were always more than a few of those knocking around Westminster.

'What?'

'Nothing, nothing.' Edgar offered a tired smile to the two advisers who had been waiting patiently in the corner. One was a pollster, the other, one of the Downing Street Press Officers.

36

'Sorry, guys, we're out of time here. Let's reconvene in the morning.' Without a murmur of complaint, the duo shuffled off. Finishing the last of his cognac, the PM decided against another one. Doubtless Christian Holyrod was getting stuck into his first bottle of Château Haut-Brion Blanc 2006, and Edgar was keen to join him. He placed his empty glass on the table and turned to Miller, who was always the last man to leave his side. 'So what do you think?'

'What have we got?' Miller shrugged. 'Bad behaviour by tabloid hacks, gleefully reported by other tabloid hacks. Is it really so surprising?'

'Of course not,' Edgar sighed.

'The plebs love scandal, simply love it. They want to be titillated one day, outraged the next.'

'It was ever thus.'

'So, I would say that it's all just a storm in a teacup.' Miller shoved his hands into his trouser pockets. 'We have to be seen to be taking it seriously, of course, but there's no need to panic. Soon enough it will all be over, and everyone will move on.'

'Absolutely,' the PM nodded. 'It just depends how many careers it wrecks along the way.' The beginnings of an idea floated across his Hennessy-soaked brain. 'Sir Gavin may well be right. Some important heads will have to roll.'

Miller thought about that for a moment. 'How many heads are we talking about?' he asked finally.

'Difficult to say,' Edgar smiled. That is the great thing about you, Mr Miller, he thought. Nothing fazes you. The Head of Security had been a key member of his team for more than seven years now. Unlike the callow youths who swarmed around Whitehall acting as special advisers, Trevor Miller was a man of the world with an extensive range of contacts. Over time, the 'security' brief had expanded as Edgar had come to rely on him for an ever-wider range of advice and services. Other people brought him problems; Miller delivered solutions.

'I would assume a relatively small number,' Miller mused.

'Not too few but not too many either; with at least one sufficiently senior, so that the whole process doesn't look too . . . tokenistic.'

'Exactly.'

'Do you have anyone particular in mind?'

Edgar glanced towards the dining room. On reflection, Christian might well be on his second bottle of Château Haut-Brion by now. 'You know that is not my style.' He patted Miller on the shoulder and headed for the door. 'I'll leave such details to you.'

EIGHT

How do I manage to get myself into these situations?

Finishing his whisky, Carlyle let his host refill the glass. He had first met Sir Michael and Veronica Snowdon about six months after their daughter Rosanna's death. They had been given his name by Fiona Singleton, a sergeant in Fulham who had worked on the investigation and knew about the inspector's connection to the dead girl. Never comfortable when it came to dealing with grieving relatives, Carlyle had uttered a few platitudes about what a great person their daughter had been, although in truth he had hardly known her.

At the time the couple had politely listened to him prattle on for several minutes, before Sir Michael placed a firm hand on his shoulder. 'Thank you for your kind words, Inspector, but I was wondering if we might trouble you for some professional advice.'

Oh, no, Carlyle thought wearily, here we go. 'How can I help?' he asked.

'We just need to understand,' said Lady Snowdon cautiously, clearly unsure of her ground, 'whether it is likely that Rosanna's case will ever be resolved?'

No, Carlyle thought, it's not likely at all. You should accept that and move on. After all, you'll be dead yourselves soon enough. 'It's hard to say,' he stammered. 'I know that my colleagues in Fulham—'

Recognizing bluster when he heard it, Snowdon gently cut across him. 'I am aware of their efforts,' he said neutrally. 'However, they cannot even confirm the cause of death.'

'These things are often difficult,' the inspector admitted, staring at his shoes. He hadn't felt this sheepish since he was thirteen and his mother had found a copy of *Fiesta* under his mattress.

'Yes,' Sir Michael agreed, 'they are.'

Over the last couple of years, Rosanna's parents had come to see Carlyle as their man on the inside. Too embarrassed to disabuse them, the inspector would give the impression of making 'discreet enquiries' behind the scenes, while waiting patiently for them to stop plying him with drink and to finally come to terms with their daughter's death.

With a theatrical flourish, Joe Szyszkowski glanced at his watch. Carlyle knew that Joe's wife, Anita, would not be happy right now. Within the normal constraints of his job, she preferred her husband's hours to be as regular as possible. Like the inspector himself, Joe was not the kind of man allowed any backsliding when it came to his family duties. The sergeant looked pleadingly at his boss but Carlyle remained impassive. He appreciated Joe tagging along with him to provide moral support on this mercy mission, but there was no scope for either of them bunking off early. Now that they were here, both officers had to stay a respectable length of time.

The inspector took another sip of scotch, desperately trying to think of something to say. The silence was getting awkward but his mind remained completely blank. Ignoring Joe's silent entreaties, he glanced up at the painting of the girls wearing bikinis. What was the artist called? Osmund something-or-other. What kind of a name was that?

'So, Inspector . . .'

Blinking, he looked towards Veronica Snowdon, who was again pacing back and forth in front of the windows.

'Yes?' he smiled.

'What do you think of the breakthrough in Rosanna's case?' she asked.

'Sorry?' *What breakthrough?* Carlyle didn't have a clue what they were talking about. 'Well . . .' Gripping his glass more tightly, he looked to Joe for some help. But none was forthcoming as, making the best of the situation, his sergeant was busily helping himself to a third slice of cake.

'After all this time,' Snowdon chipped in, his cheeks now slightly flushed from the scotch, 'do you really think they've finally got him?'

'Well . . .' Carlyle said, and gulped. 'It is a possibility.'

Feeling warm and fuzzy, Hannah Gillespie squinted at the little clock in the top right-hand corner of the screen on her mobile. 'God!' she mumbled. 'It's getting late – I need to go. Mum will kill me. And I've still got that essay to write.'

'Relax.' She felt a hand on her shoulder. 'It's still early.'

'But . . .'

The phone disappeared from her hand and was replaced by a glass almost full to the brim with red wine. 'Have another drink. There's plenty of time.'

'Mm.' Hannah wasn't sure about that, but she felt too chilled-out to argue. Brian Faulkner, Ted Heath and the Troubles could wait.

'Cheers.' There was a gentle click of glasses.

Hannah grinned. 'Cheers.'

Marc Harrington stood pummelling the Mosmans' front door, banging the oversized brass knocker, in the shape of a lion's head, until his fingers felt numb. He had been standing there for more than a minute now, but there was still no response from inside. Feeling like a prize idiot, he looked around, wondering what to do next.

'For God's sake,' he mumbled, wiping a bead of sweat from his brow. If anything, the music had got louder over the last few minutes. Surely the neighbours on the other side could hear it too – if they were home, that is, rather than off sunning themselves at their villa in the South of France.

Bloody neighbours, he thought. Why does this have to be my problem?

It suddenly struck him that he should call the police. Maybe they would arrest Horatio Mosman. That would give the little shit something to think about while he waited for his parents to bail him out of jail. Reaching into his trouser pocket, Harrington realized that his iPhone was still sitting on the kitchen table. 'Shit, fuck, bollocks . . .'

Suddenly the music stopped.

Problem solved, or just a temporary reprieve?

Taking a step away from the door, Harrington counted the following seconds in his head. After thirty seconds of blissful silence, he reconsidered his options.

Should he nip back home, refill his glass, and declare victory?

Or would the selfish little sod crank 30 Seconds to Whatever back up again before Harrington could get another glass of the Chevalier-Montrachet in his hand?

He had yet to make up his mind when the door suddenly flew open. However, rather than being confronted by a dishevelled teenage onanist, he found himself face-to-face with a tall figure dressed from head to foot in black, its face hidden by a balaclava. All that Harrington could make out was a pair of blue eyes looking out at him through the slits.

'Horatio?'

Surely the boy hadn't grown that much. From somewhere inside the house came a noise that could have been a groan, or equally could have been a scream. Glancing along the hallway, Harrington took another step backwards. It was only when he looked back at the figure in front of him that he saw the pistol in the guy's hand.

Holy shit! Harrington felt his heart try to leap straight out of his chest and his sphincter contracted. *Breathe*, he told himself. *Keep calm.* He had clearly stumbled upon a robbery. *This is none of your business.* Whatever had happened to young Horatio, there was nothing he could do about it. *Just walk away. Don't try and be a hero.*

Holding up both hands, he started retreating down the drive. 'It's okay,' he said, trying to keep his voice from cracking, his eyes meanwhile locked on the gun. As a devotee of *The Shield* and *The Wire*, Harrington liked to think that he knew his weapons. This one looked to him like a Glock or maybe a Sig Sauer.

Not that it really mattered when it was being aimed straight at your heart. A wave of angst and frustration washed over him as once more he asked himself: *Why does this have to be my problem?*

'It's okay,' he repeated, now nervously eyeing the Rolex Submariner on his left wrist. Maybe he should just hand it over. 'I'm going. I didn't see anything.'

'Good.' Standing on the doorstep, the robber lifted his aim to Harrington's head and fired.

NINE

Carlyle watched Joe Szyszkowski pacing the far side of the room, mobile glued to his ear, his free hand gesturing frantically.

'I know – I *know*. Look, there's nothing I can do . . . but yes, of course . . .' Glancing over at the inspector, Joe made a face and slipped out of the room and into the hallway. He would be speaking to Anita, the inspector thought smugly – receiving another verbal beating from his missus. He himself, on the other hand, had avoided getting an earful from his wife by simply turning off both of the phones nestling in his jacket. Helen wouldn't be happy, but at least she knew the score. Anyway, she would doubtless be fast asleep by now. They could talk in the morning, maybe over breakfast together.

'How much longer?'

Perched on the edge of the sofa, Carlyle gave Horatio Mosman a sympathetic smile. 'Not long.'

The two policemen had been less than three blocks away from the Mosman residence in Wellington Road when Joe's phone had started going crazy. Energized, the inspector had shot off the Snowdons' sofa, mouthing his apologies as he headed for the door. Happy to be rescued from his painful conversation with Rosanna's parents, he was also curious to find out whether the 999 call about a kid with an alleged bomb fastened round his neck was – as he suspected – a hoax.

Five minutes later, he knew for sure that it wasn't.

From the pavement, they entered through a metal gate with a well-tended eight-foot hedge on either side. Signalling for the uniforms and the paramedics to wait out on the street, Carlyle lifted the latch and stepped on through. Immediately he spotted the body of a man sprawled in front of the main door of the house. He had clearly been shot in the head.

'Joe . . .' Carlyle began, distracted by the blood seeping towards a nearby flowerbed.

The sergeant appeared at his side. 'Fuck.'

'Good nutrition for the roses, I suppose.'

Joe frowned. Neither of them had green fingers. 'What about inside?'

'No bang – yet. I'll go in and take a look.'

Joe eyed him doubtfully. 'Okay.'

'Go and call for some reinforcements and I'll give you a shout in a minute.'

I could really do with a piss and some fresh air, in that order, Carlyle thought. He had been trying to ignore the sour smell in the room for over an hour now.

'Want something to eat?' he asked. 'They delivered your pizza a while back.'

The youngster started to shake his head, then quickly thought better of it. 'I'm not hungry.'

'Fair enough.' The inspector smiled at young Horatio. 'You're doing fine. I'm sure it won't be too much longer.'

'I want this bloody thing off!' the teenager wailed.

'We'll be as quick as possible.'

Horatio slumped back on the sofa in slow motion. 'You don't think it'll go off, do you?'

'Nah.' This time Carlyle's grin was genuine. 'It's a fake. There was something similar happened recently in – New Zealand, I think. Somewhere like that. It was just a bullshit attempt at extortion. A guy was arrested fairly quickly. I think he confessed.'

'Uh-huh.' The boy sniffed, not really taking in what the policeman was saying.

'Look on the bright side. Once you get out of here, you'll be something of a celebrity. All the girls will want to know you.'

'I'll settle just for getting this off.' Horatio gestured at the collar, where the little red light continued to blink menacingly.

'Sure.' Carlyle glanced at a couple of explosives officers from Specialist Operations who were talking quietly in a corner. 'They just have to go through the set procedures for this kind of thing, simply to be on the safe side.'

'But it's been ages now,' the boy whimpered.

And it hasn't gone off yet. Carlyle made a final effort at the big smile. 'So far, so good.'

'Mm.'

'These guys,' Carlyle explained, 'they have detailed procedures to follow, even when they think – even when they really *know* – that the bomb's a fake. They always take it one step at a time. Better to be on the safe side.'

'Okay.' Horatio wanted to be convinced, but he couldn't quite get there.

As if on cue, the officers finished their conversation. One of them slipped out of the room while the other stepped over towards Carlyle and the boy.

'Inspector?'

'Yeah?' Carlyle looked up at the squat, well-built guy with a regulation number-one haircut that showed a hint of grey at the temples. The dark rings under his flat brown eyes made him look – to the inspector's mind – a bit like a vampire. The name stencilled on the breast pocket of his uniform said *Baldwin*.

'Well?' Carlyle prompted.

'We're good.' Baldwin reached across and patted Horatio on the shoulder. 'We'll have it off you in a few minutes.'

'Yeah!' Horatio clenched a fist in triumph.

'Thank God for that.' Grimacing, Carlyle got to his feet and indulged in a stretch. 'I need a comfort break.' The last thing he wanted was to do a Gerard Dépardieu and piss himself in public.

Grinning, Horatio pointed to the door. 'There's a guest bathroom just down the hall.'

'Thanks,' Carlyle replied. 'I'll only be a minute.'

Zipping himself up, the inspector squirted a blob of liquid soap on to his hands and turned on the wash-basin tap. After rinsing his hands, he splashed a little cold water on his face, before drying it off with a towel. It was well past midnight but the adrenalin rush had yet to wear off and he was still buzzing. 'Good effort tonight,' Carlyle told his reflection in the mirror. He could have been blown to bits out there, but he hadn't bottled it. Helen would give him shit but that was nothing new. Bottom line, he was only doing his job. He flashed himself a cheesy smile. 'When the going gets tough . . .'

He was still grinning at the mirror when there was an almighty explosion somewhere nearby.

'Fuck!' Carlyle automatically threw his hands up to protect his face as the bathroom door flew open and the false ceiling fell in on him. Losing his footing, he felt his head bounce off something cool and smooth before he landed in a heap on the floor.

Then there was only darkness.

Where the hell am I?

Blinking in the gloom, Hannah Gillespie lay staring at the ceiling, listening as the pounding in her head alternated with the hum of traffic outside. After a while, she pushed aside the grimy duvet. Heaving herself up, she slowly swung her legs over one side of the bed. Head bowed, she tried to remember the events of the previous evening, but it was all a blank. She felt dizzy and there was a chalky taste in her mouth. Suddenly nauseous, she tried to throw up, but nothing came out.

What time was it? There was no clock, but from the daylight filtering into the room, Hannah guessed that she was already late for school. *Shit!* She hadn't written that bloody essay either. Bloody hell, girl, she thought ruefully, you've really overdone it here. You'll have a job to talk your way out of this one.

A tentative sniff of her T-shirt suggested a shower was in order and she also needed to pee. Grabbing her jeans from the floor, she quickly pulled them on, before shoving her feet into her trainers. Rushing over to the door, she yanked the handle. It was locked.

'Hey!' Panic rising, she hammered on the door with her fist. 'Hey! Stop jerking around. Let me out!'

Getting no response, Hannah slumped back on to the bed. Closing her eyes, she fought back a sob.

'Mum . . .' It came out like a whimper.

Outside, the traffic slipped past relentlessly.

'MU . . . UM!!'

No one came.

TEN

'That was a good time to take a leak,' Joe Szyszkowski observed, biting into a bacon sandwich.

'Tell me about it.' The inspector drained his demitasse and signalled to the waitress for another double espresso.

The girl gestured to a menu with her pen. 'Would you like anything to eat?'

'Nah, thanks.' The caffeine was mixing with the adrenalin and Carlyle felt too pumped to contemplate any food. He looked up at the clock on the wall: 4.57 a.m. Just over three hours since Horatio Mosman had been blown to kingdom come.

Amazingly, no one else had been killed in the explosion. One of the explosives officers and a paramedic had been taken to the Royal Free Hospital with serious injuries, but the expectation was that they would survive. The ground floor of the house meanwhile was – well, it was like a bombsite. The living room was completely wrecked and the rest of the ground floor had suffered extensive blast damage. The device had clearly been designed to do more than simply remove the unfortunate teenager's head from his shoulders. Forensics would be collecting bits of his body for days, if not weeks.

And yet the explosives officer – Carlyle struggled to remember his name – Baldwin had claimed it was a fake.

Bad call.

Bad, bad, bad call.

Was the guy just trying to keep the kid calm? Carlyle

wondered. Surely not. How could he have got things so wrong? There were lots of questions but no answers. Anyway, that was something to worry about later. When Mr Baldwin came out of Intensive Care, it would be back to traffic duty for him, career over.

The waitress reappeared with his coffee and a smile. 'Anything to eat with that?' she asked again, placing the cup and saucer carefully on the table before removing the old one.

No, Carlyle thought, I haven't changed my mind during the last minute. Irritated, he shook his head. 'I'm okay.'

'I'll have another one of these, please,' said Joe, with the polite reticence of the glutton. Stuffing the last of the sandwich in his gob, he handed the waitress the empty plate.

'Sure. One bacon sandwich coming up.' She turned on her heel, shouting out the order to the cook at the back as she retreated behind the counter.

Carlyle gave him a look of mock disgust. 'That's not going to help with the diet, is it?'

Joe gave him an *As if I care* grunt. Anita had placed him on an interactive, weight-loss programme almost a year ago. So far, the result was that Joseph Leon Gorka Szyszkowski had gained almost half a stone.

'Think of your arteries.'

'Gimme a break. I get enough of that stuff at home.'

'Anita just wants to avoid you keeling over one day.'

Joe belched. 'We'll all keel over one day. Look at poor young . . . What's-his-name.'

'Horatio.'

'Christ, what kind of a name is that? Anyway, the poor little bugger didn't even make it out of his teens.' A terrible thought crossed his mind. 'Probably never even got laid.'

'Stop changing the subject. You know what I mean.'

'Overall,' Joe declared, 'I'm in good shape. Better than you.' He gestured at Carlyle's battered visage. 'At this precise moment in time, anyway.'

'That wouldn't be hard.' The inspector took a sip of his coffee and gingerly felt the bump behind his left ear. It appeared to be growing in size, but wasn't actually painful as long as he didn't prod it.

Apart from smacking his head on the edge of the toilet bowl in the Mosmans' guest bathroom, he had escaped without a scratch. After the explosion, he had been out cold for maybe thirty seconds. Even the raging headache that he had come round to had subsided through the help of four Ibuprofen tablets filched from the bathroom cabinet.

'You were in just about the safest place in that house.'

Carlyle nodded. 'Yeah.' After washing down the painkillers with some tapwater, he had sat on the toilet seat and tried to take in the chaos unfolding around him: screaming alarms, groaning people, emergency sirens in the distance, getting closer. What struck him most, however, was the smell – the acrid stench of incinerated soft furnishings tinged with the aroma of charred flesh.

After several minutes, a face had appeared in the doorway. It took the inspector a moment to focus on her features. The young paramedic had clearly been investigating the carnage in the living room. The colour had drained from her face, making her look about twelve years old – a kid trying to play the part of an adult. She looked like she was going to throw up.

'Are you okay?' she asked in a shaky voice.

'I'm fine,' Carlyle smiled. 'How about you?'

'Fine.' Taking a deep breath, she shot him a look that said *Don't question my professionalism*, then stalked off.

'See you later,' Carlyle mumbled, giving her a little wave. He was quite happy just sitting there on the toilet seat and made no effort to get up until he was hit by a sudden thought: *Where is Joe?*

The waitress placed Joe's bacon sandwich on the table and looked enquiringly at the inspector for a third time. Deeply

51

irritated, Carlyle ignored her. *How many times is she going to ask me if I want anything to eat? If I want any fucking food, I'll say so.*

He glanced around the café. The only other customers were a couple of cab drivers moaning about Arsenal's wretched run of form while quickly demolishing large plates of bacon and eggs.

'You were very lucky.' Joe added some brown sauce to his sandwich before taking a bite.

'Says the man who happened to walk out of the front door five seconds before the bloody thing went off,' Carlyle snorted.

'The other good thing is,' Joe grinned, wiping some sauce from his chin, 'I was standing behind a tree, otherwise I might have been hit by the flying glass.'

'Survival instinct?'

'Mm, I'll need that when I get home.'

Carlyle laughed. 'Well, you know what they say.'

'No. What?' Another couple of swift bites and Joe's sandwich was gone.

'Better to be lucky than smart.'

Joe wiped his hands on a paper napkin. 'If Anita hadn't been giving me such grief on the phone,' he mused, 'I could have still been standing right next to that kid.'

A grave expression descended on to the inspector's face. 'Don't ever tell her that.'

'No, of course not.'

'And don't spend too much time thinking about it either.'

Joe thought about that for a few moments. Then he remarked: 'For one thing, dicing with death makes a bacon sandwich taste even better.'

Carlyle shook his head silently.

'Who would do something like that?' Joe wondered.

The inspector sucked the dregs of the coffee from his cup. 'Someone with the skills and ability to shoot a man between the eyes at close range, vaporize a kid and then walk off down the road, apparently without a care in the world. Quite impressive when you think about it.'

'Not many people like that around,' Joe agreed.

'Not on our patch, at least.'

'So, who do you think did it?'

'No idea.' Carlyle yawned. The adrenalin was beginning to wear off and he wanted to go home, jump into bed and cuddle up to Helen for an hour before the working day formally began. Getting to his feet, he signalled to the waitress for the bill. 'But that's what we have to find out, sunshine.'

A phone started bleeping. Carlyle reached into his jacket and pulled out not one but two handsets, looking at the screen of each in turn. 'Not mine,' he grunted.

Joe already had his mobile against his ear. 'Yeah, okay. Where? . . . Yeah, I know it.' Carlyle's heart sank. 'Don't worry, I was up anyway . . . Yeah, he's here . . . Yeah, okay. Shouldn't take us long to get there – maybe twenty minutes.' Ending the call, he put the phone back in his pocket and finished the last of his coffee.

'That sounds like good news,' Carlyle said wearily.

'Missing teenager,' Joe told him.

'We've had more than enough teenage trouble for one night. Can't someone else deal with it?'

'Apparently not. '

'Fuck's sake.'

'They've sent a WPC over to babysit the worried parents. Maude Hall.' Joe grinned.

Carlyle looked blank. The name meant nothing to him.

'She's very cute.'

The inspector grunted. As an old married man, he had long since realized that it was better not to notice such things. Or, at least, not to comment on them. There were lots of pretty girls in the world and none of them had anything to do with him.

'Anyway,' Joe continued, 'it's probably something and nothing. The parents are in a bit of a state though, as you can imagine.' Pushing his chair back, he got to his feet. 'Don't worry, I can handle it.'

'You're a good man, Joe.' Carlyle looked past his colleague, towards the counter. Now that he actually wanted her attention, the waitress had disappeared. Pulling a crumpled tenner from his pocket, he dropped it on the table. 'I've done my share of social-worker shit for one night. Now, I need to get to my bed.'

ELEVEN

The mornings were getting colder and darker. Winter was on the way and London would spend the next six or seven months in its default state – fifty shades of grey, damp and chilly. Zipping up his overalls, Ryan Davison climbed the steps to the office of the Street Environment Service Depot. Inside, he nodded to the supervisor, a permanently exhausted-looking man called Danimir who had fled from the civil war in the Balkans in the 1990s. For his part, Ryan had fled from the bone-crushing tedium of provincial life in the West Midlands. Both of them had found what they needed in London, more or less.

Hopping from foot to foot, Ryan watched as the clerk checked and rechecked his list with an exaggerated caution that suggested a task considerably more complex than the daily Cockpit Yard refuse-collection rota. Every day they went through this same mini-pantomime before Ryan was allocated his truck for the day. Downstairs, his crew would be getting annoyed by the delay. The sooner they started, the sooner they finished. Working on a 'task-to-finish' basis was one of the perks of the job, along with a £4,000 annual 'productivity bonus' for undertaking the weekly recycling collection.

Ryan's five-man unit – a driver and four loaders – was one of twenty crews working out of this Camden depot. Their route took them from Covent Garden in the west, to the edge of the City of London, emptying the oversized green bags full of old newspapers, glass and plastic bottles that households had left out for them. In the three months since he'd been promoted to driving the truck, Ryan had managed to get their daily run down to just under five hours. That meant that, with a bit of luck, he could be home in time to catch a *CSI* rerun on Sky before taking his afternoon kip. They were showing series six at the moment, which suited Ryan fine. He only watched up to series nine; after that, it wasn't worth watching. In his opinion, the whole thing had taken a nosedive once William Petersen had left.

Ryan believed in time management, especially when it came to getting his truck out of the depot. A good start was essential; they had to get in and out of the West End while most people were still in their beds, otherwise they would get snarled up in the morning rush-hour.

'Come on, Dan, we're ready to go.'

'Patience, patience.' Danimir didn't look up as he scratched the tip of his nose with the end of his blue biro.

Bloody bureaucrat! Ryan glanced at the row of keys lined up on the desk. Each was attached to a key-ring. Each key-ring had a number. 'Give me number six.'

'Six needs to go to the garage.' Danimir tapped his left index finger on the top of the desk for a moment, weighing up all the options before coming to a decision. He picked up a key and tossed it to Ryan. 'Take number four. It was fixed last week.'

'Great.' Ryan caught the key with a sigh. Once a truck went into the garage, it was pretty much guaranteed never to run properly again. He thought about making a grab for one of the other keys. 'What about . . . ?'

'What about you get outta here?' Danimir waved him away with an angry frown. 'Take four, like I tell you.' He fixed the young Englishman with a hard stare. 'Why are you never happy with what you get? Now, leave me to sort out the rest.'

None of the other crews have managed to turn up yet, thought Ryan, frustrated by his boss's pedantry, so what does it matter which one I take? But the clock on the wall told him that it was almost 6 a.m. He had to get going right now or the whole day would be buggered.

Danimir gave him a searching look. 'Okay?'

'Okay,' Ryan agreed, turning and reaching for the door handle.

'And don't miss out Doughty Street this time,' Danimir called after him. 'I don't want that bloody woman at number twenty-nine ringing me up again. Pain in the arse says she's going to write to the bloody Mayor.' Danimir shook his head at the injustice of it all.

'A lot of good that will do her,' Ryan laughed.

'Bloody woman! Just make sure you empty her bag properly, put it back where she left it, and don't leave a mess.'

'Sure thing, boss.' Ryan grinned. He would make sure to tell the lads to leave number 29's recycling untouched for another week.

Halfway down the outer stairs, Ryan pointed towards the hulking Dennis Elite 2 parked at the end of a row of trucks on the far side of the yard. 'We've got number four,' he shouted to one of his loaders, Steve McKitten, a Camden veteran with more than twenty years on the bins. Giving his driver a thumbs-up, McKitten jogged over to the truck indicated.

Ryan nodded to two of the other loaders – a Hungarian and a Welshman – and headed for the driver's cab. Grabbing the door handle, he was just about to pull himself up when McKitten popped his head round the side of the vehicle. 'Ryan!' he yelled. 'You'd better come and see this.'

I knew it! Ryan thought angrily. That Serbian twat's given us a knackered truck. Jumping back down on to the tarmac, he jogged round to the rear.

'Look.' Steve pointed at the pair of legs sticking out from under a pile of soggy cardboard boxes in the loading hopper.

'Holy shit.' Ryan realized immediately that there would be no early start for them today. He wouldn't be getting home in time to catch a *CSI* rerun, even if it was one of the proper ones with

William Petersen in it. He scratched his head, wondering what to do. 'Stay here,' he eventually told McKitten. 'Don't touch anything. I'll go and tell Dan.'

'She's never done anything like this before.' Alison Gillespie stared at Joe Szyszkowski as if daring him to contradict her.

'No.' The sergeant glanced at WPC Hall, who was sitting next to Mrs Gillespie on the sofa. At this time of the morning, the sergeant decided, she didn't look quite so cute. With nothing else to do, he stared at his notes.

Hannah Gillespie. Fourteen. Five foot two. Eight stone or thereabouts. One sister, safely tucked up in bed. Attends St Marylebone C of E, a good school. Good student. No obvious problems. No boyfriend (according to her parents). Went out to see a friend but never turned up. Not answering her mobile. A list of other friends who she hadn't gone to see either.

Joe sighed. His handwriting really was terrible.

So, what about young Hannah? It was probably something and nothing. On his way over, he had checked whether the kid had turned up at a local A&E or police station. Nothing. She was probably just partying somewhere with a boyfriend that her parents didn't know about.

The parents seemed a fairly nondescript pair. Their anxiety was real enough, however.

'Would you like a cup of tea?' Roger Gillespie asked for the third time in the last ten minutes.

Joe held up a hand. 'I'm fine, sir, thanks all the same.' Flipping his notebook closed, he replaced it in the back pocket of his jeans. 'And thank you for your time. We have all the details and we will now see what we can do. I'll be in touch as soon as possible. Of course, if Hannah does turn up, let us know straight away.' A familiar look of dismay passed across the faces of both parents, and he offered them what he hoped might pass for a comforting smile. 'I'm sure there's a simple explanation,' he added gently. 'We see this kind of thing all the time. Maybe

Hannah's staying with a different friend and her mobile's simply died.'

'But . . .' Roger Gillespie wanted to protest, but he didn't quite know how.

Joe beckoned to Hall. As the WPC jumped to her feet, he handed the father a business card with his mobile number on it. 'Let us know *immediately* if – *when* – Hannah comes home,' he repeated.

'Yes.' Gillespie stared intently at the card as if in search of something – hope, maybe.

'Good.' Stifling a yawn, the sergeant stepped towards the door. 'Otherwise, I will give you a call later in the day for a catch-up.' Ducking into the hall, he quickly opened the front door and disappeared down the communal stairs before they could think of anything else to ask him.

TWELVE

Sitting in the back booth of Il Buffone, Carlyle yawned expressively. The tiny 1950s-style Italian café was located on the north side of Macklin Street, in the north-east corner of Covent Garden, just across the road from his own small apartment in Winter Garden House. Daughter Alice had left for school and he was enjoying the rare opportunity for breakfast with his wife.

'John!' Helen gestured for him to cover his mouth.

'Sorry, it was a *loooong* night.' Inhaling her perfume – Chanel No. 5 Eau de Parfum – he meekly complied. She was wearing the Paul Smith polka-dot jacket – the one he'd splashed out on last Christmas – over a conservative pearl-coloured blouse, with a single button undone at the neck. With her hair pulled back in a ponytail and minimal make-up, he caught more than a glimpse of the girl he'd fallen for, all those years ago. I'm a lucky, lucky man, he thought, with a beautiful wife who puts up with me rolling in at all hours, looking like shit.

Catching him staring at her, she gave him a quizzical look. 'What?'

'Nothing,' he smiled. 'I was just thinking how lovely you look.' There was nothing he would have liked better than for them to finish their breakfast and head back to bed for another kip, and maybe something else. *If only . . .*

'You do look very tired.'

'I look old,' he grumbled.

'No, just tired.' Reaching across the table, she ran her hand through his hair. 'With some extra grey around the temples, perhaps.'

'Comes with the territory.'

'You could always go and see my guy in Berwick Street.'

'Ha!' Carlyle studiously avoided thinking about how much Helen spent on her Aussie hairdresser in Soho.

'Scott is really good.'

'You've got to be kidding. I'm not going to get it dyed.'

'Okay, okay.' His wife gave him a consoling squeeze on the arm. 'How was it last night? What a terrible situation!'

'It was all a bit of a mess, really.' Explaining further what had happened, Carlyle was careful to imply that neither he nor Joe had been anywhere near poor Horatio Mosman when he departed this earth.

Listening attentively to her husband, Helen blew on her green tea before taking a cautious sip. When he had finished, she looked him carefully up and down, making it clear that she understood he was being economical with the *actualité*. 'It sounds appalling even by your standards.'

'It *was* fairly rough,' Carlyle admitted, reaching for his own mug. With more than enough coffee in his system already, he had passed on his usual double macchiato and gone for a green tea like his wife. There was no way, however, he was going to pass on the outsized raisin Danish which Marcello, the café's Italian owner, had placed on the table almost before they had sat down. Picking up a knife, he carefully cut the pastry into quarters. Popping one section into his mouth, he began chewing.

'Who would want to blow up a teenage boy?' Helen asked, nibbling on a slice of brown toast lightly covered in raspberry jam.

'No idea.'

'Will you catch them?'

'No idea.' Keen to change the subject, Carlyle gestured at the hardback book Helen had placed on the table. On the spine, the title *MONEY HONEY* was blocked out in capital letters. 'Any good?'

'So-so.' Helen shrugged. 'I borrowed it from someone at work.'

Carlyle grinned lasciviously. 'Mummy porn, is it?'

'No, no,' Helen said. 'It's written by an academic who argues that women should exploit their erotic assets to get ahead.'

'I thought they already did.'

She shot him a sharp look.

'Joke,' Carlyle said.

'It's just written to be provocative and get reviews,' Helen told him.

'Like that woman who wrote about her divorce?'

'Exactly. It's amazing how some people can generate ink.'

'Meanwhile, writers like Lee Child get ignored by the literary snobs. After all, writing good stories and selling books – where's the interest in that?' Carlyle was himself a Lee Child man. He gestured once more to the book on the table. 'So, how does one exploit one's erotic assets then?'

'It's all about where you draw the line,' Helen explained. 'For instance, is it okay to marry a footballer for lifestyle reasons? Should prostitution be legalized?'

Prostitution *is* legal, Carlyle thought. Kind of.

'Is surrogate pregnancy a legitimate source of income?'

'Interesting questions.'

'A lot of it is quite offensive.'

So why are you reading it then? Carlyle wondered, keeping his mouth clamped firmly shut.

'Maybe,' Helen sighed, 'I'm just a prisoner of my post-feminist Puritan Anglo-Saxon antagonism to sexuality.'

He had no idea what she was talking about. 'Good for you.'

She tapped the cover of the book. 'I don't think I'll bother finishing it.' Then after taking another sip of her tea, she asked, 'Oh, by the way, did you read the thing in the paper about your celebrity friend?'

'Which celebrity friend?' Carlyle waved a hand airily. 'I have so many.'

'Rosanna Snowdon.'

'Ah, yes.'

'Marcello?' Helen flashed the café-owner the kind of winning smile she no longer needed to waste on her husband. 'Do you happen to have a copy of yesterday's *Standard*?'

Behind the counter, the old man wiped his hands on a tea-towel draped over his left shoulder. 'Probably,' he said, ducking into the back room. A few moments later he was back, newspaper in hand.

'Thanks.' Helen began flicking through the pages, reading off various headlines as she did so. '"Madame Tussauds forced to employ guards to prevent tourists making offensive Hitler salutes next to a waxwork of the dictator" . . . It was here somewhere.' She turned another page. 'Ah yes, here you go. "TV presenter death. Suspect arrested for a second time".'

Folding the newspaper in half, she placed it on the table between them. Carlyle scanned the article. The gist of it seemed to be that new, unspecified forensic evidence had convinced the Crown Prosecution Service that they could now successfully place Rosanna's stalker, Simon Lovell, at the scene of the crime.

'Better late than never,' Carlyle said.

'If they're actually right this time.'

'Of course.' He finished reading the article. Rosanna's parents themselves had declined to comment but Lovell's current lawyer – an ambulance-chaser by the name of Nigel Bradfield – was talking a good game.

'The police and the CPS should be focused on trying to catch the real killer of Rosanna Snowdon,' Bradfield was quoted as saying. 'This attempt to railroad my client does not help anyone, including Rosanna's family. The previous trial was stopped almost even before it had begun. This time we may well not even get to court. Simon Lovell has already been a victim of this investigation. His chances of a normal life have been severely diminished and we will be seeking substantial compensation in due course.'

'Lovell did it, didn't he?' Helen asked once he'd finished reading the piece.

Carlyle placed the newspaper at the far end of the table. 'No idea. You have to assume so. The CPS is very risk-averse, so I can't believe they would come back for a second go at this guy if they weren't supremely confident. I just hope they've got it right. Apart from anything else, it would be very cruel to get her parents' hopes up again after all this time.' He popped another quarter of the Danish into his mouth and washed it down with some more green tea.

Helen smiled. 'It's good, the way you and Joe go and visit them from time to time.'

'It's not a big deal,' Carlyle grunted. Just then, his mobile started vibrating in the breast pocket of his jacket. Fishing it out, he studied the screen. 'It's Joe.'

Waving at Marcello for the bill, he hit the receive button. 'Morning.' Wedging the phone between his head and shoulder, he pulled out his wallet and handed Helen a tenner. 'Where? . . . Are you there now? . . . Okay, I'm only five minutes away. I'll be right there.'

Ending the call, he jumped to his feet.

'Problem?' Helen asked.

'Yeah. It's certainly all happening today.' Leaning across the table, he gave her a kiss on the top of her head, then scooped up the plate containing the remaining quarters of his pastry. 'Marcello,' he asked, 'can I have a bag to put these in, please?

THIRTEEN

'I'm guessing that it wasn't natural causes.'

'London's leading detective . . .' Susan Phillips gave him a cheery wave with a latex-gloved hand.

'So they say,' Carlyle answered, pleased to see a friendly face at a crime scene for once. Phillips had been a staff pathologist with the Met for almost twenty years; she was a quick, no-nonsense operator and he enjoyed working with her. He gestured towards the pair of legs protruding from under the rubbish. 'What happened?'

'I don't know yet. We've worked all the way from the front gate right here to the truck but haven't picked up anything useful so far. I'm going to have to get in there.'

Carlyle grimaced. 'Rather you than me. The smell's bad enough from here.'

'Tell me about it.' Phillips stepped away from the back of the refuse truck and wiped the sweat from her brow with the back of her left wrist. A couple of assistants hovered in the background, awaiting instruction. 'At least I'm dressed for the occasion.'

Yes you are, Carlyle thought. Slim and blonde, Phillips had a healthy glow that even her present surroundings could not diminish. In a pair of Converse All Stars, skinny jeans and a Nirvana T-shirt, she could easily have passed for early thirties rather than mid-to-late forties. All in all, she was rather glamorous . . . for the Met.

Phillips caught him checking her out and grinned. 'You like Nirvana, Inspector?'

'Nah.' He shook his head, embarrassed at being caught gawping for the second time this morning. 'A bit after my time, really. Punk was more my thing – The Clash, Stiff Little Fingers . . .' *Shut up*, warned a voice inside his head, *you're showing your age*. '. . . and The Jam.'

'Mm.' She gestured vaguely across the depot. 'Not really punk, were they, The Jam?'

'That's Entertainment' started playing in his head and he laughed to himself. 'Not really, I suppose.'

'More like Mod revivalists.'

'Yeah.'

'Anyway, Joe's up in the office, running through the CCTV footage.' From under the next truck along, a squirrel appeared and eyed them both inquisitively.

'No nuts here, mate,' Carlyle told him.

'What?'

Carlyle pointed towards the squirrel, but it was already gone. Phillips gave him a funny look. 'Are you okay?'

'Yeah, yeah.' He couldn't be bothered to explain.

'How's the family?'

'Fine. You?'

'The usual.' Phillips shrugged. 'I've been going out with a doctor for a few months.'

'Uh-huh?'

'Yeah.' She stared off into the middle distance. 'Nice guy. His ex-wife is a pain in the arse though.'

'Mm.' Carlyle had little sympathy. If you insisted on making your private life as complicated as possible, aggravation was inevitable.

Picking up on his obvious lack of interest, Phillips abandoned the topic of her love-life. Stripping off her latex gloves, the pathologist pulled a BlackBerry from the back pocket of her jeans and started typing away on its keyboard with her thumbs.

Looking up, she caught the quizzical look on the inspector's face. 'It's a twenty-four-hour tweet,' she explained. 'The PR department thought it would be a good idea if we tweeted live from our crime scenes so as to provide the public with some insight into what we do.'

'Sweet Jesus!' Hands on hips, Carlyle raised his eyes to the heavens.

'You should check it out,' Phillips grinned. 'You might learn something. The Twitter handle is @metpolice121. We've got more than ten thousand followers.'

'Good for you,' replied the inspector grumpily.

'*Arrived at scene*,' said Phillips, reading aloud from the screen, '*body to be examined.*'

'Very bloody insightful. Can we get on with it now?'

'You're such a dinosaur, John.'

That was hardly the worst thing that anyone had ever called him. 'I'm a dinosaur in a hurry.'

'Yes, yes.' She jerked a thumb at the rear of the truck. 'Give me half an hour and I'll be able to offer you some initial thoughts.'

'That would be great.' He was already heading for the stairs leading to the office. 'I'll come back and see you then.'

London was such a shitty city.

Shitty.

There was just no other word for it.

As an endless procession of grey rainclouds scudded across the sky outside the window of his office on the thirteenth floor of New Scotland Yard, Sir Chester Forsyth-Walker flicked a speck of lint from the lapel of his uniform and let out a heartfelt sigh. Being Commissioner of the Metropolitan Police Service was no fun at all. Not for the first time, he wondered just how he'd managed to get himself into quite such a pickle.

Up until four years ago, Sir Chester's career arc had appeared perfect: the 1980s on Merseyside had been spent working in uniformed policing, road traffic, personnel, Professional Standards and the Control Room; the 1990s took him to Greater Manchester Police, first as a Superintendent and later as Commander of the Wigan Division; then the first decade of the new century saw him move to Lancashire Constabulary as Assistant Chief Constable – with responsibility for Human Resources and Training – before skipping over the Pennines to become Deputy Chief Constable of West Yorkshire, Acting Chief Constable and later full-time Chief Constable.

The progression had been smooth, effortless, almost trouble-free. He had been well on the way to enjoying a near-perfect career in public service. There had even been a Queen's Policing Medal in Her Majesty's New Year's Honours List, with the promise of more to come if he kept his nose clean.

And then he'd allowed his head to be turned by a smarmy politician named Christian Holyrod. The mere thought of the Mayor of London now made him grimace. He should have known better! Running the MPS – the Metropolitan Police Service – was a bit like trying to run Tesco after a lifetime of running a corner shop. Sure, it had fast-tracked his knighthood, but he would have got one of those anyway.

Even in the beginning, Sir Chester wasn't dumb enough to think he could handle a job like this. But he wasn't smart enough to say no either. So now, at a time of life when the most taxing part of his job should be giving a speech to the local Rotarians, he instead found himself having to deal with one ridiculous high-profile mess after another.

Even by the Met's standards, today's fiasco was quite something. Only with immense effort did Sir Chester manage to pick up the sheet of white A4 paper on which was typed a summary of the Horatio Mosman case. Good God, he thought sadly, what was going on here? You would never get this kind of nonsense up in Wakefield or Batley. Pining for a return to the real world populated by normal people, he dropped the report back on to his desk and looked up.

'Well?'

'Well *what*, sir?' Despite her best intentions, Commander Carole Simpson couldn't help but sound snappy. Getting dragged out of bed for a crisis meeting with the Commissioner was never the best way to start your day. She had yet to have any breakfast; it would take a double espresso at least before her mood approached anything resembling decent.

Sir Chester shifted uneasily in his seat. One of the other things he hated about the Met was the uppity nature of many of the senior officers. Especially the women. Staff in the provinces seemed to find it easier to know their place, and to do what they were told. 'Well,' he said slowly, 'we have a child—'

'Teenager,' Simpson corrected him.

'Young adult,' giggled Simon Shelbourne, Sir Chester's Communications Director, who was standing in the corner behind Simpson.

The Commander turned sideways in her seat, in order to be able to see both men at once. This was her first chance to get a good look at Shelbourne: a weedy-looking guy in a Richard James slate-grey pinstripe suit with a ridiculous lime-green shirt. Although in his mid-thirties, the PR man looked about twelve, with pale blue eyes blinking behind chunky burgundy-coloured spectacles, sandy hair and a chin that looked like it had never seen a five o'clock shadow.

All the same, the boyish clothes-horse had more than a decade in tabloid journalism behind him, culminating in a year as Editor of the *Sunday Witness* (dubbed 'the *Sunday Witless*' by rivals). After raising the circulation by more than half a million copies, which was no mean feat in the desperately tough weekend-newspaper market, Shelbourne had surprised colleagues and critics alike by crossing over to the dark side and becoming a PR man. Even more surprising was his choice of new employer. Rather than making a killing working for some American investment firm or Chinese technology company, he had joined the police force, signing on as spinner-in-chief for Sir Chester Forsyth-Walker.

Amongst other things, Forsyth-Walker's predecessor as Commissioner, Luke Osgood, had been deemed politically unacceptable and therefore 'unsafe' when it came to handling the media. Sir Chester, on the other hand, was expected to keep a low profile and, with Shelbourne's help, say and do nothing that would contradict or embarrass the Mayor.

'Let's continue.' The Commissioner glared at both of them in turn. 'We have Horatio Mosman, who was murdered by a bomb. And we have Mr . . .'

'Marc Harrington,' Shelbourne said quietly. 'Marc with a c. No k.'

'Mr Marc Harrington,' said Sir Chester, through gritted teeth, 'no k, who was shot in the face presumably by the same person who later blew up young Horatio.' He paused, waiting for another interjection. When none was forthcoming, he ploughed on. 'Needless to say, the media are all over this.' Shelbourne nodded solemnly. 'And the good people of London need some reassurance that this . . . this crazy person is going to be caught quickly and with a minimum of fuss.'

'We have a press conference scheduled for an hour's time,' volunteered Shelbourne.

'So,' Sir Chester now gave Commander Simpson his most no-nonsense stare, 'what have you got for me?'

Now it was Carole Simpson's turn to shift in her seat. She picked up the sheet of paper on the Commissioner's desk. 'The basics are contained in this initial summary report. Our investigation is currently underway, but it is still at a very early stage. We will begin interviewing the family members later this morning.'

A grim expression crossed Sir Chester's face as a spasm of pain shot across his lower back. *Bloody slipped disc.* Not that anyone gave him any sympathy. At last he was going into hospital to get it sorted next week. 'One thing that is not in the report,' he remarked, once the pain had passed, 'is why those bomb technicians didn't manage to stop the bloody thing going off?'

'We won't be going there in the presser,' Shelbourne said hastily.

'No, but the bloody journalists will,' Sir Chester huffed.

'Don't worry,' Shelbourne reassured him. 'I will jump in if it gets tricky.'

Which it will, Simpson decided.

'It's just us two?' Sir Chester asked, glancing at Simpson.

'Yes,' Shelbourne replied. 'I don't think we need the Commander to be present at this time.'

'Fine by me,' said Simpson. She felt more than a little relieved at not having to face the assembled journalists. There had been a time when she liked nothing more than parading in front of the media. Not any longer. Ever since her husband's conviction for fraud had stopped her career in its tracks, her need for a public profile had evaporated. 'By the way, Horatio wasn't blown up by the bomb fastened around his neck,' she explained. 'Indeed, there wasn't a bomb around his neck. There was, however, a bomb that had been placed under the sofa.'

'And how, in the name of God, did we manage to miss that?' Chester's face began turning pink. 'What were your officers doing?'

'They were on the scene merely by accident,' Simpson said quietly, 'and tried to assist the victim at great risk to themselves.'

'Didn't get blown to smithereens though, did they?'

You make it sound like you wish they had, Simpson thought angrily. 'This was a terrible act of violence,' she said, 'culminating in the tragic loss of a young life. However, we are very fortunate that there were not any more fatalities.'

'That's great,' said Shelbourne, scribbling furiously in a spiral notebook. '*The tragic loss of a young life* – we can use that. And add something along the lines of *the public can rest assured that we will be devoting all necessary resources to catching the perpetrator* – no, *the evil perpetrator*.' He grinned at his boss. 'That's really all you need to say.'

'Fine,' said Sir Chester wearily.

'After that, I'll give them the tip-off hotline number, and then we can quickly move on to the rest of the agenda.'

The Commissioner groaned. 'There's more?'

'Besides the exploding teenager, we've got the garlic-bread killer and the feral youths.'

Simpson raised her eyebrows. 'Sounds like quite a briefing.'

Sir Chester shot her a dirty look before returning his attention to his Comms Director. 'Go on, tell me.'

'Good news and bad news.' Releasing his inner hack, Shelbourne jumped from foot to foot like an excited five year old with a bursting bladder as he flipped through his notes. 'Good news,' he said, finding the right page. 'Jordan Perry, aged twenty-five, walked into the Elephant and Castle police station and confessed to the murder of his girlfriend, Sally Ellis. Apparently, he stabbed her thirty-eight times after she complained that he had not made garlic bread for tea.'

Sir Chester cleared his throat. 'A man who makes the tea?'

'One thing I have learned since I joined the Met,' Shelbourne beamed, 'is that real life *is* stranger than fiction. On being arrested, Mr Perry told officers: "*It's not that I am a horrible person, but shit happens*".'

'Quite,' said Sir Chester, struggling with the various concepts that had just been raised by this sordid tale of everyday woe.

'Sounds like an episode of *EastEnders*,' Simpson observed.

'What?' The soap opera might have an audience of millions every week, but Sir Chester wasn't one of them. He genuinely had no idea what his colleague was talking about.

'Nothing.'

The Commissioner drummed his fingers impatiently on the top of his desk. 'Simon, why are we featuring this incident?'

'It goes to our anti-domestic violence agenda,' Shelbourne clarified. 'Plus, partially at least, it should help offset the *bad* news.'

'Which is?' In search of some much-needed divine assistance, Sir Chester lifted his eyes to the heavens.

'Which is the continued fall-out from your remarks about the so-called "feral underclass" blighting the inner city.'

'But they are,' Sir Chester whined.

Shelbourne smiled sadly. 'You are correct, of course, but articulating that view in an uncontrolled environment – that is, by making the observation at the Young Busker of the Year Awards ceremony – was unfortunate.'

'Tsk.'

'And it was unfortunate *in the extreme* that a bleeding-heart journalist from the *Guardian* happened to be standing next to you when it slipped out.'

'But some little sod had just put a cobblestone through the window of my Jaguar at the time.' Sir Chester glanced at Simpson, hoping to elicit a little sympathy but none was forthcoming. 'My driver got a terrible shock. He was off sick with stress for a week.'

Poor dear, thought Simpson.

'Even so,' Shelbourne mused, 'both the Mayor and the Prime Minister have publicly disowned the term "feral underclass". You're on your own, so there will definitely be a question or two on it.'

'Bloody politicians.'

This time, Simpson nodded sympathetically.

'No matter,' said Shelbourne cheerily, 'we'll take it on the chin. Just say that the time for arguing over words has long gone. What we need now is a big debate across London in terms of how we empower local communities and reduce the fear of crime, especially among young people in the inner city.'

Wasn't having a big debate the same as arguing over words? Simpson wondered.

Clearly unconvinced, Sir Chester clasped his hands together. 'A big debate?'

'Yes,' Shelbourne chortled. 'With a bit of luck, if we have a big enough debate, by the time it's finished, the *Guardian* will have gone bust. Those hand-wringing lefties couldn't find a sustainable business model if it hit them over the head.'

Sir Chester grunted. He couldn't care less about the travails of the newspaper industry. 'And what about our friend Mr Meyer?'

'You know the drill on that one,' Shelbourne replied. 'We never comment on Chief Inspector Russell Meyer, or on Operation Redhead.'

'But we'll get asked about it, nevertheless.' Feeling a further spasm in his lower back, Sir Chester allowed his eyes to close. Maybe he could wish all his troubles away. That's what Tanya would tell him to do: sit back, relax, and breathe your troubles away. His wife had been a stress counsellor, back in the days before she enjoyed the honour and privilege of becoming the second Mrs Forsyth-Walker. As such, she was a firm believer in the power of positive thinking.

Then, again, Tanya had never had to try and run the bloody Met.

'Operation Redhead is completely independent of the MPS,' Shelbourne parroted, 'and does not come under your control. We have no particular insights into its operations, and have made it clear from the start that we will never comment on its progress.'

Keeping his eyes firmly shut, Sir Chester tried to think of something positive.

'Maybe I should get going,' said Simpson, as she slid out of her chair.

'Just one final thing, Commander.'

'Yes?'

The Commissioner's eyes opened slowly. 'Your man chasing the Mosman bomber . . .'

Simpson stiffened. 'What about him?'

'Is he up to it?'

Stopped in her tracks, the Commander placed a hand on the back of the chair. 'Inspector Carlyle is a very experienced officer, sir,' she said quietly. 'If you look at his track record . . .'

Another spasm shot through Sir Chester's abdomen, causing him to wince in pain. As he waited for it to pass, his mood darkened even further. 'I don't care about his bloody track record,' he snapped. 'Even a blind squirrel manages to find the occasional nut.'

Shelbourne let out a girlish titter.

'What?' Simpson asked.

'I don't care about the past,' Sir Chester grunted. 'I care about the here and now. Is he going to sort this nonsense out?'

Simpson nodded. 'I understand the need for a quick result, sir. Rest assured, the inspector is on top of it.' Defending her colleague did not come naturally to the Commander. Their relationship had improved considerably over the last couple of years, but Carlyle still made her uneasy. His ability to get results was matched only by his capacity to be immensely annoying and totally unmanageable. Given the circumstances, she knew better than to try and take him off the case now. 'He handled the situation well, I thought.'

'We can't afford to wait too long for results.'

Simpson took a half-step backwards, towards the door. 'That is well understood. I am sure that Inspector Carlyle will deliver.'

The Commissioner looked less than convinced. 'Keep me fully informed, Commander.'

'I will, sir.'

'Good.' Turning to his PR flunky, Sir Chester ran a hand through his thinning grey hair. 'I'm all yours, Simon. Will I be doing any television?'

FOURTEEN

'It's all glamour, this job,' Carlyle mumbled to himself as he read the sign next to the door at the top of the stairs. Stepping inside, he nodded at Joe.

'Boss.'

Carlyle looked his sergeant up and down; saw he was still wearing the same clothes and hadn't shaved. 'You look like a man who's been up all night.' As the inspector got closer, he realized that his colleague didn't smell that great either, but for once he was too polite to mention that.

Joe shrugged. 'I got an hour's sleep in one of the cells at the station.'

'Comfortable?'

'Very nice.' Joe managed a tired smile. 'They even brought me a cup of tea when it was time to get up.'

'Mm.' I'm too old for that kind of thing, Carlyle thought. 'How did it go with the . . . ?' He tried to remember the name of the family of the missing girl, but his mind was blank.

'The Gillespies,' Joe reminded him. 'It went so-so. I spoke to them again about half an hour ago. Hannah still hasn't turned up, but we haven't hit the panic button just yet.'

'Mm.' That seemed about all that the inspector was able to manage at the moment.

'It's not great for the parents but we just have to wait.'

'Yes.'

'We've done all the usual checks,' Joe confirmed.

'Okay.' Parking the runaway teenager for the moment, Carlyle turned his attention to the gaunt man who sat behind a battered desk, busily tapping away at a computer keyboard.

'This is Danimir Janko,' Joe explained. 'He's the supervisor here.'

'Bastards!' Danimir hissed, apparently oblivious to the inspector's arrival. He gestured at the screen. 'See what they do?'

'We've got the security images up,' said Joe, as Carlyle walked round the desk to take a look. 'You can see pretty well what happened.'

'See?' The twenty-inch screen was split into four quarters, each showing a different grainy, green-tinged still of the depot yard at night. Danimir pointed to the top-right quadrant and clicked on the mouse. As the video began running, two figures appeared out of the gloom. One was suited and booted while the other wore a hooded top, jeans and sneakers.

'No prizes for guessing which one is the killer,' said Joe as the hoodie pushed open the gate and the duo stepped into the depot.

Carlyle leaned forward to get a closer view. 'Wasn't it locked?'

'Vandals.' Danimir shrugged. 'It's been broken for almost a month now, but the Council?' He spoke wearily. 'They do nothing.'

Carlyle just about managed not to grin. On the screen, the two figures walked across the yard before disappearing between two trucks. 'Is that it?'

'Wait,' said Danimir. 'I speed it up.'

It took only a few seconds to fast-forward through the next four minutes.

'There!' The hoodie reappeared and Danimir instantly returned the tape to normal speed. Carlyle watched as the man retraced his steps, exiting through the broken gate and disappearing back into the gloom.

'Two go in,' said Joe, 'and one comes out. That's our man.'

'Presumably there are no images of what they got up to in the meantime?' the inspector asked.

'No.' Danimir shook his head. 'You can see the pair of them coming in from different angles, then heading across the yard, but once they go between those vehicles, there's nothing. They're hidden.'

'That figures,' Carlyle sighed. 'Can we enhance the images to get a better look at the guy wearing the hood?'

'They've already been sent over to SERIS,' Joe told him. 'They're going to take a look today.' SERIS – Specialist Evidence Recovery Imaging Services – was part of Specialist Crime Directorate 4, the Met's Forensic Services Unit.

'Good.' Pointing at the time-code stamped in one corner of the screen, Carlyle looked up at his sergeant. 'This wasn't that late. What about witnesses?'

'There aren't that many residential properties around here,' Joe replied. 'It's mainly offices but there's a council block nearby. There's also a pub round the corner, and a theatre. We're getting some uniforms to go door-to-door right now, and again this evening.'

'Okay.' Carlyle straightened up. 'The bin men are downstairs?'

'Yeah.' Joe nodded. 'There's a rest room on the ground floor.'

'They're not bin men,' said Danimir huffily, looking up from his computer. 'They're Street Environment Officers.'

'Whatever,' said Carlyle, heading for the door.

The Street Environment Officers had nothing of any use to tell him. After some desultory questioning, the inspector strolled across the depot yard where, having climbed into the back of the refuse truck, Susan Phillips was standing directly over the body.

'Having fun?' he asked.

'Help me down.'

Rather reluctantly, he held out a hand. Grasping it, the pathologist jumped back down on to the tarmac.

'Thanks.'

'No problem,' Carlyle replied, carefully wiping his hand on the arse of his trousers.

Phillips scratched her nose with a gloved finger. Like Joe, she didn't smell too good but, ever the gentleman, the inspector once again said nothing. 'Well,' she said brightly, 'there's no doubt about what killed your victim; he was stabbed in the chest three times.'

'Robbery?'

'Doesn't look like it. His wallet was still in his jacket pocket.'

'Jolly good.'

'There was quite a bit of cash in it – at least a couple of hundred, I'd say. He also had a fancy-looking watch which wasn't taken.' She gestured towards one of her assistants, who was standing in the middle of the yard surrounded by a collection of police-branded transparent plastic evidence bags of differing sizes. 'Kara's got it over there. The guy's name was Duncan Brown. Looks like he was a journalist – there was a union card in his wallet.'

'Journalists and policemen,' Carlyle mused, 'the only people who are still unionized these days.' A Redskins song popped into his head – *stop, strike, unionize* – and he smiled. Forget The Jam, that really *was* punk rock.

Post-punk punk.

Or something like that.

'What?'

'Nothing.' Kicking the Redskins into touch, he gestured towards the back of the refuse truck. 'This is all great information. Can you tell me who killed him, too?'

'That's *your* job. We'll get him out of here first and I'll do my report. But you know the basics.'

'That's great, Susan, thanks.' The inspector pulled out his phone and found the number for the front desk at Charing Cross police station, where he and Joe worked. 'Where are you taking him?'

'Dunno. We haven't found a free slab yet.'

'Okay. Let me know when you do, and I'll get a formal identification of the body.'

'Thanks.'

'My pleasure. See you later.' Walking away, he hit the call button and listened to it ring. After a few moments, the desk sergeant picked up. Explaining what he wanted, Carlyle listened to the guy bash away at a keyboard for a few seconds before coming back on the line.

'We got a call at one thirty-two this morning from a Gemma Millington.' He gave the inspector the woman's contact details.

'Thanks.' Ending the call, Carlyle went to retrieve the victim's effects from Kara.

FIFTEEN

Gemma Millington's roots needed attention.

'What?' The tired-looking near-blonde had looked up from her steaming glass of jasmine tea and caught the inspector staring at the crown of her head.

'Er . . . nothing. ' How many times was he going to get caught staring at women today? Carlyle placed his demitasse on the table and pulled up a red plastic chair. They were in the canteen on the top floor of the office block where she worked on Buckingham Palace Road. It was too early for the lunchtime rush, but the place was still fairly full. In the background, there was the clack of ball on ball as a couple of staffers played at one of the blue-baize billiards tables lined up at the far end of the room. To his left, the floor-to-ceiling windows gave an excellent view over the back gardens of the royal palace itself. 'This is quite some place you have here.'

'The *Financial Times* did a piece on it recently.' She took a mouthful of tea. 'They called it "a twenty-first-century play-school for grown-ups", something like that.'

'Nice.' Trying not to make it too obvious this time, he gave her the once-over as he sipped his green tea. Late twenties slash early thirties, smartly dressed in a dark business suit and pale pink blouse, pretty enough but with a hard edge to her features that would, under different circumstances, have encouraged him to give her a wide berth.

This morning, she looked pissed off rather than upset. Indeed, he had gained an impression that 'annoyed' was Gemma Millington's default demeanour. London can do that to you, Carlyle thought. It puts you on your guard.

At any rate, she did not look like the grieving girlfriend. In truth, that was a bit of a result. The inspector hated having to do the 'my condolences' routine with the friends and family of the victims of crime. The social-worker aspect of the job was something he had never been any good at.

'Napoleon once said an army marches on its stomach,' she remarked. 'Here they just want us to stay inside the building – get more work done.' This was clearly an opinion that she had expressed many times before.

'And do you?'

She looked at him blankly.

'Stay inside the building.'

'Yes. I mean, the food's good.' She gestured at the blackboard menu which covered most of one wall, listing a wide choice of dishes from sashimi and courgette tapenade to shepherd's pie, each offering colour-coded with a little yellow, green or red dot. 'And it's all free.'

'Free? Jesus, that must cost a fortune.'

She gave him a look. 'This company made more than two *billion* pounds in profit last quarter.'

'I guess they can throw you the odd pie then.' Carlyle pointed at the board. 'What do the coloured dots mean?'

'Everything is ranked by its nutritional value. Red essentially means pudding, cheesecake and stuff. Green is the healthy stuff. Yellow is somewhere in the middle.'

'I'm a red man,' Carlyle grinned.

'Apart from the restaurant, downstairs in the basement there's a newsagent, a chemist, and even a dry cleaner's.'

'Maybe I could come and work here,' Carlyle quipped.

'All the security is outsourced,' she replied quickly.

'It was a joke.'

'Ah.'

82

Carlyle finished his tea. 'So, what is it that you do exactly?'

'I'm one of the in-house legal team.'

A lawyer and a journalist, Carlyle reflected. Her relationship with Duncan Brown must have been a barrel of laughs.

She pulled a business card from the overstuffed handbag sitting on the table between them and handed it across. 'I'm the sixth youngest VP of Legal that they've ever hired in Europe.'

'Wow!' Carlyle tried to look impressed. 'Congratulations.'

'I cover the whole waterfront: government relations, corporate development and new business development.'

'I see. That sounds . . . interesting.'

'This is a great place to be working – there is so much going on.'

'I'm sure.' He stuffed the card into his jacket pocket. 'And you're okay talking about Duncan here, at work?'

She shrugged. 'Might as well.'

Definitely not seeming heartbroken.

'Don't want to take time off?'

'No, not at all.'

'Sure?'

She gave him a hard stare. 'My decision. Let's just get on with it.'

'Fine. They explained to you what happened?'

'I got the basics from your colleague earlier. But you were there? You've actually seen him, haven't you?'

'Yes,' Carlyle nodded.

'So why don't you tell me what happened?'

Carlyle replied, 'That's what I need to find out.' He quickly ran through his visit to Cockpit Yard, not feeling any particular need to sanitize the story for the clearly robust Ms Millington's benefit.

'My God!' Millington took another mouthful of tea. 'Presumably it was some random nutter?'

The inspector looked at her carefully. 'Why would you say that?'

'You should know about these things rather better than me, Inspector,' she said somewhat reproachfully. 'Duncan must just have been in the wrong place at the wrong time.'

Carlyle thought back to the CCTV images.

She had given up on the eye-contact now, allowing herself to be distracted by the guys playing billiards on the other side of the room. 'I can't see what else could have happened. What do you think?'

'I've no idea.' Carlyle rummaged round in his jacket pocket and found a scrap of paper and a biro. This was supposed to be an interview, so he should at least pretend to take some notes.

Millington tapped an expensively manicured finger on the screen of her BlackBerry, which sat on the table. 'You must think I'm a really hard bitch,' she said, as if challenging him to deny it.

Just a bit. 'No,' he lied. 'People react to this kind of situation in different ways. Not everyone automatically throws themselves to the ground and starts wailing. There are plenty of times when you just see people kind of closing down in front of you.'

'Yes.'

'Or they try to keep going as if nothing has happened – in some sort of denial. It's all about individual coping mechanisms. There's nothing wrong with being . . . detached.'

For the first time, something approximating sadness crossed her face. 'It doesn't exactly feel real yet.'

'These things can take time to sink in.'

'The funny thing is, when he abandoned me in the theatre, I made a decision there and then to dump him. It had been such an effort to get him to come along at all, and then he buggered off before we even got to the interval.' She gave the inspector a shamefaced smile. 'Makes me a terrible person, eh?'

'Not really.' Carlyle adopted a sympathetic expression. 'Happens all the time.'

She gave him a puzzled look.

'Girls dumping their boyfriends, that is. Not the boyfriends getting stabbed and thrown in the back of a rubbish truck.'

She sighed. 'We were together for eighteen months. The relationship was just getting into a rut. Neither of us was prepared to compromise enough to move things on. I felt that if I didn't pull the plug now, things were only going to get worse. I didn't want my whole life to start ebbing away.'

'Right.'

Millington was staring off into space. 'Anyway,' she said quietly, 'I've been seeing someone else for a while.'

Carlyle tried to scribble on the scrap of paper but found that the biro was out of ink. He tossed it on to the table in disgust.

'He's a lawyer, like me.' She noticed the sudden look in the inspector's eye. 'He's been in Brussels all this week,' she added hastily.

Handy, Carlyle thought, but hardly a perfect alibi seeing as it's only a couple of hours away on the Eurostar. 'I'll need his details all the same.'

'Fine.' She picked up her BlackBerry, and Carlyle recited his own email address. A couple of taps on the smartphone and it was done. 'I've sent you his v-card.'

'Thanks.' He made a mental note to get Joe to check the guy out.

'These things happen,' she said – then seeing the scepticism in his face, she held up a hand. 'Duncan was a nice guy.'

Nice?

'But he was very narrow in his focus.'

Unlike you, Ms VP Legal.

'He liked to describe himself as a good, old-fashioned hack.'

'What did he mean by that?'

'Basically, as far as I could tell, it meant he would spend as much time as possible in pubs, talking to his "sources".' Millington let out a hollow laugh. 'He thought he was fighting against the idea that journalists should be chained to their desks twenty-four seven, simply rehashing stories from the internet.'

Carlyle glanced around. Now lunchtime was approaching, a steady stream of people began coming into the canteen to check out the chestnut mushroom, chard and pearl-barley stew and the smoked haddock. Feeling more than peckish, he wondered if his host would do the right thing and feed him. 'So . . . what kind of stuff did Duncan write about?'

Millington exhaled. 'A wide range of stuff really.' She reeled off a number of topics that covered a depressingly banal list of celebrities, reality-TV shows and politicians.

Doesn't seem such a wide range of things to me, Carlyle thought sourly, just the same old shit. As far as he could see, newspapers in general were now totally redundant, and Sunday newspapers were the most redundant of the lot. He would quite happily never buy another newspaper again. Helen, however, for reasons best known to herself, bought the *Sunday Mirror*, which seemed to be pitched at people with a mental age of eight. Every weekend he picked it up and then vowed never to read it again.

'It didn't much matter what it might be,' Millington continued, 'Duncan always said that as long as you got something you could stick an *exclusive* tag on, you were sorted.'

'So he'd sell his granny for a story, eh?'

She stared at him blankly. 'He didn't have a granny. Both of them are long dead.'

Lawyers, so fucking literal! 'What about his work colleagues?'

'I didn't meet very many of them.' She made a show of considering it for a moment. 'Maybe only one or two.'

'I'll need their names.'

'Okay. But Duncan didn't really spend much time hanging out with anyone from his work. I think he got on okay with the people there but it was a very competitive place. They didn't do team spirit at the *Sunday Witness*.'

'Mm.' Something else for Joe to follow up. The boy was going to be busy. Maybe he could get WPC Hall to help him. Anita would like that.

Right on cue, his phone started ringing.

'Joe.'

'How's it going?'

Carlyle looked at Millington. 'I'm speaking to the girlfriend now.'

'Ex-girlfriend,' she mumbled.

'Just quickly then,' said Joe, as he stifled a yawn. 'First, it looks like we're gonna get nothing from the CCTV.'

'Great.'

'There's no way we can get even a partial shot of the killer's face.'

'Was that luck? Or did he know what he was doing?'

'Does it matter?'

'I suppose not,' Carlyle said. 'What's the second thing?'

'Simpson wants to see you.'

'Oh good.' The inspector raised his eyes to the sky. 'The day just keeps getting better and better.'

'She would like you to get over to Paddington asap.'

'Okay, okay.' He gazed out of the window at the palace. It had started to rain. 'I'm in Victoria anyway. I'll finish up here, nip over and see her and then meet you back at the station in . . . let's say a couple of hours.'

'Fine.'

Ending the call, Carlyle tossed his phone on to the table.

'Problem?' Millington asked.

'Just the usual. Tell me more about last night.'

'It was very low key,' she said. 'I'd booked the tickets weeks ago. Duncan clearly wanted to watch the football instead, but he at least managed to turn up, which wasn't always the case. When his phone went off, he mumbled something about a story and disappeared.'

'Do you know what the story was?' Carlyle asked.

'No.' Millington shook her head. 'To be honest, I thought he was making it up.'

'Oh?'

'It wouldn't have been the first time he'd got one of his mates to ring up and pretend to be a work call.'

'So you were annoyed?'

She looked offended at such a stupid question. 'I should say so. I was even more pissed off when he texted me ten minutes later saying he would have to go and see some guy.'

'Some guy?'

'I assume. Don't know.' Grabbing the BlackBerry from the table, she clicked a few keys and showed Carlyle the message on the screen: *Sorry. Important meeting. C u back at urs.*

And to think people worry about the future of the English language, Carlyle thought. 'So you were expecting him to come back to your place?'

Millington nodded. 'When he didn't turn up, I tried his place a few times then I called the police.'

'It was only a couple of hours.'

'I know, but the thing about Duncan was that he was *always* contactable. It never took him more than five minutes to return a call or send an email. He was the ultimate multi-tasker.' She tutted. 'Once, he even tried to text a message to his Editor when we were shagging.'

Too much information. Carlyle felt himself blush slightly. 'So you were worried?' was all he could think of to say.

'Yes. I was pretty sure that something was up.'

'Can you tell me anything else about the guy he went off to meet?'

Another pout. Another snooty expression. Carlyle was reminded just how much he didn't like lawyers.

'Or the story that he was working on?'

'Like I said, no.'

What else should he ask? 'Was Duncan depressed? Did he seem stressed?'

'Inspector,' Millington laughed, 'everyone in this city is stressed, don't you think?'

'Okay,' Carlyle conceded. 'But being a tabloid journalist is particularly tough.'

'True,' she agreed. 'Duncan was very insecure. *You're only as good as your next story* and all that. He was on some rolling

88

freelance contract. The whole thing was so wearisome – it was one of the reasons I was going to end the relationship.'

The smells coming from the kitchen were beginning to distract the inspector from the matter in hand. Sadly, however, it looked like his host wasn't going to offer him lunch. Carlyle scooped up his scrap of paper and his empty biro. 'Final question – did Duncan have any enemies?'

'Professionally?'

'Any kind at all.'

'Not as far as I knew.'

'None at all?'

'Duncan was a likeable guy. And he had that great skill for a tabloid reporter – he could do someone over and they'd still ring him up the next day to thank him for the piece.'

'On the other hand,' Carlyle mused, 'someone stabbed him multiple times in the chest.'

Gemma Millington stared out of the window for a few moments, clearly thinking something through. Finally, she reached into her pocket and pulled out a business card. 'You might want to talk to this guy.' She placed the card in front of Carlyle. *Lene Bang, FMP LLP.*

The inspector looked suitably confused.

'That's Duncan's lawyer.'

'Why did he need a lawyer?'

'Rightly or wrongly,' Millington explained, 'Duncan was worried about getting caught up in the *Witness* phone-hacking scandal.'

Alarm bells started ringing in the back of the inspector's head.

'Some of his stories were under investigation,' she went on.

The bells were getting louder. Why couldn't he have a straightforward multiple stabbing, without any of this other crap?

'He had already been questioned under caution.'

The bells, the bells . . .

'I'm sure you know all this anyway.'

Yeah, Carlyle thought sarcastically, of course I did, which is why I hadn't mentioned it in the last half an hour.

'Lene will be able to give you more details.'

'Thanks.' Carlyle picked the card off the table and dropped it into his pocket. Pushing back his chair, he got to his feet as his stomach started to rumble. 'I need to get going. I'll keep you informed of any developments.'

'Fine.' Already tapping away on her BlackBerry, Gemma Millington looked like she could not care less.

SIXTEEN

Wondering what to do with his Greggs plastic bag containing a cheese and pickle sandwich and a Belgian bun, Carlyle sat patiently in Simpson's office in Paddington Green police station, waiting for the Commander to finish her phone call.

'Mm.' The furrows on the Commander's brow deepened as she listened to whoever was speaking on the other end of the line. 'I don't think that's necessarily possible.'

She's what, Carlyle wondered, five years younger than me? Six? And already looking old! The stresses and strains of leadership are clearly taking their toll.

'Are you sure that is the best use of resources?' Simpson held up a finger to suggest to the inspector that she would only be another minute. 'I'm not ... No, of course. I understand.' Ending the call, she shot Carlyle an apologetic look. 'Sorry about that.'

'No problem,' he shrugged.

Simpson gestured at the blue and white plastic bag resting on Carlyle's lap. 'What's that?'

'Lunch.'

'This won't take long.' She waited while he carefully placed the bag on the floor. 'That was Simon Shelbourne on the phone.'

Carlyle made a *Who's that?* gesture.

'Shelbourne is the Met's Director of Strategic Communications.'

'Ah. It's good to know that we've got one of those.'

'The Commissioner's spin doctor,' she elaborated. 'Sir Chester just took a pile of grief at a press conference to do with the Mosman boy, and now they want to know that you're on top of things.'

Carlyle nodded.

'And *are* you on top of things?'

'Not really.'

'Not really?' Simpson echoed.

'I had to pick up the Duncan Brown case this morning.'

She stared at him blankly.

'The bloke stabbed to death whose body was dumped in the back of a rubbish truck.'

Simpson grunted. She didn't want to hear about that.

'I was only with the Mosman kid by accident,' Carlyle reminded her. 'Anyway, surely it's one for the Bomb Squad?'

'They're involved, obviously,' Simpson replied, 'but they haven't exactly covered themselves in glory on this one.'

'No, I can see that.'

'And Sir Chester informed the assembled press that you're the officer leading it.'

'Me? But why?' Carlyle listened to his stomach rumbling.

Because I dropped you in it and yours was the only name he could remember when some hack put him on the spot. 'No idea.'

'Fuck's sake.'

'Look, all Sir Chester wants is to get the media off his back as quickly as possible. So why not get the wheels in motion on the . . . other thing.'

'Duncan Brown.'

Simpson nodded. 'Get things started on the Brown case and then focus your attention on Mosman. We just have to display some momentum before he goes into hospital.'

Carlyle scowled. 'Before who goes into hospital?'

'Sir Chester. He needs an operation on his back, apparently. Once he disappears into his private suite, the pressure will be off.'

'Unless someone else gets blown up.'

92

'Quite.' Simpson gave him a sharp look. 'But that's not going to happen, is it?'

'Let's hope not.'

Now it was the Commander's turn to scowl. 'That's the great thing about you, John: you always manage to stay positive.'

'Maybe I need a spin doctor of my own,' Carlyle quipped.

Maybe you need a firm smack round the head, Simpson thought. 'What else have you got on at the moment?'

'Not a lot.' The inspector scratched his head. 'Joe's been checking out a missing teenager, but that's about it.'

'Good. Focus on Mosman for the next couple of days, and then we'll see where we are.' Reaching across the desk, she pulled a sheaf of papers towards her, signalling that their meeting was over.

'Okay.' Carlyle got to his feet and turned towards the door.

'Oh – and Inspector?'

'Yes?'

Simpson pointed to the plastic bag sitting by the chair. 'Don't forget your lunch.'

SEVENTEEN

'What did you expect? A half-empty bottle of scotch and twenty Benson & Hedges?' Sylvain Bellamy fixed Joe Szyszkowski with a gimlet eye, as he finished off his green salad with a flourish.

'I didn't expect anything,' replied the sergeant defensively.

'The days of long boozy lunches are long gone.' The Editor of the *Sunday Witness* tossed the remains of his takeaway box into a nearby wastebasket and took a slug of sparkling water from a small plastic bottle. 'There's no time for bad habits any longer and you don't get anywhere in this game if you don't look after yourself.' He had the slightly emaciated, hollow-cheeked look of a man who believed in looking after himself, or at least ran regular marathons. He gestured towards a framed certificate hanging on the wall behind his head. 'They sent me to Harvard last year, to do an MBA.'

'Good for you,' Joe mumbled.

'Zenger Corporation takes the professional development of its employees very seriously,' Bellamy smiled. 'At least for those of us that make it off the news desk.'

Sitting back in his chair, Joe looked through the window that offered a view across the empty newsroom. The place looked like a DIY warehouse filled with row after row of desks and computers, their screens illuminated by the strip lighting suspended from the ceiling. The overall effect was profoundly depressing. It made Charing Cross police station look like a palace.

'Before we start,' Bellamy interrupted the sergeant's musings, 'I have to tell you that I won't be able to deal with any detailed questions about Duncan Brown or his work or about the hacking inquiry.'

Joe turned back to face the Editor. 'Can't or won't?'

'Both. You can, of course, ask me anything you like. However, if we stray into . . . difficult territory, one of our lawyers will have to be present.'

Joe nodded. 'Understood.'

'You have to realize that the amount of discretion I have here is severely limited. Indeed, if my boss knew you were here now, she would be very unhappy.'

'Maybe I should speak to your boss.'

'Maybe you should,' Bellamy agreed. 'But you won't get anywhere near Sonia Claesens without an army of lawyers getting in your way. Not to mention Trevor Miller stomping all over you.'

Trevor Miller? Joe thought. Fucking hell, what's he got to do with this? Play dumb, he told himself. In the inside pocket of his jacket his mobile started vibrating – for the third time in the past minute. For the third time in the past minute, he ignored it. 'Who's Trevor Miller?'

'Hah!' Bellamy thumped the table in amusement. 'You don't know much, Sergeant, do you?'

'That's why I'm here,' Joe smiled, careful not to rise to the bait. 'So, what can you tell me about Duncan Brown?' he asked. 'Did *he* look after himself?'

'I suppose so . . . as much as anyone here does, anyway.' Bellamy carefully replaced the green cap on his bottle of water as he paused for a moment's reflection on his dear departed colleague. 'The important thing to realize is that Duncan was a good lad, a solid citizen.'

'Why would anyone want to stab him to death, then?'

Bellamy ran a hand through his silver locks. 'As you can imagine, Sergeant, I have given that some considerable thought.'

'And?'

'No idea,' Bellamy laughed. 'I genuinely don't know.'

'But—' The phone started vibrating again. 'Fuck.' Joe pulled it from his pocket and saw Carlyle's name on the screen. 'Apologies. Excuse me a second, I need to take this.'

Bellamy gave a gracious nod and turned his attention to the screen of the computer standing on his desk.

'Where are you?' the inspector asked without preamble.

'I'm in Docklands.'

Carlyle harrumphed. 'What are you doing in fucking Docklands?'

'It's where Duncan Brown worked,' said Joe, trying to hide his irritation. 'I'm talking to his boss.'

'Well get your arse back to Charing Cross, tonto pronto,' Carlyle grunted.

'But—'

'We've got work to do.'

'But—'

'Simpson says we have to focus on Mosman.'

'But—'

'No more fucking *buts*. See you back at the ranch asap.'

Bloody Carlyle, Joe thought, irritated. Always swanning around in his own little world, acting like he was the only one trying to shovel shit. He took a deep breath. 'Okay.'

'Good. See you soon.' Without another word, the inspector ended the call.

Bellamy looked up from his screen and smiled. 'Problem?'

'We'll have to talk later, I'm afraid.'

'I'm always here.'

'Good to know.' Joe flicked through a mental checklist in his head. 'In the meantime, I will send someone to check through Brown's desk and computer. It would also be helpful to have a list of his contacts.'

Grinning, Bellamy waved a hand towards the newsroom. 'We have a hot-desking system here. Everyone moves around all the time, so we won't be able to show you a specific desk or computer terminal.'

'Great.'

'But I'm sure that the IT people will be able to sort something out – once our lawyers have okayed it.'

'Fine. We'll be in touch.' Joe jumped to his feet. Having just been beaten up by his boss, he wasn't going to let some mere hack take the piss. 'Don't bother getting up. I can see myself out.'

EIGHTEEN

Still holding the Greggs plastic bag containing his lunch, a now very hungry Carlyle skipped up the front steps of Charing Cross police station. Reaching the top, he felt the phone vibrating in his pocket. With some reluctance, he pulled it out.

'Inspector, it's Julian Richardson here.'

'Who?'

'Julian Richardson.' The young man sounded pained at having to repeat his name. 'From St John's Wood.'

'Yes, yes,' said the inspector irritably, belatedly recalling that Richardson was the sergeant placed in charge of logistical coordination for the Mosman case. 'What do you want?' If he didn't get something to eat in the next five minutes, there was every chance that the inspector would go into total meltdown.

'I have just spoken to Melvin Boduka, the lawyer acting for Horatio Mosman's parents. He says his clients will be able to see you this afternoon.' Richardson reeled off an address near Park Lane.

'Okay,' Carlyle sighed. 'Tell them I'm on my way.' Ending the call, he stepped through the automatic doors. He would nip down to the canteen, scarf down his lunch, leave a list of things for Joe to be getting on with and then head back out.

'Inspector!' Half-turning, Carlyle tried to keep walking even as he smiled at the desk sergeant. 'How's it going, George?'

'Could I have a minute?'

'Er ...'

George Patrick gestured in the direction of a thin, angry-looking, middle-aged woman who was standing in front of the desk. On first glance, Carlyle thought that she seemed vaguely familiar, but then so did lots of people. 'This lady could do with some assistance,' George explained.

'Sorry,' Carlyle tried to look sympathetic, 'but I've got to go and—'

'I've been waiting to speak to someone for almost an hour now,' the woman said huffily, eyeing the bag containing the inspector's lunch. She stepped towards him. 'It's a very serious matter.'

Burying his nose in some convenient paperwork, George Patrick tried not to laugh.

'And anyway,' continued the woman, ignoring the sniggering desk sergeant, 'don't you know who I am?'

'You talk, I'll eat.' Ignoring the look of displeasure that flitted across Margaretha Zelle's face, the inspector tore open the cellophane packaging, pulled out his sandwich and took a large bite.

Sitting back in her chair in the almost empty canteen, Zelle cradled a glass mug of jasmine tea. 'Are you sure you don't know who I am?'

Trying not to speak with his mouth full, the inspector made a non-committal gesture. The truth was that it had come to him on the way down to the basement. Margaretha Żelle was an over-exposed London celebrity. Not so long ago, he had read about her latest exploits in one of the trashy magazines that his wife brought home with alarming regularity.

Born in Antwerp in the late 1970s, Zelle was a member of that rarest breed, famous Belgians. Known, in no particular order, for being a model, singer and animal lover, she had lost an arm in a climbing accident on the Neige Cordier peak in the French Alps. Her ex-husbands included a banker, a semi-famous actor and a former England football manager. An acrimonious divorce from the last had resulted in her being awarded £8.3 million in a highly publicized court settlement.

Washing the sandwich down with a mouthful of coffee, Carlyle unceremoniously started on the Belgian bun. Pouting, Zelle picked up a copy of *Metro* that had been left by a previous diner and started pointedly reading a story about a government adviser who claimed that some police officers were barely literate.

Swallowing the last of the bun, Carlyle took another mouthful of coffee. 'Ah,' he muttered to himself, 'that's better.' If not exactly full, he was no longer starving. Zelle was still pretending to read the scathing article. Maybe he could grab a Mars bar – or maybe not. Helen would definitely not approve.

A question suddenly came into his mind. 'Do you happen to know why a Belgian bun is called a Belgian bun?'

'What?' Zelle stared at him blankly. Despite the fierce countenance, she was a good-looking woman. Tall, thin and blonde, she had high cheekbones and only the faintest of lines around her sharp blue eyes.

'Never mind.'

Tapping the newspaper with her prosthetic hand, she gave a grin. 'It says here that police officers are, quote "barely literate" unquote because the entry standards are so low. Reading, writing and maths skills have fallen significantly.'

Wouldn't surprise me in the slightest, Carlyle thought, but what concern is it of yours? 'I might not be able to read or write,' he said gruffly, 'but my timekeeping skills are still up to scratch.' He pointed at the clock on the far wall. 'I really do have to get going soon, so tell me what the problem is and let's make it quick.'

The grin widened, making Zelle look even more attractive in a dangerous type of way. 'My, my,' she teased. 'We are sensitive, aren't we?'

Fuck it, thought Carlyle, I will have that Mars bar. And a double espresso to go with it. 'You've got five minutes. Remember to keep it simple though, given how stupid us cops are.' Then, getting to his feet, he bolted for the confectionery display and came back almost immediately clutching his prize.

'My publicist suggested I should come.'

That's not a line you hear every day, Carlyle thought, chomping on the Mars bar.

'My phone's been hacked.'

'Mm.' As the last piece of chocolate disappeared into his maw, the inspector realized that he should have gone for the king-sized bar.

'It needs to be investigated.'

Finishing his coffee, Carlyle screwed up the Mars wrapper and dropped it into the empty mug. He told himself firmly that he wasn't going to lose his temper. 'There's a special task force looking into this whole issue. You should go and talk to them.'

'Don't try and fob me off!' the woman snapped. 'I've been waiting upstairs for ages.'

'I'm sorry that you had to wait,' Carlyle replied evenly. 'All I'm trying to do is ensure that you get to talk to the right people.'

'A journalist called me last week,' she continued, ignoring what he had just said. 'He was able to quote verbatim from phone messages that Sam had left for me.'

'Sam?' Carlyle asked, curious despite himself.

'Sam Grove.' Grove was the former England football manager – Mr Zelle number three, or maybe it was number four. Either way, marriage to Margaretha, combined with a run of shockingly bad results, was enough to make him public enemy number one up until the point where he was ceremoniously sacked.

'Yes?'

'Don't you follow football, Inspector?'

He shrugged. *Proper football fans don't support England, they support their club.* 'I'm a Fulham fan.'

Not knowing what to make of that, she ploughed on. 'Anyway, I told this journalist: "If you do anything with this story I'll go to the police".'

'And what happened?' Carlyle already knew the answer but asked anyway.

'The bastard ran the story last weekend.' Zelle hoisted a massive red Chloé python-skin tote bag on to the table and untied the flap. Carlyle watched in silence as she pulled out a sheaf of papers and handed him a half-page cutting. 'This is it.'

Squinting, Carlyle scanned the article. Under the headline MAD MARG BLOWS HER TOP was a not very flattering picture of Zelle wearing a bikini on a Caribbean beach. The 'story' itself involved an argument over money; just a précis of the kind of routine domestic row that any couple might have. As a 'story', it was utterly boring. No wonder newspapers were dying on their feet.

Rereading the piece, Carlyle noticed the byline and realized that the article had been written by Duncan Brown.

He looked at Zelle. 'You spoke to Duncan Brown?'

'So, you *can* read, then,' Zelle said petulantly. 'And I didn't even see your lips moving.'

God give me strength, Carlyle thought morosely. 'When exactly did he call you?'

Zelle gazed into the middle distance. 'I don't know exactly,' she said, before reeling off a number of possible dates. 'I think it was the Wednesday and I'd just come out of the gym. But you can check my phone records.'

Yes, Carlyle thought, I suppose we can. 'Did you ever actually meet him?'

'No!' Zelle made a moue. 'I only spoke to the nasty little rodent once on the phone. That was it.'

'Okay.' Carlyle glanced again at the clock. The day was slipping away from him but the Mosmans could wait a little longer. After all, he hadn't committed to turn up at their lawyer's office at any precise time. Turning his gaze back to Zelle, he tried to smile. 'What we need to do now is this . . .'

NINETEEN

'Shouldn't you be in uniform?' Louise Greco studied the warrant card carefully before handing it back to the WPC. The pretty young officer had arrived in her office only ten minutes ago, but already she had created a significant glitch in Greco's tight schedule.

When you were headmistress of St Marylebone C of E Secondary School, the bureaucracy was never-ending. Greco pined for the time – long gone – when her days hadn't been chopped up into thirty-minute blocks, each of which was completely filled with a range of wearisome tasks.

Greco checked her watch. As of right now, she had a letter to write to all parents of Key Stage 3 students regarding the use of social networks and mobile phones, as well as drafting an invite for the White Paper Consultation meeting. And the Pupil Achievement Team meeting was due to start in less than fifteen minutes. In short, the headmistress simply didn't have time for some girl who looked like a refugee from the Sixth Form Common Room waltzing into her office and demanding to be allowed to interview various pupils.

Maude Hall smiled sweetly. She had been in the MPS for barely nine months, but already she understood well enough that most people were naturally suspicious of the police. 'It's my day off.'

'So . . .' Greco peered over the top of her tortoiseshell glasses and did a double-take; the girl had a tiny diamond stud in her left nostril. The thing was so small that it looked like a spot. Surely you can't wear things like that when you are in the police? Greco pondered. Even if you are off duty?

As the girl self-consciously scratched the other nostril with her right index finger, Greco noticed that her nails were painted a bright sky-blue colour. Picking up a pencil, Greco scribbled the word 'varnish' on the pad resting on her desk. She should send out a reminder that it was not appropriate to come into school with nail varnish and that all girls must remove any before they arrived for class in the morning. That was just another task to add to the list of things she had to do. She let several moments pass before returning her gaze to meet that of the WPC. 'I should assume then that this is not official business?'

'Oh, it is,' Maude replied evenly, before briskly going on to explain the reason for her visit. 'Hannah Gillespie's parents are extremely worried about her and I didn't think that I should wait until—'

Greco cut her off with a curt: 'I would in no way wish to take a situation like this lightly, but Miss Gillespie does rather have a history of this kind of thing.'

'Oh?' Hall fished a notebook and biro from her bag.

'Yes,' Greco went on. 'I'd have to check the records for the precise dates but, to my certain knowledge, Hannah has been absent without permission at least three times during the current calendar year. I keep a very close eye on such things, as you can imagine.'

'Yes.' Head down, Hall began making notes. 'How long was she away previously?'

'Twice it was just for a day, but the third time was longer: three or maybe even four days.'

'I see. And did she explain what she had been doing?'

'Not to my satisfaction,' said Greco grimly.

'Mm. And what does that mean?'

'She said only that she was visiting friends; wouldn't say anything else.'

'Was it a boyfriend?'

'I would assume so. You know what young girls are like.' Catching Hall's eye, Greco hesitated before saying defensively, 'They sometimes lack a certain amount of self-control and discipline.'

Tell me about it. Grinning, Hall focused on her notebook.

'Although,' Greco continued, talking more now to herself than to the WPC, 'to be clear, Hannah Gillespie is a very good student with great potential. And she is a valued member of our community. She takes her studies seriously and has a particular interest in history.'

And boys, Hall supposed.

'If anything,' Greco sniffed, 'I would say that young Hannah is just a touch too independent for her own good. She doesn't know where to draw the line.'

'All part of growing up,' Hall mused.

'Precisely,' Greco agreed. 'I am sure that she will learn better – eventually. Happily, this type of behaviour is very much the exception here at our school. We have an absolutely fantastic collection of girls – and I would include Hannah in that. So we're very lucky really.'

'I'm sure.' Hall put the cap back on her pen. 'It would be great if I could speak to some of Hannah's close friends.'

Once again, Greco looked her up and down. 'If you wish to do that,' she said slowly, 'I think you will need to come back in a more official capacity.'

'But—'

'Anyway,' Greco interrupted, 'I'm sure that Hannah will be safely back with us soon. In the meantime, I do not want to cause unnecessary upset among her classmates. They have exams to prepare for, and any distractions can be most unhelpful.' Greco turned her attention back to the letter waiting on her desk. 'Now, if you'll excuse me . . .'

A chocolate tartlet and two cups of Mariage Frères tea slowly helped Maude Hall get over her irritation at the way she had been treated in the headmistress's office. Maybe she had been a bit informal by going there when off duty, but even so, the woman's attitude annoyed her.

Maybe she would come back in her uniform tomorrow. First, however, Maude needed to talk to Joe Szyszkowski about how he wanted her to proceed with the investigation. She was sure that the sergeant would appreciate the fact that she'd taken the initiative – on her day off, too. As far as she could tell, Joe was a nice bloke who treated everyone fairly. Above all, he was a team player, unlike their boss. The inspector seemed a bit of a berk. Stuck in his own little world, he probably wouldn't even notice the effort she had been making to track down Hannah Gillespie.

Sitting in Café Luc at the north end of Marylebone High Street, she poured the last of the tea from the pot into her cup and took a sip. The school day had just ended and a steady stream of girls now passed by the window, in their green skirts and jumpers, chatting happily in little groups of two and three. Hall smiled to herself, thinking that they all looked like nice kids. It wasn't so long ago since that had been her. She tried to remember back to her own schooldays, but nothing memorable came to mind.

'Excuse me.'

Putting her cup back on its saucer, Hall looked up at a pretty blonde girl who could easily have passed for twenty-something except for the school uniform she was wearing.

'Yes?'

'Are you the policewoman who was asking Mrs Greco about Hannah?'

Hall raised an eyebrow. 'How did you know about that?'

'Someone heard you asking at the front desk.' Without waiting to be invited, the girl slipped into the chair opposite. 'I'm Melanie – Melanie Henderson.'

'I'm Maude.'

'Funny name.'

Hall laughed. 'You'd have to ask my parents about that. Are you a friend of Hannah's?'

'I'm in her class,' the girl said. 'Is she in trouble?'

'Not as far as I'm concerned,' Maude smiled. 'Mrs Greco might be another matter though.'

Melanie rolled her eyes. 'Tell me about it.'

'We just want to make sure that Hannah's okay. Her parents are worried.'

The girl picked up a menu and started reading it.

'Want something to eat?'

'Nah.' Melanie shook her head, then remembered her manners. 'But thanks though.'

Hall took another sip of her tea. 'The headmistress said she's missed school before.'

Melanie nodded.

'Any idea where she is this time?'

'Not really, no.'

Finishing her tea, Hall tried not to look irritated with the girl. 'But I know who she'll be with.'

TWENTY

'Where the hell have you been?'

The inspector shrugged. The conversation with Margaretha Zelle in the Charing Cross canteen had delayed him by about an hour or so. Even so, he wasn't really that late.

At least, he didn't think so.

Short, bald and in a bad humour, Melvin Boduka obviously disagreed. The lawyer unhooked his thumb from the waistcoat of his three-piece suit and jabbed an angry index finger at Carlyle. 'Horatio Mosman's parents have been waiting here for more than three hours now.'

'Let's get on with it then,' Carlyle replied brusquely. Hopping from foot to foot, he felt himself sinking into the plush carpet of Boduka's ridiculously expensive Park Lane offices. He was feeling hyper with the buzz of trying to keep multiple investigations moving along at the same time – not to mention multiple espressos – and wasn't in the mood to take any shit from this expensive ambulance-chaser. 'Where are they?'

Boduka gestured along the hallway. 'In the boardroom.'

'Okay.' Carlyle glanced at the pair of flunkeys standing behind their boss. 'Something to drink would be good.' Wired or not, he had to keep going. Presumably, the good folks at Blutch, Boduka, Lanners & Nahon LLP could stretch to a decent cup of coffee without too much difficulty.

Boduka grunted at one of the assistants who looked at Carlyle enquiringly.

'I'll have a macchiato – make it a double.' He was tempted to ask for a pastry as well, but suspected that would be pushing his luck.

With a nod, the girl turned on her heel and hurried off down the corridor.

'Thank you.' He turned back to Boduka. 'Let's get started then.'

'Just remember, Inspector,' said the lawyer, placing a hand on Carlyle's arm as he lowered his voice, 'you were the last person to see their son alive.'

'*One* of the last people,' Carlyle corrected him.

'Yes, well, it's effectively the same thing.' Boduka resorted to a stage whisper. 'The point is, please treat them with respect.'

'I always treat people with respect,' Carlyle lied.

'But under the particular circumstances . . .' The lawyer's voice rose with his exasperation.

'Yes, yes,' Carlyle said gruffly. 'Let's just get on with it, shall we? As you said, they've been kept waiting for long enough.'

On entering the room, the first thing he noticed was the view. The vista through the floor-to-ceiling glass windows of the law firm's boardroom – directly across Park Lane towards Hyde Park – was quite spectacular. The inspector, however, was the only one enjoying it. Everyone else was on the far side of the table, with their backs to the window. Next to Boduka was Ivor Mosman, ramrod straight in an expensive-looking navy suit, with a light blue shirt. Even though he was unshaven and looked tired, Mosman was still an imposing-looking man, tall with broad shoulders, a strong chin and a full head of hair that showed only a slight sprinkling of grey. He held his wife's hand tightly as they waited for the inspector to get this unpleasant meeting under way.

Zoe Mosman was clearly not holding up as well as her husband. In a grey polo shirt, with a white sweater wrapped around her shoulders, she looked like she was heading for the

Tennis Club, but her face was crumpled and she had clearly spent much of the last twelve hours in tears. Her gaze remained lowered towards the table as she rocked gently in her seat. With her hair pulled back into a simple ponytail, she looked extremely young – easily a good fifteen years younger than her husband when, in fact, Carlyle knew that their actual age difference was less than half that.

Boduka's two assistants made up the numbers. Taking a sip of his macchiato – disappointingly insipid and cool – Carlyle arranged his papers on the table before letting the Skoob plastic bag, in which he'd transported them over, drop to the floor. Flipping open a notepad, he pulled a biro from his inside jacket pocket and began listing all the names of those present. When he'd finished, he placed his pen on the pad and looked up at the parents directly.

'My condolences for what has happened,' he said, waiting for a nod of acknowledgement from Ivor Mosman before continuing, 'and my apologies for keeping you waiting this afternoon.' Another nod. 'As you will know, there is a huge amount of effort and resource going into this investigation.' He tapped the A4 folder in front of him with an index finger. 'There is only a limited amount that I can say at this moment. However, I can assure you we are moving things along as quickly as we can.'

I can assure you: Standard Operating Gibberish as used by a policeman.

Finally, Zoe Mosman looked up. 'So, what can you tell us about who did this?'

Trying not to appear too impatient, Carlyle held up a restraining hand. 'I will come to where we are currently in the investigation in just a moment. And I will share with you as much information as I can. First, however, let me just make a few . . . personal remarks which, I trust, will go no further than this room.' He looked over at Boduka who gave his assent. 'As you know, I myself was at your home last night when the . . . incident happened.' He paused, his gaze moving along the line of faces opposite. 'I sat with Horatio while the explosives officers sought to deal with . . .'

Zoe Mosman let out a loud sob. For a horrible moment, it looked like she was going to convulse into hysterics, but her husband whispered something in her ear and she managed to regain control.

The inspector cleared his throat. 'I would just like to say,' he continued, 'that Horatio showed great courage and determination in dealing with what was obviously a very difficult and frightening situation.'

The parents looked at him blankly. Feeling like a complete idiot, Carlyle let his gaze drift towards the trees outside, swaying in the wind. 'Personally and on behalf of the Police Service, I would like to express our deepest sympathy at your loss and reassure you that we will be seeking to catch those responsible as quickly as possible.' Letting out a deep breath, he then sat back in his chair.

For a moment there was silence. Finally Melvin Boduka spoke up. 'Thank you, Inspector. On behalf of Mr and Mrs Mosman, I would like in turn to express the family's gratitude for your efforts at their house.' At this point, Carlyle glanced at Zoe Mosman, whose expression seemed to be suggesting a rather different train of thought. 'And, of course, we will provide you with all help and assistance possible, regarding your investigation.'

'Thank you,' Carlyle said quietly.

The lawyer pulled a silver-plated Waterman Carene from his inside jacket pocket and scribbled something on the pad sitting on the desk in front of him. 'I am sure you have a lot of questions,' he said. 'How can we assist you at this time?'

The inspector had been waiting for this moment. Sitting up in his chair, he addressed himself directly to the lawyer. 'What I would like to do,' he said gently, 'is to speak to both Mr and Mrs Mosman – but separately.'

Frowning, the lawyer looked over towards his clients. Ivor Mosman gave an *Up to you* kind of shrug. Zoe Mosman continued staring into space. Boduka turned back to Carlyle. 'I presume that you are happy for me to be present in these . . . meetings?'

'Of course,' Carlyle replied. 'Maybe we could start with Mr Mosman.' He smiled at one of the assistants. 'And maybe I could get another coffee? And could you make it really hot this time?'

Glancing at the expensive-looking watch on his wrist, Melvin Boduka paced the corridor while they waited for a second meeting room to be cleared. 'How long do you think all this will take?'

'Not too long.' Carlyle took a sip of his second macchiato. If anything, it was more insipid and even cooler than the first. A pang of intense frustration stabbed through his chest. *Why couldn't these people understand what the word 'hot' meant?*

'You do know,' the lawyer lowered his voice as one of his colleagues slipped past, 'that the family are considering legal action against the MPS.'

'For what?'

'For missing the bomb,' Boduka replied. 'What do you think?'

How the hell did he know about that? Carlyle wondered. 'What do you mean?'

Boduka waved an admonishing finger in the policeman's direction. 'Come, come, Inspector, don't try and play me.'

'That's not my style.' The inspector seriously doubted that Ivor and Zoe Mosman would really want to sue the Met while it was still trying to find their son's killer. Then again, stranger things had happened. If they did sue, Carlyle himself would be appearing in the dock. He made a mental note to contact his Union Rep, just in case the Met tried to hang him out to dry.

'As you well know, the device around Horatio's neck was a fake,' the lawyer persisted.

Saying nothing, Carlyle eyed the lawyer carefully. Clearly, old Melvin here was sharper than he looked. Equally, however, someone must have given him a copy of the preliminary report.

The very thought filled the inspector with something approaching despair. If the report had indeed been leaked, then it would almost certainly appear on the internet and in the newspapers before the end of the day. That would inevitably make his job a lot harder.

'But you were so busy focusing on the collar bomb,' Boduka continued, 'that nobody bothered to check for a secondary device which, it seems, had been hidden in the bottom of the sofa.' The lawyer's face crumpled into a conventional picture of disappointment and concern. 'Which was rather remiss of you, don't you think?'

'As far as I could see,' Carlyle replied grimly, 'every effort was made to save that young man.'

It sounded lame and he knew it.

The lawyer allowed himself a small smile. 'So all proper operating procedures were followed?'

'That is not what I am here to discuss,' the inspector said firmly.

Boduka arched a sceptical eyebrow.

'You know that's not my area,' Carlyle insisted. 'You need to talk to the Met's Legal Department.'

'As you wish.'

'My job,' Carlyle reminded him, 'is to catch the people responsible for this outrageous act. And I am sure that must be the primary, if not the only, concern of the boy's parents, as well. So why don't you go and fetch your client and then we can get on with it?'

Ivor Mosman sipped from a glass of carbonated water. 'Zoe and I had gone to the National Theatre to see *South Pacific*,' he explained, staring into his drink. 'Horatio was left in the house alone, but he was old enough ... there had never been any problems before.' He looked up at the inspector, who was sitting expectantly, with his arms crossed. This time it was Carlyle who had his back to the window, so that he wouldn't be distracted by the view. 'We had our phones switched off in the theatre, so we didn't know what was going on until we came out.' He shook his head. 'It took us about half an hour to get home – and then we weren't allowed near the house.'

Carlyle nodded.

'No one could tell us anything. When the explosion came . . .'

'It was a very difficult situation.' The crime scene had been left in the hands of a local detective inspector who had been none too happy when Carlyle was subsequently catapulted into the role of lead investigator. Carlyle hadn't been too happy about that either, but there you go.

'Yes,' Mosman said uncertainly.

They were clearly not getting very far. The inspector glanced over at Boduka, who was again fiddling with his pen. He turned his attention back to the victim's father. 'What I really need from you now,' he said gently, 'is any idea as to why this happened.'

Boduka dropped his Waterman Carene on the table. 'We had plenty of time to discuss this before you arrived,' he said, with more than a hint of irritation. 'Neither Mr or Mrs Mosman have any idea why anyone should want to do such a terrible thing.'

'Okay,' said Carlyle patiently, 'but this was clearly a premeditated attack on Horatio and, by extension, on the family as a whole. There was nothing random about what happened on Wellington Road. It took time, effort and knowledge, not least the knowledge that Horatio would be alone in the house. Someone went to a lot of effort here. They must have been really pissed off about something. *Really* pissed off. I'm not looking for a justification for what happened, just an explanation. You must have some thoughts – and I need to hear them.'

That was his pitch. Sitting back, he folded his arms and waited for a response.

TWENTY-ONE

After the best part of an hour getting nothing out of Horatio Mosman's father, Carlyle could feel his sugar levels dropping and his temper fraying. Ivor Mosman was unable to offer up anything of use; worse, he didn't seem to think that the inspector should be talking to him at all. Carlyle never ceased to be irritated by people's ability to somehow imagine that he could do his job by ESP. He might be many things, but he wasn't psychic; he needed something to go on.

Now it was Zoe Mosman's turn. Girding his loins, the inspector gazed across the table at the grieving mother. 'So what is it that you do, Mrs Mosman?'

There was a pause as she gave a quick glance towards the lawyer, who nodded his approval. Then her lips twitched and a mumble emerged.

Her voice was so quiet that Carlyle could hardly hear her. 'Sorry?'

She cleared her throat. 'I'm an art historian.'

Carlyle studied her carefully. Finally, he thought, someone says something interesting. Casually scratching his head, he tried to show no reaction to what he'd just heard. 'An academic?'

'Yes,' Mrs Mosman whispered.

'All this information has been provided to you already,' Boduka said sharply.

But news to me, Carlyle thought, ignoring him. 'So you know a thing or two about paintings?'

She nodded. 'I have some expertise.'

Opening the file on the desk, the inspector flicked through a series of documents. Finding what he wanted, he held up a colour photocopy. 'So, do you know what this is?'

Mrs Mosman reached into her handbag, pulled out a pair of reading glasses and slipped them on. Squinting, she leaned forward and stared at the image. It was a copy of an oil painting. Under a grey sky with patches of blue, a woman in a red cape was buying vegetables in a street market while a man rode by on a horse. In the bottom right-hand corner, a dog hovered in the hope of getting something to eat.

'Take your time,' Carlyle said impatiently.

'It looks like an eighteenth-century street scene,' Zoe Mosman said finally. 'Or something like that.' She turned back to the inspector. 'A London market maybe?'

'But you don't know what it's called?'

'No.'

'So it's not famous.'

'It depends what you mean by famous.' She let out one of the weariest sighs he had ever heard in his life. 'The point is, that this kind of thing is not my area of expertise.'

'No?'

'No. My area of specialism is contemporary art; YBAs . . .'

Carlyle looked at her blankly.

'Young British Artists . . . Britart.' She mentioned a number of names, none of which meant anything to the culturally illiterate inspector.

Boduka drummed his fingers impatiently on the table. 'What has this got to do with anything?'

'A copy of this picture,' Carlyle explained, 'was pinned to Horatio's shirt by the man who killed him.' He omitted to add: '*We managed to remove it for forensic investigation just before he was blown sky high.*'

A look of utter disgust spread across Zoe Mosman's face – as if she was about to throw up on the table.

'It looks like it was cut out of a book, or maybe a catalogue,' the inspector went on, placing the photocopy back inside his file. 'Presumably it has some relevance, at least as far as the bomber is concerned.'

'This is news to us,' the lawyer complained. 'Why weren't we told about it earlier?'

'Mrs Mosman?'

Head bowed, Zoe Mosman took a series of deep breaths as she waited for the nausea to pass. Both men waited patiently as she regained a measure of self-control.

'Sorry.'

'Take all the time you need,' Carlyle mumbled.

'Thank you. I'll be fine.' She removed her spectacles and put them into her bag. When she finally looked up, her eyes were damp. 'I would have to check. We have comprehensive databases – so, if you let me have a copy, I can easily find out what that picture is for you.'

'But you haven't seen it before?' Carlyle had a strong sense that she was holding out on him, and was now keen to see how far he could push this conversation.

'No.' She shook her head as fat, heavy tears started trickling down her cheeks. 'I don't think so.'

Glaring at the inspector, the lawyer got to his feet. 'That's enough.'

'I'm sorry.' Jumping up, Mrs Mosman grabbed her bag and ran for the door.

'It's all right, Zoe.' Shaking his head angrily, Boduka followed his client out of the room. Left alone, Carlyle allowed himself a thin smile. After a few moments, he pulled out his mobile and made a quick phone call. Once it was finished, he shoved the papers back into his plastic bag and headed out in search of something satisfying to eat.

TWENTY-TWO

'So what have we got?'

Sitting in the canteen at Charing Cross police station, Joe Szyszkowski looked up from his notes. Although he was more than miffed about being dragged back to the station only to sit around for hours, waiting for his boss to turn up, he tried not to let it show. 'Which one do you want to do first?'

Carlyle finished his second Mars bar of the day, a king-sized one this time, and crumpled the wrapper in his fist. 'The Mosman case,' he took a slurp of black coffee, 'obviously. That's what the powers-that-be want us to focus on.'

Sitting next to Joe, Maude Hall raised an eyebrow. 'Commander Simpson?' she asked.

'Precisely,' Carlyle said. He wasn't entirely sure what the young WPC was doing here, but she was certainly easier on the eye than his sergeant.

'Okay.' Joe took a deep breath. 'The bomb was made of ANFO.'

'Mm.' The inspector tried to feign some kind of interest. In truth, he always found the technical stuff rather boring. At the end of the day, a bomb was just a fucking bomb. It either blew up or it didn't.

'That's ammonium nitrate and fuel oil.'

'Good to know.'

'A fertiliser bomb,' Hall elaborated.

'Commonly used in mining,' Joe continued. 'But also handy for DIY bombers.'

Carlyle looked at both of them in turn. 'So there was nothing particularly sexy, unusual or exotic involved?'

Blank looks all round.

'Nothing,' he added, 'that makes this bomb a one-off and leads us straight to an address where we can arrest the crazed loon that did this.'

'No,' Joe admitted.

'Okay.' The inspector smiled. 'So we leave that exciting stuff to the techies and the Bomb Squad. What else?'

Hall handed each of them a sheet of paper. 'I've gone through the transcripts of the interviews with Horatio Mosman's siblings, and also with Marc Harrington's wife and daughter.'

'Harrington?'

'The neighbour who was shot dead.'

'Of course, of course,' Carlyle mumbled. 'Good.' His mood improved by the sugar rush, he was beginning to think he could get to like this girl. God knows, he could do with an extra pair of hands.

'Anything interesting come out of the interviews?' Joe asked.

'Not really. According to Madeleine Harrington – the daughter – Horatio was a bit of a geek and' – she let out a small chuckle – 'a, quote "chronic self-abuser" unquote. That's about it.'

'A normal teenager then,' Joe grinned.

'Speak for yourself,' Carlyle chided him. 'Anyway, let's not worry about that now. I want us to focus on Horatio's parents.'

'I thought you were already speaking to them.'

'I was, Joseph. And, so far, no one has told me much of any use whatsoever.'

'Those poor people,' Hall said sympathetically. 'They must be in a terrible place right now.'

'Yes, indeed,' said Carlyle cheerily, 'so I want you to get right in there along with them. I want to know about their secrets – especially the mother.'

'Okay,' said the WPC, clearly unconvinced that she could deliver.

'Why the mother?' Joe asked.

'I have a feeling,' Carlyle said vaguely.

The sergeant frowned. 'You don't normally have feelings.'

'Very true,' Carlyle conceded. 'But for once, I feel I need to trust my gut instinct – my intuition, call it what you will.'

'Are you ill?' Joe asked sarcastically.

'Not at all.' The inspector waved the idea away. 'Maybe it's just a new me.'

'Bollocks,' Joe snorted. He knew perfectly well that his boss was not the kind of copper to go along with any new age nonsense. The inspector dealt in facts – and facts alone.

'Okay, okay.' Reverting to the matter in hand, Carlyle pulled the plastic bag on to his lap. After a few moments of rooting around amongst the papers inside, he came up with the photocopy that he had shown to Zoe Mosman. 'This was the picture that was pinned to Horatio's shirt.' He handed it to Hall. 'Find out what it is, and where it lives. And find out what its connection is to Mrs Mosman, who happens to be an art historian.'

'Cool,' Hall said. 'I can do that.'

'If you have any problems, go and talk to Economic and Specialist Crime. I can give you a couple of names of people there who will help.' Carlyle rubbed his hands together in glee: he could smell progress. With a bit of luck, they would have this sorted out in double-quick time. He could then get Simpson off his back, and everyone would be happy.

Everyone except perhaps Joe.

'Could be a red herring,' his sergeant said.

'What?'

Joe gestured to the picture in Hall's hand. 'Someone clearly wants you to focus on the picture, and therefore look at the mother,' he suggested. 'It's not very subtle, is it?'

Hall looked down at the picture then at the inspector.

'I hear what you're saying, Joseph,' Carlyle tried not to grimace, 'but let's first just see what WPC Hall can uncover.

120

Take things one step at a time, cross that bridge – et cetera, et cetera.'

'You're the boss,' said Joe, not sounding too happy about things.

'Glad we sorted that out,' the inspector quipped. 'Now, tell me about all the other stuff.'

'Well . . .' Finally his moment had come. Sitting up in his chair, Joe ran through the details of his meeting with Sylvain Bellamy, Duncan Brown's Editor – and Bellamy's warning about Trevor Miller.

Folding his arms, Carlyle raised his eyes to the heavens. 'Trevor fucking Miller,' he said angrily. 'I should have known that bastard would be up to his neck in this.'

Maude looked from one to the other, like an eager kid wanting to be let in on the secret. 'Who's Trevor Miller?'

'Miller and the inspector go back a long way,' Joe grinned.

Fuck. The mere mention of the name made Carlyle feel old and tired. He looked at the WPC's expectant face and sighed. 'When I was first starting out on The Job – younger than you even – I was on the picket line during the miners' strike.'

Hall looked bemused.

'Before your time,' Joe interjected. 'Before you were even born. The inspector's older than he looks.'

Carlyle frowned. 'Anyway, I was in duty one day when Miller sexually assaulted a woman.' He could remember her name even now: Jill Shoesmith. 'She launched a civil action and I was the only witness. Miller didn't think I did enough to cover his back.'

Hall thought about that for a moment. 'So you wouldn't lie for him?'

'No. Trevor had to go through a formal disciplinary hearing. I told them what I saw.'

'And?' Hall asked, trying to drag it out of him.

'The woman got her payout, Miller got a promotion, and I got my card well and truly marked as someone who couldn't be trusted by his fellow officers.'

'How did he get a promotion?'

Carlyle shrugged. 'Good bloody question.'

'These things happen,' said Joe

'So you regret the way you handled it?' Hall asked.

No, Carlyle thought. Telling the truth is always the easiest option. Just don't expect any thanks for doing it. 'Maybe.' He looked at them both. 'If you're playing the game, you might as well play the game. By doing what I did, I made a few enemies and was seen as being unreliable – not a team player.'

Joe quickly brought the story up to date. 'Mr Miller eventually left the Met to set up his own private consultancy. Dipped below the radar for a while. Then he reappeared as Edgar Carlton's security man, just before the last election.'

'Wow.'

'And then,' Joe continued, 'the inspector here managed to get into *another* pissing contest with him.'

'I wouldn't say that.' Carlyle turned back to Hall. 'Miller was involved in the death of a young man. It was something that was never investigated properly.'

A bemused look passed across Hall's face. 'Why not?'

Once again, Carlyle shrugged.

'These things happen,' Joe repeated.

'The thing now,' said the inspector, 'is that we will have to move very carefully on the Duncan Brown thing. Ironically, it probably helps that we are supposed to be focusing on Mosman.'

'So what do you want to do?' Joe asked.

'Dunno.' Pushing back his chair, Carlyle got to his feet. 'Maybe I'll go and talk to Simpson.'

'Hey, hey.' Joe motioned for him to sit back down. 'We haven't finished yet.'

'No?' Reluctantly, the inspector did as he was told.

'No,' Joe said firmly. 'We still have to talk about Hannah Gillespie.'

'Who?'

'The young girl who went missing from the Peabody Estate,' Hall reminded him.

'Yeah, yeah. She's not turned up, then?'

'No.' Hall glanced at Joe.

'There's good news and there's bad news.' The sergeant gestured to Hall. 'You tell him.'

'I went to Hannah's school,' Hall explained. 'It seems like she's a bright kid, quite mature but a bit restless. She's done things like this before, but always turned up again after a few days.'

'Shouldn't her parents have mentioned this?'

'Maybe,' Joe reflected, 'they don't have her on as short a leash as they liked to imply.'

'Anyway,' Hall said, 'our best guess still is that she's out and about somewhere, having fun.'

'Best guess isn't good enough,' Carlyle snapped. 'We need more than that.'

Hall lowered her voice slightly. 'Well, we know that Hannah's been checking her voicemails on her mobile phone. She listened to her new messages as recently as two hours ago.'

Frowning, Carlyle looked at Joe. To intercept someone's phone messages required a warrant. That could normally take several days.

'We're using our initiative,' Joe said. 'Don't ask.'

'Okay. I won't. So if she's listening to her messages, she must know people are looking for her. But she still can't be arsed to even phone home? I thought that you said she was bright?'

Hall shrugged. 'Maybe she's worried about the reception she'll get when she returns.'

Kids. At least his own daughter, Alice, wouldn't do anything like that – he hoped. 'So, what's the bad news?'

'Two words,' said Joe. 'Francis Clegg.'

The inspector gave him a look that said *Who he?*

'According to one of Hannah's schoolfriends,' Joe explained, 'Mr Clegg is her boyfriend.'

'How reliable is this friend?'

'Melanie Henderson seems a nice girl,' Hall interjected. 'Keen to help.'

'Nice girls,' Carlyle sighed. 'They're always the worst.'

'She says she's seen them together a couple of times.'

'Mr Clegg,' announced Joe, 'is thirty-two.'

'Ah.' As both a copper and a parent, the inspector didn't much like where this was going.

'With two previous convictions for sex with underage girls, and he also beat one of them up quite badly.'

'That's just fucking great,' Carlyle groaned. 'How long have we known about this?'

'A couple of hours,' Joe replied.

'So why haven't we found this bastard yet?'

TWENTY-THREE

After silently counting to a hundred, Carole Simpson reopened her eyes. Sadly, the troublesome inspector was still sitting in her office. 'I thought that I specifically asked you to focus on the Mosman case?'

'I *am* focusing on the Mosman case.'

'John . . .'

'I'm multi-tasking,' Carlyle said, conscious that the words sounded too much like an excuse, 'just trying to be more efficient.' It went against all his instincts to keep his boss in the loop, and he was already regretting making such a quick return to the Commander's office in Paddington Green. 'That's what we're all meant to do these days, isn't it? That's what the Cochrane Review is all about, if I understand it correctly.'

'Mm.' They both knew that Carlyle didn't give a hoot about the government's report into what a twenty-first-century police force might look like. 'I suppose I should be grateful to at least receive a briefing.'

Yes, he thought, so you should. 'Things are moving quickly on all fronts,' he said briskly. 'I might therefore need a bit of assistance on one or more of them.'

'What you mean,' Simpson grinned knowingly, 'is that you're going to need me to save you when you jump into the shit.'

At least she didn't say '*again*'. Carlyle gave his protector and benefactor a grateful smile. 'Precisely.'

The humour vanished from Simpson's face even faster than it

had appeared. 'It goes without saying that I'll want you to give Trevor Miller a wide berth.'

'I'm not interested in Miller,' Carlyle replied primly.

'John,' Simpson scolded, 'you are a terrible liar; truly terrible. I am warning you now: leave that man alone. If you don't, all it will do is create more trouble – for both of us.'

Carlyle slumped in his chair. 'You know me, anything for a quiet life.'

'As if. Look, do I really need to spell it out for you? Miller is close to Simon Shelbourne, who is Sir Chester's media strategist.'

'Uh-huh.'

'Shelbourne used to work for Sonia Claesens, the head of the Zenger Corporation. Apparently, they are still close.'

The inspector gave her a blank stare.

'Do I need to draw you a bloody map?'

'Yes, you do,' he said obtusely.

Gritting her teeth, Simpson continued, 'All they want to do now is find a way of closing down the hacking inquiry.'

'But,' Carlyle frowned, feigning confusion, 'it was Miller's boss – the Prime Minister, no less – who set it up.'

'Yes,' Simpson said heavily. 'And they set it up so that they could be seen to be doing something.'

'How jolly cynical of you,' he joshed, adopting a mock-posh accent.

'That is rather rich coming from the self-proclaimed "most cynical man in the world".'

'Me?' Carlyle raised his hands in surrender. 'Never.'

Simpson gave him a nasty look. 'Do you want me to proceed or not?'

Lowering his arms, the inspector said graciously, 'Go on.'

Simpson sighed. 'No one realized that this thing would just keep growing. And an election is not so far away. The independent police investigation, Operation Redhead, was supposed to have been and gone by now. Instead, it could drag on for ages.'

'Surely that's okay,' Carlyle said, 'if they can kick it into the long grass.'

'Maybe. They would much rather kill it though. And Sir Chester is increasingly worried about how it might all play out. In fact, he's as nervous as hell.'

Carlyle looked at her carefully. 'How do you know all this?'

'You're not the only one with sources, John.'

'So, what do you want me to do?'

Simpson started counting off with her fingers. 'Number one, wrap up the Mosman case asap. That's still the priority. Do what you have to do; and if you want to go after the mother, that's fine.'

'Okay.'

'Number two, keep the Brown thing nice and focused. If I had more bodies I'd give it to someone else, but I don't. These bloody budget cuts are killing us.'

'Twenty-first-century policing.'

'Don't I know it.'

You could always get out from behind that desk, Carlyle thought. The top brass are always moaning while they sit about on their arses. He mumbled something that he hoped sounded vaguely sympathetic.

'So that means you're still on Brown,' Simpson repeated, 'but it *doesn't* mean I want to see you wading into the phone-hacking mess and creating even more problems for everyone. The Met is under enough scrutiny as it is.' He made to say something but she held up a restraining hand. 'The last thing we need is the usual John Carlyle bull in a china shop routine. Just focus on the precise question of who stabbed that journalist and dumped his body in the back of a rubbish truck.'

'Understood,' Carlyle nodded. 'The blinkers are on.'

'Good. Keep them on. Focus is important in an investigation. Now, is there anything else?'

'What about Hannah Gillespie?'

The Commander gave him an exasperated look. 'Who?'

'Hannah Gillespie is the schoolgirl who has gone missing.' He quickly filled her in on the details.

'Do we think she's okay?'

'She's still checking her phone messages.' The inspector immediately regretted letting slip the fact that they had been tapping the girl's phone but, happily, Simpson either didn't pick up on the point or she let it pass.

'We'll just have to hope that she turns up.'

'The parents aren't very happy.'

'Well, they wouldn't be, would they?' Simpson snapped.

'My sergeant spoke to them just as I was coming over here. He says they're talking about going to the press.'

'Christ, that's all we need.' Simpson drummed her fingers on the table. 'What are they like?'

'The parents?' Carlyle shrugged. 'Dunno. Haven't met them. Joe's been handling it all.'

'Well, you'd better bloody well pay them a visit, then.'

'But you told me to prioritize Mosman,' he protested.

Simpson's eyes narrowed. 'Just as well you're so good at multi-tasking then, isn't it?'

'Yes, boss.' Hoist by his own petard, Carlyle got to his feet. 'I'll add it to the list.'

TWENTY-FOUR

'Are you sure this is the place?' The inspector strode out on to the balcony of the Soho flat and let the chill evening air wash over him.

'Yeah.' Joe Szyszkowski held up a stack of envelopes that he'd picked up off the floor. 'They're all addressed to Francis Clegg.'

'Well, he's not here now.' Leaning over the railing, the inspector gazed at the newly refurbished Marshall Street Baths across the road. They were barely a one-minute walk from Oxford Circus. The 2,000 square foot loft-style apartment with three bedrooms and direct lift access to an underground car park had to be worth several million. 'The bloke's obviously doing well.'

Clearly thinking the same thing, Joe gave a rueful shrug.

'Go and have a word with the concierge and see what he can tell us. We need to find this guy.'

'Will do.' As Joe headed for the door, the chirp of a mobile sounded in his pocket. He lifted it to his ear. 'Hello? . . . Yeah.' He turned to face the inspector. 'No, when do you need it by? . . . Okay, I'll see what I can do . . . Yeah, I've got your number.'

'News?' Carlyle looked at him expectantly.

'That was Bernie Gilmore.'

Carlyle's heart sank. Gilmore was a freelance journalist who chased down crime and political stories for a range of different newspapers and websites. You never wanted to get a call from him; invariably it meant he was on to something that was best kept under wraps. He eyed his sergeant suspiciously. 'How did he get hold of your number?'

'He's got everyone's number,' said Joe wearily. 'I'm only surprised that he didn't call you first.'

Right on cue, Carlyle's official, MPS-issue Nokia began vibrating in the breast pocket of his jacket. Scooping it out, he squinted at the screen: BG. Hitting the reject button, he let it fall back into his pocket. Looking up, he saw Joe eyeing him inquisitively. 'Just the missus,' the inspector smiled. 'What did Mr Gilmore want?'

Joe let his gaze drop to his shoes. 'He's on to the Hannah Gillespie story.'

'Fuck!' Carlyle stomped his foot in frustration. 'How the hell did he manage to get that?'

'Dunno,' Joe replied, 'but he's spoken to the parents. They gave him my name.'

'And?' Carlyle demanded, sensing there was more.

'And he's also got Clegg's name.'

'You are fucking kidding me!' The inspector's face turned an unpleasant shade of red until, for a moment, it looked like his head might actually explode.

'And he's even got this address.' Fearing that his boss was about to rush over and throttle him, Joe took a couple of precautionary steps backwards. 'I know,' he said, holding up both hands. 'I know, I know, I know. Someone's blabbed. But we are where we are. He's going to be here in ten minutes. What do you want me to tell him?'

After a succession of deep inhalations, Carlyle's face slowly began to return to something approaching its normal colour. 'Just go and speak to the bloody concierge. I'll deal with Bernie myself.'

Carlyle intercepted the journalist at the front door of Clegg's apartment building. Bernard Wynstanley Gilmore was a bear of a man: six foot two and twenty stone, he had a shock of black

130

hair and an unkempt beard flecked with grey. His Depeche Mode *Sounds of the Universe* sweatshirt was covered in stains of an indeterminate nature, and his jeans were torn at both knees.

'How's it going, Bernie?'

'Inspector.' The journalist greeted him, wheezing as if he'd just climbed ten flights of stairs. 'Can I come in?'

'Of course not,' Carlyle smiled.

'Why not?' Gilmore raised an eyebrow. 'Is it a crime scene?'

'No.' At least not yet anyway. Carlyle gestured down the road, towards Ganton Street. 'Let's go to the Shaston Arms.'

'Mm.' Gilmore thought about that for a moment, patting his belly as he did so. 'D'ya think they'll have Tyrell's crisps?'

'I'm sure they do,' Carlyle said, leading the way.

Bernie Gilmore looked genuinely hurt. 'They didn't have any Tyrell's.'

'Ah well.' Never a connoisseur, the inspector smiled as sympathetically as he could. As far as he was concerned, one bag of crisps was pretty much the same as another. It wasn't as if the pub didn't have any kind of crisps, so surely the hack could make do.

Gilmore ripped open a bag of Thai Sweet Chicken and another of Sizzling King Prawn and laid them on the table. 'Help yourself.'

'Thanks.' Carlyle took a sip of his Jameson's and waited while the journalist sampled the different flavours. Listening to the happy buzz of the conversations around them, he considered how he should play this meeting.

After washing the crisps down with a couple of gulps of Greene King IPA, Gilmore placed his pint glass on the table and happily wiped some crumbs from his beard. 'Ahh!!'

'Good?' Carlyle finished his whiskey. He should have asked for a double. Already he felt like another.

'I think I prefer the Sweet Chicken,' Gilmore said solemnly. 'Anyway, what's the story?'

'That remains to be seen.'

Gilmore lifted the glass back to his mouth. 'Hardly.'

'Pardon?'

'As you well know, Inspector, these days, *wait and see* is never an option.' Gilmore paused to demolish the rest of his beer. 'If you're going to ask me to just sit on this, there's no chance. Pretty girl, a top student, goes missing in the middle of the big city? It seems very surprising that the police haven't gone public on it already. Meanwhile, the parents, as you would expect, are worried sick. So, what are you waiting for?'

What do you know about the parents' worries? As far as Carlyle knew, Gilmore didn't have any kids. Even if he did, it was a fair bet he never got to see them. Being an in-your-face, muckraking journalist was a 24/7 gig; it did not sit easily with family responsibilities. 'We don't actually know that the girl is in danger.' He kept his voice low, his tone even. 'So far, this is just a missing person inquiry.'

'Is that so?' Gilmore raised an eyebrow. 'Interesting. The Missing Persons Bureau hasn't heard of her.'

'Okay,' Carlyle grimaced. 'Maybe – and this is not for quotation – we're a bit behind on the paperwork.'

Folding his arms, Gilmore sat back in his seat. 'Look,' he said, 'I'm not interested in giving you a hard time.'

Carlyle shook his head disbelievingly. 'No?'

'No, really, I'm not. But the point is, I've got more than enough material to go with this story. I've spoken to the parents, and to the best friend. By all accounts, Hannah was a smart kid.'

'*Is*,' Carlyle corrected him, hoping that he was right.

'Very smart,' Bernie continued, ignoring the interruption. 'Her parents were already dreaming of a scholarship at Stanford. That's an American university.'

'Yes, yes,' Carlyle snapped. 'Silicon Valley and all that.'

'You can hardly blame them,' Bernie mused, 'what with tuition fees here going through the roof. Who'd want to scrape together nine grand a year to send their kid to some shitty polytechnic that no one's ever heard of?'

'Do they still have polys?' Carlyle asked.

Bernie thought about that for a moment. 'Maybe they changed their names,' he offered finally. 'Still, no match for the Ivy League, though.'

'No,' Carlyle agreed.

'So the boyfriend was obviously a bit of a fly in the ointment when it came to the grand plan.'

'True.'

'Teenage hormones,' Bernie shrugged. 'They're a killer.'

A thought struck Carlyle. 'Did you tell the parents about Clegg?'

'You really are off the pace on this one, aren't you?' Gilmore shot him a pitying look.

Fuck, the inspector thought, as he realized that he would have to talk to Mr and Mrs Gillespie asap. That was something else to look forward to.

'So you did tell them?' Carlyle asked again.

'Well, I'm not going to let them read about it in the paper, am I? I've even got a photo of young Hannah posing with the Mayor.'

'Christian Holyrod?' Carlyle felt himself shudder. 'When did *he* manage to find his way into the story?' He had a sudden nasty thought. 'He hasn't been shagging her too, has he?'

'No, no, no.' Bernie tutted in disgust. 'She was introduced to him at a Peer Workers' Outreach event. Hannah is a member of the Link Up Crew.'

What the hell are you talking about? Carlyle wondered.

'The Link Up Crew,' Gilmore explained, 'are kids who are supposed to go out and spread the word about the Mayor's good deeds, informing young Londoners on what's happening in the capital and sending their views, opinions and feedback to City Hall. It's all part of the Mayor's policy of engagement with the youth of today – trying to stop the little buggers looting sneakers next time there's a riot.'

'What a load of old crap,' Carlyle snorted.

'Quite. But the fact that Hannah signed up to take part shows she's trying to be a good corporate citizen. In other words, she is not just some feckless chav.'

'No one ever said that she was,' Carlyle replied defensively.

'No, but equally, she's not the kind of middle-class kid with connected parents for whom the forces of the state would be deployed in the blink of an eye without any of this *let's wait and see* stuff.'

'Eh?'

Giving up on the social commentary, Bernie spelled it out. 'Maybe you could be doing a bit more.'

'Like what?'

'You tell me. You're the policeman.'

'Thanks for pointing that out.'

For a few moments they sat in uneasy silence, until Gilmore gestured to Carlyle's empty glass. 'Want another?'

The inspector let out a deep sigh. 'Why not?'

Returning from the bar, Gilmore handed Carlyle his whiskey. 'Got you a double this time.'

'Thanks.'

'You look like you need it. I saw how the last one didn't touch the sides.'

'There's a lot going on.'

'There always is.' Gilmore sat down heavily, dropping a packet of Flame-Grilled Steak crisps on to the table. 'Dinner,' Bernie said succinctly, noting the policeman's dismay.

'Fair enough.' Lifting the glass to his lips, Carlyle took a modest mouthful, letting the Jameson's slide across his tongue.

Gilmore sat back, waiting for the negotiating to begin.

'Look,' said Carlyle, returning his glass to the table, 'I know that we might be playing catch-up . . . but I can trade.'

Now it was the journalist's turn to shake his head. 'Not your style.'

That was true enough. It was well known that the inspector was not a great one for cosying up to journalists. Here and now, however, it looked like he was going to have to make an exception. 'Circumstances change.'

Gilmore contemplated his new pint for several moments. 'I've got the girl, the boyfriend and the worried parents,' he said, not looking up. 'That's everything I need; more than enough, in fact.' Carlyle nodded, letting him say his piece. 'What's more, it's an exclusive.'

The inspector patted the phone in his pocket. 'It wouldn't be for long if I gave it to someone else.' But it was a feeble threat, and they both knew it.

'What would be the point of that? It would hardly solve your problem.'

'I'm also working on Horatio Mosman . . .'

'Big deal!' Gilmore scoffed. 'Everybody knows that. And it's been done to death already.' Opening his new packet of crisps, he arched an eyebrow. 'No pun intended, of course. And anyway, I am perfectly well aware that you have no progress to report.'

'Then there's the Duncan Brown case.'

'Mm . . .' Gilmore dropped a handful of crisps into his mouth and chewed thoughtfully. 'That may be a little bit more interesting. What have you got so far?'

'You'll have to wait.'

'A bird in the hand, Inspector.'

Looking around, Carlyle lowered his voice. 'I will give you a full heads-up on both Mosman and Brown – in due course. Also, if anyone else starts sniffing around the Gillespie story I will let you know straight away, so that you can still get it out there first.'

Gilmore took another crisp from the packet and contemplated it carefully. 'You have my mobile number?'

'Of course.'

'Don't forget to use it.'

When he returned to Clegg's apartment, Carlyle was surprised to find WPC Maude Hall there, talking to Joe.

'How did it go?' Joe asked.

'He'll give us a little time,' Carlyle replied, not wanting to go into the details. 'Did you get anything of use from the concierge?'

'Nah,' Joe said. 'The guy says that Clegg travels a lot; hasn't seen him in the last week or so. He doesn't recognize the girl – says he hasn't seen her coming or going from the flat.'

'Or doesn't want to let on,' Carlyle grumbled.

'Either way, it's the same situation.' Joe gestured towards the WPC. 'Anyway, Maude's come up with something interesting.'

'On Mosman,' Hall clarified, 'not this.'

'Okay.' Carlyle was more than happy to accept good news wherever he could find it. He looked her up and down: out of uniform she looked so very young. And was that a stud in her nose?

'Inspector?'

'Yes?' He belatedly restored eye-contact.

'Zoe Mosman told you that she was an art historian?'

'Yes.'

'Well, that's not quite the whole story. She is, in fact, Creative Director for the Government Art Collection.'

'That's the thing Sir Michael Snowdon was talking about,' Joe reminded him.

'Yes,' Carlyle nodded, 'the bikini picture. But is that of any significance?'

'I think so,' said Hall. 'The picture that was pinned to Horatio's shirt was a view of Covent Garden, painted by a Flemish painter called Joseph van Aken in the 1700s. The GAC bought it back in 1929 and the last record of it being on display was in an exhibition put on by the British Embassy in Lagos in 1986.'

Carlyle looked at Joe and Maude in turn. 'How did you find this out?'

'It's all easily accessible,' Hall smiled, 'if you know where to look.'

'Good. Well done.' The inspector turned to Joe. 'So, it looks like we need to go and have another word with Mrs Mosman.'

'Yes.' His sergeant looked eager at the prospect.

The inspector thought about it for a moment longer. 'But maybe I should talk to Sir Michael first.'

TWENTY-FIVE

Trevor Miller shovelled the last forkful of Cumberland sausage into his mouth before pushing away his empty plate with a satisfied sigh. Wondering what he could stuff down his gullet next, the Prime Minister's Senior Security Adviser noticed that his dining companions had barely touched the food on their plates. Sonia Claesens had ordered the caviar omelette (sixty quid!) and Simon Shelbourne the haggis with fried duck eggs (only a tenner). Twenty minutes waiting for their orders to arrive, and then the two of them spent another ten minutes pushing the food around their plates, waiting for Miller to finish eating so that they could finally get down to business. The bill would come to more than a hundred quid and all they would actually get out of it was a cup of herbal tea.

It all seems like a terrible waste of good food, Miller thought idly. But what did he care? It wasn't like he would be picking up the tab.

Smearing a slice of white toast with butter and adding a layer of Dundee rough-cut marmalade, Miller took a large bite, before washing it down with a mouthful of coffee. Detecting more than a hint of impatience in Sonia's eyes, he quickly squashed the rest of the toast into his mouth, chewed and swallowed. Finishing his coffee, he placed the cup back on its saucer and pushed his chair an inch or so away from the table, signalling that the eating part of the proceedings was at an end.

'Very nice breakfast,' he smiled, holding in a small burp.

An officious-looking waiter appeared at the table. Sonia Claesens glared at him balefully and he scurried away.

'Amazing service in this place,' Shelbourne mused. 'And always so busy!' He gestured to the people queuing at the door, waiting for a table to become available. 'You'd never know that there was a recession on.'

'And has been for the last six years,' Claesens added somewhat resentfully.

Miller stared at them blankly. Small talk wasn't his forte. 'Mm,' was all he could manage. Amazingly, he still felt rather hungry. He wondered if he could have some more toast.

'Of course,' Shelbourne trilled, 'I used to come here all the time – before I started working for Sir Chester, that is.'

Before you started having to get your expenses through the Met's Accounts Department, Miller thought. The Warham would never have been his first choice for this meeting. The Piccadilly café-restaurant in the grand European tradition – a former car showroom with lots of Venetian and Florentine influences; pillars, arches and stairways all over the place – was too busy, too noisy and too showy for his own taste. Looking around, it seemed that everyone else was busily checking out their fellow diners; or tapping away on their BlackBerrys and iPads while holding desultory conversations. It was a place to be seen, rather than somewhere for a discreet tête-à-tête. There was no semblance of privacy. A journalist working for Claesens had even been banned for prowling the tables, hassling the great and the good over their food in his relentless search for 'exclusive' stories. The venue made the veteran security consultant feel distinctly uncomfortable. It had been chosen by Shelbourne's PA and Miller belatedly wondered if he should have insisted on somewhere else. By now, the fact that the three of them were breakfasting together was probably already a matter of record on some social networking site.

Fucking Twitter, Miller thought with a sigh. You never had to worry about that kind of shit in my day; you could go about your business in peace. Social media provided a limitless platform for voyeurs, the ego-crazed and the criminal. If his boss, the Prime Minister, had any sense, he would just close the whole internet thing down. Maybe Miller should suggest it once he got back to Downing Street. It wouldn't be that difficult – or, at least it wasn't for the Chinese and the bloody Iranians. He poured himself some more coffee. It was too late to worry about the location now, so he would just have to make the best of it. If the meeting ever did become public, perhaps he could hold up the venue as evidence that they were being totally open and transparent. Hiding in plain sight had a lot to recommend it.

Gazing around the room for the hundredth time, Miller picked out various familiar faces, a banker here, a newspaper editor there; a chat-show host complaining to his waiter about something; a couple of actresses looking bored in one corner as a television executive wittered on. No one caught Miller's eye or returned his gaze. Deciding against extra toast, Miller folded his mauve cotton napkin and placed it on the table. 'So . . .'

'So . . .' Shelbourne blinked once, twice, before turning to his former boss for help. Encased in a Moschino red tweed bouclé jacket buttoned to the neck, Sonia Claesens fixed Miller with a steely glare. She had the pinched features and dead eyes of someone who had spent the last two decades subsisting on half-rations.

'I think,' she said solemnly, 'that we will be able to find an agreement on an intelligent way forward.'

Shelbourne nodded enthusiastically. 'Absolutely.'

I very much doubt that, thought Miller. He smiled. 'The PM would welcome that.'

'Good.' A well-preserved, forty-something platinum blonde, Claesens was Senior Managing Director at the Zenger Corporation. This role gave her responsibility for the *Sunday Witness* and other British assets owned by the global new media conglomerate. In such an elevated position, she had become used to sharing a table with prime ministers, rather than slumming it with their minions. Now, however, with Zenger enmeshed in scandal, Sonia's stock was sinking at an alarming rate. Edgar Carlton, the current PM, had appointed Trevor Miller as Number Ten's 'gatekeeper' on the phone-hacking issue. To her immense chagrin, Claesens found herself in the position of having to mix with the bag carriers.

Dabbing the corners of her mouth with her napkin, she glanced at her Omega Ladymatic. Time, as always, was precious. 'Broadly speaking, Mr Miller, is Edgar happy about where we are now?'

'The Prime Minister is in Birmingham today,' Miller grinned, 'visiting some widget factory or other and having to mix with the plebs. So, no, I don't suppose that he is very happy at all.'

Claesens grimaced at the feeble quip.

'Shouldn't you be with him then?' Shelbourne asked. 'Given that you do his security?'

Miller shook his head. This boy was clearly an idiot. 'There is a team of more than seventy who cover the PM's security detail. I'm not one of the guys who stand next to him, wearing an earpiece, ready to take a bullet.' He smiled indulgently. 'I'm too old for that.'

'But you would if you had to,' Shelbourne persisted. 'Take a bullet, I mean?'

Not in a million years. 'Of course,' Miller said. 'If the situation arose, I would definitely step in.'

Shelbourne removed his spectacles and began cleaning the lenses with a napkin. 'You were previously in the police, weren't you?'

Miller stiffened. The less people enquired about his past, the better. 'A long time ago.'

'In the Met?'

'Yes. I was born here in London. I started out in the mineworkers' strike up north in the eighties.' He gave the little scrote a dismissive look. 'I guess that was before you were born.'

'Almost,' Shelbourne said, steadfastly not taking any offence.

'But we did it at school. Or at least, I remember seeing something about it on the telly. So I know a bit about it. The whole thing looked pretty brutal – the "enemy within" and all that. Good to know that you were there, standing up for law and order.'

'We cracked a few heads,' Miller replied, smiling at the memory.

'But it's rather a long way from the coal mines to Downing Street. How did you end up as the Prime Minister's Security Adviser?'

'It just happened,' Miller shrugged. 'After leaving the Met, I set up my own consultancy . . .' He suddenly remembered his Downing Street media training and a pre-prepared soundbite popped into his head. 'Edgar Carlton is the best leader we've had in a long time – certainly the best since Margaret Thatcher put the country back on track. I am very lucky to have had the chance to work for him.'

Shelbourne smiled wanly. As an ex-journalist, he knew when he was being spun a line. So did Sonia Claesens, who looked like she was in pain.

'And I also have a very interesting job,' Miller continued, 'taking an overall view of different issues . . . general situations and specific threats, trying to neutralize them before they become active.' God alone knew what that guff meant, but it was a well-rehearsed explanation. He regularly used it around Westminster, where the lame-brained politicians always lapped it up.

'Well, then,' Claesens looked like she would happily shoot both of them, given a chance, 'getting back to our particular *specific* threat . . .'

Leaning forward, Miller realized that he had taken a visceral dislike to this woman that would never be reversed. He lowered his voice and went into the little speech he had composed on the way to the restaurant. 'Edgar has asked me to make it clear that he is all too aware of the current situation. None of us' – the word *us* reminding them that he, Miller, had risen to become a player here in his own right – 'are happy about the latest turn of events.'

142

Shelbourne gave Claesens a concerned look. 'What "latest turn of events"?'

'Duncan Brown's murder.'

'Who?'

'Jesus, Simon,' Claesens snapped, 'you don't ever pay any attention, do you? He worked at the *Witness* for almost five years. He was there when you were still the Editor.'

'More than two hundred people worked on that paper,' Shelbourne replied huffily.

'He was a news reporter; won Best Newcomer of the Year at the Press Awards three years ago.'

'You're still not ringing any bells,' Shelbourne said tightly.

'Anyway,' said Claesens, turning her attention back to Miller, 'it is all very unfortunate, I'm sure. But, equally, it had nothing to do with our current situation.'

'Maybe not, but at this stage the possibility of some kind of connection can't be totally ruled out.' Having done a little discreet digging, Miller was aware that Brown had been placed under investigation after it leaked out that Metropolitan Police Officers were selling confidential information to Zenger reporters. Worse still, these were the very journalists who were championing the government's re-election prospects. The whole tawdry mess needed to be nipped in the bud before the start of the campaign was formally announced. Edgar Carlton wanted to call an early poll and have a second term in the bag before the Opposition managed to get their act together. The last thing he needed was them sinking their teeth into a nice juicy scandal.

Without warning, Shelbourne suddenly seemed to tune into the significance of their conversation. 'Oh, God!' he mumbled. 'This thing is a total nightmare. And it's just getting worse and worse.'

'Pull yourself together, Simon,' Claesens snapped.

I bet she's said that to him plenty of times before, Miller thought.

'The whole business is just too horrible for words,' the PR man groaned.

'But we are where we are,' Claesens said firmly.

'But we are where we are,' Miller echoed, a shark-like smile crossing his lips. 'Of course, ultimately, *we* are not exposed to the potential fallout from this in the way that *you* people are.'

'Is that a threat?' Claesens picked up her fork. Gripping it tightly, she looked like she was getting ready to stab him in the chest.

'Not at all,' Miller said evenly. 'It is just the reality of the situation.' He turned to Shelbourne. 'Where are you with the Meyer investigation?'

A look of panic flashed across the young man's face. 'Well,' he stammered, 'the Chief Constable's inquiry is independent of both the Commissioner and—'

Miller cut him off with an impatient wave of his hand. 'Spare me the PR guff, sonny. Sir Chester knows that if he allows himself to be outmanoeuvred by some Nottinghamshire plod, he will be straight out the back door, to be replaced by the Mayor's latest pet.'

For the first time, a smile tickled the edges of Claesens' lips. 'But surely it was the government's decision to set up Operation Redhead? And didn't Edgar take the credit for parachuting in Chief Inspector Russell Meyer to head it up? "A clean pair of hands" was the phrase he used, if I remember correctly.'

'It was indeed,' Miller nodded. 'The PM has personally taken a firm lead on this thing. But, as you well know, Meyer is letting the whole thing get out of control. He now has seventy officers working on it and they spend their whole time taking calls from bloody lawyers who claim to be representing "victims" and are greedily eyeing up big fat compensation pay-outs.'

'Bastards,' Claesens clucked.

Miller shot her an angry look. 'Maybe if you'd kept your people under control in the first place,' he snapped, 'we wouldn't be sitting here having to worry about this mess.'

Sonia Claesens didn't like the security man's tone one little bit. 'But I knew nothing about any of this before it came to light,' she pouted. 'Did I, Simon?'

Hiding behind his teacup, her former underling said nothing.

'I wasn't even aware that we were using those people,' she continued.

Those people meaning Wickford Associates: a group of former police officers now working as private detectives.

'Is there any way that I could have had any idea that they were hacking people's phones? Of course not!'

No, love, Miller thought sarcastically. Of course not.

'As soon as I heard about what was going on, I ordered it stopped,' she trilled. 'And I have the emails to prove it.'

'I bloody hope so,' Miller snorted. 'But we still have to clean up the mess so that we can draw a line in the sand and move on.'

Shrugging, Claesens took another sip of her lemon tea.

'The point is,' he said, 'there are now literally thousands of people coming out of the woodwork claiming that their phones have been hacked. Not all of them can be z-list celebrities that no one cares about. Some of them must be real people.'

Another theatrical shrug. 'Real' people rarely, if ever, featured on Sonia Claesens' radar.

'If there are real people involved,' looking around, he lowered his voice even further, 'it appears that the Metropolitan Police Service and the government have been turning a blind eye to what you've been doing.'

'You don't need to spell it out,' Claesens said crossly.

Behind his goofy glasses, trying to keep up with the conversation, Shelbourne looked like he was about to burst into tears.

Miller took a deep breath. In an ideal world, he would take the pair of them into a windowless room and slap some sense into them. But, sadly, it was far from an ideal world.

'The Prime Minister,' he said slowly, 'values the working relationship that exists between Zenger Media, the Metropolitan Police Service and the government. It has been very productive, on many levels, and has made several important contributions to the evolution of our civil society.' They looked at him blankly, but he ploughed on; it was amazing how easily this meaningless crap just rolled off the tongue. He supposed that was what happened when you spent too much time hanging around politicians. 'However, if it is discovered that there have been aspects of the relationship that were somehow dysfunctional or less than transparent, then, well . . .' He spread his hands to signify *You're on your own*.

Claesens pulled an iPhone6 from her large combo tote and began tapping angrily at the screen. 'Of course,' she said, not looking up, 'the next election is on the horizon.'

'Edgar is well aware of that,' Miller said flatly, 'and he is grateful for your continued support.'

Claesens dropped the iPhone back in her bag and looked up. 'Which he should not take for granted.'

'We would never do that.' Miller held her gaze. 'As I said, the PM values what all parties bring to the table here.' He gestured to Shelbourne. 'Simon here will keep his man under control.' The boy looked doubtful but nodded anyway. 'And you have to sort out *your* people.'

'They are not *my* people,' Claesens protested.

'They are now,' said Miller.

Claesens glared at him but made no reply.

'I will let Edgar know that we have had a productive meeting,' Miller told them, 'that everyone's on the same page . . . and that this matter will be dealt with speedily, efficiently and quietly.' He paused. When there was no response from either of his eating companions, he got to his feet. 'Thanks for breakfast. Let's keep talking.'

Claesens did not seem particularly pleased at the thought of a continuing dialogue on this subject. Then she remembered something and perked up a little. 'Tell Edgar I'll see him at the weekend.'

Miller frowned.

'We're all going to the Harvest Food and Music Festival,' Claesens explained. 'It's in his constituency, after all, and Edgar gave a great speech last year. There is excellent street food, too. Anastasia and I are looking forward to getting together.'

146

'Mm.' Miller didn't want to get into an argument with the PM – or the PM's wife – about their weekend arrangements. He knew how keen Anastasia Carlton would be to be seen out and about with her husband, if only to try and stem the gossip about Edgar's extra-curricular activities. On the other hand, the last thing he wanted at the moment was his boss being caught in public with the toxic Ms Claesens. Worse still, what if there were horses around? The press were still having fun with George Canning, the ex-police horse that Claesens had adopted. A new picture of Edgar, Claesens and some horse – any bloody horse – would appear on every front page.

That was simply unacceptable. It could not be allowed to happen. Even Edgar himself could see that, surely?

'It's been in the diary for months,' Claesens said.

'I'll let him know,' Miller said, 'but there may be some, er, scheduling issues.'

Claesens gave him an icy stare. 'There had better not be.'

147

TWENTY-SIX

Carefully announcing his arrival, Sir Gavin O'Dowd gave a loud cough as he stepped through the soundproof doors of the Cabinet Room. Rising through the ranks to the role of Cabinet Secretary, Sir Gavin had seen a lot in his time. At the same time, he had managed to *not* see a whole lot more. A man of the world, O'Dowd prided himself on the fact that he had let little faze him over the years. Yet, in all his time in the Civil Service, he'd never come across a situation like this.

'Prime Minister . . .'

Painted off-white, with floor-to-ceiling windows looking out on to Downing Street, the Cabinet Room was bathed in a traditional English 60-watt gloom. Edgar Carlton sat at his usual place, underneath the only painting on any of the walls, a copy of the portrait of Sir Robert Walpole by French portrait painter Jean-Baptiste van Loo. Dressed in a navy Ozwald Boateng single-breasted, two-button navy suit, with a cream shirt and a chocolate brown tie, he lounged in his mahogany chair. It was positioned facing the windows, at the centre of the boat-shaped table introduced by Harold '*You've never had it so good*' Macmillan in the 1950s.

'Yes?' Less than pleased at the unexpected interruption, the PM glared up at Sir Gavin. Sitting next to him in the seat usually occupied by the Chancellor of the Exchequer, Edgar's artist girlfriend Yulissa Vasconzuelo sat grinning wolfishly.

'Your eleven o'clock,' O'Dowd said, 'with the Vice President of Afghanistan. The delegation has arrived a bit early.'

'Bloody foreigners,' Edgar snapped. 'They have no sense of time. Can't we buy him a Rolex out of the aid budget, or something?'

'Hey!' Yulissa smacked him playfully on the arm. 'I'm a foreigner, you know.' Her sleeveless Elie Tahari lace and leather dress crinkled provocatively. In search of divine inspiration, Sir Gavin lifted his gaze to the chandeliers.

'Yes, well.' Scratching his groin, Edgar looked at the civil servant. 'Where are they?'

'They're waiting in the Terracotta Room.' O'Dowd glanced optimistically at the door. 'The meeting is scheduled to take place in the White Drawing Room.'

'And where is the bloody Foreign Secretary?'

'Stuck in traffic, I believe.'

Edgar sighed in exasperation. 'Well, serve them some tea, and tell them we'll be along in a short while. In the meantime, they'll have to bloody well wait.'

Giggling, Yulissa kept her gaze on the Cabinet Secretary as her hand disappeared under the table.

Was it his imagination, Sir Gavin wondered, or did the PM actually stiffen?

'I've got some important business to attend to here,' Edgar spluttered as he shifted in his chair. 'Miss Vasconzuelo is looking at making some additional gifts to the nation from her hugely impressive . . . body of work.'

'The nation?'

'To the Government Art Collection, man.'

'Ah, yes.' Sir Gavin looked pleadingly at Sir Robert Walpole for some assistance. None was forthcoming.

'So, maybe,' Edgar continued, 'you could leave us to it. Tell the Foreign Secretary, when he manages to get here, to start the proceedings. I will be along shortly.'

'Of course,' said Sir Gavin, quickly retreating out of the room.

Nodding to Sir Gavin on the grand staircase, Trevor Miller bounded across the entrance hall and burst into the Cabinet

Office with his usual aplomb – and stopped in his tracks. Slumped in his official chair, the only one in the room possessing arms, Edgar Carlton rolled his tongue across his lower lip. His eyes were half-closed and a glazed expression occupied his face. His gentle moans could have denoted pain; or they could have equally denoted pleasure.

Miller's trained eye noted the PM's dishevelled appareil, as well as signs of movement under the table.

'Excuse me?'

Still, the Prime Minister didn't seem to realize that he was there.

'Shall I come back in five minutes?'

'No need,' replied a muffled voice from under the table. 'We're done here.'

With a final grunt, Edgar shook himself awake. Slowly his eyes began to regain focus. Miller discreetly averted his gaze while his boss rearranged himself, making no comment when Yulissa Vasconzuelo appeared from under the table.

'I need to get going now.' Yulissa kissed Edgar on the top of the head, though keeping her gaze firmly on his Head of Security. 'I've got an art exhibition benefit at the ICA this lunchtime. Tiresome people but it has to be done. The food is terrible, as well.'

'Sounds more fun than my lunch,' Edgar said ruefully, still ignoring his staffer. 'I've got to go and make nice to . . .' he made a face as his mind went blank '. . . somebody or other.'

'The Vice President of Afghanistan,' Miller reminded him.

'Yes, indeed.' Edgar zipped himself up and gave his balls a hearty scratch for good measure. 'Thank you, Trevor.'

'Enjoy!' Yulissa grinned as she skipped from the room.

'What a girl!' Edgar enthused as the door closed behind her.

Miller smiled but said nothing.

'If only we could make her Minister for the Arts, or something.'

Miller pretended to give the idea some thought. His boss's flights of fancy were becoming more frequent; as if the job was eating into what little brain he possessed to start with. Or maybe it was too many blow jobs? 'She's a foreign national,' he pointed out eventually. 'I think that would be a problem.'

Edgar waved a hand dismissively. 'Couldn't we just give her a passport and stick her in the House of Lords or something?'

'Perhaps.' Miller had no idea. 'Anyway, I thought that you might want an update on my breakfast with Simon Shelbourne and Sonia Claesens.'

'Mm.' Not wanting to hear about it at all, Edgar pushed himself out of the chair. 'But the Afghan guy—'

Trevor stepped in front of the door to block his way. 'You've kept him waiting twenty minutes already. Another five won't make any difference.'

'All right,' Edgar said huffily. He began pacing in front of the fireplace.

Not mentioning Duncan Brown, Miller gave his boss a quick recap of the mess they were in. Even at the best of times, Edgar wasn't a details man. 'They are not happy about the way things are going,' was his conclusion.

'None of us are,' Edgar grumbled.

'Sonia Claesens, in particular, thinks that we should be doing something more.'

'That woman . . .' Edgar shook his head sadly.

'They understand,' Miller continued, 'the need to progress carefully but I'm worried that she may turn out to be a loose cannon.'

Edgar gave him an exasperated look. 'Trevor,' he said, 'you're not telling me anything new here.'

'Sonia says she's going to the Harvest Food and Music Festival. Apparently she's already spoken to your wife about it.'

At the mention of Anastasia, Edgar flinched.

Miller ploughed on. 'Clearly, all the papers would love to get a picture of you and Sonia socialising.'

'That bloody horse . . . I should never have ridden that bloody horse.'

151

'As far as I know,' Miller said gently, 'George Canning isn't going to be there, but that isn't really the point. Getting photographed consorting with such a high-profile Zenger Media exec while the phone-hacking scandal is still in full swing would not appear good.'

Edgar raised an eyebrow. 'And when did we suddenly become an expert in PR?'

Miller shrugged. 'It's not exactly rocket science, is it? Anyway, I've spoken to your Communications Director, and he agrees that it would be a very bad idea for you to be present.'

Edgar grimaced. 'I'm sorry, but that is impossible. The festival is one of the highlights of my constituency year.' A vague imitation of the same dreamy look that had taken flight once Yulissa Vasconzuelo left the room returned to his face. 'Organic beefburgers, twenty-seven types of cheeses, over a hundred real ales . . .'

You wouldn't know a real ale if you drowned in one, Miller reflected.

'It is a truly unique British event,' Edgar continued, sounding like he'd swallowed the advertising brochure. 'Face-painting for the kids. Lots of celebs – people that I *do* want to get photographed with. Jeremy Clarkson's going to be there. Hugh Fearnley-Whittingstall. KT Tunstall, for God's sake!'

'The point remains,' Miller said firmly, 'that there will be dozens of photographers looking to get just one particular shot – the picture of you socializing with your chum, the media executive currently accused of breaking the law on an industrial scale.'

Edgar's eyes narrowed. 'Well, you'll just have to make sure that you keep us apart then, won't you?' Stepping forward, he said more kindly, 'I hear what you're saying, Trevor, and I know that you are just trying to be prudent, but I have to go to that festival. I am sorry, but it is simply non-negotiable. There is no way that Anastasia and the kids are going to let me pass on this one. Anyway, if I was to spend my whole life running from photographers I would never go anywhere. You'll just have to sort it out somehow. Now, if you'll excuse me, I think . . . whoever it is has waited long enough. I'd better go and make my appearance.'

Carlyle pointed to a sign in the window that said *Strictly over 18s*.

'Dad!' Shaking her head, Alice dug into her Creamy Banana flavour ice cream with banana ripple sauce. 'Don't be embarrassing.'

'I'm a policeman,' her father shrugged. 'I can't be seen to encourage law-breaking.'

'What law?'

'Well . . .' the question had him stumped.

'Hah!' Alice waved an accusing spoon in his direction. 'How can you be under-age in an ice-cream parlour?'

'Good point.' They were sitting at a table on the sunny side of Maiden Lane, outside *Sweet & Creamy*, the self-proclaimed 'world's first gay ice-cream bar', complete with its own masseur offering massages and ice-cream facials.

Only in London.

Inside, Lady Gaga was singing about being on the Edge of Glory. Outside, however, it was just another glorified café. Helen had gone to a kundalini yoga class, leaving Carlyle to spend some quality time with his daughter. As Alice got older, they seemed to be spending less time together. He felt sad about that, but at the same time realized it was inevitable.

'Anyway, Mum says that you are always breaking the rules.'

Carlyle played with his empty demitasse. 'Well,' he said cheerily, 'first, you should never listen to your mother on things like that. And second, I *do not* break the rules . . . I just bend them occasionally.'

'That's not what Mum says.'

'How would she know?' Carlyle asked, his good humour beginning to crumble at the edges. He sat in silence for a few moments, watching his daughter polish off the last of her ice cream. 'Want anything else?'

'No.' Licking the spoon clean, she placed it in the bowl. 'That was good.'

'So,' said Carlyle, 'I was wondering . . .'

Alice shot him a look. 'If you were going to ask me about Stuart, don't.'

'No, no, no,' he lied. Stuart Bowers was Alice's first boyfriend, and Carlyle was more than curious about what was going on.

'I dumped him weeks ago,' Alice explained.

'Ah.' Result! Carlyle started to grin then managed to check himself.

'He was so immature, it was really annoying.'

'That's boys for you. If I were you, I'd think about ignoring them until you reach your thirties, at least.'

She made a face.

'Ideally, it should be your *late* thirties.' His mobile phone started vibrating in his pocket. Thinking it might be Helen, he pulled it out but there was no number on the screen. He brandished the handset at Alice. 'Might be work.'

She gave him a smile. 'Take it, Dad, I don't mind.'

Carlyle hit the receive button. 'Hello?'

'Inspector . . .'

Damn! He immediately recognized the precise tones of Sir Michael Snowdon and was conscious that he still hadn't checked on the Rosanna investigation. His recent visit to the Snowdon residence – their stilted conversation over a glass of Bladnoch, until the unfolding Mosman fiasco offered a chance of escape – seemed like half a lifetime ago. So much had happened since that he had simply been overwhelmed by events.

'I'm sorry,' he stammered, 'but I haven't yet been able to speak to anyone at Fulham.'

'Don't worry, Inspector,' Snowdon said amiably. 'That wasn't why I was ringing.'

'No?' *Thank God for that.*

'No, this is about the other thing.'

What other thing?

The older man continued, 'There's someone I think you should meet.'

Leaving Alice to enjoy the sunshine, Carlyle headed towards Soho. Less than twenty minutes later, he was sitting in the first-floor dining room of a private members' club on Wardour Street. All the other tables were empty, the lunchtime rush being long over.

A waiter hovered in the background while Sir Michael Snowdon ordered a glass of La Grace de l'Hermitage 2007. 'Are you sure that I can't interest you in something to drink, Inspector?'

Carlyle held up a hand. 'I'm fine, thank you.'

The former Permanent Secretary waited for the waiter to retreat before gesturing towards the third man at their table. 'Apologies if I seem to be interfering in your investigation,' Snowdon smiled.

'Not at all.'

'I am confident that you would have got round to speaking to Harris here soon enough . . .'

Having no idea where this was going, Carlyle nodded firmly.

'. . . but I assumed that sooner might be better than later, as it were.'

Waiting for Sir Michael to finish his preamble, Harris Highman looked Carlyle up and down, as if reluctant to make up his mind about the policeman too quickly.

'Thank you.'

Highman couldn't quite manage a smile. 'I'm glad to be of help in any way I can.' He was a small, pale man of indeterminate age, wearing an old-fashioned, double-breasted grey wool suit with a white shirt and a navy tie. 'When I saw the news about poor Horatio Mosman, I realized immediately.'

'Realized what?' Carlyle felt unable to hide his curiosity any longer.

'That – at some level – it had to be related to what his mother was up to.'

'Why?'

'Because of the van Aken.'

His mind blank, the inspector turned to Snowdon for help.

The waiter arrived with Sir Michael's wine and he sniffed it appreciatively. 'Joseph van Aken's *View of Covent Garden*,' he declared.

'Yes, yes,' Carlyle said, recalling the conversation he'd had with Maude Hall. 'You mean the picture pinned to the boy's shirt.'

Highman scratched his nose. 'It is one of a number of government-owned paintings which have gone missing.'

'As in stolen?'

'As in unaccounted for.'

Snowdon took a mouthful of the wine. 'When Her Majesty's Government decided to sell off some of the works in its collection, it realized that it didn't really know what it had. Quite sensibly, therefore, it decided to conduct an audit of the entire collection. Poor old Harris here was tasked with trying to track them all down. Quite a few, a rather shocking number, in fact, remain "unaccounted for", as the dear fellow so euphemistically puts it.'

The inspector thought about that for a moment. 'How does this connect to Zoe Mosman? When I showed her a copy of the painting, she didn't even recognize it.'

Snowdon glanced at Highman, who allowed a pained expression to dance across his face. 'That would be hard to believe, Inspector. In fact, it is impossible, simply impossible. I have had three meetings with Zoe over the last year concerning the missing paintings. We have discussed the van Aken at least twice.'

'So someone was trying to drop her in it,' Carlyle mused.

'Yes, indeed,' said Snowdon solemnly. 'It certainly looks as if someone was trying to give you a very big clue.'

* * *

Wondering how best to deal with Zoe Mosman, Carlyle wandered up Drury Lane, heading for home. Turning into Macklin Street, he fumbled in his pocket for the fob that opened the front entrance to Winter Garden House. On the step, he flicked it across the small black entry pad and heard the heavy door click open. Stepping inside, he breathed in the powerful smell of pine disinfectant that Daniel, the caretaker, used on the stairwell every day. The LCD display above the lift doors said it was currently on the third floor, heading upwards. Maybe he should take the stairs instead.

'Hello, John.'

Slowly turning round, Carlyle smiled. 'Trevor. I was wondering when you'd show up.' He glanced towards the CCTV camera positioned above the door, which covered the lobby area. Someone had yanked the cable out, which was not a good sign.

Squaring his shoulders, Trevor Miller moved forward. The man was six foot plus, giving him a height advantage of four inches. These days he also had a weight advantage of four or five stone. 'Our paths cross again.' It came out like a line he'd been rehearsing for a while.

'It seems so.' Carlyle tried to hold his irritation in check. Despite the fact that the guy was hopelessly out of shape, Miller could beat him to a pulp with one hand tied behind his back. He would therefore have to let him have his say, respond calmly and face him down. 'What can I do for you?'

Miller shook his head. 'I can't believe that you, of all people, ended up on the Duncan Brown case.' In a grey suit and with a white shirt open at the neck, he looked more tanned and relaxed than Carlyle could ever remember him. But, carrying so much weight, he still looked like a heart attack waiting to happen.

If only, Carlyle thought. Half-turning away, he pressed the call button for the lift. 'A bloke gets stabbed and dumped in a rubbish lorry in my patch, so what do you expect?'

'And it's just my luck that the world's most fucking offside plod happens to get the case.'

Carlyle watched his former police colleague slowly ball his fists. 'Do you perhaps have some information that you would like to share with the investigation?' he asked evenly.

'Yes, I do.' Miller stepped even closer. The strong whiff of alcohol on his breath made Carlyle wonder if he'd had a few in the Rising Sun across the road, while waiting for his quarry to arrive. But he held his ground and tried to retain eye-contact, which was difficult now that Miller was actually towering over him. 'Even you have to realize that this is one time when you need to try and understand the bigger picture,' Miller told him.

'Oh?' Carlyle said. 'And what's that?'

'Don't play stupid with me.' Miller jabbed a meaty finger towards his face. 'Brown, as you very well know, was up to his neck in this phone-hacking business. It is very important for the MPS to be—' The entrance door to the building buzzed open and Miller suddenly shut up. A small boy in the uniform of the nearby St Clement Danes Primary School heaved it open, struggling with his oversized backpack. The boy, who was called Samuel Bajwa, looked at the two men suspiciously.

Carlyle suddenly wondered if Alice had made it home yet. He didn't want her to walk in on this nonsense. Stepping away from Miller, he gave the boy a cheery smile. 'How's it going, Sam?'

'Okay, Mr Carlyle.' But the boy looked less than reassured.

'School all right?'

Samuel's face brightened a little as he waved the sheet of A4 paper that he was carrying in his left hand. 'I am Star of the Week.'

'Good for you,' Carlyle said. 'Your mum will be really pleased.'

Wiping a bead of sweat from his brow, Miller glared at the boy.

The inspector pointed to the lift, which was now back at the third floor. 'It's really slow today. Why don't you take the stairs?'

The boy didn't look thrilled about that idea, but Carlyle knew that he only lived on the first floor. The exercise would do him good.

'Go on.'

Samuel made his way to the first step and began climbing up with the help of the handrail. Slowly his footsteps grew quieter and then there was the sound of a door slamming shut.

With some satisfaction, Carlyle realized that he couldn't even recall what Miller had been saying. 'This is neither the time nor the place,' he declared. 'I don't know what you think you're going to achieve by—'

Leaning forward, Miller gave an instant response, by way of a sharp punch to Carlyle's gut. As the inspector staggered backwards, he followed it up with another, and then a swift kick between the legs. Sinking to the concrete, Carlyle took another two quick blows to the side of his head.

I guess that means I've won the argument, he thought, trying not to puke all over himself.

The concrete floor was cool, with that reassuring smell of disinfectant. Carlyle didn't try to get up. Concentrating on breathing, he wiped a tear from his eye and waited for the pain to subside.

Stepping forward, Trevor Miller wiggled the toe of his boot right in front of Carlyle's face. 'Remember last time.'

The inspector said nothing. Last time, Miller had drowned a young man in a swimming pool. Carlyle had watched it happen. But, still, he hadn't been able to put the bastard away for it.

'You know the drill,' Miller hissed. 'For once in your life, don't be a stupid cunt. Remember, I'm on to you. Push things too far, look into anything that is beyond your immediate brief, and I will make sure you are fucking dealt with once and for all.' He aimed a final kick at Carlyle's ribs, before stomping away.

The inspector listened to the leather soles of Miller's boots on the concrete, the click as the main door was opened and then the clunk as it shut again. A few moments later, the returning lift finally reached the ground floor. As the doors opened, two women he didn't recognize stepped out, chatting away about something on last night's television. Each was pushing a stroller containing a small child. If they were surprised to see him lying there, they didn't let it show. Without interrupting their conversation or otherwise acknowledging his presence, they expertly manoeuvred the buggies past the prone policeman and headed out of the door.

Slowly, the buzzing in his head started to subside. I should get up, Carlyle thought. A quick check suggested that nothing was broken. He would end up with a few bruises, nothing more. Struggling to his feet, he stepped towards the lift just as the doors started to close.

'Shit!' He tried to catch it but was too late. Reluctantly he limped towards the stairs, hoping that, like Samuel, the exercise would do him good.

The welcoming sound of The Clash coming from Alice's bedroom made Carlyle smile. His daughter had expropriated large chunks of his music collection, and he took considerable pleasure from the fact that she took an interest in the music he himself liked; not least because Joe Strummer, Mick Jones et al had, for the most part, stood the test of time very well indeed.

Sitting on the living-room sofa, nursing a small glass of Jameson's whiskey, he mumbled along to 'London Calling' while he pondered the implications of his visit from Trevor Miller. Miller had never been the most sophisticated individual but, even by his standards, such a clumsy intervention in a murder investigation was surprisingly crass. By coming to Carlyle's home, he had definitely crossed a line.

From the bedroom, 'London Calling' gave way to 'Safe European Home'.

'All the classics,' he grinned. The whiskey was easing the pain of his beating nicely; so, finishing his drink, he reached for the bottle sitting on the coffee table. Refilling his glass, he sat back and closed his eyes, trying to organize all the information strewn around inside his brain.

He quickly realized that was impossible. Everything was a jumbled mess, overlapping and confused. Yawning, the thought suddenly occurred to him that Trevor Miller and Rosanna Snowdon were connected, kind of. When Miller had murdered one of Edgar Carlton's advisers, drowning him in a swimming pool on election night, Carlyle had taken the story to Rosanna Snowdon. She had listened to him explain how the crime would never reach court, and then gently told him that no journalist would touch a story like that. Reluctantly accepting her advice, the inspector was thereafter in her debt – just as he now owed her father.

Ah, yes, Sir Michael – another member of the Snowdon clan who deserved better from J. Carlyle Esq. The inspector resolved that he would definitely speak to his colleagues in Fulham about the latest on the Rosanna Snowdon case.

Definitely.

In the morning.

The front door clicked open, then was slammed shut.

'Turn that down!' Helen shouted.

Carlyle opened his eyes as the introductory crescendo of 'I Fought the Law' quickly fell away to a low-level growl. His wife appeared in the doorway, her gaze falling first on the open whiskey bottle on the table, and then on the bruises that were beginning to appear on his face. 'What the hell happened to you?' she asked, her concern sounding rather more like an accusation than Carlyle would have liked.

'Shit day,' he said wearily. 'Let me make you a cup of tea, then I'll tell you all about it.'

'There you go.' Carlyle handed Helen a cup of decaf green tea, recovering his glass of whiskey before taking a seat next to her on the sofa.

'Thanks.' Helen balanced the cup on her knee. 'So, have you been in some kind of fight?'

'Not exactly.' Carlyle explained what had happened.

'He came here?' was Helen's first reaction, once he'd finished.

Carlyle nodded.

161

She placed the teacup on the table and folded her arms. 'Bloody hell, John.'

I'm the one who got a beating, he thought grumpily. 'It won't happen again,' he said, emptying his whiskey glass for the second time. 'It was a stupid move on his part.' Pouring himself another drink, he let her think things through.

'Well,' she said finally, 'Miller's clearly spooked. It's now well known that there is an uncomfortably close relationship between the police, the government and the Zenger journalists – almost certainly inappropriate and possibly corrupt. But for the PM's security guy to go blundering about like this means there must be something more to it than that – some kind of smoking gun he's trying to hide.'

'Uh-huh,' Carlyle grunted. He didn't believe in smoking guns, reckoning that life was never that simple.

'What about Duncan Brown?'

'What about him?'

'Is there a connection linking him to Miller?'

'Not as far as I know. Not directly, at any rate.'

'Maybe the killer is the common link.'

'Maybe.'

'Maybe Miller is the killer?'

Carlyle thought back to the CCTV pictures. 'Nah.'

'But he could be connected to it somehow?'

'Sure.'

'It's simple, then,' Helen announced, reaching over and picking up her cup of tea. 'All you have to do is find the killer.'

'Brilliant!' said Carlyle sarcastically. 'Why didn't *I* think of that?'

The door to the hotel room clicked open. With a deep sigh, Zoe Mosman dropped the key card into her Marc Jacobs leather satchel, pushed it open and stepped inside.

'Come in. Help yourself to a drink.'

Zoe dropped the bag on to the floor and tried to wish away the monster headache that was building at the base of her skull.

Scanning the hotel room, she forced herself to confront the scene before her; a flashback to a former life.

The man lying on the bed, his erection clearly visible through his underwear, kept his gaze on the football match playing on the muted TV.

For the briefest moment, the sense of déjà vu was overwhelming. It was like she was nineteen years old again.

Almost.

'Get me another vodka, will you?'

Zoe reached into the minibar, pulling out a handful of 5cl bottles. Tossing a Grey Goose towards the bed, she slipped into the bathroom and dumped two miniatures of Hendrick's gin into a glass standing by the washbasin. Throwing back her head, she downed them both in one. Her headache was getting worse. Turning on the tap, she splashed some cold water on her face and gazed into the mirror. *A little girl lost.*

'What are you doing in there?'

'I'm just coming.' Burying her head in a towel, she fought back a sob. A small box of paracetamol sat by the basin; popping three, she washed them down with some water. 'Pull yourself together, girl,' she hissed. 'Pull yourself together.'

'Zoe?'

Feeling sick to her stomach, she stepped back into the bedroom. He was naked now, sitting on the end of the bed, cradling himself with one hand while holding a scalpel in the other.

'Come.'

Obediently she stepped in front of him, her eyes flicking from his erection to the blade. Her obvious discomfort seemed to excite him even more; she could see the pre-cum glistening on the tip of his penis, and she worried that he was about to ejaculate all over her Iro Svevalia leather skirt.

'Do you remember the first time?'

Zoe nodded. It was the greatest misfortune of her life; probably the last thing she would remember on her deathbed.

163

He waved the scalpel airily. 'That was what? Twenty-three years ago?'

'Something like that.' Her throat was dry and it came out like a whisper. The blade definitely had her full attention now.

'You were the best thousand dollars that I ever spent. *Ever*. You know that, don't you?'

She opened her mouth but no words came out.

'Real value for money.' The accent that she used to find so sexy now made her skin crawl.

'You've told me before,' she mumbled, determined not to start crying.

'And you are still as beautiful as ever.' He patted his soft belly. 'Me? My cock might still be hard but I'm going to seed. For a man, that's inevitable. But women, they fight it. And you . . .'

Blinking back a tear, she dropped to her knees.

'No, no.' He gestured for her to get back up. 'Not yet.'

Slowly, Zoe did as she was told.

'We've come a long way together.'

'Yes.'

'And I am sorry that it has to end like this.'

As she nodded, great heaving sobs welled up inside her chest.

'There, there,' he said, making no effort to dry her tears. 'At least we can part as friends.'

Stroking himself gently, he waited for the crying to stop. 'Poor Horatio. Did you know he was addicted to pornography? Or maybe he was just an average teenage boy these days. You know, there have been times when I have wondered: maybe he was mine?'

'Fuck you,' Zoe hissed, lunging for the scalpel. But she was too slow. Pulling the blade away from her grasp, he caught her on the jaw with a sharp jab from his free hand, sending her sprawling backwards. Before she could get to her feet, he was dragging her by the hair towards the bed.

'Come here.' Breathing heavily, he pushed her on to the duvet, waving the blade in front of her face. If anything, her attempt to fight back had excited him even more. 'There is no need for that. You have to be pragmatic.'

Pragmatic? That was the story of her life.

The sobs came again but no more tears. She was all cried out.

'I am sorry about Horatio, truly I am. But you have to realize how serious this is. We have got ourselves into this situation – yes, "we", because I include myself in that – and now *we* have to sort it out. If we are successful, no one else needs to get hurt.' He smirked. 'At least, no one else in your family.'

'And if not?'

He looked at her with a mixture of lust and contempt. 'I wouldn't think like that, if I were you.'

'I only ever did this for Ivor and the kids,' she whimpered. Squirming on the bed, she suddenly felt a desperate need to pee.

'Zoe, Zoe, Zoe . . . don't lie to yourself. You did it because of who you are. You needed the excitement, the drama, the money and the drugs. Remember how it made you wet. Don't lie to yourself about it now, because it isn't worth it. You've got to be true to yourself.' Leaning forward, he brought the scalpel down towards her abdomen, slitting the skirt so that it fell from her like the dead skin of a snake. With the tip of the blade tickling the inside of her thigh, he traced the outline of her Coco Blues briefs. 'And you know what you are, don't you?'

'Yes.' Zoe could barely hear her own voice over the furious beating of her heart.

'It was clear that motherhood was always going to be the wrong choice for you.' The big man let out a theatrical sigh. 'And why you married that English loser will always be a complete mystery to me. God! You must have been bored out of your skull for years now!'

Saying nothing, she tried to struggle off the bed.

'Not now,' he warned her, grabbing her arm with his free hand.

'But—'

'But nothing!' As he pulled her roughly towards him, she felt her bladder give way. The arc of golden urine spilling across the linen sheets only seemed to excite him more. 'Do I scare you that much?' His eyes sparkled with delight. 'Surely not.' He gestured to the side of the bed that was still dry. 'Lie back.'

Engulfed in shame, Zoe did as she was told. Pushing her legs apart, he sliced open the sodden briefs. Carefully peeling the scraps of silk from her skin, he lifted them to his face and inhaled deeply. 'Ahhh!' Tossing the destroyed underwear and the scalpel on to the bed, he barely managed to force himself inside her before delivering a shuddering climax.

TWENTY-SEVEN

Sliding off the wet bed, Zoe Mosman skulked into the bathroom. After cleaning herself up, she returned to inspect the tattered remains of her clothing. Her skirt was now unwearable, not to mention her panties. How the hell was she going to get home?

A loud fart came from the direction of the bed. 'There are some jeans you can use.'

Zoe reached for the wardrobe door.

'Not yet. When we've finished.'

'But—'

'Take off your shirt. And the bra.'

Descending into a fresh circle of hell, Zoe once again did as she was instructed.

He let out a low whistle. 'God, you really are in great shape. You must starve yourself.'

Momentarily lost in thought, she ran a finger round her belly button.

'It's amazing how you can still excite me after all these years.'

In spite of everything, a small grin crept across Zoe's face. Hands on hips, she stood at the end of the bed watching him try, and fail, to restore his erection. Finally, tiring of this losing battle, he propped himself up with a pillow. It was time to get down to business.

'So,' he began, trying to sound casual, 'how are we going to solve this little problem of ours? Do you think you can handle the police?'

'Maybe the police wouldn't have gotten involved if you hadn't—'

'Don't be silly. It was only a matter of time. Better to deal with it and move on.'

'You don't know that.'

'I know that if you hadn't been so determined to bury your head in the sand, I wouldn't have had to take such . . . drastic action.' He held her eye. 'Now: can you deal with the police?'

Thinking about it, she scratched an itch between her legs. 'They know nothing. I would be more worried about the CAG investigation. Harris Highman should be able to complete his audit in a matter of weeks. Then they will know what's missing. It will come back to me eventually – probably sooner rather than later.'

'But this guy Highman is just some tiresome old civil servant. We can handle him, don't you think?'

Feeling tears rising up again, she said nothing.

'Zoe?'

Wiping her nose on the back of her wrist, she nodded.

'Yes?'

'Yes.'

'Good,' he smiled. 'That's settled. Now come back over here.'

Slowly, slowly, slowly, Carlyle slid back into the here and now. The disconcerting noise that he could no longer ignore meant that either the mice were back or his mobile was dancing on the table next to the bed. Sticking a hand out from under the duvet, he answered it.

'Hello?' said a man's voice. In the background he could hear traffic noises. 'Were you asleep?'

'No, no.' Carlyle yawned. The clock by the bed said 10.02, so he must have slept in. How did that happen?

'Why didn't you give me a call?'

'Well . . .' He still wasn't quite sure who he was speaking to.

'Have you got anything for me yet? I can't sit on this Hannah Gillespie thing forever, you know.'

One small mystery solved. Needing a piss, he rolled out of bed and padded towards the bathroom. 'I know, Bernie, I know.'

'Where are you now?' Bernie Gilmore demanded.

'Drury Lane.' It was close enough.

There was a pause while the journalist scanned his mental A–Z. 'Okay, do you know a place called Il Buffone?'

'Yeah, yeah,' Carlyle mumbled as he entered the bathroom, navigating his way around the piles of clothing that Helen had left on the floor.

'Good. I'll see you there in ten minutes.'

He was somewhat perturbed by the idea that one of his favourite haunts was known to a hack like Bernie, but that couldn't be helped. 'Fine. See you there.' Ending the call, he pushed up the toilet seat with his big toe and took aim at the porcelain.

In the event, Gilmore took almost half an hour to reach the café. By the time he arrived, the inspector was on his second macchiato and already buzzing nicely. Apart from the two of them and the café's owner, Marcello, the place was empty.

'What happened to you?' Bernie asked, as he slipped into the back booth. Today, he was wearing a T-shirt featuring Bert and Ernie from *Sesame Street*, under a black leather biker's jacket. His beard looked even more out of control than Carlyle remembered it. The overall effect was of someone who had spent the previous night in a hedge.

For his part, having been somewhat refreshed by his extended sleep, the inspector had almost managed to forget about his run-in with Trevor Miller the day before. His face still looked a mess, but Marcello, busy preparing for the lunchtime rush, had been too polite to mention it.

Carlyle gave a half-hearted grin. 'You should see the other guy.'

'Mm.' Gilmore gave him a look suggesting that he didn't think the inspector could give anyone a run for their money in the fisticuffs department, before turning his full attention to the menu. 'It's been a long day already,' he mused. 'I think I'll go for the all-day breakfast.'

'A heart attack on a plate,' Carlyle observed, *sotto voce* so as not to offend Marcello.

'All the best things in life come at a price.'

Wiping his hands on the tea-towel draped over his left shoulder, Marcello appeared from behind the counter to take Bernie's order. 'Another coffee?' he asked the inspector.

Carlyle shook his head. Any more caffeine and his head might explode. 'I'm fine, thanks, Marcello.'

'Okay.' Marcello disappeared into the back and almost immediately the sound of bacon sizzling in a pan could be heard.

Gilmore returned the menu to its holder. 'So I'm guessing that you had a visit from Trevor Miller.'

How the hell did you know that? Carlyle wondered. Trying to hide his surprise behind his demitasse, he drained the last of the coffee from the cup.

Marcello reappeared from the kitchen with some slices of buttered white bread and a mug of milky tea.

'Maybe I will have another, Marcello,' Carlyle decided.

'Sure.' The café-owner scooped up the cup and saucer and disappeared again. At that moment, the door opened and a young woman came in. She took a long look at Carlyle before turning on her heel and walking out. Maybe I look worse than I thought, Carlyle guessed. He felt a small pang of guilt. It was hard enough for Marcello to make ends meet as it was, without the policeman scaring away potential customers.

Gilmore folded up one slice of bread and pushed it into his mouth, chewing it twice before swallowing. 'What do you know about Wickford Associates?' he asked, before washing the food down with a mouthful of tea.

'Never heard of them,' Carlyle said.

Marcello reappeared with Bernie's breakfast and Carlyle's coffee, placing each carefully on the table before retreating to a discreet distance behind the counter.

'Wickford Associates', Gilmore informed him, 'was set up by Trevor Miller after he left the police force. It employs ex-police officers and also some Army types. They provide a range of services to private-sector clients. It's quite a lucrative business.'

Sitting up straighter on the banquette, Carlyle blew on his coffee before taking a sip. The smell of the sausage and bacon was making him feel a bit sick. 'So how did he end up working for Edgar Carlton?'

'For such a dullard, old Trevor really has been quite successful.' Gilmore unwrapped a serviette and pulled out a knife and fork. 'And lucky, of course.'

'Of course.'

'Trevor was great mates with a man called Will Clay.' Gilmore held the cutlery over his plate while looking for some flicker of recognition on the inspector's face. Seeing none, he went on, 'Clay was one of Edgar's cronies, as Party Chairman and a major fundraiser. He was found dead in a toilet at the Glastonbury Festival a couple of years ago.'

'Unusual.'

'According to the coroner, he died of natural causes – heart disease, apparently. There was no sign of foul play, which is a shame.'

Carlyle frowned, not comprehending.

'That would have made it a much bigger story,' the journalist explained.

'Ah.'

'The poor bugger was only in his mid-fifties.' Gilmore shook his head as he cut into a pork sausage. 'Anyway, Clay had hired Miller's company to work for the Party on various things – conferences, fundraisers and so on. Remember the row about private dinners being held in Downing Street?'

'Vaguely.'

'Make a donation of two hundred and fifty grand to the Party and the PM's wife will cook your tea.' Popping the sausage into his mouth, he chewed happily.

'Money well spent.'

'No doubt. Anyway, Clay organized some of these, and he got Miller to handle the security. That's how good old Trevor got to know Edgar Carlton so well.'

'I don't really know much about this,' Carlyle admitted as he watched Gilmore work relentlessly through the food on his plate. 'I know Trevor isn't the sharpest tool in the box, but why is he trying to interfere so crudely in a murder investigation?'

Gilmore waved his fork airily in front of his face. 'Because,' he said, having finally managed to swallow, 'he's playing both sides of this particular game.'

'What particular game do you mean?' Carlyle asked, feeling even more stupid than usual.

Gilmore speared a couple of chips with his fork. 'Once he went to work for Carlton, Trevor had to stand back from Wickford. He was no longer running the company, but he was still the owner or, to be more precise, the largest shareholder. And his broadening list of political contacts proved very handy when it came to landing the Zenger Media contract.'

'And you know all this stuff how, exactly?' Carlyle was playing for time while he tried to work out where the story was leading.

'It's my job to know things,' Gilmore smiled.

'But you haven't written about any of this?'

'Lawyers, my friend, lawyers,' Bernie sighed before the last of the bacon disappeared into his mouth.

'Said you couldn't publish?'

Bernie nodded. 'Always worried about getting their arses sued off, even though what I write always stands up in a court of law.'

The inspector raised an eyebrow.

'Well,' Bernie chuckled, 'almost always. Anyway, even if we were to come a cropper in front of the beak, there's always the libel insurance to fall back on. The bloody lawyers just don't want to make a claim, even though that's what it's there for.'

'Worried about their premiums.'

'Precisely! The useless buggers are just put on this earth to drive the rest of us mad.'

'Okay.' Carlyle was finally beginning to understand what their conversation was all about. The journalist needed him to try and flush out Miller, so that he could publish his story. That was fine by the inspector. All he wanted was to nail the evil bastard any way he could. Whether that was in a court of law, or in the court of public opinion, didn't really matter.

Dropping the cutlery onto his plate, Gilmore fished another paper napkin from the dispenser on the table and began clearing the detritus that had collected in his beard. When he was satisfied with the job achieved, he crumpled up the napkin in one meaty fist and dropped it on the table. 'For years now, Wickford has been working with journalists like Duncan Brown, tapping people's phones in order to get stories.'

Carlyle thought about Margaretha Zelle. 'You have proof?'

Gilmore nodded.

'So why don't you go and talk to the good people at Operation Redhead? This is specifically their thing.'

Sitting back on the bench, Gilmore pawed at his T-shirt, scratching Bert on the nose – or maybe it was Ernie. 'Because, Inspector, I'm not simply a concerned citizen, I'm a man who needs to make a living.'

Fair enough, Carlyle decided.

Shifting in his seat, Gilmore settled into lecture mode. 'These days,' he said, 'there's no real money to be made from conventional journalism. No money at all, in fact.'

Aware that he needed to get up to speed, Carlyle sat and listened, happy to let the other man talk.

'Most information isn't worth shit. There's far too much of it about – in fact, we spend all our time trying to fight it off. No one wants more of it. There's more information in one single edition of a daily newspaper – a broadsheet anyway – than an ordinary person would have been exposed to in their whole lives, two hundred years ago.'

All of it crap, too, Carlyle reflected.

'And that's just newspapers. Then there's television, radio and the universe's great intellectual garbage dump known as the internet.' He looked the inspector up and down to make sure he was keeping up. 'Know what I mean?'

'Yes,' Carlyle lied.

'So,' he continued, 'your basic law of supply and demand tells you that information is now effectively worth nothing. That's bad news for someone like me who sells information for a living.'

'You could always become a plumber,' Carlyle smirked. 'Or even a copper.'

Gilmore ignored this feeble attempt at humour. 'Of course, some types of information will always be worth something . . . in particular circumstances. But even the stuff that is worth something is only worth something if you *know* that it's worth something.'

'Mm.'

'And even *then*, that same information may have a value that changes over time.'

'Right.'

'So,' said Gilmore, finally getting to the point, 'what I knew about Trevor Miller wasn't really that useful – until I ran into you.'

TWENTY-EIGHT

Sir Chester Forsyth-Walker winced in pain. The operation on his bad back had been declared a success but it didn't feel much like that to him. The painkillers provided by the hospital were simply not up to the job. Even after downing four of them in quick succession, it still felt as if someone was stabbing him repeatedly in the lower spine with a hot needle.

Noting his boss's obvious discomfort, Simon Shelbourne adopted a solicitous demeanour. 'Are you okay?' he asked. 'Maybe you shouldn't have discharged yourself for another day or two.'

'Nonsense.' Looking round the room he had been given, Sir Chester dismissed his spin doctor's concerns with as imperious a wave of the hand as he could manage. The Laura Ashley décor did nothing to improve his mood. 'It's like a bloody twelve year old's bedroom in here.'

Shelbourne nodded sympathetically. 'It's the best room they had available,' he said. 'I double-checked. Anyway, the wallpaper is the same in all of them.'

'And how much do people pay to come here?'

'About twelve hundred a night.'

'Good God!' At least he wasn't having his bank account raped as well as having his senses assaulted. Another spasm of pain shot through the Commissioner's back and his face crumpled in distress.

Shelbourne gestured towards an armchair in the corner of the room. 'Why don't you take a seat?'

175

No fear, thought Sir Chester. If I sit down, the pain will only get worse. 'It's nothing,' he insisted. 'At least, nothing that a large scotch won't sort out.'

Lowering his gaze, Shelbourne shook his head sadly. 'I'm afraid that's not possible.'

'What?'

'The doctors were very clear. No alcohol allowed until you come off your medication.'

'Bugger that!' Sir Chester eyed the sideboard sitting by the wall. 'Where is the booze in this place anyway?'

'That's the other thing,' Shelbourne said. 'This is a one hundred per cent dry facility. There is no alcohol at Laanti's.' He tried not to smirk. 'Zero tolerance of booze is a cornerstone of their "guaranteed detox" policy.'

With increasing impatience, Sir Chester listened to his minion run through a series of rules and regulations that the younger man had seemingly learned off by heart.

Having reached the end of his recital, Shelbourne gave a shrug. 'This code of conduct extends to the customers as well as to the staff.'

'It sounds more like a bloody prison than a health farm,' Sir Chester said grimly.

'Anastasia Carlton can't speak highly enough about it,' Shelbourne remarked.

'Yes, well,' Sir Chester mumbled, 'the Prime Minister's wife has plenty of time on her hands for swanning around spas these days, from what I hear.'

'Sonia is a big fan too.'

'Sonia Claesens?' The faintest of alarm bells began ringing in the back of the Commissioner's fatigued brain.

'Yes,' said Shelbourne, 'she comes here all the time. At least, she used to when I was working on the *Sunday Witness*. Her ex-husband built the kriotherapy centre here. It's considered state of the art.'

Sir Chester frowned. 'I thought the former Mr Sonia Claesens was a farmer or something?'

'He's in agribusiness,' Shelbourne nodded, as if that was one and the same thing. 'This is just a sideline. I think it was Sonia who got him interested in it in the first place. She might have ditched him for a toyboy, but she is still a big kriotherapy fan.'

The bells started ringing louder but Sir Chester dismissed them angrily as he fought to process the random bits of information his PR man was now throwing at him. Dammit, all he wanted was a bloody drink! Was that really too much to ask?

'Kriotherapy,' Shelbourne droned on, 'comes from the Greek word *cryo* meaning "cold" and *therapy* meaning "cure". It involves using extreme cold to reduce pain and inflammation.'

This idiot has swallowed the marketing brochure whole, the Commissioner reflected.

'I've even booked you in for a session, since it should be good for your back.'

'I'll try anything,' Sir Chester decided. A thought suddenly hit him: 'Is it expensive?'

'Don't worry,' Shelbourne smiled, 'everything is being taken care of. Hannes was absolutely clear that this isn't going to cost you a penny.' He was referring to Hannes Laanti, the owner of the eponymous spa. 'You will get an itemized bill at the end of your stay, but that is simply so that you can place it on the Official Register of Interests when you get back to work.'

Sir Chester harrumphed. This kind of so-called 'transparency' was all the rage these days. He could barely go to the bloody toilet without having to report it to someone or other. The whole thing went against all his old-school principles. Why he couldn't let a friend do him a favour without having to tell the whole world about it was beyond him. He felt his mood darkening by the minute. He really did need that damn drink. 'I've got to ring Tanya,' he said gruffly, 'and tell her to bring me a bottle of Royal Lochnagar.' He patted his pockets, searching in vain for his mobile.

'The use of mobile phones is not allowed here either,' Shelbourne chirruped. He had a cheeky glint in his eye which irritated the Commissioner even further.

'Simon,' he said wearily, 'just give me your bloody phone, so that I can call my good lady wife.'

'The reception's crap as well,' Shelbourne pointed out. Nevertheless he fished an iPhone out of the back pocket of his jeans and handed it over, before politely retreating to the far corner of the room to allow his boss some privacy. After struggling with the number, Sir Chester listened to the phone ring for what seemed like an eternity before Tanya's cheery voicemail kicked in. Stifling a curse, he mumbled a brief message, hung up and forcefully bowled the handset back to his lackey.

'Is she on her way?' Shelbourne asked brightly, plucking the phone out of the air just before it smashed against the wall.

'She's taking her own sweet time about it,' Sir Chester grumped. He imagined that she was probably tied up with her Pilates class, or the Bikram yoga, or whatever the latest fad was for this week. He sighed deeply. No sense of priorities, that woman; no sense of priorities at all.

Stepping over to the window, Shelbourne looked out across the carefully manicured front lawn which extended in front of the original manor house around which the spa had been developed. A small group of fat, middle-aged women were waddling across the grass under the watchful gaze of a couple of young instructors dressed in army fatigues. Obviously, the luxury boot-camp brigade were heading off on their country hike.

'Look at that lot,' he giggled. 'Let's just hope none of them suffers a heart attack.'

'What?'

'Nothing.'

Still focused on the matter of refreshment, Sir Chester eyed his aide thoughtfully. 'Maybe,' he said, 'you could go and find me an off-licence?'

'What?' Shelbourne turned away from the window and frowned at his boss. 'Er . . . well, not really,' he stammered. 'For a start, we're in the middle of nowhere. And anyway, I need to get going.'

Resisting the urge to throttle the useless little shit, Sir Chester's eyes narrowed. 'So, remind me, why exactly *are* you here?'

Shelbourne stole another glance out of the window. A couple of the fattest women in the group were struggling to reach the far side of the lawn without collapsing; it looked like the bootcamp had been a bit too ambitious. Maybe the cost of their stay would have been better spent on liposuction or on having a gastric band fitted. 'I just wanted to make sure that you were settled in okay,' he lied.

The reality was that he had been called into a strategy session by Hannes Laanti himself, for whom he moonlighted as a freelance adviser. After three hours' talking crap in a tiny room, Shelbourne was more than ready for a stiff drink himself. Turning back to face his boss, he smiled. 'And also to talk to you about my meeting with Sonia Claesens and Trevor Miller.'

Mention of Miller's name made Sir Chester wince yet again. By some margin, Miller had turned out to be the most annoying individual the Commissioner had come across since arriving in London. As head of the MPS, Sir Chester had assumed, somewhat naively as it turned out, that his job had included responsibility for the security of the Prime Minister. Instead, he was horrified to discover that the job had been entrusted to a grubby private contractor. A man who had barely risen above the rank of constable when he was serving in the Force now had the ear of the most powerful man in the country. The whole situation was a total disgrace.

'What did that oaf have to say for himself?'

'He was particularly brusque.' Shelbourne shook his head at the memory. 'Even Sonia was given short shrift.' He allowed himself the briefest of peeks out of the window. Two of the hikers were now lying on their backs on the lawn, surrounded by staff dressed in white coats. It looked like they were receiving extra oxygen. 'I thought she was looking terrible, by the way; a bit like Cruella De Vil on crack.' He sniggered at his own joke.

Not picking up the reference, Sir Chester gingerly lowered

himself on to the bed. As his buttocks made contact with the duvet, a now familiar pain shot up his spine and he immediately jumped back to his feet. 'What precisely is Miller suggesting in terms of a course of action?'

'He basically told her that she's on her own,' Shelbourne replied, trying to ignore Sir Chester's signs of discomfort.

'And us?'

'The clear implication of what he said is that the PM considers that we' – meaning *you* – 'are also expendable.'

'We're all expendable.' His gaze focusing on the patterned carpet, Sir Chester began pacing from the bed to the armchair and back again. 'The question is whether there is anything we can do to try and retrieve the situation?'

Damned if I know, Shelbourne thought. Outside, an ambulance had appeared. One of the hikers was being lifted on to a stretcher.

'Where are we on the other stuff?' Sir Chester asked, realising that this boy was not about to deliver anything useful or insightful on the phone-hacking front.

'Other stuff?'

'I don't know . . .' Sir Chester racked his brain, trying to remember what concerns had been current before he had gone under the surgeon's knife. That had been less than forty-eight hours ago but it felt like weeks, if not months. 'The teenager who was blown up?'

'Horatio Mosman,' Shelbourne reminded him. 'I haven't had any update. Do you want me to ring Commander Simpson?'

'We need news,' the Commissioner mumbled, ignoring the question. 'Good news. Something to show that we are moving things forward.' He eyed the other man hopefully but even his spin doctor, who could always be relied upon for a vacuous phrase or a meaningless soundbite, seemed lost for words.

Salvation came in the form of a knock at the door. Before either of them had time to respond, it opened and a pretty blonde girl appeared in the room.

'Sir Chester?'

The Commissioner suddenly felt his spirits rise.

'I'm Sally,' the girl said cheerily. 'It's time for your kriotherapy.'

Having let the polite ripple of applause die away, Carole Simpson stepped quickly off the stage in the gymnasium of the Bernard Rhodes South Camden Secondary School. There was a time when the Commander would have given awards ceremonies like this the widest of berths, but nowadays she was more relaxed about such events. All she had to do was hand out a few prizes, then have a quick cup of tea with the headmistress in the staffroom; undemanding if somewhat boring, it was the Met's idea of winning hearts and minds.

'Boss.' Carlyle emerged from behind a curtain just as she reached the bottom step.

Simpson took a half-step backwards, almost falling over. 'Jesus! Why do you have to creep up on people like that?'

'Sorry.' The inspector glared at a timid-looking woman in a cheap business suit hovering a few yards away. 'We won't be a moment,' he told her. The headmistress gave a nod and retreated to a respectful distance. The kids had already fled, along with the rest of the teachers, leaving the cavernous hall empty apart from the three of them.

'Nice speech,' said Carlyle feebly.

'What do you want?' If the Commander noticed the bruises on his face, she chose not to comment on them. Instead, she glanced theatrically at her watch. 'I need to get going.'

'Your office said I would find you here. I need to update you on various things.'

'Okay.' Simpson shot the headmistress a look that was more of annoyance than apology. 'Make it quick.'

Carlyle quickly took her through the highlights, careful to focus mainly on the Mosman case.

'So,' she said, cutting him off before he had finished, 'when are you going to bring the mother in?'

It was the obvious question. At the very least, Zoe Mosman had some explaining to do. 'I'm not in any hurry,' he said.

Simpson tugged at a button on her uniform. 'You might not be but the bloody Commissioner is.'

'How's his back, by the way?'

'He's recuperating.'

'At Laanti's, I hear.'

Simpson looked off into the middle distance, signalling that she didn't want to discuss the matter.

'Mrs Mosman,' said Carlyle, returning to the matter in hand, 'is already lawyered up. Plus, I suppose, she thinks she can bluff us about the missing picture.'

Simpson gave him a blank look.

'Joseph van Aken's *View of Covent Garden*.' Carlyle went on to explain the significance of the painting to his investigation. 'First, I want to see what more we can find out from Harris Highman's GAC audit before jumping in and trying to force a confession from her.'

'A confession to what?'

'Exactly.' Carlyle smiled, as if she had just made his argument for him. 'I dunno yet.'

He thought he heard Simpson mumble something that sounded like 'smug bastard' under her breath but he let it slide.

'Okay,' she said finally, 'do it your way. But don't leave it too long. Sir Chester is still enjoying his spa treatments, but it won't be long before he's back at his desk in New Scotland Yard and wanting to see some progress.'

'Understood,' Carlyle said. The headmistress reappeared in the corner of his vision and hovered. 'Just a couple of other things,' he said quickly, as the Commander turned towards her.

'Yes?' Simpson did not seem at all happy at the prospect of extending their conversation.

'It won't take long at all,' said the inspector emolliently. Guiding his boss by the elbow, he moved them away from their host, saying, 'Excuse us just one moment longer.'

The woman struggled to come up with a smile. This was her school and she wasn't used to being kept waiting.

'Quickly,' Simpson hissed.

'Right.' Lowering his voice, Carlyle skipped through his conversation with Gilmore about Trevor Miller and Wickford Associates.

Folding her arms, Simpson assumed what Carlyle felt was a rather schoolmistressish air of her own. 'All this is in the public domain,' she said dismissively. 'It has been known about for a long time. As far as I know, Mr Miller gave up the day-to-day running of his business when he first went to work for Edgar Carlton.'

'But he still owns it.'

'He may still be a shareholder,' Simpson conceded. 'So what?'

'But there's a clear conflict of interest.'

Frustrated by her underling's enduring blockheadedness, Simpson pawed the ground impatiently with her left foot. 'That is a very elastic term, as you well know, John. One man's conflict of interest is simply another man's synergy.'

For a moment he thought that she sounded like the old Carole Simpson: the over-ambitious officer still trying to climb the greasy pole and to cosy up to politicians; becoming a fellow-traveller on the Edgar Carlton bandwagon.

The old Carole Simpson that he had known and hated.

The same one that he thought had evaporated when her career had crashed and burned at the hands of her husband. He looked at her carefully. 'That's a very relaxed point of view.'

Simpson simply shrugged.

'Bernie Gilmour reckons . . .'

Simpson raised an eyebrow.

'According to his sources,' Carlyle continued, 'Wickford Associates does work for both the Zenger Corporation and the Metropolitan Police Service. They worked closely with Duncan Brown on the *Sunday Witness*; and Brown's stories are being investigated by the phone-hacking inquiry.'

'Hand it over to Operation Redhead, then.'

Carlyle made a face. 'It's a murder inquiry.'

Simpson lifted her gaze to the heavens and closed her eyes, thinking things through. 'It's a can of worms,' she decided finally.

'Aren't they all?' Carlyle laughed emptily.

'Not like this one, John.' Simpson opened her eyes and stared at him with a mixture of annoyance and compassion. 'Not like this one.'

'So?'

'So – do what you have to do. Keep digging away like the grubby little dung beetle that you are, but don't forget that your priority remains the Mosman case.'

Grubby little dung beetle? Was she trying to insult him? If so, it was water off a duck's back to Carlyle; over the years he'd been called a lot worse. 'For sure.'

'You need to have another conversation with Mrs Mosman, and sooner rather than later.'

'Yes,' he nodded. 'Now, about Hannah Gillespie.'

Simpson stared at him blankly.

'The missing schoolgirl with the dodgy boyfriend.'

But the Commander was already walking away. 'John,' she said firmly, 'I don't have time for any more right now. Use your discretion. Let's talk again later.'

Fine by me, Carlyle thought. He watched her apologize to the headmistress before they wandered off in search of the refuge of the staffroom and a cup of tea.

Francis Clegg tossed the empty Coke can towards the bin in the corner of the room, missing by a considerable distance, and began fiddling with his ponytail. After a few moments, he abandoned that activity and began picking his nose.

On the other side of the glass viewing window, Joe Szyszkowski made a sound of disgust. 'Nice.'

WPC Maude Hall watched as Clegg wiped a large bogey on

his red T-shirt, which had *narcissist* printed on it backwards in white letters. 'At least we found him.'

'Yeah.' Joe turned to the stocky man standing between them. 'Thanks for the tip.'

'It's our pleasure.' Sergeant Declan Formby of the Aviation Unit gestured towards the glass. 'He was getting on to a flight to Ibiza but we managed to stop him at the gate.'

'Nice one,' Joe smiled. It was a lucky break. Hundreds of thousands of people passed through Heathrow Airport every day. If it hadn't been for an exceptionally alert security officer, Mr Clegg would have been enjoying his first bottle of San Miguel in the sunshine by now.

'Sorry about the room,' said Formby, 'but all the cells are full. A bunch of boozed-up chavs started a riot on a flight from Barcelona.'

'Ah, the joys of modern travel,' said Joe. 'That's why we stay at home for the holidays. Go to Devon.'

'Wise man,' Formby nodded. 'What do you want him for, anyway?'

'We're looking for his girlfriend,' Hall explained.

Formby looked puzzled. 'Who would go out with a muppet like that?'

'She's fourteen,' said Hall grimly.

'Ah.' The colour leached from Formby's face as he thought about his own daughters of a similar age. 'I'll leave you to it then,' he mumbled, as he headed for the door.

'Can I have another Coke?' Squinting under the strip lighting, Clegg looked up as they entered the room. His right index finger was still firmly ensconced in his right nostril, and he continued rooting around robustly while the officers each took a seat on the opposite side of the table.

'For God's sake!' Joe gestured towards the finger. With some reluctance, Clegg removed it, shoving the offending hand into the pocket of his jeans instead.

185

'I'm still thirsty.' Thin and pasty-faced, he had twenty-four hours' worth of stubble on his chin and dark rings under his eyes. The overall effect was of a man who had been partying hard for several days.

Joe placed his hands on the table. 'I don't want to waste any of your time, Francis.'

'You already have,' Clegg shot back. 'I've missed my flight.'

'Where is Hannah?'

With a snort, Clegg sat back in his chair and folded his arms. 'Who?'

'Hannah Gillespie,' Hall said flatly. 'Your girlfriend.'

'Never heard of her,' Clegg smirked. He made a show of looking Hall up and down. 'Have *you* got a boyfriend, sweetheart?'

'Let's stick to the point,' said Joe. 'When did you last see Hannah?'

'Like I said,' Clegg replied, not taking his eyes off the WPC, 'I don't know her.'

Hall's eyes narrowed. 'One of Hannah's friends named you. She says she's seen the two of you together several times.'

'I know a lot of people.' The smirk got wider. 'And I wanna drink.'

'The girl is missing,' Hall said slowly, leaning forward in her chair. 'Her parents are extremely concerned.'

'Not my problem.'

'In that case,' Joe sighed, 'we'll have to take you back to the police station.'

'Wrongful arrest, man. Police harassment.'

'We'll sort that out at the station.' Pushing back his chair, Joe got to his feet. As he did so, Hall's right arm shot across the table, grabbing Clegg's T-shirt and dragging the paedophile out of his seat.

'Hey!' Joe stumbled backwards as he watched her drag Clegg across the table and throw him on to the floor, administering three quick kicks to his head and torso as he went down.

'Maude . . .'

Ignoring the sergeant, Hall gave the prostrate man another swift kick. Groaning, Clegg adopted the foetal position. Crouching down, she grabbed him by the ears. 'Look at me, fucker,' she hissed. 'Open your fucking eyes.'

Resisting the urge to laugh, Joe looked hurriedly around the room. No CCTV – thank fuck for that. The corridor outside was empty. Fingers crossed, therefore, no one had seen what had happened. 'Maude!' Jumping forward, he put a hand on her shoulder. Shrugging it off, she jabbed Clegg in the eye with a thumb.

'Aawww!' Clutching his face, Francis Clegg began rolling round on the floor like a footballer looking for a penalty.

Standing up, Hall wiped a loose strand of hair from her face. 'Tell us where she is,' she said quietly, 'or you might not even make it back to Charing Cross.'

'Tell her to stop,' Clegg whimpered.

At a loss over what to do, Joe stepped backwards until he was leaning up against the window, blocking the view of anyone who might come wandering along the corridor outside. 'I would advise you to tell the lady what she wants to know,' he said smoothly. 'Otherwise, you're on your own.'

TWENTY-NINE

At least there was one person in Charing Cross police station who looked like they had taken more of a kicking than he had. After getting Francis Clegg to sign his statement, the inspector retreated back up to the third floor. Joe was sitting at his desk, drinking a mug of coffee, while WPC Hall was perched on the edge of a nearby desk, munching happily on a banana. Since returning from Heathrow, each of them had maintained an exaggerated air of innocence; just as if butter wouldn't melt in their mouths.

Carlyle put the statement on his desk and eyed his sergeant carefully. 'So he sold her?'

Hall quickly swallowed the last of her banana, dropping the skin into the cardboard box on the floor that served as a makeshift bin. 'Not really,' she said. 'He just kind of passed her on to one of his mates.'

'As one does,' Joe said, looking sick.

'Do we believe him?' Carlyle asked.

'I think so.' Joe brightened. 'Once Maude had a little word with him, he rather quickly decided to lose his attitude and tell us what was going on.'

Blushing, Hall looked at the floor.

'The Krav Manga worked a treat,' Joe smirked. 'I'm thinking of taking a few classes myself.'

'Krav Maga,' Hall corrected him, still blushing. 'It's a fighting technique developed by the Israeli Defence Forces,' she explained, seeing that Carlyle was at a loss. 'It's their official martial art – a form of hand-to-hand combat originally developed to defend Jews against Nazi attacks in the 1930s. I go to classes in Westminster twice a week. It's good fun. You should give it a go.'

Not me, Carlyle thought, but it might be good for Alice. His daughter already did a weekly karate class at Jubilee Hall on the south side of the piazza; maybe this Krav Whatever would help her take her self-defence skills to the next level.

'What d'ya reckon?' Joe asked.

'Nah,' Carlyle said. 'I'm too old, too slow.' He waved an admonishing finger towards Hall. 'Just make sure you keep it for outside, in future. You're very lucky that Clegg didn't make a complaint. The stupid bastard didn't even ask for a lawyer.'

'We got a result,' Joe protested.

'Yeah,' Carlyle agreed. 'But at the very least, the pervert could have tied you up in disciplinary hearings for months.' He gave his sergeant a disappointed look. 'You should have known better.'

Staring into his coffee, Joe said nothing.

Turning to the WPC, Carlyle gave Hall a hard stare. 'Don't do it again.'

'Okay,' she said meekly.

'Good.' Carlyle dropped into his chair and placed his hands behind his head. 'Now, the new guy we think Hannah Gillespie has ended up with. What do we know about him?'

Joe put his coffee cup down on the desk next to the sheet of A4 paper containing his notes. 'Alexander Montague Laws. Known as Monty. No record. Some kind of freelance IT guy. He's not at the address that Clegg gave us. So far, he's in the wind.'

'Okay. See if you can extract any more useful information from Clegg' – Carlyle looked up at Hall – 'without smacking him around. Just tell him he's stuck in that cell until we find Mr Laws.'

'And then?' Joe asked.

Having no idea, Carlyle shrugged. 'Let's worry about that later. Meantime I've got to chase something else up. Keep me posted.'

'What happened to you?' Detective Inspector Vanessa Valette asked as she handed Carlyle back his warrant card.

'Walked into a door.'

'Mm.' Valette, a slightly built brunette, rolled her eyes to the ceiling. 'Come into my office and we can talk there.'

Following her inside, Carlyle sat down and glanced around. The DI lived and worked in a glass cube, measuring about eight feet by twelve, in the corner of a large, open-plan industrial space. Rows of computer screens waited patiently for someone to start using them. Yet, apart from a group of five officers crowded round one desk about twenty feet away, the place was empty. In the background, he could make out the general hum of traffic on the Commercial Road, six floors below them.

'A bit out of the way here, aren't you?'

'We wanted a bit of space well away from the Commissioner and his guys, for obvious reasons.'

'Mm.' It must be a really shit job working on Operation Redhead, Carlyle thought. A complete hospital pass. Sooner or later, someone will come along and nobble you. And in the meantime you're stuck out here in the arse end of nowhere: glamorous East London, where the Luftwaffe was as near as things ever got to urban planning.

Barely five feet two, Valette disappeared behind a mound of files resting on her desk and sat down. Carlyle waited patiently while she cleared a channel through which they could re-establish eye-contact. 'Sorry about that.' Under the harsh lighting, she looked tired and frail.

'No problem,' Carlyle smiled.

'So, what brings you here again?'

It took some considerable effort for Carlyle to suppress a

grimace. He had already explained his involvement in the Duncan Brown murder case to four different lackeys, in order to get this meeting with Valette. Now it seemed that he would have to start all over again.

'Duncan Brown.'

'Sorry.' Valette gestured to the paperwork surrounding her. 'He's not one of mine.'

'Huh?'

The DI leaned forward between two piles of documents, each at least a foot high. 'This investigation is so large – and growing all the time – that we have had to divide it up among half a dozen of us.' She scratched her head. 'I think Brown belongs to Inspector Walters but, to be honest, I'm not entirely sure.' She gestured to the largely empty room beyond the window. 'Anyway, I fear he's not around right now.'

Christ, Carlyle thought, if the Commissioner really is worried about the possibility of this investigation causing him any grief, a quick look round here should put his mind at rest. Clearly, Operation Redhead was going nowhere. 'But this is a murder investigation I'm talking about,' he said, finally letting his exasperation show.

'Yes, well.' Valette disappeared behind one pile and switched on her computer, which began slowly wheezing into action. 'Interesting thought. Do you think there's any connection with what we're doing here?'

Carlyle bit his lip in frustration. 'I believe I have to work on that assumption.'

'You do? Why?'

'Too much of a coincidence, don't you think?'

'I've no idea.' Somewhere behind all the paper, she began tapping on a keyboard. I should get going, Carlyle thought. This is a complete waste of time.

A few more taps.

He pushed himself out of his chair. 'Sorry for wasting your time.'

'Hold on.' Valette reappeared with a pair of rimless spectacles now balanced on her nose. They made her look at least ten years older. She held up a finger. 'One minute.'

Reluctantly, Carlyle sat back down. Retrieving a mobile from her jacket pocket, Valette made a call. Almost immediately, someone picked up at the other end.

'Duncan Brown,' said Valette by way of introduction, sounding very businesslike. 'Yeah.' She glanced at Carlyle. 'Right, one minute.' Ending the call, she got up and headed for the door. 'Wait here.' It was an instruction, rather than a request.

Despite himself, Carlyle nodded meekly.

'I'll be back in a couple of minutes,' she added.

Just shy of twenty-five minutes later, Valette reappeared in the doorway. 'You check out,' she announced.

That's good, Carlyle thought, not knowing what she meant.

Holding the door open, she signalled for him to stand up. 'Come on.'

The inspector jumped to his feet. 'Where are we going?'

'To see Meyer.'

Standing at a window, staring down at the slow-moving traffic, Russell Meyer looked round as Carlyle shuffled into the room. The chief inspector was a small man, maybe five foot four, with a light frame and greying bouffant hair. Carlyle was somewhat surprised to see him wearing a single-breasted suit in a Prince of Wales check, rather than a uniform. Then again, hardly anyone seemed to wear a uniform these days. That's what happened when you went from being a Police Force to becoming a Police *Service*.

A look passed between Valette and Meyer. The latter eyed Carlyle suspiciously, then waved towards the three chairs lined up in front of an oversized desk. 'Please.'

Carlyle took the middle seat and Valette took the one on his left.

'Vanessa here tells me that you are on the Brown investigation.' Meyer stepped away from the window and sat down behind the desk. The desk itself was bare – not even a phone to be seen. Unlike Valette's office downstairs, there were no papers at all, no computer even; nothing to suggest that anyone actually worked here. By comparison, it made Simpson's office back in Paddington look positively homely.

'That's right,' Carlyle replied.

Meyer clasped his hands together as if in prayer; as if the Good Lord Himself was going to provide the right words for him to utter.

Ever the atheist, Carlyle waited patiently.

'I want you to lay off.'

Carlyle frowned. This was not what he had been expecting to hear.

Meyer glanced at Valette, who was staring determinedly out of the window. Slowly, he returned his gaze to Carlyle. 'Well, perhaps not lay off exactly, but don't push too hard.'

Holding Meyer's gaze, Carlyle forced himself to say nothing for ten seconds. The Detective Inspector didn't blink.

'This,' Carlyle said finally, 'is a murder inquiry.'

Meyer shifted uncomfortably in his seat. 'I know that, Inspector, but your investigation into Duncan Brown cuts across Operation Redhead, and that, as you will appreciate, must be given priority.'

Knowing better than to protest, Carlyle sat back and folded his arms. 'Explain that to me.'

'Operation Redhead is not just about investigating a bunch of celebrities who've had their phones hacked. It's much wider than that. It affects real people as well.'

'And I am dealing with a murder inquiry,' Carlyle repeated. 'That profoundly affects a number of real people, too.'

'This involves something', said Meyer, 'that goes beyond any single police case. It goes to the very heart of the way we do business in this country. It involves the way in which the press operates, yes, but also the media's relationship with the government and even the Police Service. It involves our standards of behaviour.'

Spare me the speech, Carlyle thought.

Seeing the less than impressed look on the inspector's face, Meyer decided to change tack. 'You know what the really shocking thing is?'

'Shock me.'

Valette suddenly coughed; it sounded like she was trying to stifle a giggle.

'I'm fairly certain that the practice is still going on.'

'Phone hacking?'

Meyer nodded.

Bollocks, Carlyle thought. 'That would be fairly stupid, given what's happened.'

'These things tend to develop a momentum of their own,' Valette interjected. 'It can be hard to get out of the habit. When the furore about phone hacking first kicked off, Zenger Corporation looked at closing down the *Sunday Witness*, which was where most, if not all, of the stories were appearing. After a bit of hand-wringing, they decided against it. Ironically, their sales have gone *up*. Readers assume that they're still busy hacking phones, so they must have the best stories.'

'Makes sense, I suppose.' Carlyle tried to think back to the last time he'd properly read a Sunday newspaper himself. Not in the last couple of years, at least. Life, he had decided, was too short.

'So, we're fairly sure that they're still doing it,' Valette continued. 'They still need to find exclusive stories.'

'And,' Meyer jumped in, 'they're still using Wickford Associates.'

Is that so? Carlyle, however, kept his thoughts to himself.

'Duncan Brown was involved in the tapping of more than a dozen people's phones before he was killed,' Valette added. 'Indeed, that's *why* he was killed.'

Carlyle looked at her, then turned to Meyer. He spoke slowly, keeping his tone even. 'You know who killed Duncan Brown?'

'We have a good idea.' Valette couldn't resist a smirk.

'And?'

'And nothing,' Meyer said sharply. 'Are we doing business here, or not?'

'We're doing business.' Carlyle would work out precisely how to shaft this self-important little prick later. For now, he just needed the information.

'Very well.' Meyer seemed a little uncertain, but he ploughed on. 'Bear in mind though, that we don't currently have anything that would definitely stand up in a court of law. And anyway, it is not technically part of my operation.'

'Technically,' Carlyle repeated.

'Not unless you go the whole hog,' Meyer smiled, 'and decide to join us.'

Carlyle stared at Meyer and then at Valette. The Chief Inspector's smirk had grown, and he was beginning to find DI Valette more than a little annoying. He sat up straighter in his chair. 'Why would I want to join Operation Redhead?'

They looked at him with a mixture of pity and dismay. 'This is an extremely high-profile investigation,' Valette explained. 'It's all over the newspapers.'

'Which is quite ironic, when you think about it,' Meyer quipped.

Carlyle wondered just how often the man had used that line over the last few months.

The Chief Inspector waved his hands in front of his face. 'This thing is getting bigger all the time. More people are coming forward; there are more cases to investigate. Our budget has been increased but the single biggest threat to this investigation is not political interference, but simply the risk of us disappearing under a mountain of material. Every day I worry that it could all simply collapse under its own weight.'

Not my problem, Carlyle thought happily.

'We need more people,' Meyer went on, 'meaning good people. People who can take this investigation forward, wherever it goes, without fear or favour.'

'Outsiders,' Valette added.

Meyer assumed his most sincere expression. 'People like you.'

Holding the Chief Inspector's gaze, Carlyle sat in silence, not liking at all the way they had teamed up on him. Nor did he like the idea that they assumed they could flatter him into shovelling their shit for them. He recalled that the Americans had an appropriate phrase for it: *blowing smoke up your ass.* John Carlyle didn't like in the least the idea of anyone blowing smoke up his ass.

'No,' he said finally.

Meyer looked pained. 'Why not?'

Carlyle shrugged. 'Because I've got plenty of my own stuff to deal with, not least Duncan Brown.' Meyer started to say something, but the inspector held up a hand. 'And also because, ultimately, I'm not really that bothered about phone hacking. Even if it's not just a bunch of witless celebrities who are being affected. '

Meyer drummed his fingers angrily on the table. 'So you're the kind of copper who likes to pick and choose what kind of alleged criminal he investigates?'

'We all pick and choose,' Carlyle said, 'all the time. Some politician chose to set up Operation Redhead. You chose to take it on, for whatever reasons. In the process, you will have turned down something else.'

'I'm not a dilettante,' Meyer protested.

'Neither am I. I'm just a run-of-the-mill police inspector who is trying to deal with a number of cases where the victims have suffered fates much worse than having their phones hacked.' Realizing he was sounding a bit pompous, Carlyle tried to lighten the tone. 'Anyway, everyone knows what the British press is like, so why would anyone expect they *wouldn't* be tapping people's phones?'

'This is a very serious issue,' said Meyer, trying to sell the job one last time. 'The relationship between Zenger and the MPS needs to be cleaned up. The connections with the political elite are also complex and troubling. Our job is to sort it all out.'

You sound like a politician yourself, Carlyle thought. If this whole thing is so very important, why did they put the investigation into the hands of a Chief Inspector no one had ever heard of? You're trying to operate way above your pay grade and it won't work. All these people you are supposed to be investigating can bury you at any time they want.

Folding his arms, Meyer sat back in his chair. 'I have carte blanche with this investigation. I will get to the bottom of things.'

'Good luck with that.' The inspector couldn't resist a chuckle as he pushed himself out of his seat.

Meyer watched him get up. 'Carole Simpson warned me that you were extremely cynical.'

'You've talked to the Commander?' Carlyle sat back down.

'Carole and I go back a long way,' Meyer told him. 'She is very supportive of you – *too* supportive according to some people.'

What people?

'But even she recognizes that there are long-standing concerns about your attitude.'

Fuck my so-called 'attitude', Carlyle thought. If he hadn't come here for a job interview, he certainly hadn't come for a lecture either.

'She was quite amusing about it, in fact.'

Oh, was she? He was intending to have words with Commander bloody Simpson.

'She said that you could start a fight in an empty room.'

'Just another macho cop,' Valette agreed.

'Carole warned me that I would struggle to get you on board,' Meyer said. 'Not very good as a team player, are you?'

Having heard enough, Carlyle stuck up a hand. 'Hold on, hold on. I appreciate the feedback but I merely came here to share information and to find out more about Duncan Brown.' He took a deep breath. 'Now, whatever my personal opinions, I understand and respect what you are trying to do here. Nor have I any interest in doing anything that would in any way compromise your investigation. But if you have any information about who killed Mr Brown, you need to share that with me immediately. And you can have confidence that I will use it carefully and appropriately.' He paused, waiting for a response. None was forthcoming. 'Look, if you've spoken to Simpson about my ... attitude, she must have also told you that I'm a safe pair of hands. I'm clean.'

After satisfying himself that the inspector had said his piece, Meyer finally replied. 'Yes, yes,' he said, 'but it comes down to one simple fact: you're either with us or you're not.'

Carlyle shook his head. 'Sorry, but I'm not.'

Valette made to get up but Meyer gestured for her to remain seated. 'Because what we are doing, it's not important enough for you?' he sneered.

Carlyle gave an apologetic gesture. 'No, because I don't think it will make any difference. All the time, effort and money. All of those "victims" coming forward to tell their story. All the guys seconded to your investigation. The years and years and years of work ...'

Meyer jabbed an angry finger across the desk. 'Heads *will* roll.'

'Okay, so a few people may get the chop. Even a few terribly important people. So what? They'll all be replaced sooner or later, anyway. And what will that leave us with? Same circus, different clowns.'

'What?' Meyer snapped.

'That's exactly what we have here,' Carlyle went on. 'The names of the clowns may change, but it's still the same bloody circus. That's just the way the Establishment works.'

'Bravo!' Valette gave him a quick round of mock applause. 'The most cynical man in the room speaks. So we're banging our heads against a brick wall?'

Carlyle said nothing.

'But isn't it just the same with all the cases you condescend to investigate?' she demanded.

He thought about Duncan Brown's friends and family, Hannah Gillespie's parents, the Snowdons, and he said, 'I can either make a difference to the lives of a small number of people or I move on.'

Arrogant, ego-driven little prick, Meyer thought. 'So . . .'

'So tell me who killed Duncan Brown.'

'Or?'

'Or I'll come back with a warrant.'

Meyer stared vacantly into space for a few moments. 'We had Mr Brown under surveillance,' he said finally. 'We watched him go into the Cockpit Yard depot with another man.'

'Who?'

'A guy called Warren Schwartz,' said Valette.

Carlyle thought about it for a moment but the name didn't ring any bells. 'Who's he?'

'He is a freelance consultant,' Meyer explained, 'a former soldier who provides a range of ill-defined services to clients. Last heard of in Montevideo, but he is known to have worked for Wickford Associates at least three times in the last eight years.'

The inspector couldn't prevent himself from breaking into a smile.

'That's right,' said Valette. 'He is a known associate of Trevor Miller.'

'So,' Meyer sighed, 'finally do you see why we want you to leave it alone?'

'No,' Carlyle said quietly. 'Quite the reverse.'

'It will get sorted in due course.'

'Mm.'

Meyer pulled a mobile from his jacket pocket. 'Do you want me to speak to Commander Simpson again? She has already agreed that you may not act on anything we have told you here today. If there is a problem with that, I can have you taken completely off the Duncan Brown case in less than a minute.'

'No, it's fine.' Trying to look suitably chastened, Carlyle stood up for a second time. 'I understand.'

Meyer looked at Valette and then back to the inspector. 'If anything significant develops, let Vanessa know straight away.'

'Of course.'

'This is *our* investigation and you cannot be allowed to compromise it in any way.' Meyer dismissed him with a wave of his hand. 'Vanessa will see you out.'

'No need,' said Carlyle, already halfway to the door and pondering his next move.

THIRTY

By the time he got back to the station, Carlyle had managed to put all thoughts of Meyer, Valette and Operation Redhead behind him. Walking through reception, he was surprised to find Gemma Millington, Duncan Brown's girlfriend, waiting patiently for him. Dressed for work in a grey trouser suit and cream blouse, she didn't look any more upset about her boyfriend's death than when they last spoke. Head down, she was typing furiously on her BlackBerry in one corner of the room. Carlyle was just thinking about leaving her there, when she looked up and saw him.

'Good job you showed up,' she began, getting up and moving briskly towards him. 'I was only going to give you another couple of minutes.'

'What can I do for you?' he asked.

She finished typing her email and hit send before dropping the handset into an outsized black leather bag. 'I've got something to show you.'

Aware of his stomach growling, he took her gently by the arm and propelled her towards the front door. 'We can talk outside. Let's go and get some coffee.'

Five minutes later, they were sitting in a new café called Cactus that had sprung up on Monmouth Street. After careful consideration of the menu, Carlyle ordered a double macchiato and a mozzarella, tomato and basil panino. Millington settled for a Diet Coke with ice, no lemon.

Not having previously patronized the establishment, Carlyle gave it the once-over, quickly concluding that it wouldn't last a year. 'Not quite as fancy as the canteen in your offices,' he observed. 'If you'd given me a call, I'd have happily come over for lunch.'

Millington smiled. She looked less tired and more relaxed than the last time they had talked; in fact, she looked like she'd had a few days off in the sun. 'I thought this would be better dealt with off-site.'

'Fair enough.' The waitress arrived with the Diet Coke and his macchiato. After taking a sip, Carlyle winced: it should have been hotter and sharper. He briefly thought about complaining but decided that he couldn't be bothered, satisfying himself instead with revising the café's life expectancy down to nine months.

Millington reached into her bag. After a few moments rummaging around, she pulled out a white A5 envelope and placed it on the table. 'This is some stuff of Duncan's that I found in my flat.'

Trying to feign interest, Carlyle eyed the envelope. It was unlikely to contain anything of note. After spending the best part of a day searching Brown's own flat, he and Joe had come up with precisely nothing. The guy had clearly been very careful about covering his tracks. And, even if they did find something, the inspector was less than sure what he'd be able to do with it. After his conversation with Meyer and Valette, it was clear that his murder investigation had become merely a pawn in a wider game.

Tugging at the ring-pull on the can, Millington poured some of her Coke into a glass. 'Aren't you going to open it?'

'Back at the station.' He held up his right hand and wiggled his fingers. 'When I've got some latex gloves on.' *Where was his sandwich?*

'Ah, yes.' She sipped her Coke demurely, placing the glass carefully back on the table, next to the envelope.

Carlyle smiled. That's the good thing about *CSI*, he thought; everyone who's watched it on TV thinks that they know how things get done.

A frown crossed her face. 'Have you got any?'

'Gloves? Sure. I always keep a pair on me, just in case.'

'Just in case what?'

'Just in case.' He pointed at the envelope. 'First off, why don't you give me a quick rundown of what's inside. Was there anything that you were surprised to find?'

She thought about it for a moment. 'No, not really. Just notes for some of his stories, a few business cards and a USB stick. I don't know if any of it is going to prove useful, but I thought that you still might want to have a look.'

'Thanks.' The panino arrived, looking rather anaemic. The waitress put the plate down right on top of the envelope, ignoring Carlyle's irritated glare as she walked away. 'What's on the USB stick?' He took a bite of the sandwich and shook his head in disgust. It was too cold and there wasn't enough tomato. If he hadn't been so bloody hungry, he might have left it unfinished. By now, he was convinced that this place would struggle to last three months.

'I don't really know.' Millington finished the Coke in her glass and carefully poured some more from the can. 'Transcripts of interviews, some notes . . . Duncan always kept various drafts of things that he had on the go at any one time.' She sighed. 'For a guy writing for a newspaper which requires a reading age of eight, he spent forever fiddling with his copy.' She reached back into her bag to pull out her BlackBerry and check the time. 'Shit! I really do have to go.' Pushing back the chair, she got to her feet. 'Anyway, I hope it's useful. And thanks for the Coke.'

'No problem,' Carlyle told her. 'Thank you for taking the time and effort.'

She hoisted the bag over her shoulder. 'Are you any closer at all to finding out who did it?'

Carlyle gave an apologetic shrug. 'I can't really talk about that.'

'No, no, of course.'

'But murder is really quite rare in London – and the clear-up rate is very high. So you can assume that we will catch whoever did this to Duncan.'

'Yes.' Nervously juggling her BlackBerry, Millington didn't look as though she quite believed him.

'And, of course, as far as possible I'll keep you posted.'

'Thanks.'

Finishing off his panino, he watched Gemma Millington walk out of the door and disappear down the street. Once she had turned the corner, he grabbed the envelope from under his plate and opened it with a knife. Clearing a space on the table, he carefully emptied out the contents.

On first glance, it was basically as Millington had described. Pulling a pair of latex gloves from his jacket pocket, he slipped them on, ignoring the funny look he received from the waitress as she cleared away his plate. The USB stick was unbranded: a small blue plastic rectangle missing its removable cap from the end. There was nothing he could do with it right now, so he put it back in the envelope. Next, he glanced through Duncan Brown's notes. A dozen or so sheets of lined A4 paper, torn from a notebook, were covered from top to bottom in a tiny, undecipherable script. 'Someone else will have to check that out,' Carlyle mumbled to himself, shoving the papers back inside the envelope. That left five business cards. While looking quickly through them, one caught his eye.

'Bingo!'

Dropping the card in his pocket, he signalled to the waitress for the bill.

On the third floor of the police station, the inspector tossed Joe Szyszkowski the envelope that he'd just been given by Gemma Millington. 'There's a USB stick in there. Don't get your prints on it. Check it out first then hand all that stuff over to Forensics.'

'What is it?' Joe tipped the contents on to his desk.

'Stuff Duncan Brown's girlfriend found in her flat.' Carlyle flopped into his chair. 'We should have gone round there and had a look, really.'

'Mm.' Both of them knew that was an oversight. But, badly overstretched, there was no way that they could hope to cover all bases on the various investigations that were ongoing. Using a paper napkin, Joe lifted the memory stick from his desk and stuck it into one of the USB slots in his computer. 'What about the other stuff the girlfriend handed over?'

'Not worth worrying about, as far as I could see.'

'Okay.' A window opened on the screen and Joe clicked on the *Open folder to view files* icon. 'So what have we got here?' He scrolled down through a series of Word documents, clicking on a couple at random. Carlyle's gaze wandered to the TV screen suspended from the ceiling nearby. Sky News was running a report about an HM Inspectorate of Constabulary report into undercover policing. The report had been delayed – again – after allegations of officers taking part in trials using aliases. Personally, the inspector couldn't see what all the fuss was about. It was just the kind of shit you had to do to get the job done.

'Looks like copies of his stories,' said Joe. He started laughing. '"I had a sex swap on my sixteenth birthday"! "Zoo-keeper lets killer animals loose"!'

A thought popped into Carlyle's head. 'Anything about Margaretha Zelle?'

'Not as far as I can see. We've got some pictures on here as well though.' With a couple of clicks of the mouse, he pulled up the first image. 'Whoa!'

Carlyle stepped over to the desk. 'What have you got?'

'Look at that,' said Joe, reducing the size of the picture so that it wasn't quite so obvious to anyone passing by what they were looking at.

'Bloody hell!' Hands on hips, legs apart, a rather drunk-looking Gemma Millington smiled back at him wearing nothing but a pink wig and a black bra.

'The Forensics boys will love this,' Joe grinned.

'That's the girlfriend,' Carlyle told him. 'At least we know she didn't delete anything before she handed the stick over. She can't have bothered to check it.'

'Silly girl.'

They were so busy gawping at the screen that they didn't notice Maude Hall approaching. 'What's that?' she asked, placing a hand on Joe's shoulder.

'Er . . . nothing important,' Joe stammered, quickly closing down the window. Carlyle stared intently at his shoes.

'You guys aren't breaking the standard HR guidelines on inappropriate computer use, are you?' Hall grinned.

'Probably,' Carlyle mumbled, feeling himself blush.

'It was just a picture on a memory stick belonging to Duncan Brown,' Joe explained, 'the guy who was found in a rubbish truck in Cockpit Yard. The girl is his girlfriend.'

Maude frowned. 'And you think she did it?'

'No.' Carlyle shook his head. 'Not at all.'

'But she's still worthy of some careful investigation?' Hall's grin grew wider. 'It's good to know that I am working with a pair of dirty old men.'

The inspector was about to protest but thought better of it. *When in a hole* . . . and all that.

'By the way,' Hall added, 'Bernie Gilmore called.'

Carlyle groaned. Why couldn't people just leave him alone?

'He says you owe him a phone call.'

'Okay.' Bernie wanted his pound of flesh, which was fair enough. But a bit more patience wouldn't hurt. Right on cue, he felt a vibration in his pocket. Pulling out his mobile, he stared at the blank screen, puzzled. Then he pulled out the private mobile he used alongside his police-issue device.

'Yeah?'

'Inspector? It's Bernie Gilmore.'

Carlyle looked at the handset. The Nokia 1800 was one of the cheapest, most ubiquitous pay-as-you-go models currently on the market. Carlyle had bought it for cash and then topped it up for cash at random newsagents well away from his usual haunts. The number was shared with as few people as possible; even then he would change both the phone and the SIM card every three or four months. This didn't guarantee him complete secrecy, but it meant that no one in the MPS could check his calls as a matter of routine. It gave him some measure of privacy and for that it was worth the hassle and extra cost involved.

'How did you get hold of this number?'

'I've been waiting for you to call,' Gilmore replied, ignoring the question. 'What have you got for me?'

'Hold on a sec.' Carlyle made a gesture to Joe and Maude indicating that he would be back in a minute, then headed off to one of the small meeting rooms that lined the far wall of the room, playing for time while he pondered how best to play Bernie.

'Okay.' Stepping inside the room, he carefully closed the door behind him and perched on the single desk that took up 80 per cent of the floor space. Through the wall-to-ceiling glass, he could see there was no one within twenty feet of him. Regardless, he was careful to lower his voice before resuming the conversation.

'You still there?' he asked.

'Yes.'

'Right, this is what I think you should do.' The inspector filled Gilmore in on the developments with Clegg and Monty Laws. 'I would go with the Gillespie story tonight. We'll hold a presser tomorrow, so you'll be ahead of the game.'

There was a grunt of acknowledgement. 'Okay. So, what else have you got?'

Carlyle sighed. He should have known that Bernie would drive a hard bargain. At the other end of the line he heard car horns blaring and someone shouting.

'Duncan Brown,' he said finally, once the noise had died down, 'is going to cause a storm.'

'Tell me more.'

'Later,' said Carlyle as firmly as he could manage. 'I need to nail down a few things first.'

'But we have a deal?'

'Of course, Bernie, absolutely. I'll keep my side of the bargain. You'll get a heads-up well before anyone else.'

'Okay, but keep me firmly in the loop.'

'I will.'

'Good.'

After checking a few more details on the Gillespie case, Gilmore hung up. Making a mental note to change SIM cards straight away, the inspector put the phone back in his pocket.

As Carlyle returned to his desk, Joe was scrolling through one of the Word files on Brown's USB stick.

'No more photos, then?'

'There were plenty more photos.' Joe kept his eyes on the screen. 'I must say, that girl is really quite uninhibited in front of a camera.'

'Maybe she was just drunk,' Carlyle mused. 'Or high.'

'I've found the Zelle story.' Joe was pointing at the screen. 'Nice headline: *MY HELL WORKING FOR RANTING PARANOID MARG.*'

'Not a favourable piece, then?'

'Hardly. It goes: *Queen Bitch's nanny tells how she was driven to thoughts of suicide by threats and bullying.* It's a story that appeared a few weeks ago.'

'But nothing that tells us any more about the phone hacking?'

'Not as far as I can see.'

'Okay.' Carlyle glanced over at Hall, who sat working away at a nearby desk. It struck him that he was beginning to really quite like this girl. Maybe she could be a good addition to the team; he would have to talk to Simpson about that. 'Maude, what are you doing this afternoon?'

The WPC looked up at him and smiled. 'That depends. What do you have in mind?'

'Don't worry,' Carlyle grinned. 'It doesn't involve a pink wig.'

Hall narrowed her eyes. 'Shame.'

'I was wondering if you could check something out for me.'

Perched on the edge of the sofa, Sir Gavin O'Dowd appeared a study in concentration as he slowly peeled the skin from a Cox's pippin, letting the peel drop on to the table.

'I hope you're going to clean that up after you,' Edgar Carlton, sitting in an armchair opposite him, said huffily.

Ignoring him, Sir Gavin continued carefully wielding his Swiss Army knife.

I know what I'd like to do with that, thought Trevor Miller grimly. Standing by the window, he was playing Angry Birds on his smartphone, while watching the rain fall on Downing Street.

After finishing his task, the Cabinet Secretary took a modest bite from the denuded apple, and chewed happily before swallowing. 'You know,' he said, waving the knife airily, 'the study is my favourite room in Number Ten. Lady Thatcher used to work in here on important documents from her red boxes until late into the night. Sir Winston Churchill apparently used it as a bedroom.'

Enough of the bloody history lesson. Stepping away from the window, Miller looked at his boss. 'We need to decide on your schedule.'

Crossing his legs, the PM looked up. 'My schedule has already been decided,' he whined, 'by Mrs Carlton.'

Miller tried not to let his irritation show. 'But my advice—'

'I'm well aware of your advice, Trevor,' Edgar snapped. 'And also of the advice of the Communications Director – *and* the advice of the Party Chairman, and so on and so forth. And it's not as if I want to go to any bloody harvest festival. But Anastasia has decided that she must go. And that's that. I have to indulge her on this.'

Seeing as you're banging some Peruvian bird behind her back, Miller reflected.

'And you will just have to make sure that nothing embarrassing happens.' Edgar waved a finger towards his security chief. 'Make absolutely sure I'm never standing close enough to Sonia Claesens for anyone to get a picture of us together, and things will be fine.'

Sir Gavin placed the remains of his apple on the table, pulled a handkerchief from his pocket and began cleaning the knife. 'The formidable Ms Claesens will make a beeline for you, of course.' Closing the knife, he put it back in his jacket pocket. 'Even if Trevor has already warned her off, she is a very determined lady'

Closing his eyes, Edgar began massaging his temples vigorously. 'Well, you'll just have to manage it somehow.'

'Fine,' said Miller unhappily. His mobile phone began vibrating in his hand. He didn't have to look at the screen to know who it was, and they could wait.

'Good.' Re-opening his eyes, Edgar stood up. 'Now, you'll have to excuse me. I've got to go and see Yulissa. She's hanging one of her paintings in the White Drawing Room. It's called *Final Voodoo* or something. Worth three to five mil at auction, apparently, but now another gift to the nation.'

'Your . . . *friend* is too generous,' Miller smiled.

Saying nothing, Sir Gavin stared intently at the table. *Three to five mil?* The work in question looked like something cobbled together by a rather backward six year old. Nevertheless, if Edgar was right, the damn thing was worth more than he had earned in total, over almost a quarter of a century as a high-ranking civil servant. As he fought to keep the rising tide of self-pity at bay, an idea popped into the mandarin's head: *Perhaps I should turn the remains of my apple into a work of art?*

'Simon?'

Shelbourne blinked through the smoke of his Ramon Allones Extra. His lunch was settling heavily in his stomach and he was more than a little pissed. Even so, the appearance of such a pretty girl at his table managed to perk him up somewhat. 'Yes?'

'How are you?' The girl smiled broadly before sliding into the booth opposite. His gaze was instantaneously drawn to her handsome décolletage.

Men! They were the most predictable creatures on the planet. Wondering if she had maybe undone one button too many, Maude Hall let him stare for a few moments. 'You don't remember me, do you?'

Placing the cigar in his ashtray, he pulled his chair closer to the table. 'Of course, of course.'

'Jenny Southerton,' Maude purred. 'I was an intern on the *Sunday Witness* when you were still Editor.' Crossing her legs, she brushed the back of his calf with her foot. 'When the paper was in its heyday.'

'Of course,' Shelbourne smiled. How could he have forgotten? So many girls, so little time. That was one thing he certainly missed about Zenger: the women in the MPS just didn't compare – didn't even come close. 'How could I forget?'

'It must be hard . . .'

It's certainly getting there, Shelbourne smiled inwardly.

'. . . keeping track of so many people when you are the Editor, right at the top.'

Picking up his Ramon Allones, Shelbourne took another drag. 'Certainly the responsibilities of office are considerable.'

Wrinkling her nose at the smoke, Maude sat back in the booth. 'Are you allowed to smoke in here these days?'

'Balmoral is a private members' club – "the epitome of fine English dining since 1743", so they say. Therefore, technically, they have more leeway,' Shelbourne told her, 'or something like that.'

That's nonsense, Hall thought, but she let it slide.

'Anyway, they allow a few select patrons like myself some special privileges.' And so they bloody should, Shelbourne thought, given that I drop a hundred and fifty quid or more in

211

here almost every day. Stubbing out the half-smoked cigar in the ashtray, he lifted the bottle of Massaya Gold Reserve that was sitting in the middle of the table and pointed it towards an empty glass. 'Would you like some? It's from the Bekaa Valley . . . not bad.'

Maude gestured vaguely towards the front of the restaurant. 'I was having lunch with some friends,' she said. 'I just thought that I'd come over to say hello.'

'Don't worry about that.' Shelbourne poured the red wine into the waiting glass. 'Let's have a drink and you can tell me what you're up to these days. And then maybe I can show you the rest of the club.'

'But what about your table companion?' Hall gestured at the remains of the Burnt Cambridge Vanilla Cream pudding on the plate in front of her.

'Ah, yes.' Shelbourne gestured to the fat, sweating, middle-aged man in a Marks & Spencer suit who was now approaching. 'Trevor was just leaving.'

Trevor Miller scowled at the bimbo who had stolen into his seat while he was off having a slash in the bogs. His attempts to get Shelbourne to persuade Sonia Claesens to stay away from the harvest festival had proved futile, but at least he had managed to get a good lunch out of it. Whatever Simon bloody Shelbourne might tell the girl, he had every intention of helping finish off the wine before he left.

'Who's this?' he asked sharply.

Shelbourne waved a hand in Hall's direction. 'Trevor, this is . . .'

'Jenny Southerton,' Hall reminded him, taking a sip of her wine.

'A former colleague at the *Sunday Witness*,' Shelbourne explained. 'Jenny, this is Trevor Miller.' Adopting a tone of mock secrecy, he lowered his voice. 'Trevor is the Head of Security for the PM.'

I know exactly who he is, Hall thought, smiling sweetly at the former policeman.

212

Realizing that he was not about to get his seat back, Miller could barely manage a grunt in reply.

'I know that you have to get moving,' Shelbourne said to Miller, his eyes looking glassier by the minute. 'Regarding the thing we were talking about – I'll see what I can do.'

Bollocks, thought Miller sourly. Giving up on any more wine, he started towards the door. 'Keep me posted.'

'Yes, indeed,' Shelbourne murmured as he watched him leave. Turning back to Hall, his eyes once again fell on to her chest. 'Now,' he smiled, slurring his words slightly, 'where were we?'

THIRTY-ONE

Lifting the glass to his lips, Carlyle took a gulp of Jameson's, letting it sit on his tongue for a few seconds before swallowing. It tasted good; he should have ordered a double. From the speakers above the bar came the familiar refrain of 'Rock the Casbah', the volume turned low so as not to interfere with the animated chatter of the early-evening customers. The Clash as background music? Sacrilege. At the same time, he liked the idea that his favourite band had survived the test of time so well.

'How did you know I was here?' From behind a large glass of Company Bay Sauvignon Blanc, Commander Carole Simpson eyed her subordinate suspiciously. Her friend, a glamorous forty-something interior designer called Laura, had tactfully gone outside for a smoke while the two of them talked business.

'Your PA told me this was one of your usual haunts.'

'That girl . . .' Simpson shook her head. All she really wanted from an assistant was someone who kept their own mouth shut and kept other people's noses out of the Commander's business. How difficult could that be? Rather difficult indeed, judging by the turnover in administrative support that she'd had to endure in recent years.

The inspector finished his drink and signalled to a passing waitress that he'd like another, 'a double'. At £8.50 a pop, he was trusting that his boss would be picking up the tab. 'I went to visit Meyer at Operation Redhead,' he said.

'Mm.' The look on Simpson's face suggested that she already knew what was coming next.

'He's got quite a set-up over there.'

Sipping more wine, the Commander said nothing.

'He said you'd spoken to him – about me.'

Placing her glass carefully on the table, Simpson asked, 'And did he offer you a job?'

'Yeah. And I refused it, just like you told him I would.'

Simpson said, 'I did try and warn him, but Russell never was very good at listening.'

'You know him well?'

'Not really. I've met him a few times – at conferences and so on. I was somewhat surprised when he gave me a call.'

'He seems like a bit of a prick. Why would they put someone like that in charge of such a high-profile operation?'

'John,' Simpson said drily, 'you know the answer to that perfectly well. Meyer is there solely to provide the necessary sound and fury.'

'Meyer doesn't seem to think so,' Carlyle snorted. 'He sees himself on a mission to change the world.'

'Like you said, he's a prick.' Simpson's eyes sparkled and he wondered how much she'd already had to drink.

'I thought I was supposed to be the . . . what was it?' He tried to recall one of her previous put-downs. 'The "self-styled most cynical man in the room"?'

'Yes, you are – but I'm slowly catching up.' Simpson took another mouthful of wine just as the waitress reappeared with his whiskey.

'Thanks.' Carlyle waited for her to go before he turned back to his boss. 'Meyer wants me to back-pedal on the Brown investigation.'

'Doesn't surprise me,' Simpson sighed. 'He always was the kind of officer who thought the ends could justify the means.' She laughed. 'In the end, he's probably even more cynical than both of us combined.'

The Clash gave way to Marc Cohn's 'Walking in Memphis'. The crowd continued with their chatter.

'Maybe.'

'What did you tell him?'

'I promised I wouldn't do anything that would compromise his investigation.'

Simpson looked surprised. 'That was very diplomatic – by your standards.'

'The way I see it, my own enquiries are proceeding quite nicely.'

'Oh, are they?' Simpson arched an eyebrow.

'And I don't need to tread on his toes to get a result.' The inspector filled her in on the materials recovered from Gemma Millington's flat – omitting mention of the photo of Ms Millington in a pink wig – and outlined his planned next steps.

'Fine,' said Simpson, refilling her glass from the bottle on the table.

'So, I was wondering if I might be able to take WPC Hall off the shift rota for the next few days?'

Simpson eyed him quizzically. 'I thought that you already had. The desk isn't too pleased about it.'

'Sorry.' The inspector tried his best to sound apologetic. 'But she's doing a good job.'

'She's pretty, too, I hear.'

'Which is why,' he smiled, 'she is in good hands with two tired, old married men like me and Joe.'

'Let's see how it goes over the next few days. Now, seeing as you are here, you can tell me something useful.'

Uh oh.

'How is the Mosman case going?'

Good bloody question, he thought, gulping down a sizeable slug of whiskey.

'You know the case – the one that I said should be your top priority?'

Yes, yes, yes. 'I'm going to speak to Mrs Mosman again

tomorrow,' he said evenly, glossing over the fact that he had done nothing of note regarding her since they had last spoken.

'Good.'

'And,' he added, belatedly remembering why he had come here in the first place, 'I want to hold a presser about Hannah Gillespie.'

'Why?'

'The media have started running with the story. In particular, a journalist called Bernie Gilmore.'

The Commander eyed him suspiciously. 'I know Gilmore. I never return his calls.'

'Me neither.'

'Mm.'

'The parents have got to him. He's already put something online. The girl has been missing for days now, and some of her known associates give us cause for concern. We need to get on the front foot regarding this. We've played it by the book so far, but you know as well as I do that, until the kid turns up safe and sound, we will always be accused of not doing enough.'

'Fine. Organize a presser. But you'll have to handle it without me.' Simpson's days of mugging for the cameras were over. Until not so long ago, she would have run a mile to get in front of a microphone. Now she couldn't keep far enough away. 'Just keep it short and sweet.'

'Sure.'

'Do you think the girl is still okay?'

'Hopefully – but I've no idea, really. If nothing else, we'll be covering our own backs.' Everyone knew that covering one's back was always a good reason for action. Out of the corner of his eye, he saw Laura reappear at the door and begin making her way towards their table. Carlyle drained his glass and gave his boss a big smile. 'Lots to be getting on with,' he said cheerily, and stood up. He could feel the effects of the alcohol as he swayed slightly on his feet. 'I'll keep you posted. Thanks for the drink.'

'My pleasure,' Simpson replied tartly.

He nodded at Laura. 'Nice to meet you.'

'You too, Inspector,' she said. 'It's always fun to meet some of Carole's more interesting colleagues.'

Curiously disconcerted by his uncharacteristic show of politeness, Simpson watched her underling head for the door.

Placing her iPhone and Marlboros on the table, Laura reached for the bottle of Sauvignon Blanc. 'Seems like a nice guy.'

'Mm,' Simpson replied. 'He has his moments.'

Walking in Memphis . . .' Hoping to clear his head, Carlyle inhaled deeply as he walked down the Edgware Road, heading towards Marble Arch where he could get a bus home to Covent Garden. Passing a kebab shop, he felt a sharp pang of hunger just as one of his phones started vibrating in his pocket.

'Carlyle,' he announced.

'Inspector, it's Snowdon here.'

Shit. Another job he hadn't done. If it wasn't for the drink, he would have had the wit to leave his phone unanswered. Grimacing, he cleared his throat. 'Good evening, sir. How are you?'

'I was just wondering if you had managed to speak to your colleagues in Fulham yet?' Even with all the background noise, Carlyle could detect that the old man sounded drunker than he was himself. Looking up in the nick of time, he narrowly avoided walking into a lamppost.

'I haven't been able to get hold of them yet, but I'm hoping to go down there tomorrow.'

'I see.'

'Don't worry, I hadn't forgotten,' he lied. 'And thank you for setting up the meeting with Mr . . .'

'Highman.'

'Yes, thank you. That was very useful.'

'Harris is a good chap.'

'Indeed.' His attention was distracted by a takeaway called Hell's Pizza located, appropriately enough, on the corner of Church Street. His stomach rumbled insistently. 'Look, my apologies but I have to go. I will give you a call with an update tomorrow.'

'Very good,' Sir Michael said wearily.

Ending the call, the inspector switched off his phone and headed straight towards his culinary salvation.

Sitting back in his chair, Harris Highman contemplated his gloomy, cluttered office. This was the nearest thing he'd had to a home for more than thirty years. Thirty years! Not for the first time, he reflected that he had spent almost half a lifetime sitting in one little room. Now that retirement was looming, he was at a loss as to what to do about it. Where had the time gone? It was such a banal lament.

Through the window, he could make out the London Eye, lit up now as it carried its last tourists of the evening. A cleaner stuck her head round the door but Highman waved her away with a flick of his hand. Loosening his tie, he took a sip of his lemon and ginger tea before scanning the list of names on the sheet of paper resting on his lap.

'Mm.' Reaching across his desk, he put down his *Book of the Dead* souvenir mug and picked up a copy of *UK in Germany*, the glossy bi-annual newsletter published by the British Embassy in Berlin. The centre spread was given over to an interview with the Ambassador, Michael Murphy, which had been conducted by Zoe Mosman six months earlier. In it they had discussed works from the Government Art Collection which were then on display in the Embassy on Wilhelmstrasse and also in the Ambassador's residence. Highman tut-tutted. '*Iconic works by some of the greatest sculptors working in Britain today*, indeed!' he scoffed. Anish Kapoor and Tony Cragg were definitely not to his taste.

On the next page was a series of a dozen or so photographs from a reception held to celebrate the CAG. Zoe Mosman appeared in three of these: one with the Ambassador and his boyfriend; another with two other women, one of whom was the ubiquitous Yulissa Vasconzuelo, the Prime Minister's floozy, who seemed to attend every party known to man; and the third with a dark, unsmiling man with cold eyes who looked decidedly unhappy about having his picture taken. Dropping the newsletter on to his desk, Highman checked the list of guests attending the event for the tenth time. 'Well, well,' he mumbled to himself. There could be no doubt: he had the name. He even had the photo to prove it. 'What a very interesting development.'

Harris felt a delicious shiver of self-satisfaction slip through him. He had acquired knowledge. And knowledge – as Sir Francis Bacon had pointed out – is power.

But what was he going to do with it?

His first inclination was to call Zoe Mosman and confront her with what he had discovered. However, he quickly discounted that idea. Under the circumstances, that was not the best approach. Not when he had other options. Flicking through the Rolodex standing on his desk, he found the card that the policeman had handed him when they had met in Wardour Street. Picking up the phone, it took him three attempts to dial the number properly, only for it to immediately go to voicemail. Sighing, he waited for the beep.

'Inspector, this is Harris Highman. We were introduced recently by Sir Michael Snowdon.' Slowly and clearly he recited his mobile number and then repeated it. 'I would be very grateful if you could give me a call at your earliest convenience.'

'Sit up.'

Sniffling, Hannah Gillespie did as she was told. She no longer noticed the unpleasant smell or the buzzing in her head.

'Can you stand up?'

She shook her head. Her legs felt like jelly.

'Never mind.'

'Please . . .' Her voice, barely audible over the traffic, sounded small and far away.

'Just keep still. This won't hurt.'

'Mum,' she whispered, closing her eyes. 'I'm sorry.'

THIRTY-TWO

As usual, the Media Centre at Charing Cross was cold, harshly lit and filled with the smell of stale food from the canteen next door. With Joe Szyszkowski following behind, Carlyle entered the room from a side door, making a quick headcount as he marched towards the platform. To his relief, a handful of hacks had managed to make it out of bed: a news reporter from the *Evening Standard*, a guy from the *Daily Mail*, a local radio reporter, and local television in the shape of Independent Television's *London Tonight* and BBC London. The small group sat waiting with *Impress me* looks on their faces, idly scribbling on copies of the Hannah Gillespie press release or tapping away on their assorted mobile devices. Bernard Gilmore Esq was nowhere to be seen. That was not a surprise; Carlyle knew Bernie wouldn't bother turning up just to gloat at rivals that he'd already scooped. He might be a hack, but he was a classy hack.

Carlyle waited for a few extra minutes beyond the appointed start time, in the vain hope that someone else might turn up.

'Let's get on with it,' Joe mumbled, as the clock on the far wall ticked on towards five past ten.

'Okay.' With a sigh, Carlyle switched on the microphone in front of him. 'Good morning.' Once he was sure he had their attention, or at least as much of their attention as he was ever going to get, he launched into a scripted introduction which explained the background to Hannah's disappearance and concluded with an appeal for her to get in touch with her anxious parents as soon as possible.

After he finished there was a pause before an emaciated-looking man in a red Berghaus jacket, sitting in the middle row, raised his hand.

'Yes?'

'Edgar Smith, the *Mail*.' The skeleton looked up from the pad on which he had been scribbling furiously and pinned the inspector with a hostile gaze. 'Why did you bother calling this press conference when you'd already leaked the story to Bernie Gilmore last night?' A murmur of approval for the question spread among the other hacks.

And why did you bother coming, if you weren't interested in the bloody story? Carlyle thought sourly. 'We didn't leak anything.'

Smith shook his head in mock disbelief.

'I think you'll find,' said Joe firmly, 'that it was Hannah's parents who spoke to Mr Gilmore.'

'Is that why they're not here?' asked another man at the back. 'Because they're not happy with the lack of action so far on the part of the police?'

Conscious of TV cameras rolling at the back of the room, Carlyle bit his tongue. 'There has been no lack of action on our part,' he said finally. 'Hannah's parents are understandably concerned . . .' As he watched the hacks struggling to find enough enthusiasm to write down these words, he wondered about the wisdom of holding this presser at all. 'What we are basically asking is . . .' Just then, he was distracted by a hand landing on his shoulder. Maude Hall had appeared at his side and handed him a note. Reading it quickly, he nodded and gave it back to her.

'What we are saying is that all everyone wants is for Hannah to get in touch with her parents as soon as possible.' He jumped to his feet, signalling for Joe to follow. 'So, if there are no more questions, let's leave it there. Thank you for your time. We will let you know of any further developments in due course.'

Not waiting for any additional responses, he skipped off the platform and ducked through the door, heading for the lift.

The inspector picked up the business card and made a show of reading it carefully. *Charles W. Ross, Life President, Wickford Associates.* What did the W stand for? Carlyle wondered. He let a somewhat uncharitable but appropriate word float through his brain as he considered the address underneath. An office on New Bond Street in the West End: the same address as on a similar card he'd taken from the envelope of goodies that Duncan Brown's girlfriend, Gemma Millington, had recovered from her flat.

Well, well, well.

Sitting in a fourth-floor meeting room, Charlie Ross eyed the inspector carefully while sipping slowly from an outsized Starbucks beaker. Happy to have escaped the press conference, Carlyle could do with a coffee himself. He placed the card back on the table and looked up.

'Do you remember me?' he asked.

Ross fixed him with a sharp gaze. Well into his eighties, his blue eyes were still clear and alert behind a pair of fashionable rimless glasses. 'Aye, son, I remember you well.'

Happy to go along with the fiction, Carlyle nodded.

'At Cortonwood and Orgreave,' the old man continued.

'Right.'

'That business with Trevor Miller.'

'Indeed.' Maybe the old sod genuinely did remember. Or maybe he'd done some homework before bowling up here.

'Bloody hell!' Charlie chuckled. 'That was something like thirty years ago now. I was still a young man back then – almost.'

'Time is a bastard,' Carlyle agreed. 'You're looking good though.' It was true. On first inspection, apart from the fact that his hair was now pure white, Sergeant Charlie Ross didn't appear that much older than when he was dodging half-bricks on the Yorkshire picket lines. Indeed, tanned, relaxed and carrying a

223

few extra pounds, he looked considerably healthier than Carlyle remembered him back then. The expensive-looking suit he was wearing only added to an overall impression of well-being and prosperity.

'Thanks.' The old man grinned ruefully. 'I wish I could say the same for you.'

Carlyle smiled. This was still the same old Charlie: always in your face. Born in Burnbank, South Lancashire, Charlie Ross's police career had been going nowhere until it was given a late lease of life by the 1980s miners' strike. For John Carlyle, a young PC dumped out in the provinces to take on a paramilitary role on behalf of an extremist government only too keen to go to war against the 'enemy within', it was an uncomfortable education in more ways than one. For Charlie Ross, with almost twenty-five years' service under his belt, it had instead been a memorable swansong.

'We gave those bastards a right shoeing,' Ross recalled happily, his harsh accent defiantly unaffected by more than fifty years of living in London.

'Mm, what can I do for you, Charlie?'

Placing his cup on the table, Ross sat back in his chair and folded his arms. The look on his face said *Don't fuck about with me, son.* For someone who was an old man, he still managed to create an air of menace – especially when he smiled. 'I thought I'd come and see you before you came to see me.'

'Oh?'

'In fact, I'm surprised you haven't been over to see us already.'

'I've had a lot on.'

'I bet you have. And I thought I might be able to help you in that regard.'

'That's very kind of you.'

'My company has nothing to hide.'

Your company, the inspector wondered. I thought it belonged to Trevor Miller? It was a detail that he let slide. 'That's good to know.'

'I'm assuming that you know all about our connection to Duncan Brown and the Zenger Corporation?'

Carlyle nodded.

'That is all in the public domain. Like I say, we have nothing to hide. If there has been any breach of our well-documented procedures and guidelines, then we will take all the appropriate steps to weed out the guilty parties and do everything necessary to beef up our systems and processes.'

Spare me the corporate bullshit.

'As you would expect, we are already cooperating fully with Operation Redhead and your friend Russell Meyer.'

'He is not my friend,' Carlyle snapped, his meagre reserves of patience already used up.

'Whatever you say.' Ross held up his hands in supplication. 'You have, however, compared notes, I take it?'

'That is *my* business,' said Carlyle huffily. He really needed some caffeine. 'What exactly do you want?'

Ross held his gaze for one, two, three seconds. 'What I want, son,' he said finally, 'is to give you Trevor Miller's head on a fucking plate.'

Unsure what to make of his conversation with Charlie Ross, Carlyle watched the old man skip down the front steps of Charing Cross police station and slip into the back seat of a black Lexus sedan which had been ostentatiously idling in front of a *No Parking* sign.

'Who was that?' Maude Hall appeared at his shoulder, carrying a file stuffed with documents. Wearing jeans and a washed-out red T-shirt under a grey cardigan, she looked about sixteen.

'His name is Charlie Ross,' said Carlyle, watching the Lexus nose out into the traffic. 'He works with Trevor Miller.'

'I met Miller yesterday.'

'Oh?' Trying not to look concerned, the inspector took a half-step backwards.

'Yeah. Simon Shelbourne introduced us.'

'Mm.' Maybe sending the girl to spy on the Commissioner's PR man hadn't been such a good idea, after all. 'Let's go to the canteen and get a coffee,' he suggested. 'Then you can tell me what happened.'

Three small crumbs were all that remained of his chocolate doughnut. Feeling better and worse at the same time, Carlyle looked guiltily at his plate before finishing off his coffee. Munching on an apple, Hall said nothing.

'So,' he said, waiting for her to finish chewing, 'how did it go with Shelbourne?'

'What a creep!' Dropping the apple core on her plate, Hall wiped her hands on a paper napkin. 'He was obviously pissed and offered to give me the guided tour of his club. They have bedrooms on the top floor, and he thought . . .'

A couple of male officers at the next table began tuning into their conversation, so Carlyle signalled for Hall to lower her voice.

'He thought,' she whispered, 'that I would go up there with him and – well, you know.'

Gritting his teeth, Carlyle told himself, *Sending Hall off to act as your spy was definitely not one of your better ideas*. Apart from anything else, Simpson would have a fit if she ever found out.

'Not that I was falling for that,' she grinned. 'I let him show me round quickly, and then legged it.'

'Good for you.'

'My dad boxed for the Army. I can look after myself.'

'I'm sure you can,' Carlyle nodded, not sure what the connection there was.

Her grin widened. 'And then, of course, there is the Krav Maga.'

'Yes.' Carlyle smiled, remembering the unfortunate Francis Clegg. Hall's obvious ability to look after herself made him feel a little better about having sent her to try and butter up the deeply unpleasant Simon Shelbourne. 'What did you two talk about? Did he tell you anything useful?'

Hall shook her head. 'Not really. He moaned about Miller being on his case the whole time, clearly because of the phone-hacking business, but he didn't go into any details. Oh, and apparently Sir Chester's stay in a health farm is costing almost thirty grand.'

'Thirty grand?'

'I know. Simon says he's particularly keen on the colonic irrigation, and he's also having kriotherapy for his back twice a day.'

'What's that?'

'No idea. Just some kind of treatment.'

'So how can Sir Chester afford thirty k?'

'He doesn't have to. The guy who owns the health farm is letting Sir Chester and his wife stay for free.'

'Interesting.' Pushing back his chair, the inspector got to his feet. 'Do you know when he's back at work?'

'Probably sometime next week. Depends on how his recovery is coming along.'

'Have you told anyone else about the thirty grand?'

Hall looked vaguely affronted. 'No.'

'Good. Then keep it to yourself.'

'Okay.'

Carlyle wondered if she would really be able to keep her mouth shut. In his experience, coppers were terrible when it came to gossiping. 'Right, go and see what Joe needs help with. We really have to find Monty Laws. Now that Hannah Gillespie has hit the press, we'll have to keep feeding the beast.'

Not really sure what the inspector was wittering on about, Hall nodded enthusiastically.

'And let's give Shelbourne a wide berth for a while.'

'With pleasure!'

'Tell Joe I'll catch up with you guys later on.' Should he have another doughnut? Unable to make his mind up, Carlyle sent Hall on her way. At least he would have some more caffeine. Heading back to the coffee machine, he pressed the button for a double espresso and waited.

THIRTY-THREE

The BBC's news channel was showing live coverage of the House of Commons' Select Committee hearing into the slowly emerging phone-hacking scandal. Yawning, the inspector was surprised to see Margaretha Zelle's pixellated face suddenly appear on the TV screen. 'What the fuck's she doing?'

'Playing the victim.' Leaning across the sofa, Dominic Silver picked up the remote control from the floor and muted the sound. Sitting in an armchair in the far corner of the room, Gideon Spanner momentarily looked up from his book – a paperback copy of *GB84*, David Peace's novel about the miners' strike – before returning to his reading without otherwise acknowledging the inspector's arrival. Spanner, an ex-soldier, was Dom's right-hand man, and he was not the kind of guy to waste his words.

'Talking a load of rubbish,' Dom continued, 'as per usual. Lots of guff about how she's been violated by the invasion of her privacy . . . yada, yada, yada. All that happened was someone listened in to her poxy messages.'

'Why do people bother?' Carlyle wondered aloud. 'Half the time, I can't be bothered to listen to my own bloody messages.'

'Half the time you don't *remember* to listen to your own bloody messages,' Dom chided him.

'Fair point,' Carlyle conceded.

Dom waved airily at the screen. 'Just as well for her that the media didn't hack any of her messages from me,' he chortled.

The inspector raised an eyebrow. 'She's a client?'

'Now and again,' Dom sighed. 'A pain in the arse, basically.'

'I can imagine,' said Carlyle sympathetically.

'Having given it some thought, I would have to say that she is one of the most stupid, self-obsessed people that I've ever met in my life.'

'That must be saying something.'

'And I find it impossible to believe that she's ever had any conversation worth listening in to, ever.'

'Phone hacking is a serious crime,' Carlyle mused, slipping into an empty chair, 'apparently.'

Silver shot him the kind of amused stare that had been perfected over several decades. A former policeman turned drug dealer, he had a somewhat ambivalent attitude towards matters of law and order. In that respect, he wasn't so different from Carlyle himself. 'Now that we've cleared *that* up, Inspector, what is it that I can do for you?'

'Trevor Miller.'

A look of disgust swept across Silver's face. 'That wanker! What's he up to now?'

While Margaretha Zelle prattled away silently, Carlyle quickly ran through a potted history of the Duncan Brown case and its connection to Operation Redhead, omitting the bit about Miller turning up at his block of flats to give him a shoeing.

'It's amazing what people get wound up about,' was Dom's only response.

'Yeah. But at the end of the day, we are talking about murder,' Carlyle reminded him.

'Of a bloody *journalist*,' Dom sniffed. 'Mitigating circumstances personified.'

'Journalists have rights too,' the inspector said primly.

On the TV, Ms Zelle pulled a handkerchief from the sleeve of her jacket and wiped away a tear. Dom waved an exasperated arm at the sobbing celeb. 'This shows what a fucked-up society we are. In other places, when journalists get killed it's because they are trying to uncover some big story, trying to shine a spotlight on some social injustice, or whatever. A newspaper editor in Mexico was decapitated last week for trying to write about the drugs war.'

'Mm.' Where did that come from? Carlyle wondered. And aren't you with the other side in that particular war? But their successful long-standing relationship was built on an understanding, among other things, that life was full of ironies.

'Over here, on the other hand,' Dom complained, 'journalists are just lobotomized morons. Everything's just about who's fucking whom or promoting whatever shit show is on the telly on Saturday night.'

'That's just the way of the world.' Leaning forward in his chair, Carlyle held up a hand. He didn't have time for his mate going off on one about the shortcomings of contemporary British society. In small doses, Dom's drug-dealer-as-sociologist shtick was interesting enough – but there was a time and a place. 'Do you remember Charlie Ross?'

Dom thought about it for a moment. 'Sergeant Charlie Ross?'

'The self-same,' Carlyle nodded.

'Rucking at Orgreave Colliery.'

'Amongst other places.'

'Hard bastard.'

'I reckon he's somewhere in his eighties now, but still looking good. He came to see me this morning. Said he could offer me Miller's head on a plate.'

'What's he got to do with Trevor?'

'They run a private security and investigations firm together, called Wickford Associates.'

'So why would good old Charlie want to fuck over his business partner?'

'That,' Carlyle smiled, 'is what I need some help in working out.'

A horn blared in the distance and the sounds of a passing argument came up from the street below. Lost in thought, Dom stared out of the window at the grey Soho sky, as a plane whined overhead on its approach to Heathrow. All the reassuring sounds of the city.

Carlyle checked his BlackBerry. He was slightly disgruntled to find that no one had sent him a message since he'd last looked.

'You should leave it alone,' Dom said finally. 'Let the Redhead guy . . .'

'Meyer?' Carlyle put the BlackBerry away and looked up.

'Yeah. Let Meyer deal with it. Don't own other people's problems. Don't be ruled by your ego.'

'What?'

Getting to his feet, Dom began pacing backwards and forwards in front of the window. 'You've been obsessed by Miller all through your career.'

'No, I haven't.'

'Yes, you have – ever since that bloody Shoesmith woman sued him for sexual assault.'

Carlyle was surprised that Dom remembered her name but he kept his mouth shut.

'I told you at the time, you should have just said you saw nothing.'

'Look the other way, you mean?'

'Ye-es. And it's exactly the same now as it was back then. Trevor Miller is not your problem, so leave him alone.'

'Fuck that,' said Carlyle angrily.

'Be careful, Johnny boy. Remember – you're getting old. These days, I'm not sure I'd be able to offer you alternative employment.'

'Hah!' Carlyle laughed. It had been a running gag down the years that Dom had a place for Carlyle in his organization, should the inspector ever leave the Force. They both knew though, that it was something that would never happen.

Dom spread his hands wide. 'Behind the carefully constructed exterior of a useless fat cunt, Trevor has always been quite a shrewd operator. Whatever he's been up to, he's made sure that he has contacts, and that his back is covered. Now he works for the bloody Prime Minister, for fuck's sake!'

'He'll crash and burn in the end,' said Carlyle grimly.

'Exactly!' Dom did a little jig of triumph. 'So sit back and enjoy the fucking show. It's like the old Japanese proverb . . .'

Fuck me, Carlyle thought, here we go now with the bloody proverbs. On the TV, Zelle had finished her testimony. Her place in front of the Committee had been taken by a middle-aged suit he didn't recognize. The clock in the bottom left-hand corner of the screen told him it was time to go.

'If you sit by the side of the river long enough, you will see the body of your enemy floating past.'

'Thanks for that.' Carlyle stood up. 'So will you help me or not?'

Dom laughed. 'You're not going to sit on the river bank?'

'No.'

'What a big fucking surprise,' Dom cackled.

'It's been thirty years already.'

'You never fucking grow up, do you?'

'You going to help me?'

Dom held up his hands in surrender. 'Don't I always?'

'Thanks.'

'No promises – but I'll see what I can do.'

THIRTY-FOUR

'Boss, it's me. What exactly do you want me to do on this Hannah Gillespie thing? I'm worried that it's dragging on and we are just not getting anywhere. She's still checking her voicemails, so that's kind of okay, but she's not responding to any of them. With the benefit of hindsight, people are gonna say there's just not enough people on the case. At this rate, we're not going to find her. And Simpson'll go mad if we end up getting sued by the parents. Give me a call.'

'What do you want *me* to do about it?' Carlyle grumbled to himself. It was late and he simply didn't have the energy to respond to Joe Szyszkowski's voicemail, not least because he didn't have any answer.

'Dad, you're on TV!'

'What?' Carlyle ambled out of the kitchen with a cup of green tea in his hand. By the time he'd flopped down on the sofa next to Helen, the news had moved on from his presser to a story about a new lion cub in the London Zoo.

'Missed it,' Alice grinned from her armchair. 'You looked old.'

'Thanks,' Carlyle groaned.

'And knackered,' Helen added for good measure.

'How kind of you to say so.'

Alice stood up. 'I'm off to listen to some Clash.' Bending over, she kissed her father on the forehead. 'Maybe you should take a holiday.'

'Maybe I should.'

'Anyway, I hope you find that girl.'

'Thanks.'

'*Will* you find her?' Helen asked him, once Alice had gone.

'Sure,' said Carlyle, blowing on his tea, 'one way or another.'

Wearing nothing but a towel, Trevor Miller sat in a booth in the Treasures of Heaven sauna on the Euston Road waiting for 'Melissa' to come and give him his executive deep-tissue Swedish massage. Struggling to get into the right frame of mind, he looked up at the TV that hung from the ceiling above the bed. Rather than the usual porn, it was showing the local news. The cable feed must be down again, he thought sourly, picking up the remote control. He was just about to change channels when a shot of Charing Cross police station appeared, quickly followed by pictures of a press conference hosted by a familiar face.

'That cunt Carlyle,' he grunted to himself, watching as his one-time nemesis made an appeal for finding a missing teenager. At least it wasn't about the Duncan Brown fiasco.

A shot of a plain-looking girl in her school uniform flashed up on the screen, along with a phone number. Then back to some closing shots of the presser. Suddenly a woman appeared on the platform and whispered something to the inspector. Recognizing her immediately, Miller's eyes narrowed. 'What was your name?' he asked himself, thinking back to their brief meeting in the Balmoral Club at the end of his lunch with Simon Shelbourne. 'Jenny – Jenny . . . *Southerton*.' He was pleased with himself for remembering. 'Is that right? We'll have to see.'

As he was making a mental note to check out the name that the woman had given, the door opened and a tired-looking brunette in hot pants and a London 2012 Union Jack T-shirt entered. Without saying a word, she placed a large bottle of Johnson's Baby Lotion on the table by the bed. Removing Miller's towel, she looked down and smiled. 'Looks like we've got a bit of work to do there, sweetie.'

After pushing out a rather fruity fart, Miller scratched his arse. That's what I'm paying you for, he thought.

Wrinkling her nose, the girl pointed to the bed. 'Better lie down for me and we'll get started.'

Alice and Helen had already gone to bed. Sprawled on the sofa, Carlyle was working his way steadily through *Return of the Last Gang in Town*, the monster biography of The Clash which Alice had picked out for him at Holborn Library. It was slow going – Helen had already twice extended the loan period – but he was making steady progress. Deep in the messy detail of the recording of *London Calling*, he became conscious that his mobile had started vibrating its way across the coffee table. With a deep sigh, he put the book down and picked up the phone.

'Carlyle.'

'Inspector, it's Melvin Boduka.'

With his head full of thoughts of rock'n'roll, the inspector struggled for a moment to place the name.

'The Mosmans' lawyer,' Boduka reminded him. 'Sorry to be ringing you so late.'

'That's okay,' said Carlyle, sitting up. 'What can I do for you?'

There was a pause. 'Mrs Mosman would like a meeting.'

'*Mrs* Mosman?'

'That's what I said,' Boduka replied testily.

The inspector leaped up and began prowling the room. 'She has something to tell me?'

'Yes.' The lawyer didn't sound too happy about it. 'I am not party to the details, but she has indicated that she now believes she may be able to help you further in your investigation.'

About bloody time, Carlyle thought. He could feel the adrenalin buzz building in his system. 'She wants to meet now?'

'No, no, I was wondering, could you come to our offices in the morning?'

'Now would be good,' Carlyle replied, trying to take control of the situation.

Boduka was having none of it. 'She suggested the morning.'

'Fine, fine. What time?'

'How about ten?'

'Okay.'

'That's agreed, then. We will see you tomorrow.' Without another word, Boduka rang off.

'*Yes!*' Tossing the phone on the sofa, Carlyle adopted a Joe Strummer-type pose, clenching his fist in triumph while hopping from foot to foot.

Progress at last.

As he continued his little jig, Helen suddenly stuck her head round the living-room door, a sleepy scowl on her face. 'What are you doing?'

'Sorry.' Carlyle stopped jumping around like an idiot and retrieved his phone.

'Come to bed,' she commanded, disappearing back down the hall.

'Okay.' Looking at the handset screen, he noticed the message icon and frowned. That wasn't there earlier, he was sure. Hitting 901, he waited for it to play.

'*Inspector, this is Harris Highman. We were recently introduced by Sir Michael Snowdon. I would be very grateful if you could give me a call at your earliest convenience.*'

Immediately, Carlyle hit 5 to call Highman back, only to get a recorded message telling him that the callback facility was not available for that number. 'Bollocks!' Stumbling into the kitchen, he pulled open a succession of drawers until he found a pen. Then he played the message again, writing down the number on a copy of yesterday's *Standard*. Punching in the numbers, he listened to Highman's phone ring, knowing in his gut that it would inevitably go to voicemail.

When it did, he kicked the fridge in frustration.

'*Mr Highman, it's John Carlyle here. Apologies for missing your call. Try me again at any time.*'

From down the hall he could hear the complaining tones of his wife. 'John, for God's sake! It's late. Stop playing with your bloody phone.'

'Okay, okay.' Dropping the phone into the back pocket of his jeans, he headed for bed.

'Harris?'

Highman looked up from his reading – a *Frieze Magazine* article on Italian photographer Luigi Ghirri – to see Zoe Mosman standing in the doorway of his office. It was after 10 p.m. and the first time he had seen her in the place since the horrific incident with her boy. The idea that she was, technically speaking, his superior, made Harris shudder with disgust. He had never felt comfortable around her and now, after her bereavement, it was worse. Families, they were so . . . problematic.

'Zoe,' he mumbled, trying to look sympathetic. 'How are you?'

She gave him a wan smile. 'Bearing up.'

'I was extremely sorry to hear about what happened to Horatio.' Irritatingly, his phone started ringing in his pocket. He killed the call without even checking to see who it was.

'Thank you.' She dropped her gaze to the floor.

'I'm sure that you've had to listen to a lot of people say that recently.' Unsure of how to handle this, he stayed behind his desk.

'Yes, but it is still kind of you to say it, Harris.'

What else am I going to say? he wondered, suddenly feeling irritated at having been put on the spot.

'I thought I might come in tonight and catch up on some paperwork,' Mosman explained. 'I hoped it might help to take my mind off things.'

'I understand,' Highman nodded. She's losing it, he thought, more than a little put out that he no longer had the place to himself.

Mosman gestured along the hall in the direction of her own office. 'I've got a bottle of ten-year-old Springbank in my desk. I thought I might have a glass. Would you care to join me?'

Not really, Highman thought. Gin had always been his thing, more than whisky at least. Even so, now was not the time or place to be churlish about such things. Taking a deep breath, he forced an appropriately sombre smile on to his face. 'Why not? That would be nice.'

Looking round the room, Highman estimated – not for the first time – that Zoe Mosman's office had to be at least twice the size of his own. However, where his, stuffed full of books and papers, had the look and feel of an absent-minded academic's lair, hers was largely empty. Even with a selection of family photographs scattered across the various bookcases, it retained the antiseptic air of a doctor's consulting room. All that would change, of course, when he moved in here. He looked down at the glass of Springbank in his hand. 'I don't suppose you've got any ice, by any chance?'

'No, sorry.' Seated behind her desk, Mosman lifted her own glass to her lips. She was about to say 'Cheers', but under the circumstances, thought better of it. For appearances' sake, Highman took a mouthful of the whisky. Swallowing quickly, he tried not to make a face.

'You don't like it?' That was one of the many annoying things about Zoe Mosman; she had always been able to read him like a book.

'No, no,' he coughed. 'Very nice.'

Putting down her glass, Mosman sat back in her chair and lifted her stockinged feet on to the desk top, increasing Highman's level of discomfort still further. Beside the big toe of her left foot, he noticed a tear in the stockings.

'So,' she said, wiggling her toes in what frankly seemed a rather provocative manner, 'how is your audit of the collection coming along?'

'Well, um . . .' He lifted the glass back to his mouth, then thought better of it. 'I would say that it's coming along as well as can be expected, under the circumstances.'

'Under the circumstances?'

'Yes.'

'Well, that's good. You must be pleased.'

'Yes, I think we have made reasonable progress. There is light at the end of the tunnel now. In fact, the whole thing is almost complete.'

'I see.' Taking her feet off the desk, Mosman sat up in her chair. 'And what will your conclusions be?'

'My conclusions?' Highman stared again into his glass. 'Well, I really think that I would like to wait until the whole thing is finished before—'

'Come on, Harris,' she snapped. 'I have more than enough on my plate right now without having to worry about what you're cooking up.'

'I am not cooking up anything,' Highman protested. He could hear the tension in his voice, and hated himself for it. Why did he let this woman browbeat him so?

'In that case,' she said, effortlessly slipping back into smooth CEO mode, 'why the secrecy?'

'There is no secrecy,' he whined, reflexively gulping down another mouthful of scotch.

Mosman smiled sadly. 'If I didn't know better,' she said quietly, 'I might think there is something of a conspiracy developing here.'

'There is no secrecy,' he repeated, 'and there is no conspiracy. What there *is* . . .'

Placing her hands on the desk, Mosman leaned forward. 'Yes?'

'What there is,' he began again, 'is a rather significant discrepancy between what we believe should be in the collection and what we can actually account for.'

'Which means what?'

Highman let out a deep sigh; so much for keeping his own counsel. 'Which means that, so far, there are more than a hundred paintings – having an estimated total market value of more than thirty million pounds – which we cannot find.'

Mosman stared at him. 'And what do you think happened to them?'

'We don't know.'

'But you must have some ideas?'

Highman looked her in the eye. 'I am not going to sit here and speculate.'

'But presumably you will be required to indulge in some speculation when it comes to your final report?'

Highman shrugged. 'The National Audit Office will inevitably demand some kind of explanation.'

'I'm sure they will,' she sniffed.

'No doubt we will all then have questions to answer.' *Some more than others.*

'Mm.'

'A collective failure of control and monitoring would appear to run all the way through the organization.'

'All the way to the top?'

Surprised to see that his glass was now empty, he looked up. 'Yes.'

Mosman drained her own glass and poured herself another. She didn't offer him a refill. 'So I'm going to be hung out to dry?'

'I wouldn't like to pre-empt what might happen.'

There was a sound in the doorway and Mosman lifted her gaze past her colleague's shoulder. 'Can I help you?' Before Highman could turn round to see who it was, he felt a cool pressure in the hollow at the base of his skull. A look of horror flashed across Mosman's face as she jumped from her chair. There was a grunt, followed by a metallic click, and then Highman felt himself pitching forward into darkness.

Pulling a box of Handi Wipes from a desk drawer, Zoe Mosman began furiously wiping Harris Highman's blood splatter from her face. 'What the hell did you do that for?' She reached instinctively for her glass of whisky but her hand was shaking so much that she only succeeded in knocking it to the floor. 'Fuck it!' Unscrewing the cap, she took a long hard swallow directly from the bottle. And then another. She would have a monster fucking hangover in the morning, but right now that was the least of her worries.

The man standing over Highman's body said nothing. She had no idea who he was but she knew perfectly well who had sent him.

Feeling distinctly woozy, Mosman placed a hand on the desk for some support. 'How are we going to clean this mess up?'

'We're not.' Slowly the man lifted the gun, giving her time to finally understand what was going on, before firing twice.

Bringing the Audi A3 to a halt at the side of the kerb, Toby Gray tried to keep his voice sounding casual. 'Any chance of a coffee?'

Maude Hall smiled. Toby was okay but it was only their second date, and he was a long way from getting invited into her flat 'for coffee'. She yawned theatrically. 'It's late and I've got an early start in the morning. Maybe next time.'

'Sure, no problem.'

'Thanks. I had a nice time.' Undoing her seatbelt, she reached across and gave him a peck on the cheek.

'Me too,' Toby blushed.

'I'll give you a call.' Opening the door, she slipped out into the cold night air.

Standing in the entrance hall of Murdoch Mansions, Maude listened to the Audi pulling away from the kerb. Picking up her mail, she slowly climbed the stairs to her first-floor flat. Reaching the door, she carefully placed the key in the lock.

'Jenny . . .'

Frowning, she turned to face Trevor Miller.

'Or should I say Maude?'

'What the fuck is someone doing, out riding a bike at this time of night?' Marcus Evans made a vigorous hand gesture through the windscreen. 'Oi, fuckface! Get out the way.'

Gripping the steering wheel tightly, Dennis Smith swerved

round the cyclist and accelerated across the otherwise almost empty Blackfriars Bridge, heading north.

'Fucking hell, Den, how fast can this thing go?'

'I've had it up to over ninety,' Smith grinned, 'but don't tell the boss.' Foot to the floor, he started drumming on the steering wheel of the Vauxhall Combo. 'Spurs were good tonight.'

'For a fucking change.'

'Against shit opposition though.'

'You can only beat what's put in front of you,' Evans mused. Right on cue, a caller on 5Live was making the same point, before concluding, 'We're only two or three quality signings away from being a great team.'

'We're *always* two or three quality signings away from being a great team, you dick,' Smith grunted towards the radio. Flicking on the indicator light, he lifted his foot off the accelerator. 'How do I get on to Queen Victoria Street? Can I turn left up here?' Looking for a sign, he didn't see the man in the suit step out from behind the number 63 bus, which was heading south. Head down, he was talking into his mobile phone as he wandered into the middle of the road.

'Fuck!' Evans screamed. Before his mate even had time to touch the brakes, there was a huge thud and the windscreen shattered.

'Fuuuuccccckkkkk!!!' The steering wheel spun out of his hands and Den watched in horror as the van roared across on to the wrong side of the road, heading directly for the water.

Standing on Blackfriars Bridge, the inspector gazed east, past St Paul's and the City, towards Docklands. The sky was a deep blue, full of promise, and there was a pleasing nip in the air. Another day: busy people simply getting on with their lives. 'What a great city.' Breathing in deeply, he turned to his sergeant. 'What a fucking *great* city!'

'I beg your pardon?' Joe Szyszkowski was nowhere to be seen. Instead, Carlyle found himself talking to a pimply youth whom he had never seen before. In an ill-fitting suit, with an appallingly bad bog-brush haircut, the kid stood maybe an inch or two taller than the inspector himself. Hopping from foot to foot, he had a pained expression as if he urgently needed the bathroom.

'Who are you?' Carlyle asked, suitably unimpressed.

'Eric Peterson.' Fumbling in the pocket of his raincoat, the youth pulled out a business card. 'Transport for London and Special Adviser to the Mayor.' He tentatively offered the card. Hands kept firmly in his pockets, the inspector ignored it.

'What are you doing here?' Carlyle gestured towards the south end of the bridge and the yellow police tape flapping in the wind. 'You should be behind the cordon.'

The youth stood his ground. 'We need to get this bridge open.'

Carlyle's eyes narrowed.

'There are roadworks on Waterloo Bridge,' Peterson explained, 'and London Bridge is closed for repairs. If we don't get Blackfriars open there's going to be total chaos.'

'There's always chaos,' Carlyle grunted.

'Improved transport routes are one of the Mayor's key deliverables. We are already six percentage points down on where we were projected to be this month, in terms of improved traffic flows. That means we are on course for having to provide the Assembly with a written explanation. It is imperative—'

What the fuck is the little sod talking about? Stepping forward, the inspector cut Eric Peterson off with an angry wave of his hand. 'This,' he said slowly, 'is a crime scene.'

Folding his arms, the young bureaucrat shook his head, annoying Carlyle even more.

'The point is—'

'The point *is*,' Carlyle stepped right up to the guy and jabbed a finger towards his face, 'people have died here. My job is to find out what happened, and that will take however long it takes. So kindly fuck off behind the tape there, or I will have you arrested for obstruction and wasting police time.'

'The Mayor will not be happy,' Peterson huffed.

'The Mayor will not be happy,' Carlyle parroted. Out of the

corner of his eye, he noticed Joe approaching. Even at this distance, it was clear that his sidekick had the deathly pallor of a man who had done a full night's work.

'Not in the slightest.' Confronted by the policeman's full-on hostility, Peterson's bottom lip had started to quiver and it looked like he might burst into tears at any moment.

'Well, tough shit. The Mayor's re-election prospects are not my concern.' For a second time, Carlyle pointed towards the tape. 'Now *fuck off.*'

'Who was that?' Joe asked as he watched Eric Peterson slouch off towards the tape.

'Just another fucking idiot sent by the powers-that-be to try my patience,' Carlyle sighed. 'What have you got for me?'

Gesturing in the direction whence he had come, the sergeant held up a clear plastic evidence bag containing a mobile phone. 'We found this in the gutter back there. It's been fairly bashed up but the SIM card should still be fine. We think it must belong to our guy.'

Our guy. Carlyle smiled. 'That's a fucking result.'

'And a half.'

'So, tell me what happened.'

'What we *think* happened?'

'Yeah, your best guess.'

'Okay.' Joe took a deep breath. 'Based on what we've pieced together so far, from CCTV and a couple of eye-witnesses, the assumption is that our guy went into the Government Art Collection building over there,' he pointed past the statue of Queen Victoria towards an office block on the north-east corner of the bridge, 'and shot both Harris Highman and Zoe Mosman. Then he waltzes out and starts crossing the bridge, heading towards where we are now. After tossing his gun into the river, he makes a call on his mobile. Deciding to cross the road, he walks out from behind a bus and gets taken out by Fred's Fabulous Fruit 'n' Veg van, which is coming the other way at somewhere north of eighty miles an hour.'

Fred's Fabulous Fruit 'n' Veg? The name vaguely rang a bell but Carlyle couldn't immediately place it, so he let it slide.

Joe pointed towards the ragged hole in the fencing almost exactly in the middle of the bridge. 'The van careers across the road, taking the pedestrian with it, then crashes through the barrier – and *splash*!'

The pedestrian, meaning the shooter.

'Out-fucking-standing,' Carlyle grinned, gazing down at the pontoon from where police divers were trying to recover the bodies. 'How long till we get an ID?'

'Dunno,' Joe shrugged. 'If we can work it out from the phone, maybe a couple of hours. If not, we'll have to wait for the river to give him up. They reckon there are two guys still inside the van but they haven't found the pedestrian yet.'

'All three are sleeping with the fishes?'

'Not down there, they're not,' Joe laughed. 'They probably died of poisoning rather than drowning.'

'I thought the Thames was supposed to be cleaner these days?'

'I dunno about that.' Joe pointed at the murky grey-brown water. 'I mean, look at it.'

'Fair point.' Carlyle returned his attention to the bridge itself. 'Anyway, this is probably the most excitement they've had here since Calvi in the early eighties.'

'Eh?'

'Roberto Calvi, God's banker.'

Joe still looked at him blankly.

'He was an Italian banker, with links to the Mafia, the Masons and the Vatican, yada, yada, yada.'

'Clever boy.'

'Yeah. His bank went bust and he was found hanged underneath the arches, weighed down with bricks and fifteen grand still in his pockets.'

'Before my time,' said Joe with the air of a man having more pressing things to worry about.

'Mine too,' Carlyle mused. 'Just.' A thought suddenly struck him. 'Where's Maude, by the way?'

'Haven't been able to get hold of her so far this morning.' Joe held up the battered mobile again. 'I'll go and get this checked out.'

'Fine,' Carlyle nodded. 'Then go and see Mrs Mosman's lawyer. Tell him, if he's withholding anything from us, I will make sure that he faces conspiracy charges.'

'Conspiracy to do what?'

'We'll work that out later.'

'Fine,' Joe laughed, walking away.

Considering his next move, the inspector turned his attention back to the vista in front of him, ignoring the angry horns of snarled-up traffic on both sides of the bridge. Right here, right now, London was his.

What a great fucking city.

THIRTY-FIVE

'What we are doing here, in a very real sense, is parlaying food into a branch of performance art.' Standing in the mud of the Funky Food Field, Liam Shakermaker popped a cube of his award-winning *Everything's Gone Green* brand of organic goat's cheese into his mouth and began chewing thoughtfully. In his deerstalker hat, tweed jacket and plus fours, he looked like a country squire from a 1950s Ealing comedy.

'Mm, yes,' Edgar Carlton mumbled, uncomfortably aware of a journalist hovering on the edge of their conversation, digital recorder in hand. At least it wasn't raining – yet – and there was no sign of Sonia Claesens. But he felt horribly exposed, all the same. Where the hell was Trevor Miller? Anastasia had taken the kids off to have a go at milking some goats, while he suspected that his Head of Security had sneaked off to the real ale tent.

Shakermaker finished chewing and offered Edgar a taste from the plate of samples sitting on a beer barrel that doubled as a table. 'Why don't you try some? It's delicious.'

'I'm sure.' Edgar tried not to grimace. He wasn't a cheese man.

'I make it at my organic farm in East Sussex. One hundred per cent natural ingredients, and we follow a traditional recipe used by Ancient Britons since the time of Stonehenge.'

Edgar held up a hand. 'I've already tried some,' he lied. 'Very nice.' Somehow, he managed to drag a smile across his face. 'Very nice indeed.'

'Food is the new rock'n'roll,' Shakermaker mused, dropping

another cube into his maw. 'In fact, it's why I gave up rock'n'roll.'

'Of course,' said Edgar, looking round desperately for someone to save him from this idiot. 'You were in the . . . ?'

'Heathen Physics,' Shakermaker grinned, naming his largely forgotten band. 'I played keyboards and tambourine. And the occasional triangle.'

'Ah, yes,' Edgar nodded. 'Of course.'

'Kings of Britpop.'

'Mm.' The PM was more a Spandau Ballet man himself: anything after 'Gold' left him rather cold.

An idea floated through Shakermaker's brain. 'Maybe you could start serving *Everything's Gone Green* cheese at Number Ten.'

Edgar frowned.

'You know, at receptions and that.'

'Well . . .'

'It could be part of a celebration of the new wave of British cuisine,' continued Shakermaker, slipping into marketeering mode. 'You know that we already export to more than twenty countries.'

'It's an idea,' Edgar agreed. 'I will talk to the Cabinet Secretary about it.' It would give Sir Gavin O'Dowd something to do.

'Cool.' Winking at the journalist, Shakermaker gave Edgar a hearty slap on the back. Christ, thought the PM sourly, I'm being set up by a bloody cheese maker.

'It's a bit early for that, isn't it?'

'We're stuck in the middle of a muddy field, waiting for a KT-fucking-Tunstall concert.' Sonia Claesens defiantly downed the rest of her large glass of Pinot Auxerrois and signalled for the bartender to pour her another. 'It's time to either get pissed or throw yourself under a tractor.'

Seymour Rowntree tried to recall who KT Tunstall was but couldn't quite manage to place her.

'Or maybe walk straight into a combine harvester.'

Seymour realized that he was getting seriously bored with this cougar thing. The fact that his girlfriend here was only two-and-a-half years younger than his mother didn't bother him; after all, Sonia was a good-looking woman, she had cash, and she got invited to cool parties every night of the week. But she could also be bloody hard work. And her moods recently had become terrible. Maybe it was time to go back to his Spaces and Objects course at Central St Martin's and start fucking some girls his own age, or thereabouts.

'Folk rock is such *shit*.'

'Stop winding yourself up.' Seymour looked around nervously. Fortunately there was no one around to listen to her ranting. 'We didn't have to come here.'

'That bastard flunky of Edgar Carlton's can't tell *me* what to do,' Sonia hissed. 'He can't tell me what to do and where to go. What next? House arrest? Fucking politicians, we own them. We fucking *own* them. And the moment there's any turbulence, they think they can just run off and pretend they've got some fucking principles.' The bartender placed a fresh glass of wine on the bar. Sonia fished a fifty-pound note out of her purse and slapped it down. 'Just leave the bottle. Thanks.' Dropping the purse into her Chloe Marcie python tote, she took out a packet of Regal King Size and a lighter.

The bartender shook his head. 'I'm sorry, but you can't smoke in here.'

'What do you mean, I can't smoke in here?' Sonia squawked. 'We're in a fucking *tent*! I haven't seen this much fresh air since my bloody Duke of Edinburgh course.'

'Sonia . . .' Seymour placed a hand on her arm and she shook it off. This damn toyboy was becoming more hassle than he was worth. He might be hung like a donkey but he had the brain of one as well.

'Just fuck off.' Lifting her glass, she tilted back her throat and downed the contents in one, before storming towards the exit.

* * *

Liam Shakermaker squinted at Edgar from behind his Tom Ford aviator sunglasses. 'You know, I never realized just how interesting cheese could be. I can honestly say that it gives me as much pleasure as cocaine did twenty years ago.'

Edgar simply had no idea how to respond to that. A female TV presenter wandered past and he tried, unsuccessfully, to catch her eye. Taking matters into his own hands, he pulled out his phone. 'Excuse me for a second.' Looking for a quiet corner of the field, he scrolled through his contacts. But who to call? He was the Prime Minister, therefore other people usually called *him*. Finding Yulissa's number on the screen, he hit the call button, staring with resigned dismay at the mud on his Loake tan brogues as he listened to the ringtone.

'Edgar.'

'What?' Turning to face his wife, he quickly ended the call. 'Yes?'

Anastasia had one of those stock 'cross looks' on her face. 'Why are you hiding over here?'

'I wanted to ... er ... check out some of the gardening workshops.' He gestured lamely at a handwritten sign that read: *Success with seeds and cuttings*.

Anastasia ignored this blatant lie. 'The children want you to take them to *Charlie & Lola Live!*'

'Why can't Pammi do it?' he whined. 'Isn't that what we bloody pay her for?' The thought of having to sit through a stage version of some kiddies' cartoon made his heart sink to a new low.

'Because,' said Anastasia firmly, 'lovely though she is, the children have already spent all week with the au pair. At the weekend, believe it or not, they would like to spend some quality time with their father.'

'I seriously doubt that,' Edgar grumbled.

'Anyway, if they spend any more time with that girl than they do already, they're going to sound as if they come from Sydney!'

'Well, whose fault is that? You're the one who hired a bloody

Australian nanny off Skype!' He shook his head at the folly of it all. It had taken the *Daily Mirror* about ten seconds to find Pammi Kewell on Facebook – complete with pictures of her smoking the biggest spliff you had ever seen in your life. His wife might have laughed it off, but it was another PR disaster he could have done without.

'For God's sake,' Anastasia nagged, 'pull yourself together. We both agreed she was the best one for the job.'

Edgar grunted non-committally. He had been secretly hoping for some blonde East European hard body, a cross between Mary Poppins and a Moscow call girl, but the au pair agency had singularly failed to deliver on that one. Taking a deep breath, he told himself that there really was no point in going over this same old argument for the umpteenth time. He was just about to cave in and head off dutifully to see *Charlie & Lola*, when he caught sight of Sonia Claesens steaming out of the Wonderful Wessex Wine tent on the far side of the field, with her callow boyfriend trailing after her. Spotting her quarry, Sonia made a beeline towards the Carltons, a look of grim determination on her face.

'Oh, no.' Edgar was about to turn and run when he felt a firm hand on his shoulder.

'I'm very sorry, Mrs Carlton,' said Trevor Miller, bowing ever so lightly, 'but I need to get you and your husband out of here right now.'

The Prime Minister's wife contemplated Miller as she might inspect some cow shit on her shoe. The man had cuts and bruises all over his face, looking like he'd recently been in a fight. 'What happened to you?' she asked.

'We need to go,' Miller repeated.

'But I wanted to see KT Tunstall,' Edgar objected.

'Sorry, sir,' said Miller, already pushing him towards a waiting Range Rover. 'Maybe next time.'

'I was wondering when you were likely to turn up.' Sitting in a largely empty Starbucks situated a block from the Fulham police station, Sergeant Fiona Singleton cradled her grande cafe mocha carefully, as she settled back into her seat.

'It's been on my "to do" list for a while,' Carlyle admitted apologetically, 'but stuff keeps getting in the way.'

'I know what you mean.' She nodded sympathetically. 'And anyway, it's not as if Rosanna Snowdon is really your problem, is it?' A thin, thoughtful woman with a rather unflattering pageboy haircut, it was over a year since Carlyle had last seen her. Although she had to be a good fifteen years younger than the inspector, it crossed his mind that she seemed to have aged considerably during that time. The ring on her wedding finger suggested that she'd got married as well. Maybe the two things were not unconnected.

'No,' Carlyle shrugged, 'but you know how . . .'

Singleton understood. That didn't mean, however, that she had much time to help him out. She glanced at her watch. 'I can't hang around, I'm afraid. Got a case meeting about a bunch of car thieves who have been relieving the locals of their Chelsea tractors at an alarming rate.'

'Poor dears,' Carlyle scoffed. SUV owners were not high on his sympathy list. In fact, they weren't on that list at all.

'We'll get 'em soon enough,' Singleton grinned. 'Anyway, where do you now want to start?'

Carlyle looked down at the small cup that had previously contained his double espresso. It was already empty, he noted sadly. 'Simon Lovell,' he said. 'Have you actually seen him?'

'A couple of times.' From behind her own outsized cup, Singleton made a face. 'If anything, he seems even weirder than the last time round.'

'If his original confession to the Snowdon killing was ruled inadmissible,' Carlyle said, 'the new DNA evidence must be strong?'

'I don't know about that. There's still a lot of pressure to get a result on this one, coming from the media and the family.'

'I thought that Rosanna's parents were dealing with it quite well.' *Under the circumstances.*

'Oh, they are,' Singleton agreed. 'Very dignified, indeed, but you know what it's like. The father still has some political clout, and Rosanna was herself a bit of a celebrity.'

'Yeah, yeah,' Carlyle sighed. 'Who's Lovell's lawyer these days?'

'He's acquired a few, as you could imagine, but the main one's still a woman called Abigail Slater.'

Carlyle shook his head. 'Never heard of her.'

'Ambulance-chasing bitch. She'll have made a real killing on Legal Aid by now, but she's only going through the motions, if you ask me. It's a high-profile case and she likes that kind of attention – wants all the publicity she can get.'

'Lawyers,' Carlyle groaned. He didn't like them any more than anyone else did.

'Slater will string this thing out for as long as she can, but she's only delaying the inevitable. You can tell the parents that they'll probably get a result this time.'

'Probably?'

Singleton thought about it for a moment. 'Almost certainly.'

'That's not the same as saying he did it,' Carlyle grumped.

Singleton's eyes narrowed. 'Whose side are you on?'

'I'm not on anyone's side,' Carlyle replied, rather too sharply. 'The Job is not about taking sides. I want this case closed – for Rosanna and for her parents, of course.'

'But?'

'But it comes down to reasonable doubt. Unless I'm missing something here, we still don't actually know that he did it.'

'The DNA?'

'Maybe.'

'Well,' Singleton sniffed, '*I* think that he probably did it.'

Carlyle gave her an enquiring look. 'Fair enough, but is that good enough? You don't *know*. No one does.'

'No,' she said, reasonableness personified, 'but *you* can't say for sure that he didn't do it either, can you?'

The inspector felt a bubble of frustration growing in his chest.

The ability of people to believe what they wanted to believe – what it suited them to believe – annoyed the hell out of him. 'If this is bullshit, we're just going to end up making ourselves look stupid again.'

'I honestly don't think it is bullshit,' Singleton said stubbornly. 'Look at all the other crazy theories knocking about – Russian hitmen, angry viewers, and all that crap. Dear old Mr Lovell was always the only credible suspect. It wasn't like we had to beat the crap out of him to get his original confession either.'

Carlyle nodded. The sergeant had a point.

'Anyway, you're not the one who's had this case sitting on your desk for the last couple of years.' Singleton was then distracted as her mobile began vibrating across the café table. 'Shit.' Putting down her cup, she grabbed the phone and answered it. 'I'm coming,' she said quickly, before whoever was on the other end of the call had time to say anything. 'I'm just round the corner. I'll be there in two minutes.' Ending the call, she said, 'Sorry, but I'm really under the cosh today.'

'No worries.' Carlyle held up a hand. 'It was good to have a catch-up.'

'This might be of more use.' Rooting around in her shoulder bag, Singleton pulled out an A4 manila envelope stuffed with papers. 'These are copies of some of the stuff we found in Rosanna's flat. They might be of interest – and if nothing else, the parents might want to have them. But make sure these get properly looked after. After all, the case has still to be concluded.'

'Of course,' said Carlyle, accepting the envelope from her. He was grateful for her thoughtfulness, because Singleton needn't have bothered. She was putting herself out here and he was genuinely grateful. 'Thanks.'

'No problem.' Hoisting the bag over her shoulder, she got to her feet. 'You can return the favour one day.'

'It'll be my pleasure,' Carlyle smiled.

As she disappeared out of the door, his gaze fell on the largely untouched mocha. *What a waste of an expensive cup of coffee.* With an unhappy sigh, he ripped open the envelope and pulled out a stack of papers more than an inch thick. 'That's a lot of reading,' he mumbled to himself. Top of the pile was a selection of stories printed off from the BBC website. The inspector was just about to start reading when his phone vibrated in the breast pocket of his jacket. Looking at the screen, he saw that he had already accumulated four missed calls.

Bloody phones. How the hell did that happen?

Tutting, he answered it. 'Yeah?'

'Boss, it's Joe.' His sergeant's voice sounded strained. 'Where the hell are you?'

Filled with light, the flat was spartan but not depressing; 550 square feet on the top floor of a converted Victorian mansion block in Tufnell Park, divided into a bedroom, bathroom and tiny kitchen/living room. Hands resting on hips, Carlyle stood behind the breakfast bar, trying to stay out of the way of the technicians as they went about their business.

Inside, he wanted to cry.

'It looks like she put up a hell of a fight.' Joe Szyszkowski appeared from the landing, looking ashen-faced.

The inspector nodded. He couldn't bear to go and view the body. All he could think about was that, in all likelihood, he himself was responsible for her death.

'What about the neighbours?'

Joe shook his head. 'Nothing.'

'For fuck's sake!' Carlyle threw up his hands in despair. 'Someone must have seen something!' The general public were never of any help when you needed it, always in your face when you didn't.

Joe dropped his gaze to the floor. 'Her father . . .'

Carlyle grimaced. 'Yes?'

'He's waiting downstairs.'

* * *

For a man who must have been somewhere in his late fifties, Mervyn Hall was in good shape. Stocky but without any signs of middle-age spread, he looked like he could step back into the boxing ring at a moment's notice. It had taken Carlyle a good ten minutes to persuade Maude's father that they should stay away from Maude's flat and leave the crime scene to Forensics. He felt sick to his stomach telling the man that he couldn't see his daughter, but it was for the best. The poor bastard would have to formally identify the body soon enough. For now, they sat in uncomfortable silence in an empty café on Brecknock Road, a block away from the flat, both lost in their respective thoughts. Meanwhile the rest of the city continued about its business as usual, untroubled by the violence that had turned their world on its head.

Shit happens.

Life goes on.

No one really gives a fuck.

After an eternity of staring into his greasy black coffee, Hall looked up, clearing his throat. 'So what happens now?'

Carlyle finished his espresso. It was disgusting. What he really wanted, he decided, was a large glass of Jameson's, or maybe more. His gaze lingered on Willy's Saloon Bar, the Irish pub across the road, before returning to Hall. 'Now,' he sighed, 'we have to find out who did this.'

Leaning across the table, Hall placed a hand on the inspector's forearm. 'Make sure you do. And then, let me know.'

'Of course,' Carlyle nodded.

'And I will kill the fucker.'

The inspector really did need that drink. 'I didn't know Maude for very long,' he said finally, 'but I really enjoyed working with her. She had great energy and charm, and she was an excellent police officer.' Looking round, he realized that Hall wasn't listening to him. He was busy typing a text message on his mobile.

'I've got to go and see Maude's mum,' he said, hitting the send button. Pulling a pen from his jacket pocket, he scribbled down a mobile phone number on a napkin and handed it to Carlyle. 'Let me know when I can see my daughter.' Slowly getting to his feet, he looked down on the inspector, his expression more detached than grim. 'And remember what I said.'

'Mister . . .'

Carlyle looked up from his papers to see a blonde girl in a red Michael Jackson T-shirt, green bikini bottoms and a pair of brown cowboy boots standing at his table with an impatient look on her face. 'Pardon?'

She began waving a pint glass in front of his face. The glass was empty apart from a couple of pound coins and a fifty-pence piece, which rattled about noisily. 'Put some money in the glass and I will do a dance.' She gestured with the glass towards the tiny stage that had been raised maybe eight inches off the floor at the far end of the room. In the middle of the stage was a pole. Another girl, in a grubby yellow evening dress, was giving it a clean ahead of the next performance with some Cif anti-bacterial spray and a rag.

'A pound,' the girl repeated. He guessed that her accent was West Country, or maybe Welsh.

Embracing the warm, comforting buzz of the whiskey, Carlyle looked around the bar. The lunchtime rush was over and the only other patron he could see was an old guy sitting at a nearby table with his head stuck in the *Racing Post*.

'I don't want to watch a dance.'

The girl shook the glass angrily. 'It's only a pound, you cheap git.'

With a sigh, Carlyle brought out his warrant card and waved it at the girl. 'Fuck off and leave me alone.'

Muttering to herself, she turned and stalked off, wiggling her ample rear as she did so. If you're going to make it as a stripper, Carlyle thought to himself, you'll have to work on that arse. Finishing his drink, he returned to the stack of papers that Fiona Singleton had given to him earlier in the day. Delving back into the Rosanna Snowdon case offered him some kind of excuse for delaying his return to Maude Hall's flat, and he was more than happy to accept it.

On top of the pile was one of the stories that had been printed out from the BBC website. At the top, in red pen, was written *LC?*

LC – that was fairly straightforward since Rosanna had presented a television show called *London Crime*. Presumably she had been considering this as a potential item at the time of her death.

The inspector began reading further.

The article was the best part of three years old. It concerned the unsolved murder of a private investigator called Anton Fox. The inspector thought about that for a moment, but the name didn't ring any bells. Apparently, five years ago, Mr Fox had been found in the car park of a West London pub with an axe in his head. The vague suggestion in this BBC piece was that Fox had been chasing down alleged police corruption. However, no one had ever been brought to trial.

Reading the story, Carlyle had the frustrating sense of lots of pieces of unconnected information floating round in his brain. He knew that somehow he had to try and find a common thread that would pull everything together.

And then he reached the crucial paragraph.

There it was, also ringed in red pen – the name of Fox's employer at the time of his untimely demise: Wickford Associates.

Wickford Associates.

Carlyle smiled.

Wickford fucking Associates.

It was time to give Charlie Ross a call.

Without warning, Spandau Ballet's 'True' started blaring from the speakers above the bar. The girl in the cowboy boots skipped on to the stage, the Jacko T-shirt now discarded to reveal a pair of nipple tassels attached to her over-inflated breasts. As she reached for the sparkling pole, the grandad did not look up from his form guide. Scooping up his papers, Carlyle got to his feet and jogged to the door.

'The shit I have to put up with . . .'

It's not just me then, Carlyle thought happily.

Carole Simpson read aloud from the report in the evening paper. '*Scotland Yard revealed that a detective sergeant was demoted to constable, and three constables were formally reprimanded for having taken, quote, "an overly aggressive approach to stopping a suspect with unauthorized equipment", unquote.*'

The inspector frowned. He liked to think he was up on the latest in MPS crime-fighting techniques, but this particular fiasco had passed him by. 'What does that mean?'

Simpson flashed him the photo accompanying the story. 'Officers attacked a guy's Mini with baseball bats. In the middle of the rush hour! And they bloody filmed it, of course, so it's all over the sodding internet.'

Despite everything, Carlyle couldn't help but laugh. 'Why?'

'Despite a three-year, two-million-pound investigation that involved – amongst other things – bugging Southfield police station to listen in on their private conversations, we never actually got to the bottom of that,' Simpson grumped.

'Surprise, surprise.'

'Anyway, that's done. Now we have other things to worry about.' Closing the newspaper, Simpson folded it in half and dropped it into the cardboard box sitting on the floor by Carlyle's desk that served as a waste-bin. 'I understand that you spoke to Maude Hall's father?'

'Yeah.' Carlyle glanced at his watch. 'He should have formally identified the body by now.'

The look on the Commander's face – a mixture of sadness and concern – was deeply unsettling. Carlyle found her anger much easier to deal with. 'I truly hope, John, that you didn't do anything that contributed to the poor girl getting killed.'

Sitting back in his chair, Carlyle lifted his gaze to the ceiling, but said nothing.

'The investigation into Hall's killing has to be fast and flawless. We simply cannot drop the ball on this.' Simpson mentioned the name of a DI – some woman whom Carlyle had never heard of. 'She is in charge now, and whatever it needs, she gets. Make sure you provide every possible cooperation, while staying well out of the way.'

'Sure,' Carlyle nodded vigorously. Standard operating procedure dictated that he couldn't be seen to take part in the investigation because of a potential conflict of interest. But reading between the lines, Simpson was giving him the green light to get on with finding Hall's killer. 'With the Mosman thing out of the way, I can clear the decks.'

'What do you mean?' Simpson asked sharply.

Carlyle paused. Maybe he was misreading the signals, after all? *What the hell.* He ploughed on regardless. 'Well, with Zoe Mosman murdered, I think we've reached a dead end.'

'Don't give me that crap,' Simpson snorted. 'Whoever put a bomb under Horatio Mosman, it wasn't his bloody mother.'

'I don't know,' Carlyle shrugged. 'Not everyone is naturally cut out to be a parent.'

'Now is simply not the time for any of your juvenile humour, John.' Simpson looked like she wanted to reach over and give him a good hard slap. 'How many times do I have to tell you that the Mosman case is your priority? Why do you never bloody listen? Why can you never just focus on the cases you've been given rather than running off elsewhere like an incontinent puppy?'

Now might not be the best time to mention Rosanna Snowdon and Anton Fox either, Carlyle thought, stifling a nervous laugh. 'An incontinent puppy?'

'You know what I mean.'

'Okay, okay.' He held up a hand. 'We're on the case.'

'Good,' said Simpson sternly. 'Get on with it or I'll go and get one of those baseball bats out of the Evidence Room and beat you round the head with it.'

Gripping his pint of London Pride so tightly that it felt as if the glass might disintegrate, Charlie Ross tried to remember the last time he'd felt this angry. Probably not since his second wife had run off with one of the neighbours. In the event, that had turned out to be a blessing in disguise. This, however, was a total car crash, pure and simple.

The temptation to take his glass and smash it into Trevor Miller's stupid mug was almost overwhelming. The boy had always been a liability – all the way back to the miners' strike when he attacked that woman. How Miller had ever made it through the door of Downing Street would forever be one of life's great mysteries.

It's your own bloody fault, Charlie reproached himself. When Miller had come to him with the idea for Wickford Associates, he should have known that it was always going to go tits-up. At the time, however, he had been happy enough to come along for the ride.

'So what are we going to do now?' Miller asked, hiding behind his bottle of Mexican lager.

'Keep your voice down,' Charlie hissed. The pub, a dive off the Gray's Inn Road, was largely empty but there was no harm in being paranoid.

Miller adopted an appropriate whisper. 'What do you think?' His face had the worried look of a ten year old who'd been caught stealing sweets from his local newsagent. A monster ten year old, but a little kid all the same. 'Is it all going to blow over?'

It was questions like these that had left Charlie tossing and turning all night. At his age, sleep was hard enough at the best of times. At the moment, he couldn't be getting more than a couple of hours a night. He felt weary to his bones.

'What are we going to do?'

Having reached no kind of conclusion, Charlie just shrugged. 'Well,' he murmured, 'I don't see what else we can do except press on with the current plan.'

THIRTY-SIX

'Have you ever heard of a guy called Anton Fox?'

'Yeah,' Carlyle said. 'He was a private investigator who got murdered in a pub car park.'

'That's right.' Dominic Silver yawned. Nine-thirty in the morning was still a bit early for him, given the nocturnal company he kept.

'You need some coffee?'

'Peppermint tea is fine.' Sitting in a Dean Street café, they were comparing notes. 'The Fox case remains open, as you are doubtless aware – you being a police inspector and all.'

Carlyle scowled; he was in no mood to have his leg pulled. 'All right, all right, get on with it.'

'Okay.' Dom placed his cup on the table and spread his arms wide. 'Gideon tracked down Bella Fox, Anton's sister. That didn't take him long.'

Carlyle nodded: they both knew that Gideon Spanner was extremely efficient and totally reliable.

'She's a teacher, living in Southend.'

'Nice.'

'I went to see her last night.'

'You know,' Carlyle laughed, 'you might make a decent copper yet.'

'Wish I could say the same for you, sunshine,' Dom grinned. 'Anyway, Bella says that, just before he was killed, Anton was convinced he was being targeted by the *Sunday Witness*. He told her that they had him under surveillance.'

'But wasn't he working for them?' Carlyle frowned. 'Indirectly, I mean, through Wickford Associates?'

'Yeah. This is where it all gets rather messy. What I *think* happened is that Anton, off his own bat, had been chasing down evidence of police corruption: officers taking backhanders from journalists in exchange for information and also for phone numbers that could be hacked.'

'A bit close to home,' Carlyle mused.

'For sure,' Dom agreed. 'Of course, if he did have evidence, the irony was that the only thing he could usefully do with such information was to give it to someone else in the press.'

And that someone would doubtless be Rosanna Snowdon, Carlyle thought, and her *London Crime* show. He felt a jolt of adrenalin; things were finally falling into place.

'But that meant that Anton was going up against both his employer and the company's number-one client.'

'So they killed him?' Carlyle still wasn't convinced.

Dom shrugged. 'He went to the Princess Ottoline pub in Hammersmith to meet a contact, and ended up with a terminal headache.'

The inspector let out a long breath. 'It's all speculation.'

'Absolutely. But you know Trevor Miller. You know Charlie Ross. Both of them are nasty bastards in the extreme. They had stumbled into a nice little business and wouldn't want anyone to mess it up.'

Carlyle let his gaze lose focus as he stared out of the window, realizing that they still had a way to go to join all the dots. He thought of Anton Fox, Rosanna Snowdon and Maude Hall. 'Do you think he could have killed them all?' he asked, keeping his voice low.

'Trevor?' Dom wrinkled his nose. 'Why not? That fucking idiot is capable of anything – anything stupid, that is.'

'Fu-uck! What a mess.'

'Yes, but you might be able to get your man.'

'How?'

Dom took another mouthful of tea. 'I would lean on Simon Shelbourne.'

'The Commissioner's PR man?'

Dom nodded. 'Before he became Editor of the *Sunday Witness*, he covered the crime beat for the paper. Bella says that he was close to Anton. She says that Shelbourne promised Anton fifty grand for some big story just before he died.'

'What story?' Carlyle demanded.

'Dunno. What I *do* know, however, is that our Mr Shelbourne has been interviewed by Operation Redhead officers . . . twice.'

The inspector smacked his head. 'Fuck's sake!' Bloody Chief Inspector Russell Meyer, why hadn't he mentioned any of this?

'Both times,' Dom continued, 'he denied having any contact with Fox.'

'So why do you think *I* would be able to get any more out of him?'

'Shelbourne is weak,' Dom continued, 'both physically and mentally. I could get Gideon to have a word with him. He'd crumble in less than five minutes. Tell you whatever you want.'

'Mm.' Carlyle had to admit, the idea had much to commend it. As he contemplated Gideon getting to work on the ex-Editor, his phone started vibrating. 'Hold that thought. In the meantime, keep on digging. See what else you can find out.'

'Inspector?' said a familiar gravelly voice. 'It's Charlie Ross.'

'Charlie.' Carlyle shot a glance at Dom.

'Are you busy?'

'I'm always busy. What can I do for you?'

'I was wondering if we could meet up.'

On his way to see Charlie Ross, Carlyle took a detour in order to drop in at the Holborn police station on Lamb's Conduit Street. He wanted to speak to Susan Phillips. In the event, he had to wait more than half an hour before the pathologist made an appearance. Sweeping through the reception at a clip, she headed straight for the entrance door, signalling with the slightest nod of her head that he should follow. Carlyle chased after her, but she was going at such a pace that they were halfway towards Coram's Fields before he caught up.

'What are you doing here?' Phillips snapped, not slowing down.

'Nice to see you, too,' Carlyle quipped.

'John, now is really not the time.' Skipping out in front of a taxi, she crossed Great Ormond Street and dived into the Starbucks on the corner, leaving him still standing on the kerbside. By the time he made it inside, she had already ordered a double espresso and a latte and was paying for them with her credit card. 'Get a seat. I'll bring the coffees.'

Stepping back outside, the inspector grabbed a small table that had just been vacated by a couple of tired-looking hospital workers. From his seat, he watched her through the window, chewing nervously on her thumb as she waited for their order. Given that Phillips was just about the most laid-back colleague Carlyle had ever known, it was clear that something must be up.

Sitting back in his chair, Carlyle placed his hands behind his head and smiled to himself.

If something was up, that meant they must have found important new evidence.

'Just don't ask me anything about Maude Hall.' Phillips took a mouthful of her latte as soon as she had handed Carlyle his espresso.

'Thanks.' The last thing the inspector needed was more caffeine, so he placed the small paper cup carefully on the table without taking a sip.

'Because I know that it's not even your case,' said Phillips, lowering herself into the other chair.

'No,' he had to agree.

'Not that you've ever let minor details like that stop you in the past.'

Carlyle held up a hand. 'It's just the way I am, sorry.' He knew

Phillips well enough. Despite the complaining, she would tell him what was going on in her own time.

'Yes, well . . .' Phillips looked around, before leaning across the table, tension etched on her face.

Fuck me, Carlyle thought, I've just walked into a John le Carré novel.

'The shit has really hit the fan on this one,' she whispered.

Or maybe not. Le Carré's characters always spoke so much more eloquently. All that public school and Oxbridge education; money well spent. He tried not to laugh at his own musings.

'Poor Maude Hall put up a hell of a fight.'

'That doesn't surprise me. She was an expert in self-defence.'

Phillips nodded. 'We found traces of skin and blood under her fingernails.'

Carlyle knew where this was going, but he should let her tell it at her own pace.

'And we've got a match.'

I've got the fucker! He wanted to leap in the air and start running down the road, arms pumping in triumph. Instead, he restrained himself.

She looked at him suspiciously. 'What's up?'

'Nothing. Go on.'

Phillips did another sweep of the street, as if looking for spies. 'We've got a match – to a guy who does security for the Prime Minister.'

'Trevor Miller.' Carlyle's self-restraint buckled and he couldn't resist dropping the name in first.

Phillips's eyes narrowed even further. 'You know him?'

'Yeah. How did you make the match?'

'Everyone who works in Downing Street has to go on a DNA database. It took us about ten seconds to find him.'

'Trevor Miller fucks up again.' He had to fight the urge to give Phillips a big kiss. 'Nice.'

The pathologist finished the last of her coffee and tossed the paper cup into a nearby bin. 'But why would he kill a police officer?'

'Because he's a total bastard. And a complete fucking moron.' Carlyle was going to be late for his meeting with Charlie Ross and he didn't have the time – or the inclination – to take Phillips through the whole backstory. 'Who else knows about this?'

'When the results came in, it had to go straight to the top. All the way up to the Commissioner.'

Fuck, he hadn't thought about that. 'When?'

'I dunno, maybe an hour or so ago.'

'Tell me at least that you haven't put it on bloody Twitter.'

'Don't worry,' Phillips chuckled. 'The tweetathon's finished.'

'Thank God for that.' The inspector thought things through for a moment. 'I should give Simpson a heads-up,' he said, making the call there and then. 'And I need you to do me a favour,' he added to Phillips, as he listened to Simpson's phone ringing.

A dark look crossed the pathologist's face. 'But—'

Grimacing, Carlyle held up a finger as the Commander's voicemail kicked in. 'It's me,' he said curtly, 'and it's urgent. Bloody urgent. Call me as soon as you get this message.'

Returning his attention to Phillips, he began talking quickly, keen to override her likely objections to his latest disregard for protocol. 'There's a case that Fulham have been working on for a couple of years, concerning the death of a woman called Rosanna Snowdon.'

'The TV presenter?' said Phillips cautiously, not sure where the inspector was going with this.

'Exactly. I want – I *need* you to check the evidence that they collected and do a read-across from Hall.'

Staring at the sky, Phillips slowly let the implications of what he was asking for sink in. 'That's going to be very tricky.'

'I know.' Fighting his own excitement, Carlyle waited for her to resume eye-contact. 'But speak to a sergeant there called Fiona Singleton. Tell her I suggested it. She's solid.'

'Mm.' Phillips looked dubious.

Carlyle gave her his most earnest stare. 'I've been chasing this bastard for a long time, Susan. I want to get him for *everything*.'

'Okay,' she sighed. 'I'll see what I can do.'

Simpson's phone was still going to voicemail. Without leaving another message, Carlyle put his phone away and scanned the bar of the Adam Tavern, just south of the Euston Road. It took him a few moments to locate Charlie Ross, sitting on his own in a booth at the back, nursing a pint of beer, and then the best part of ten minutes to get served at the bar. By the time he returned to Ross's table with the drinks, the old sergeant's previous glass was empty.

'Thanks.' Ross accepted the pint of Morse Ale and placed it on the table. Still holding his glass of Jameson's, the inspector pulled up a stool.

'My pleasure,' Carlyle lied.

'Your health,' Ross mumbled, lifting the fresh glass to his lips for a modest sup.

'So,' Carlyle asked, keen to get down to business, 'what did you want to talk about?'

Charlie tried – and failed – to do an impersonation of a guileless old man. 'I just wanted to see where you are with your investigation.'

'Don't fuck me about, Charlie,' Carlyle snapped. 'I thought I was getting Trevor Miller's head on a plate.'

'Patience, patience. All in good time.'

Carlyle downed his whiskey in one. He wasn't going to sit around and talk nonsense with this old bastard. 'Trevor is living on borrowed time,' he said, smacking the shot glass down on the table. 'So, give him up – *if* you can give him up – and the better it'll be for you.'

A shit-eating grin spread across Ross's face. 'I know about Anton Fox.'

'Not that crap again.'

The grin ebbed away as Ross placed his glass on a beer mat advertising a gambling website.

'We've been hearing all these stupid stories for years,' Carlyle scoffed. 'That's old news. Who cares who brained that stupid bugger?'

'I also know who did Duncan Brown.'

'Charlie, I know the whole story,' Carlyle told him. 'Not just Fox, not just Brown . . . but the whole fucking thing.'

'You can know what you like,' the old man growled, 'but you have fuck all when it comes to actual evidence.'

The inspector said nothing.

'Otherwise you'd have a fucking warrant,' Charlie's eyes narrowed, 'and I'd be behind bars by now. Am I right?'

Busted. All Carlyle could do was to try and brazen it out. There was no appealing to Ross's better nature because the old sod didn't have a better nature.

'Please,' he said finally, 'don't waste my fucking time. We are talking about multiple murders here – and by former police officers, for Christ's sake. Trevor goes down, you go down too, along with anyone and everyone associated with Wickford Associates and God knows who else. Either you cooperate now or you will die in jail.'

Leaning forward, Ross jabbed a finger towards the inspector's face, the anger clear in his eyes. 'Don't threaten me, sonny. You don't know shit. Without me, you have nothing – and Miller will slip through your hands yet again.'

A voice inside the inspector's head told him to stay calm. He would deal with Charlie Ross in due course. In the meantime, he had to stay focused. 'Okay,' he conceded, letting out a long breath. 'What do you want?'

'Me?' Sitting back on the banquette, Ross folded his arms. 'I don't want anything. Why should I? At my age I'm untouchable.'

'So why are you doing this?'

'Because, given what has happened, I want to fuck Trevor up just as much as you do. This is supposed to be my retirement.

Now I'm having to run about here, there and everywhere, trying to clear up all his shit while he ponces about like he's God's bloody gift.'

The inspector wanted to believe what Ross was saying, but maybe the old bugger was setting him up. Or maybe he was just a bored old man who wanted some attention and someone sitting with him in the pub. 'So where is Trevor now?'

'Somewhere safe.' Ross took another mouthful of beer. 'Waiting for me to tell him what to do next.' He clocked the look of concern that flashed across Carlyle's face and grinned malevolently. 'Don't worry, he's still in the country – for now. He knows that things are going tits-up big time though. If we don't move fast, he'll try and do a runner for sure.'

'So when do I get him?' Carlyle asked, sounding way too eager.

'When the time is right,' Ross replied vaguely.

'And when will that be?'

'When I bloody say so.' He nodded towards the bar. 'In the meantime, why don't you go and get me another pint.'

Licking his lips, Sir Chester Forsyth-Walker eyed the generous glass of Martell XO clutched in the Prime Minister's hand. I've come all the way over to your club to tell you in person about this, he thought, so the least you could do is offer me a bloody drink.

Sadly for the Commissioner, hospitality was not high on Edgar Carlton's current agenda. As a waiter approached, the PM shooed him away with an imperious wave of his free hand. 'How many people know about this?'

With a look of dismay, the Commissioner watched the flunky retreat. 'Not that many. The officer in charge was smart enough to bring it straight to me.'

'Mm.' Edgar knew that wouldn't count for much: news like this would leak faster than the *Titanic* after it had hit the iceberg. Some bugger will have tweeted the news by the time I sit down for dinner, he thought grimly. If they haven't already. 'And there's no doubt about all this? We're sure Miller's guilty?'

Still trying to catch the waiter's eye, Sir Chester replied, 'Yes. The evidence, from what I understand, is fairly compelling.'

'Fine.' Edgar lifted the heavy crystal glass to his lips and drank deeply. He should have known this day would come. That was the thing about politics: all of your people fall by the wayside sooner or later. Then, when you – the chief! – are the last man standing, someone steps up to take you out as well. The actual circumstances might come as a surprise, but the narrative was as inevitable as it was predictable.

In the PM's book, Trevor Miller had always seemed solid, dependable. Obviously, the guy had flipped. Something must have short-circuited in his brain. This was what his spin doctors liked to call 'a game changer'. Edgar had never known what exactly the term meant until now.

Out of the corner of his eye, the PM saw Sir Gavin O'Dowd slip into the room. Waiting until the Cabinet Secretary was within discreet earshot, he asked: 'Is it done?'

'Yes,' Sir Gavin nodded. 'Your new interim Head of Security has been appointed as of,' he looked at his cheap-looking watch, 'twelve minutes ago.' He mentioned a name but Edgar swatted it away. At this moment, the precise details of Trevor Miller's replacement were irrelevant.

'Good. And what are you going to say about Mr Miller himself?'

'When the calls start coming in, the Press Office has been told to adopt a strict "no comment" policy. We will hold to that for as long as possible.'

Sighing theatrically, Edgar looked under-impressed.

O'Dowd gave an apologetic shrug. 'I know that it is less than satisfactory.'

'Even by your exalted standards of insight,' the Prime Minister said drily, 'that is something of an understatement.'

'It is far from satisfactory,' Sir Gavin repeated, the rictus grin

272

on his face looking like it was about to crack. 'But we are where we are. The press team will hold to the line for as long as they can.'

Which will be about six seconds, Sir Chester estimated grimly.

'Only if someone starts running a story about Miller being suspected of murder and on the run will we go to a line against inquiry saying that this is a police matter and that he has been relieved of his duties pending their enquiries.'

A look of extreme annoyance crossed Sir Chester's face as he noticed the large G&T that had just been placed in the Cabinet Secretary's hand. 'What do you want me to do?' he asked.

'You?' Sir Gavin shot the police chief a patronizing smile. 'I think it's probably best if you try to do nothing.'

'Nothing?'

'Just do what you can to stop the information from leaking out. When it eventually does, get your guy to give the press something suitably bland that doesn't make things even worse.'

'You think you can manage that?' Edgar demanded.

'Of course,' said the Commissioner stiffly. Privately, he wondered if even that much was achievable. The whereabouts of 'his guy' was currently a mystery. Much to his boss's annoyance, Simon Shelbourne's mobile had been switched off for the last hour. This was easily the biggest crisis of Sir Chester's career and the stupid little bugger had gone incommunicado.

'Good.' Sir Gavin tasted his gin and gave a small grunt of approval. 'How long do you think it will take to place the . . . er . . . suspect in custody?'

'Impossible to say.' Suffering from the chronic lack of alcohol in his bloodstream, Sir Chester wasn't going to stand there and try to pretend that they had any clue as to Miller's location. 'We are trying to track him down at this very moment, but we have yet to pick up his trail.'

'Pick up his trail?' Edgar complained. 'This is not a bloody fox hunt. He can't have gone far, so get your officers off their arses and damn well find him!'

Sir Gavin shot his boss a look that said *Calm down*. 'I am sure that the Commissioner is making this his number-one priority at the present time.'

'That is absolutely the case,' Sir Chester confirmed. 'Yes.'

'And, as this is a police matter,' Sir Gavin continued, 'we should be doing nothing more than assisting the police in dealing with this most serious and grave situation.'

'Miller's clearly gone totally crazy,' Edgar mused. 'With a bit of luck, he'll do the decent thing and top himself. Save us all a lot of time and trouble, as well as a bundle of taxpayers' money.'

The Commissioner's face brightened slightly. 'Maybe that's what's happened. Maybe he's lying face down in a pool of his own blood somewhere, which explains why he's proving so difficult to find.'

The PM tried to shoot his underling a meaningful look. 'That would be a *result*, as they say.'

Not responding, Sir Gavin stared into his drink.

'Yes, well . . .' Uncomfortably aware of his latest orders, Sir Chester began retreating towards the door. 'I will let you know of any developments.'

'You do that,' said Edgar sternly, signalling to the waiter that his glass needed refilling.

Once the Commissioner had slunk off into the night, the Cabinet Secretary pulled a letter from the inside pocket of his jacket and handed it to Edgar.

The PM took the envelope but didn't open it. 'What's this?'

Sir Gavin O'Dowd cleared his throat. 'I've decided that it is time for me to retire.'

Edgar angrily stomped on the carpet. 'Bloody hell, Gavin, not tonight.'

Sir Gavin stood his ground. 'The letter is undated. We can action it in due course, once this problem is out of the way.'

'So *you* are bailing out on me, too?'

'Not at all.' Sir Gavin smiled. 'It's simply time for me to do some other things.'

'Lucrative non-executive directorships,' Edgar grumped.

'I was thinking more along the lines of some travel and a bit of birdwatching.'

'Mm.'

'I'm planning a trip to the Mahananda Wildlife Sanctuary to try to spot the Lesser Adjutant stork.'

'For God's sake, Gavin.'

The Cabinet Secretary shrugged. 'The bottom line is that my heart's simply not in it any more. We all reach our sell-by date and I've now reached mine.'

Nodding sadly, Edgar held out his glass for the hovering waiter to add some more cognac. He was already feeling a little drunk, but now was most definitely not the time to stop drinking. *Where the hell is the Mahananda Sanctuary?* he wondered. *Maybe I should consider a trip there myself.*

Crawling on to his Jensen Ophelia Continental bed, Simon Shelbourne placed the cool glass of the Jack Daniel's bottle against his fevered brow, in the hope that it could relieve his bastard migraine. He'd been suffering from raging headaches and nausea for hours now – ever since he'd clocked the story in the *Standard* about the dead policewoman.

A youthful Jenny Southerton had smiled up at him from the front page. Only her name wasn't Jenny, it was . . . somebody else. Simon almost dropped the newspaper in shock. He couldn't believe it. He could feel his heart-rate accelerating as he read through the story of the woman's violent death. Thinking back to their meeting in the Balmoral Club, he realized that everything the little tease had told him was a lie. She hadn't worked on the *Sunday Witness*. She was a cop.

An undercover cop, who had been spying on *him*. And now she was dead. There was no doubt about it: he was totally fucked.

Dealing with this calamitous situation in time-honoured fashion, Shelbourne had decamped to Wade's Wine Bar and promptly done three lines of charlie in the bog before settling in for an extended session of continuous drinking. Five (or was it six?) hours later, having somehow made it back to his Wapping flat, he bounced on the patented Hourglass Zoned Spring System – which, mercifully, provides consistent support to your ever-changing position and weight distribution – while trying to wriggle out of his Citizens of Humanity Adonis slim jeans.

'Have you got any more coke?' The bottle blonde he'd dragged home with him – Rebekah or Rachel or something – dropped her bag on the floor. Shrugging off her denim jacket, she jumped on to the bed, pulling her Mumford & Sons T-shirt over her head as she did so.

'Fucking first,' declared Shelbourne, 'drugs second.' Eyeing her sheer lime-green bra he was relieved to feel a comforting twitch in his groin. The stress of recent events had been impacting on his ability to perform of late, but hopefully tonight he would be okay. The girl reached behind her back to unclasp the bra but he gestured for her to stop. 'Leave it on.' The anticipation, he reckoned, was always better than the reality. Shrugging, she did as she was told. Kicking off his jeans, he pulled down his Spanx boxers with his free hand while unscrewing the top of the whiskey bottle with the other. 'Suck me off.'

'Gimme some Jack,' said the girl, grabbing the bottle. Before he had time to react, she poured half the contents of the bottle over his crotch.

'Hey!' Shelbourne objected.

The girl gave him a sly grin. 'If I'm gonna eat it, I want it to taste good.' She took two long slugs.

Seems reasonable, Shelbourne thought, falling back on to the mattress.

He couldn't have been asleep for long. Slowly, slowly, slowly, the room came into focus. Shelbourne found himself staring at the crown of the girl's head as she vigorously worked on his whiskey-flavoured member. Her roots need doing, he thought. Gingerly, he reached out to grab her hair.

'Fuck off,' was the muffled reply as she slapped his hand away, digging her teeth ever so slightly into his skin as a gentle reminder of who was in charge.

'Maybe we should just fuck,' he grumbled.

Her response was to pitch forward on to his chest, before sliding off the bed.

'Jesus,' Shelbourne laughed, 'you're even more fucked than I am!'

'Not for long,' interjected another voice. Standing in the doorway, Trevor Miller took in the sordid scene.

Simon Shelbourne sobered up in an instant once he registered the silenced gun in Miller's left hand.

'What are you doing here?' he asked. Forcing himself into a sitting position, he could now see the two bloody holes in the girl's back. He tried to scream, but only succeeded in vomiting into his own lap.

Trevor shook his head. 'This isn't going to look good when the police get here.'

'Hold on,' Shelbourne whimpered, trying to shuffle off the bed. 'You can't do this. I didn't tell that girl anything.'

'I can't hold on any longer,' Miller said grimly. Then he lifted the gun and fired four shots into the naked man's chest.

THIRTY-SEVEN

Yawning, Carlyle stepped into the R6 newsagent on Drury Lane, nodding at Suraj behind the counter, who was patiently waiting for one of the local drunks to count out sufficient copper coins to pay for a can of Red Stripe.

Easy like Sunday morning . . . Covent Garden style.

It's 9:30 a.m., Carlyle thought groggily, a bit early to be hitting the booze. Sucking on a latte from the Ecco café up the road, he scanned the front covers of the newspapers laid out by the till. It was the usual mix of celebrities, sex, drugs and disaster. As he did every weekend, Carlyle wondered why his family bothered purchasing newspapers any more. In his book, they were just a waste of time and effort – a bloated mix of no news and the noxious opinions of ridiculous columnists that you would happily cross the road to avoid if they ever came walking down your street. It was Helen who insisted that they keep buying them; more out of habit than anything else. Somehow, he still managed to waste an hour or so of his free time restlessly flicking through pages brimming with bile and manufactured outrages in a vain search for something that might catch his interest.

Finally coming up with the right cash, the dosser grabbed his lager and shuffled towards the door, giving off a rather nasty niff as he did so.

'The usual?' Suraj pulled a *Sunday Times* and *Sunday Mirror* from their respective piles and set them in front of the inspector.

'Thanks,' Carlyle smiled, handing over a fiver. Waiting for his change, his gaze fell on the front page of the *Sunday Witness*.

HANNAH PARENTS: 'CALL US'

Carlyle's heart sank as he reached for a copy. 'I'd better have one of those as well.'

'What did you get that for?' Helen asked, as he dropped the pile of newspapers on the living-room floor. Sitting on the sofa with a cup of green tea, she carefully considered which bit of which paper she wanted to read first.

'Work,' Carlyle grumped, annoyed that his wife would think he would have bought the *Witness* through choice. Grabbing the tabloid, he slumped into an armchair and began reading. Under an 'Exclusive' tag, the front page was dominated by a picture of a smiling Hannah Gillespie, along with a strapline that said: Full story, pages 4, 5 and 6. 'Jesus,' he mumbled, 'misery sells.'

'Nothing new in that,' sniffed Helen, as she tore open the plastic wrapper containing the *Sunday Times* magazines.

'Thank you for that stunning insight,' said Carlyle, flicking to page four and starting to read:

The parents of a missing schoolgirl yesterday begged her to come home as the police admitted they didn't have enough men available to find her.

Fuck, Carlyle thought, Simpson isn't going to like that comment. He quickly scanned down through the article.

Accused of being slow to react, police have admitted that they are no closer to finding Hannah. Despite listening in to her phone messages, they still have no idea where she is. One said: 'We are just not getting anywhere on this. There's simply not enough officers deployed on it. At this rate, we're not going to find her – and we'll end up getting sued by the parents.'

Carlyle frowned as he reread the quote. 'You have *got* to be kidding me.'

'What?' Helen asked, looking up from her article on winter soups.

Carlyle gestured at the phone sitting on the arm of the sofa. 'Throw me my mobile, will you?'

Reaching over, Helen grabbed the phone and handed it to him.

'Ta.' Carlyle pulled up 901 and hit call.

You have no new messages and twelve old messages.

Quickly deleting the first three, he came to the one that Joe had left for him a couple of days earlier.

'*Boss, it's me. What do you want me to do on this Hannah Gillespie thing? I'm worried that it's dragging on and we are just not getting anywhere on this. She's still checking her voicemails, so that's okay, but she's not responding to any of them. With the benefit of hindsight, people are gonna say there's just not enough officers on the case. At this rate, we're not going to find her. And Simpson'll go mad if we end up getting sued by the parents. Give me a call.*'

Carlyle replayed the message. Then he looked back at the newspaper. 'Bugger me,' he groaned. 'It looks like my phone's been hacked.'

'Hah!' Helen chuckled. 'Who'd want to hack *your* phone?'

'You'd be surprised.' Right on cue, the mobile started vibrating in his hand. It was Joe. Mightily relieved that it wasn't Carole Simpson, Carlyle squeezed the receive button with his thumb. 'I've seen it,' he said, by way of introduction.

'What?'

'The *Sunday Witness*.'

'Well, forget about that,' Joe replied brusquely. 'Sorry to interrupt your Sunday-morning reading but we've found a body.'

Standing behind the police tape in an Army surplus jacket, Bernie Gilmore caught Carlyle's eye. Filled with an overwhelming sense of grim resignation about the turn of events, the inspector left his sergeant dealing with the pathologist, and wandered slowly towards the journalist.

'Bernie.'

'Inspector.'

A few yards away, a small knot of hacks eyed them suspiciously. 'Not really a great place to talk,' Carlyle mumbled, pawing the greasy cobbles with the sole of his shoe.

'No. You wouldn't want to be marked out as my bitch, would you?'

Carlyle smiled grimly. 'I'm not sure I'd quite like that either but no, I certainly wouldn't want our ... relationship to be misconstrued.'

'Do you know the Constitution on St Pancras Way?'

'I can find it.'

'Okay. I'll see you there in ten minutes.'

'Make it twenty.'

'Fine. I'll have a Jameson's ready for you.'

Turning on his heel, Carlyle trudged back towards the crime scene. 'Make it a double.'

'So ...' Sitting underneath a muted 50-inch TV screen showing Sky Sports News, Bernie at least had the good grace not to say, *'I told you so.'*

'So ...' Carlyle took a mouthful of whiskey and placed his glass on the table. 'It's Hannah.'

Saying nothing, Bernie supped at his pint of IPA.

'The parents haven't been formally told yet, so you'll have to hold off for a while.'

'Of course,' Bernie said, returning his glass to the table, where it sat next to a blue biro and an unopened notebook.

'The body was discovered in the boot of a Vauxhall Vectra that was reported stolen two days ago. The vehicle was found dumped in the alley earlier this morning. The boot was already open. We think she's been dead for at least a day.' Grabbing his glass, he took another swig. 'That's all I've got at this stage. I don't know precisely how she was killed or any other . . . details.' Details like whether the girl had been sexually assaulted, which was always the first thing that the hacks wanted to know.

'Okay, where do you go from here?' Bernie listened to Carlyle run through the backstory which had so far been kept from the press, concerning Francis Clegg and Monty Laws. 'You gonna go public on that?' he asked when the inspector had finished.

'Dunno yet. Not my call.' Carlyle finished his drink. He wanted another but that was not advisable, given that he had a long day in front of him. 'We've urgently got to find Laws, but if we go public now, we're gonna get a lot of shit.'

Bernie looked disapproving. 'Are you a cop or a PR man?' he snorted.

'Both. You know the way it works. The girl is dead. Whose fault is that?'

'You tell me.'

'It's the fault of the bastard who did it, obviously . . .'

'Obviously.'

'But *we* get the shit for not stopping it.'

'That sounds more than a little self-pitying to me,' Bernie commented. 'And it doesn't leave me with much in the way of a story.'

'I would have thought you'd have moved on by now,' said Carlyle, keen to return the barb with one of his own, 'seeing as how you always seem to be so far ahead of the game.'

'Now, now,' Bernie waved an admonishing finger, 'let's not descend into acrimony. Don't forget you need all the friends in the media you can get. Did you see the *Sunday Witness* this morning?'

'Yeah,' Carlyle said dolefully.

'What idiot copper admitted that they were fucking up?' A sly grin spread across his face. 'It wasn't you, was it?'

'No, no,' replied Carlyle defensively.

'Whoever said it – *if* they said it – it was a strangely unguarded remark.'

'I wonder,' Carlyle mused, trying to sound as if it was a casual thought that had just popped into his head, 'if they're now tapping *our* phones.'

Bernie pondered. 'Possible. It would be an incredibly stupid thing to do, under the circumstances, but it's certainly possible. What makes you think that's happened?'

'No reason.'

'Anyway,' Bernie went on, 'the real problem is that you really are seriously off the pace.'

'Thanks.'

'Sorry, Inspector, but sometimes the truth hurts. This has all been a complete pile of shite.'

'Constructive criticism, please.'

'On the bright side, things will move on quickly enough.' Gilmore paused, looking round the pub. 'By the way, Trevor Miller's been sacked by Number Ten.'

Carlyle raised an eyebrow. 'That's news to me.'

'Yes?' queried Bernie, eyeing him suspiciously. 'They're trying to stonewall me at the moment but something's definitely going on.'

'Bernie,' Carlyle quipped, 'there's always something going on.'

'You wouldn't happen to know anything about it, would you?'

'No,' Carlyle shook his head, 'but I'll see what I can find out.'

'Thanks. What else is happening?'

'Well, there's Sir Chester's trip to the health farm.' The words slipped out before he had the chance to properly consider the wisdom of using them.

'Everyone knows about that,' Bernie said dismissively.

'I hear the bill was thirty grand.'

'Mm.'

'Which he didn't pay for.'

'So who did?'

'The guy who owns the place. Can't remember his name. I've no idea why he'd do that.'

'That's certainly a nice present. Has he declared it yet?'

'Dunno.'

Bernie thought about it further for a moment. 'In the current febrile atmosphere, if he hasn't, he will be in trouble, silly boy. Things like this can make you look either bent or naive.'

Sitting patiently, Carlyle watched the cogs turning in the journalist's brain.

'Does anyone else know about this?'

Happy to be gaining some credit with the Bank of Bernie, the inspector smiled. 'Not as far as I know.'

After his conversation with Bernie Gilmore, the inspector simply wanted to go and hide. The best place to do that was at work. As expected, the third floor of the Charing Cross police station was empty, as he sat down at his desk and switched on his computer. It was a Sunday and, nominally at least, he was off duty but he felt agitated, and with this agitation came the need to at least feel like he was doing something effective. Helen had sent him a text saying that she and Alice had gone to Brighton to see Helen's mother, so there was no pressure for him to get home. Sitting back, he suddenly felt overwhelmed by tiredness. 'I shouldn't have had that whiskey,' he mumbled to himself, closing his eyes.

'What a great way to spend a Sunday,' came a voice from nearby.

'Huh?' Jerking awake, it took him a moment to focus on the grinning face of Susan Phillips, standing by his desk. She was dressed in jeans and a black leather biker's jacket over a green Noah & The Whale T-shirt; and altogether it was a rather fetching ensemble.

'Nice kip?'

'I was thinking,' said Carlyle, massaging a crick in his neck.

Phillips's grin grew wider. 'You were snoring happily away.'

Whatever. 'How did you know I was here?'

'I rang the desk. They told me that you'd come in about an hour ago.'

Shit, had he been asleep for an hour? 'And what are you doing here?'

'Richard is taking me to see the Leonardo Da Vinci exhibition at the National Gallery.'

'Mm.' Carlyle didn't ask her who Richard was. He didn't keep track of the Phillips men; there was no point, as they never lasted long. 'I hear it's really good.' He didn't have a clue on the score, but it was Leonardo, so what were the odds?

'Yes. But we've got timed tickets, so I need to get going.'

'What can I do for you?'

'It's more what I can do for you, Inspector.' Taking a step backwards, Phillips perched on the edge of Joe's desk.

'That's what I like to hear,' Carlyle grinned.

'I checked out the Rosanna Snowdon evidence.'

'That was quick.'

'That was *very* quick,' she smiled, clearly pleased with herself. 'I had to call in a couple of favours . . .'

'Thank you.'

'But it was worth it.'

'Yeah?' Sitting up in his chair, Carlyle already knew what was coming but wanted to hear her say it.

'We got a match: Miller's prints both inside and outside the dead journalist's flat.' She folded her arms. 'So it seems you were right.'

'It happens – every now and then.'

'What I don't understand though, is why they weren't checked at the time.'

'This whole thing has been a complete balls-up from the start. The officers investigating Rosanna's death were so fixated on Simon Lovell that they simply didn't bother to check all the other leads properly.'

'Someone will cop some flak for that now,' Phillips said.

'Let's hope so.' He wondered, however, if that someone would be Fiona Singleton. The sergeant had helped him and now she could get dropped right in it. Nothing much he could do about that. 'Who else knows about this?'

'No one yet.'

'Okay, can you sit on it for now? I'm going to get Simpson to deal with it.'

'Fine.' Phillips pushed herself off the desk. 'I'm supposed to be having time off, anyway. I'll get Richard to take me to Suffolk for a couple of days.' She gave him a sly grin. 'You have to make your own entertainment there, as there's no mobile coverage. I'll write up my report when I get back.'

'Perfect,' Carlyle smiled. 'And thanks again.'

'No problem. You can get back to having your nap now.'

'Ha! Enjoy the exhibition.' As he watched her saunter towards the lifts, his mind drifted to thoughts of a couple of days' R&R in Suffolk with Susan Phillips. 'Richard,' he mumbled to himself, 'you are a very lucky bloke.'

For once, Simpson picked up on the first ring. 'Where the bloody hell have you been?' she snapped. 'I've left you three messages already.'

Nice to speak to you, too, Carlyle thought. Jumping to his feet, he inspected his phone as he began pacing the room. There were no missed calls listed on the screen. The vagaries of the network? 'Sorry, none of them came through.'

'Mm.'

'Your messages will probably turn up the day after tomorrow.'

The Commander let out a deep sigh which suggested she wasn't interested in any of his technology-based excuses. 'What are you up to, then?'

Quickly, Carlyle explained about Trevor Miller and Maude Hall. Not quickly enough, as it turned out, for she cut him off with a curt: 'Enough.'

'What?'

'I know all about this. Sir Chester's gone into overdrive. Someone also shot Simon Shelbourne last night.'

The inspector momentarily struggled to place the name.

'The Commissioner's PR man,' Simpson reminded him.

'Yes, yes.' He took a breath, trying not to sound too excited. 'Miller has totally lost it.'

'We don't know that it was him.'

'It's got to be.' Carlyle then ran through the backstory of Anton Fox, Charlie Ross and Rosanna Snowdon. 'The guy has been out of control for years. Now it's all coming down around his ears.'

There was a long silence at the other end of the call.

'Carole?'

'Don't sound so bloody smug,' she said finally. 'This is all your fault.'

Carlyle managed a nervous chuckle. '*My* fault?'

'You were supposed to be focusing on the Mosman case,' Simpson said grimly.

'That's well in hand,' Carlyle lied airily.

'Instead, you go chasing old enemies and stir up a total shit storm that is going to take months, if not years, to clear up. Never mind that moron Miller, this mess is going to do serious damage to the reputation of the Met and you just stand around, stirring the pot.'

Bollocks to this, Carlyle thought. 'Don't give me that crap,' he hissed by way of a response. 'I'm just doing my fucking job, going where the evidence takes me – and if you don't like it, that's tough.' Simpson tried to protest, but he ploughed on. 'I didn't put Duncan Brown in the back of that bin lorry and I didn't get Maude Hall killed.' *Well, maybe I did, but now is not the time.* 'What I'm going to do is catch the bastards responsible. If that means bringing down the whole fucking circus, fine. And after all this time, if I get Miller – well, I fucking deserve it.'

'Have you quite finished?' Simpson said quietly.

'I'm not going to cover this up.'

'For God's sake, John, no one is suggesting a cover-up.'

'That'll be a first, then.'

'As you said, we go where the evidence takes us,' Simpson said firmly.

'Good. Now that the whole thing is falling apart, maybe you and your mate Meyer should step up to the plate.'

'I've already tried to contact him. Apparently he's on leave.'

'Good timing.'

'I tried calling him at home. Funnily enough, his wife said she knows nothing about his whereabouts.'

'What about his sidekick?' He managed to pluck the name from his memory. 'That woman Valette.'

'We can't get hold of her either.'

'Fucking excellent,' Carlyle harrumphed. 'It's all about to fall into their laps and Operation Redhead goes on holiday. I always knew that they were idiots.'

'That, Inspector,' Simpson deadpanned, 'is one of your many talents.'

'Eh?'

'You're such a good judge of character.'

'Ha ha. Maybe you could stop taking the piss for a minute and tell me what *you* think we should do next?'

'You're asking me?' Simpson asked grumpily.

'I wondered if you could speak to the powers-that-be at Fulham about Snowdon. Phillips's findings are going to be a big problem for them.'

'Of course,' said Simpson. 'After all, that's what I'm here for, isn't it – to clean up your mess.'

'Thanks,' said Carlyle, choosing to ignore her acid tone. 'By the way, there's a Sergeant Singleton down there who's involved in this. She has been very helpful, above and beyond. If we can stop her being dragged into the mess . . .'

Simpson cut him off. 'I'll see what I can do.' The tone, however, was very much *Don't push your luck*. 'Meanwhile, what will you be doing?'

'I need to chase up some loose ends on the Mosman case,' Carlyle replied, throwing her a bone.

'I see.'

'And,' he added, in the spirit of openness and transparency for which he was famous, 'I am obliged to go and see Rosanna Snowdon's parents. To give them a heads-up that everything is about to explode. It's the least they deserve.'

'Very well, but please impress upon them the need for total discretion at the present time.'

Carlyle smiled. When she picked up speed, the Commander could start spouting police jargon with the best of them.

'This is an *extremely* tricky situation,' she continued. 'They simply can't speak to anyone about this until the matter is further resolved.'

Further resolved? 'Of course.'

'Good.' Simpson sounded like she had finally grasped the situation. 'Just one other thing.'

'Yes?'

'Where is Mr Miller?'

'That's what everyone's trying to find out.'

'Well, be careful. If he has totally lost the plot,' Simpson said, 'he might end up coming after you.' It didn't sound as if she found that such an unappealing prospect.

'Let him try,' said Carlyle grimly.

'Just be careful, is all I'm saying,' Simpson chided. 'And keep me posted.' Without further ado, she ended the call, leaving Carlyle continuing to pace his office undisturbed.

'It's worse for me. I was the one quoted in that bloody paper.' Folding his arms, Joe sat back in his chair, gazing up at a painting of a bowl of fruit.

'No one knows it was you.'

'How long do you think that will last?'

'Well, if *you* don't tell anyone,' Carlyle said evenly, '*I* won't.'

'Deal.' Joe sounded unenthusiastic.

'You didn't leave your name, so how could it get out?'

'Mm.'

Squinting, the inspector read the short description that had been discreetly positioned next to the painting. *A Festoon of Fruit hung above a Stone Table, a view of a Mountainous Landscape beyond.* It was by an artist called Jan Mortel. 'Nice.'

'Yeah,' Joe laughed, 'it would look really good in my living room.'

'How much, do you think?'

'No idea,' Joe replied. 'You know what they say: if you have to ask the price, you can't afford it.'

'Story of my life.' Carlyle glanced along the corridor towards the empty reception desk. The girl who had let them in had disappeared now, and showed no sign of returning. 'You think they'd at least offer us coffee.'

'There was a Caffè Nero down the road. Want me to go and get some?'

'Nah, it's fine.' For a few moments, Carlyle forced himself to contemplate Mortel's work but, try as he might, the inspector had never been able to relate to paintings. You looked at them and then you didn't; that was that. He otherwise didn't have much time for them. Even Helen had long since stopped trying to drag him round various exhibitions and galleries, finding Alice a far better companion. Within three seconds, he felt overwhelmed by boredom. A bowl of fruit was just a bowl of fruit. It might have been a big deal in the eighteenth century or whatever, but life had moved on. He glanced at Joe, whose eyes were similarly glazed. 'So,' he asked, keeping his voice low, 'how do you hack a phone?'

Joe shot him a sideways look. 'Bloody hell, you must be the only person in the country who doesn't know how it works by now.'

Carlyle gave a small bow.

'Don't you read the papers?'

'Only when *you're* quoted in them.'

'Ha-bloody-ha. Have you got your phone there?'

'Sure.' Carlyle fished out his mobile.

'Right,' said Joe. Taking his own phone from his jacket pocket, he pulled up the inspector's number on the screen, then hit the call button. After a moment, Carlyle's handset started vibrating in his hand. 'Don't answer it. Just let it go to voicemail.' Tapping a few numbers, Joe lifted his own handset to his ear and started to listen. 'You've got a message from Helen . . .'

'Hey!' Carlyle made a grab for the phone, but Joe ducked away.

'She's pissed off about something.'

'Nothing unusual there,' Carlyle grinned. 'How did you do that?'

Joe tapped a few more keys before ending the call. 'If you dial that number, you can access voicemail remotely.'

'You can?'

'The factory setting for the security code is four zeros. If you don't change it, anyone can go in and listen to your messages.'

'Shit.'

'Don't worry,' Joe smiled. 'I've changed it.'

'To what?'

'Four ones.'

'Thanks.'

'My pleasure.'

'I'll give you a call when I forget it.'

'No worries.'

Carlyle looked back towards the empty desk. 'Where the fuck is that girl?'

'Do you want me to go and look for her?'

'Give her another minute,' said Carlyle, happy enough to sit on his arse doing nothing for a little while longer. 'Tell me about the bloke who owns this place.'

Joe pulled out a small notebook and flicked through the pages until he found his notes. 'Dario Untersander. Swiss national. Educated in England. Worked in Sotheby's before setting up his own business twelve years ago.'

'Mm.'

'No record.'

'Obviously.'

'He is a former Chairman of the Society of London Art Dealers and an executive committee member of the European Fine Art Foundation.'

'Good for him,' Carlyle said sullenly.

'Mr Untersander,' said a voice from down the corridor, 'is also a leading light in the British Antique Dealers Association and the Grosvenor House Art and Antiques Fair executive committee.'

The inspector looked round to see a well-fed, middle-aged man with rosy cheeks and a head of thinning silver hair. 'And who are you?'

'Daniel Brabo.' The man advanced towards them, proffering a business card. 'I'm Mr Untersander's legal adviser.' Carlyle shot Joe a disgusted look as Brabo gestured towards the rear of the building. 'My client will see you now.'

'Nice coffee.' Resigned to the fact that it was all he was going to get from this visit, the inspector resolved to appear as magnanimous as he could manage.

Dario Untersander nodded. He was a tall man folded up behind an antique desk that was rather too small for his lengthy frame. Groomed to within an inch of his life, in an expensive-looking suit, with a red and white striped shirt and a red tie, he looked every inch the New Bond Street salesman. 'Harrods Heritage Blend'. His accent was 100 per cent Sloane Square. 'We only like the best.'

'I'm sure,' Carlyle smiled. He gestured towards the lawyer sitting on a chair to the right of the desk, who was busily demolishing a shortbread finger. 'Thank you for agreeing to see us on a Sunday.'

'Happy to oblige,' Untersander said pleasantly. 'Many of our clients are from the Middle East and this is a working day for them. So it is a working day for us, too.' He glanced at Brabo, who accelerated his chewing and swallowed quickly. 'And, under the circumstances, we were expecting your visit.'

'And what exactly were those circumstances?' Joe jumped in.

Surprised at the underling asking a question, both Untersander and Brabo shot the inspector an enquiring look. Taking another mouthful of coffee, Carlyle gestured that he was happy for them to answer.

'The circumstances, as I understand it,' said Brabo, 'are that you are interested in a series of phone calls that appear to have been made—'

Giving the waffle short shrift, Joe cut across him. 'A gentleman now believed to be responsible for three murders,' he interrupted sharply, 'made a succession of calls to a phone number belonging to your client. We want to know why.'

A sickly smile passed across Brabo's face. Maybe the shortbread had gone down the wrong way. 'And who is this gentleman you refer to?'

'That's one of the things we were hoping *you* would be able to tell us,' Carlyle said smoothly. This lawyer clearly had an inside track on the police investigation, but where had he got his information from? No point in worrying about that now. The inspector eyed the pile of biscuits on Untersander's desk. Shortbread wasn't his favourite but he was still tempted.

'We really have no idea,' Brabo replied, injecting just the right amount of dismay into his voice to suggest the disappointment of an honest citizen unable to be of more assistance with the police's enquiries. 'The phone you are referring to was bought by Mr Untersander for his daughter. But unfortunately, the young lady lost it several months ago.'

How very convenient, Carlyle reckoned. 'So why didn't you cancel the contract?'

Untersander gave a sheepish grin.

'Apparently,' Brabo explained, 'Sofia – Mr Untersander's daughter – forgot to mention it.' He shook his head sadly. 'You know what children are like.'

'I do indeed,' Carlyle agreed. He turned to face Untersander. 'So you know nothing about these phone calls, but you do admit to knowing Zoe Mosman?'

'Yes, professionally speaking,' said Brabo, 'which should be no great surprise. Both are important players in the London art world, which is not that extensive.'

'Do you do business with the Government Art Collection?'

'I believe,' said Brabo, 'that the gallery has sold them the odd piece over the years.'

'Oh? I thought that the government were sellers, not buyers?'

The lawyer shrugged. 'Recently, yes, they have sold some things, but we have not been involved in that.'

'What the GAC has been putting into the market lacked quality,' Untersander explained. 'They keep the good stuff well under lock and key.'

Brabo shot him a plaintive look that said *Leave the talking to me*. 'The main thing is that it was not the kind of thing the Untersander Gallery has been looking to acquire.'

'Okay.' Carlyle frowned, keen to move the conversation along. 'So the man who kills Mrs Mosman calls a phone number that *was* yours . . . before you lost it. That's quite a coincidence, don't you think?'

Keeping his face blank, Untersander held the inspector's gaze.

'That,' Brabo snapped, 'is not something you would reasonably expect us to comment on.'

Having despatched Joe back to the station to check on the ongoing search for Monty Laws, Carlyle headed towards Green Park underground station, pondering his next move. He was just about to descend towards the tube when a call came in from Dominic Silver.

'What have you got for me?' the inspector asked brusquely.

'Not a lot,' Dom admitted glumly. 'Over the years, it looks as if Trevor Miller really has turned into a Grade A bastard.'

'I knew that already.' In the middle of a relentless stream of pedestrians at the entrance to the tube, the inspector was not inclined to stop and chat. 'The question now is: where the bloody hell is he?'

'I'm still asking around.'

'Thanks.'

'But I think you need to be careful.'

'I'm always careful.'

'Seriously. This guy is way past caring. *I am in blood/Stepped in so far that, should I wade no more/Returning were as tedious as go o'er.*'

'You what?'

'*Macbeth.*'

Carlyle grunted. He wasn't in the mood for Shakespeare.

'Miller's just ploughing ahead,' Dom explained, 'in the hope that he can somehow escape the mess he's in. A few more bodies – yours, for instance – is neither here nor there to him now.'

'He's running, I'm chasing; not the other way round. That means he'll want to steer well clear of me.'

'I hope you're right – but it wouldn't do any harm to have someone watching your back.'

'I've got plenty of support. Don't worry about that. Let me know if you get any lead on his location.' Not waiting for a reply, Carlyle ended the call, before skipping down the steps and into the station.

The Rolodex standing on Harris Highman's desk was open at Carlyle's card. Taking a seat in the dead bureaucrat's chair, the inspector looked around the grey office, searching for some kind of inspiration. 'What was it you wanted to tell me?' he mumbled.

On the desk was a mug from the British Museum's *Book of the Dead* exhibition. Carlyle recalled Helen dragging him to see it several years earlier. If he remembered correctly, he had trailed round the exhibits with a distinct lack of good grace. Dead people didn't interest him that much; an amusing thought for a policeman.

Next to the mug, a glossy magazine lay open. Idly picking it up, Carlyle glanced at the photos displayed in the centre-spread and frowned. 'Shit!'

'Excuse me?'

A sickly-looking young man in a suit and tie stood in the doorway. He was clutching a collection of files to his breast and there was a pained expression on his face. 'What are *you* doing here?' he asked.

'Police,' said Carlyle sharply, closing the magazine and tossing it on the desk.

'Ah.' The man edged backwards.

'Sit down.' The inspector pointed to the chair in front of Highman's desk. Reluctantly the young man did as he was told. Keeping his eyes on the cop, he slowly lowered himself into the seat.

'Who are you?'

'Mark Segel. I'm one of Mr Highman's assistants.' The voice was quiet, the accent American. 'I've been working here for a year, on secondment from the Brooklyn Museum.'

Good for you, Carlyle thought. 'Have you been interviewed by us already?'

Segel nodded. 'I don't know why anyone would want to kill Harris.'

'No,' Carlyle sighed, 'I suppose not.'

'He was a very . . . quiet man.'

'What about Mrs Mosman?'

Segel let his grip on the files loosen slightly. 'I didn't know her.'

'No? But what about gossip, tittle-tattle . . . stuff like that?'

The youngster frowned. 'Why would you be interested?'

'I'm interested in everything,' Carlyle smiled. 'That's the only way you find out why someone got shot.'

'Well,' lowering his voice, Segel leaned forward slightly, 'she had a reputation for being a bit of a bitch.'

'Why was that?'

'Just in general.' The kid shrugged. 'I didn't really have any personal experience of that; she was never around. Anyway, I was working full-time for Harris.'

'Were you involved in the GAC Audit he was working on?'

296

'Yes.' Segel's face brightened a little. 'We were working on a final draft of the report. It was due to go to Mrs Mosman, and then to the Arts Minister. I guess it will go on hold now until Zoe's successor is announced. I gave a copy to Sergeant Si . . . Si . . .'

'Szyszkowski.'

'Yes. Do you work with him?'

Carlyle nodded. He realized that he hadn't got round to looking at the material Joe had collected regarding the shootings here. Did that make him sloppy? Or just overworked? 'In a nutshell, what does it say?'

'The report?'

'Yes.'

Segel gave him a thoughtful look. 'It was only a draft.'

'I understand that,' Carlyle said patiently, 'but what does it say . . . in draft form.'

Segel glanced over his shoulder before lowering his voice to the level where the inspector had to concentrate hard to hear him. 'The audit shows that there are more than one hundred and twenty paintings unaccounted for in the collection.' He let out a nervous giggle. 'Art worth tens of millions of pounds has . . . disappeared.'

'Stolen?'

'Most likely, I'd say. Stolen or lost. Probably a bit of both.'

Carlyle thought about that for a moment. 'Can't you track these things?'

Segel shook his head. 'Not in this case. The systems and controls were either rudimentary or non-existent. That was quite amazing really.'

'Sounds like a mess.'

'Yes,' Segel nodded. 'When the news gets out, it'll be quite a scandal. I think that Mrs Mosman would have resigned, for sure – if she hadn't been shot, that is. Otherwise the Minister would have certainly sacked her.'

'Interesting.' The phone in Carlyle's pocket started vibrating:

he had a text message from Joe. Reading it, he jumped to his feet, grabbed the magazine, shoved it under his arm and hurried towards the door. 'Thank you for your time . . .'

'Mark.'

'Yes, Mark, that was very helpful.'

THIRTY-EIGHT

'This way. Be careful and watch your footing.' MPU Sergeant Ian Sidbury signalled for Joe Szyszkowski to follow him down a narrow metal gangplank running alongside the north bank of the river, by Wapping. With some considerable reluctance, Carlyle brought up the rear.

The wind whipped off the water and the inspector stopped to button up his overcoat, complaining about the cold.

'If you fell in here,' Sergeant Sidbury remarked cheerfully, 'we'd only have a couple of minutes in which to fish you out.'

'Fucking great,' Carlyle grumbled as he tiptoed along carefully.

'The Thames is two hundred and thirteen miles in length,' Sidbury explained, sounding more like a tour guide now than a member of the Marine Policing Unit – the Met's river police.

'Interesting.' Joe nodded politely.

'We normally get a dead body washed up about once a week, but there's been more of them than usual so far this year. This one is DB32.'

'Okay,' said Carlyle, trying to inject some cheeriness into his voice, 'let's just hope Dead Body Thirty-Two is our man.'

'That'll be for you to decide,' Sidbury replied. Shuffling between a pair of Targa 31 fast-response boats, they came to a stop in front of a small wooden jetty. On the jetty was a single-storey structure about ten feet high and eight feet wide, built out of metal scaffolding poles and covered with blue plastic sheeting.

'This is where we bring all the bodies we find,' Sidbury continued. 'We wash 'em down and do a preliminary examination, looking for anything suspicious and that, before they go to the morgue for a proper post-mortem.'

Great, thought Carlyle. Squeamish at the best of times, he reckoned that he had seen more than enough dead bodies just recently. Worried about puking, he took a series of deep breaths as a precaution against the onset of nausea.

'Do you want to go inside?' Sidbury gestured towards the blue-covered structure. 'This one's definitely a bit of a mess, I'm afraid. We've got nothing left below the waist.'

Nothing below the waist? The inspector inhaled again, trying hard not to make it obvious.

'Where's the rest?' Joe asked casually.

Sidbury waved a helpless hand across the shit-coloured waters. 'Could be anywhere. The size of the river down here and the strength of the current will make it impossible to search for it. I doubt if we'll ever find any more. Shall we go and take a look?'

This was definitely time to delegate. Half-turning back in the direction whence they'd come, Carlyle gazed thoughtfully at Tower Bridge and, beyond that, the London Assembly building.

'I'll do it,' said Joe, finally picking up his cue.

'Thanks,' said the inspector, already making his way back towards dry land.

Twenty minutes later, Joe was looking more than a little green around the gills himself. Carlyle shot his sergeant an amused look as he entered the canteen in the Wapping police station. 'Feeling okay?'

'Not nice.' Joe made a face. 'I need a coffee.'

'Good idea,' his boss nodded. 'Get me another espresso while you're at it.'

By the time Joe returned with their drinks, the colour had begun to come back to his cheeks.

'Well?' Carlyle asked. 'Is it our guy?'

'Could be. There are bruises on the face and chest consistent with being hit by a vehicle.'

'Mm.'

'But that doesn't matter much if we can't get an ID.'

'Yeah,' Carlyle agreed, sipping his espresso. 'If we can't work out who it was that shot Zoe Mosman, we're fairly fucked.'

'The MPU are running his prints through the system. I've asked them to do Interpol as well. We should know in a couple of hours.'

'What about his phone?'

'For some reason, we couldn't get any usable prints from that.'

'No, no. I mean did the phone have a service contract?'

'Nah.' Joe shook his head. 'It was just a cheapo pay-as-you-go.'

'Okay,' Carlyle sighed. 'So what have we got now? We know that Dario Untersander was acquainted with Mrs Mosman.' He gestured to the magazine he'd taken from Harris Highman's office, which lay on the table between them. 'There's a photo of them together there, looking very friendly. Maybe there was more to their relationship than he's letting on.'

'She was shagging him, you mean?'

Carlyle adopted a philosophical demeanour. 'That kind of carry-on is not unheard of, Joseph, particularly in *artistic* circles.'

'No, but—'

Ignoring his colleague's reservations, Carlyle went on, 'Indulge me here. Zoe Mosman was responsible for the GAC. There have been significant thefts from the collection. So, maybe Mosman was nicking them for Untersander to sell?'

'Thin.'

'Maybe they were worried that the thefts were about to come to light as a result of Highman's audit . . .'

'Getting thinner.'

'. . . and they had some kind of falling-out.'

'Thinner than Kate Moss after a three-month detox.'

'It's possible,' Carlyle insisted. 'Business deals go wrong all the time.'

'So he got a hitman to blow up her son and shoot one of the neighbours?'

'It's just a theory.'

'It's just a totally crap theory. Why would Mosman get into bed with a Euro-sleazeball like Dario Untersander?'

'Physically or metaphorically?'

'Whichever way you like.'

'Money.' Carlyle rubbed together the thumb and index finger of his right hand.

'You saw Mosman's house,' Joe protested. 'Why would she need the money?'

'She could have been living beyond her means. Did we check her finances?'

'Not as far as I know.' Joe scratched his head. 'And I'd be surprised if we were allowed to. Technically we are investigating her son's murder and I doubt if we could get a warrant.'

Carlyle waved away this objection. 'Let's try. Go to a friendly judge.' He mentioned a couple of names. 'If you don't ask, you don't get. Check the husband's bank accounts, as well. Doesn't he run some business or other?'

'Yeah, a vehicle-leasing company.'

'Okay, let's find out about that, too.'

'Fine,' Joe sighed, 'but this is a fairly scattergun approach. We need more help on this one if we are going to know what to focus on.'

'Fair point,' Carlyle agreed. 'I'll speak to Sir Michael Snowdon about how best to approach the GAC end of it. It's another reason to go and see him. I've put it off for too long already.'

'I'll come with you, if you want.'

Getting to his feet, Carlyle smiled at him. Joe clearly didn't want another excruciating visit to Rosanna's parents any more than he did, but it was good of him to offer. 'It's okay, I can handle it.'

A look of relief washed over the sergeant's face. 'Thanks.'

'I've got someone else to see first, then I'll head up to North London and report in with the old man. Let me know if we get a lead on the floater's fingerprints.'

'Sure thing.'

'And remember, next time there's a body to be fished out of the river, you're on your own.'

Standing in a semi-derelict fruit warehouse just south of Covent Garden's piazza, Carlyle waited patiently while a tiny make-up girl fluttered around the D-list celebrity Margaretha Zelle. Finally satisfied with the job done, the girl bounced off, leaving the two of them alone in the makeshift changing room. Under a red Puffa jacket, Zelle was dressed in a white silk maxi-dress with crystals scattered around the neck. Her hair had been cut short and the inspector had to admit that she was looking good.

A sly grin crossed her face as she caught him gawping. 'Armani.'

'You look like you're going to the Oscars.'

'Hardly,' she sighed. 'I'm supposed to be an ordinary hostess. Imagine you're a guest at my Christmas drinks party . . .'

'Thank you.' Carlyle gave a small bow.

'And I am introducing you to the delights of Prince Percy's Perfect Peanuts.' Shifting round in her chair, she grabbed a 500g tin from the table behind her and waved it in the air. 'They're be-*yond* tasty!'

'Mm, I'm not really a nut man myself.'

'I don't blame you,' said Zelle, tossing the tin back on to the table. 'But this was the only thing that my agent could get for me, useless cow.'

Why did a woman who had made millions from her divorce have to do adverts at all? And why would anyone go out and buy a tin of nuts on the basis of her *endorsement?* Keeping his questions to himself, Carlyle gave her a sympathetic nod.

'I mean, I should be doing Ferrero Rocher – craftsmanship, perfection, excellence. Or maybe Disaronno. In other words, products with class.'

'Yes.'

'It's not like I'm even getting paid properly for this. We recorded the original ad months ago, but then the British Nutrition Foundation complained that we'd oversold the health benefits and the Advertising Standards Authority made us pull it.'

'Health benefits?'

'I don't know the details,' she said airily, as a hassled-looking man with a beard stuck his head round the dressing-room door.

'We're ready for you now, Margaretha.'

'I'll be there in a minute,' she snapped, gesturing towards the inspector. 'Can't you see that I'm helping the police with their enquiries here?'

The bearded man glared at Carlyle, who gave an apologetic shrug. 'As soon as possible then, please,' he muttered.

'Yes, yes.' Zelle turned her attention back to the inspector. 'I suppose I should thank you, really.'

Carlyle frowned. 'Why?'

'Now that the police have broken open this phone-hacking scandal, I'm in line for a nice payday.' Reaching forward, she gave his arm a gentle squeeze. 'Zenger Media is going to have to pay out compensation for all the victims. My agent reckons I should get something in the low hundreds of thousands – maybe even half a million.'

'Wow.' Carlyle let out a low whistle. 'Not bad for letting someone listen to your voicemails.'

Sitting back in her chair, Zelle shot him a sharp look. 'It's for misuse of private information,' she rebuked him, 'for breach of confidence, publication of articles derived from voicemail hacking and a sustained campaign of harassment over a period of more than eighteen months.'

'Of course,' Carlyle said stiffly. 'Anyway, that's not what I came to talk about.' From his jacket pocket, he pulled out the pages that he had carefully cut from the magazine he had found in Harris Highman's office. Opening them out, he showed her one of the smaller photos they contained.

'God, I remember that!' Zelle squawked. 'It was *soooo* totally boring. No one in Berlin seemed to know who I was.' She pointed to one of the other women in the picture. 'They were all fawning over that stupid bitch Yulissa Vasconzuelo. Just because she's fucking the Prime Minister doesn't mean she's any good, you know.'

Trying to stick to the point, Carlyle put his finger against the third woman in the picture. 'You knew Mrs Mosman?'

'Zoe? Yes, I've known her forever.' Zelle's face darkened. 'Terrible what happened.'

'Indeed.' Carlyle showed her another photo. 'What about this guy?'

'Dario, yes. We all go back a long way.'

'So he knew Zoe, too?'

Zelle shot him an amused look. 'Oh, yes, he knew her intimately.'

'Before she was married?'

'Before . . . and after.' Zelle waved her hand in the air. 'It wouldn't surprise me if he even fucked her on her wedding day. That kind of thing would have amused Dario,' she arched a heavily pencilled eyebrow, 'and aroused him considerably.'

'Did her husband know about the affair?'

'Ivor Mosman,' Zelle sighed, 'is not a man of any great passion. He's a bit of a wimp, really. Altogether very English.' She thought about that for a moment. 'With a tiny dick – I can vouch for that.'

Carlyle didn't want to know about that.

'I think,' Zelle continued, 'that he decided at an early stage that he could just ignore what was going on. I'm sure it bothered him, but he could live with it. In my experience that's quite common; a lot of people just decide to put up with things.'

That particular situation seemed rather a lot to put up with, but the inspector said nothing.

She noticed the scepticism in his face. 'Maybe it was more than that. Maybe he found it convenient, especially as the kids grew older. The couple lived fairly separate lives. After all, Zoe was financially independent. Indeed, I know for a fact that she bankrolled his business for a while, when things were tough. But as a marriage it was fairly hollow.' She shook her head. 'They'd had separate bedrooms for years.'

'Mm.'

'Marriage is tough,' Zelle said ruefully, and then she grinned. 'A man in your life is like a car – you need to change them every couple of years.'

The inspector was wondering quite how to respond to this when the door reopened and a woman's voice shouted, 'Margaretha! We're ready. They're all waiting for you.'

'All right, all right,' Zelle grumbled. 'I'm coming.' Getting to her feet, she slipped off the Puffa jacket. 'Prince Percy's Perfect Peanuts,' she mumbled under her breath 'They're be-*yond* tasty!'

'What do you think about Dario?' Carlyle asked her, as she reached the door.

Zelle didn't miss a beat. 'I think he's easily the biggest bastard I ever met.' She said it quietly but with feeling. 'If you're looking for someone who might have killed Zoe, I would start with him.'

'For you.'

Simpson eyed the party-sized tin of peanuts, which the inspector had just placed on her desk, with a mixture of suspicion and disgust.

'Apparently, Prince Percy's are all the rage if you are hosting a drinks party,' the inspector explained innocently.

Ignoring the nuts, she fixed him with a wary look. 'Why are you here?'

'Mosman,' he said cheerily.

'You mean the case that you were supposed to be prioritizing?'

'The case that I *am* prioritizing.'

'Oh?' Simpson frowned. 'Did I miss an arrest? Can we put another tick in the "case-solved" box?'

Ignoring his boss's sarcasm, Carlyle told her, 'The guy we

think is responsible is called Dario Untersander, a Swiss national. He and Zoe Mosman go way back. The suggestion is that she did a bit of escorting to pay her way through university and—'

Simpson held up a hand. 'Are you saying that she was a hooker?'

'Grey area.' Carlyle shrugged. 'When she was younger, it seems that there were lots of parties and expensive holidays paid for by rich boyfriends of various ages and tastes. Was she on the game? It's a matter of semantics. The point, however, is that it was at this time she met Untersander.'

'And who told you all of this?'

'A reliable source,' Carlyle said. For the purposes of this conversation, he was prepared to stretch his definition of *reliable* to include someone as flaky as Margaretha Zelle. 'Someone who has known both of them reasonably well.'

Simpson grunted, unconvinced.

'Anyway,' Carlyle ploughed on, 'Mrs Mosman and Untersander had a sexual relationship which apparently was continuing, sporadically, despite both of them since being married to other people.'

Simpson gave him a *Get on with it* look.

The inspector took a deep breath. 'Sooo . . . the theory is this. Mosman stole a significant number of middling-quality paintings from the Government Art Collection for Untersander to sell under the counter in his gallery. Then the government decides to do an audit, so that it can start flogging some of the pictures itself. Mosman and Untersander are naturally worried about their little scam being uncovered. They argue about what best to do and have a falling-out. Untersander first threatens Mosman through her son, then he kills her.'

It didn't sound any more convincing than when he'd run it past Joe earlier. In fact, second time round, it sounded even flimsier.

'And you can put Mr Untersander at either crime scene?'

'No.' Carlyle shook his head. 'He used a hitman.' Simpson began to say something else, but he held up a hand to cut her off. 'We have a series of phone calls and we have the hitman – at least, we have the top half of him.' Simpson's eyes rolled heavenwards as he explained about his trip down to the river. 'We are now waiting to see if we can get an ID.'

'And Untersander?'

'All lawyered up and sitting tight.'

For a moment they sat in unhappy silence.

'In reality,' Simpson said finally, 'you've got bugger all.'

'It's going to take some time,' Carlyle admitted. 'But, then again, look at the Snowdon case. There are times when you have to be patient.'

'Speaking of Snowdon, Simon Lovell is due to be released any time now. Have you spoken to Rosanna's parents yet?'

'Next on the list. I assumed you'd want the update on Mosman first.'

'Good news would have been better, John.'

The inspector spread his arms wide. 'It is what it is.'

'Okay, okay.' Closing her eyes, Simpson began massaging her temples with her fingers.

'What we really need,' Carlyle said gently, 'is to track down some of these missing paintings.'

'Yes ... so here's what we'll do. You keep on with your enquiries and I will speak to Specialist Crime.'

'Good idea,' Carlyle nodded, pleased that she'd taken the bait.

'I'll get them to put the Arts and Antiques Unit on the case.'

Then if we continue to get nowhere, Carlyle thought happily, we can transition the investigation over to them. 'That,' he beamed, 'makes perfect sense.'

Standing in a corner of the packed State Dining Room, Edgar Carlton took a mouthful of Penfolds Yattarna Chardonnay as he watched Sir Gavin O'Dowd, less than fifteen feet away, holding court before an attentive group of government ministers.

'Look at him,' he muttered unhappily. 'The way he carries on, you'd think *he* was the Prime Minister.'

Might be better if he was, Christian Holyrod thought. Stopping a passing waiter, the Mayor held out his glass for a refill. 'You're not jealous of a soon-to-be-retired bureaucrat, are you? This time next week he'll be standing knee-deep in some bog studying blue tits or whatever.'

'I'm not jealous at all,' Edgar harrumphed.

'You just sound like it, then.' Chortling at his own joke, the Mayor swallowed a large mouthful of wine.

'That man's nickname may be GOD,' Edgar whined, 'but that doesn't mean he has to act like one.'

Holyrod put his free hand on his esteemed colleague's arm. 'Edgar,' he said, keeping his voice low despite the general hubbub, 'it's the man's farewell party.' He gestured around the throng. 'By this time tomorrow no one here will remember his bloody name, never mind his nickname.'

'I suppose not.'

'So, stop carrying on like a teenage girl.'

'I'm not.'

'Yes, you are,' said Holyrod, smiling through clenched teeth. 'You need to develop a sense of perspective.'

'This job is just *so* demanding,' Edgar complained. 'It never stops.'

Who'd have thought it? The Mayor suppressed a smile.

'You never get any time to yourself. I can't afford to get burnt out. I really need to chillax.'

'No,' said Holyrod firmly, 'that is one thing you *don't* need to do. There's more than enough of that going on around here as it is. Everyone already thinks that you are far too—' he was about to say 'lazy' but quickly corrected himself, '*easygoing*. You're the Prime Minister, after all. If you're not well on the way to a nervous breakdown, people will assume you can't be taking the job seriously enough.'

'These days, I can't even go down the Cock and Bottle for a

nice foaming pint of Spitfire Ale without a dozen snappers running around, trying to catch me out.'

'Well,' Holyrod grinned, 'if you hadn't abandoned your youngest child in the pub one Sunday morning, people might be a bit less interested in what you get up to at weekends.'

Edgar winced at the memory. Leaving a five year old in the boozer didn't get you any Parent of the Year Award. It was front-page news and Anastasia had been furious. If they had been living on a council estate, he would have already had a knock on the door from Social Services. 'It was an easy mistake to make,' he mumbled. 'I thought she was with her mother. Anyway, no damage was done.'

'Mm.'

'It could happen to anyone. People leave their kids in different places all the time – in supermarkets, DIY centres, lots of places.'

'Not when they've got six bodyguards in tow.' The Mayor knew that he shouldn't be winding Edgar up like this, but he simply couldn't resist.

'Bloody Close Protection Officers,' the PM wailed, 'they're totally useless. What would happen if my bloody life was actually in danger? Anyway, we sent the buggers packing and got a new lot in.'

'Oh, really?'

'Yes.' Edgar smiled malevolently. 'The others have been demoted to traffic duty in the Orkneys or something. Teach them a damn good lesson.' Suddenly energized, he waved an angry finger at the Mayor. 'No one loses one of my kids.'

'No.'

'Anyway, we can't allow any more of this nonsense. We need to get a grip.'

'Quite,' Holyrod nodded. 'By the way, did you see the poll in *The Times* this morning? You're trailing by twelve percentage points.'

'Of course I bloody saw it!' Edgar exclaimed. 'But it's just one bloody poll. We'll be fine. Twelve points is nothing at this stage.

However crap the voters think we are, they know the opposition is worse.'

'It's a point of view, I suppose,'

'Stop being so negative, Christian.'

'Just remember, the result is by no means in the bag,' the Mayor said slyly. 'If it was, I would have taken your job by now.'

'Good to know that we're all in it together.'

'Just so you're aware.'

Finishing his drink, Edgar looked around for somewhere to deposit the empty glass. 'From what I hear, London's more than enough for you to handle already. You can't even run the bloody police properly.'

'At least,' Holyrod shot back, 'my Head of Security isn't a suspected killer on the run.'

'*Ex*-Head of Security,' Edgar corrected him. 'And he wouldn't still be at large if your people were capable of catching him.'

'That's all in hand.'

'All in hand?' Edgar let out a shrill laugh. 'So where is he, then? And it's not just that, is it? I hear that Operation Redhead itself is on the brink of collapse.'

Holyrod gave a shrug. 'It appears that Chief Inspector Meyer couldn't keep it in his trousers. In true provincial style, his wife caught him in flagrante in a Travelodge with one of his colleagues, a detective inspector called Valette. She didn't take it at all well apparently; proceeded to beat up poor old Meyer quite badly.'

'The wife, you mean?'

'Yes,' Holyrod tittered. 'Seems like she's into kickboxing, or something like that. As far as I know, he's still in hospital.'

'Oh dear.'

'The girlfriend wanted to have the wife charged with GBH, but was persuaded that would not be a good idea.'

'Good God, no. The media would have a field day. On top of everything else, it would make the police look like complete idiots.'

'Quite. Anyway, it seems as if that particular own goal has been avoided.'

'And Meyer?'

'As soon as he's well enough to sign a letter of resignation, he will be standing down – for personal reasons.'

'Bloody hell!' Edgar shook his head. 'And to think he was my appointment. I really have been so badly advised on these things.'

'Never mind,' said Holyrod. He gave the PM a consoling pat on the shoulder. 'You can hardly be blamed for the man's irresponsible libido.'

'No, I suppose not.' Edgar handed a passing waiter his empty glass, declining a fresh one as he did so.

'And look on the bright side. By the time we get a replacement, and the whole inquiry thing gets going again, it will be after the General Election.'

Edgar's expression lightened up somewhat. 'Good point.'

'Speaking of libidos,' Holyrod grinned, 'how is the lovely Yulissa?'

Edgar's face darkened again. 'She's becoming a bit of a pain in the arse, to be honest. The latest thing is that she wants a seat in the House of Lords.'

Sipping his wine, Holyrod stared thoughtfully at his shoes. 'Well, she'd certainly liven the place up a bit. And it would be very handy if you fancied a quick bunk-up in the Derby Room.'

'Ha, ha,' was the hollow response. Edgar glanced at his watch. 'Enough of this chatter. I need to go and say a few carefully crafted words about GOD's impending departure.'

THIRTY-NINE

By the time he looked up it was too late. 'Ah, there you are,' said the familiar voice. 'I was wondering when you would get here.'

Oh fuck.

'John bloody Carlyle – God's gift to the Metropolitan Police Service. Better late than never, I suppose. Come on in.'

Taking a step into the Snowdons' living room, the inspector took a moment to compose himself. Sitting on the sofa, Veronica Snowdon looked even more pale and sickly now than he remembered. Barely acknowledging his arrival, her eyes remained firmly fixed on her other visitor. Resting his ample arse against the dining table, Trevor Miller stood, arms folded, with a smug grin on his face. In his right hand he held a Glock 19, silencer affixed to the short barrel, which was pointing towards the ceiling in a rather dissolute James Bond-type pose. He was wearing jeans and a brown Kappa hoodie; the overall effect was that of a monster five year old.

A monster five year old brandishing a loaded weapon.

So much for me being the bearer of good news, Carlyle thought glumly.

'Sit,' Miller commanded.

After a moment's pause, Carlyle did as he was told, parking himself next to Lady Snowdon. By the sideboard, beneath Osmund Caine's *Bathing Beach*, Sir Michael hovered next to the Bladnoch single malt. Ever the gracious host, the old man gestured towards the bottle. 'Would you like a drink, Inspector?'

313

Despite his situation, Carlyle smiled. 'Under the circumstances, why not?'

Miller frowned. 'On duty? I think not.'

'As you wish,' the inspector sighed. His desire for a drink was acute but not acute enough to risk getting shot. 'Why are you here, anyway?'

'I thought that would be obvious,' Miller snorted.

'Trevor,' Carlyle said gently, 'nothing you do is ever obvious – at least not to normal people.'

There was a flash of rage in Miller's face. His arms dropped to his sides and it looked like he was going to spring forward and pistol-whip the insolent cop. But the moment passed and he restricted himself to a threatening movement with the gun. 'I've been keeping a close eye on you, and now it's time to get this thing sorted.'

'Good idea.' Carlyle gestured to Veronica and Sir Michael. 'So, when were you going to tell the Snowdons here that you murdered their daughter?' To his right there was a whimper and for a second he was worried that Veronica Snowdon had collapsed. Then he felt her fingernails dig into his flesh, as she grabbed hold of his hand and held on for dear life.

Sir Michael took a half-step forward until a wave of the Glock warned him to come no further. 'Is this true?'

It wasn't clear who the question was directed at, but Carlyle decided to jump in. 'Rosanna was investigating a case for her TV show: the murder of a private detective called Anton Fox. Fox worked for Trevor here, but when he started looking into police corruption someone stuck an axe in his head.' He looked up at Miller. 'Was that you, too?'

'Anton was a complete berk,' Miller grunted. 'He never knew when to leave well alone. Neither did the girl, for that matter.'

That doesn't sound like the Rosanna I knew, Carlyle thought. With the best will in the world, the girl had never been much of an investigative journalist. But now wasn't really the time or the place to debate the point.

'You bastard!' Sir Michael shouted. Rushing at Miller, he was stopped in his tracks by a meaty fist which sent him to the floor, blood oozing from a gash above his right eyebrow.

'Michael!' Dropping Carlyle's hand, Veronica Snowdon jumped up from the sofa and went to comfort her groaning husband.

Staying seated, Carlyle glared at Miller, who had retreated to the window, his Glock now pointing directly at the inspector's head.

Miller ran his tongue across chapped lips. 'He's got a bit of bottle, for an old fella.' His trigger finger was visibly shaking and the inspector sincerely hoped that the safety catch was still on. 'Unlike *some* people here.' He gestured at his ex-colleague with the gun. 'You never did have any bottle, did you?'

He's totally and utterly round the bend. Carlyle knew that he would have to try and rush the crazy bastard. But what were his chances of doing any better than the old man?

Miller read his thoughts. 'Want to give it a go?'

The inspector said nothing.

'Up you get, dear.' Veronica Snowdon helped her husband from the carpet. The bleeding seemed to have stopped, but Sir Michael still wore the glazed expression of someone who didn't really know where he was. Shuffling sideways, the inspector made room for the two of them on the sofa.

'Stay where you are,' Miller barked.

Carlyle held up a hand. 'Relax, Trevor. I'm not going anywhere.' Out of the corner of his eye, he registered a flicker of movement in the hallway. Miller caught it too. Keeping the pistol trained on the inspector, he edged his way across the room. Reaching the doorway, he stuck his head tentatively into the hallway. It's now or never, Carlyle thought, moving to the edge of his seat. He tried to catch Sir Michael's eye, but the old man was still in a daze. The gap between himself and Miller was about eight feet, so he'd just have to hurl himself forward and hope for the best.

Stop thinking about it, you stupid bastard, and just do it!

Rocking forward, he had just transferred his weight to the balls of his feet when a shabby-looking grey cat sauntered into the room.

'Silvio,' Veronica gasped, 'what are you doing here?' The cat prowled along in front of the sofa, eyeing the three of them suspiciously.

'Silvio?' Carlyle enquired, happy enough for any distraction which gave him a little more time to play with.

'Next door's cat,' Veronica Snowdon explained, as if this was a normal conversation. 'He's a bit of a ladies' man but they don't have the heart to give him the snip.'

'Stupid bloody animal,' Miller huffed. Taking a step forward, he aimed a kick at Silvio's ribs, but the cat was too quick for him and darted under the table.

'Still quite nimble,' Veronica mused, 'for his age.'

Carlyle grinned at Miller. 'Maybe you should shoot it.'

'Fuck you.'

'No, fuck *you*.'

There was an audible click. 'What the—' Miller froze as he felt some cold steel nuzzle the back of his neck.

'That was me releasing the safety on my Browning.' Gideon Spanner, Dominic Silver's lieutenant, stepped out from behind his target to get a better view of the trio lined up on the sofa.

Where the hell did you come from? Carlyle wondered. Not that I bloody care! With his heart thumping in his chest, he had to resist the urge to let out a hysterical laugh.

'I don't want to blow your head off,' Gideon murmured quietly in Miller's ear, 'because apart from anything else, it would make a terrible mess, and I think you've caused these good people more than enough trouble for one night, don't you?'

Miller's mouth opened slightly but no sound came out.

'So drop the gun, please,' Gideon instructed, 'and that's one less problem for us to worry about.'

Miller did as instructed and the Glock hit the carpet with the gentlest of thuds. Intrigued, Silvio appeared from under the table to give it a sniff, before nonchalantly wandering back into the hall.

'Good. Now kick it towards the inspector over there.' Again, Miller obliged, carefully side-footing the pistol towards the sofa.

Carlyle, whose bemusement had rapidly turned to relief, made no effort to pick it up. He glanced at the Snowdons, who seemed to be taking it all in their stride.

'Who are you?' Miller demanded. It was less a question, more of a wail.

'Never you mind,' said Gideon sharply, giving him a prod on the back of the neck with the gun. 'On your knees, hands behind your head.' As Miller slowly lowered his bulky frame, Gideon glanced at the inspector. 'Cuffs?'

Carlyle made a face. 'Sorry, no.' He had left them in the station – or maybe at home. A look of weary resignation passed over Gideon's face.

'There's some washing-line cord in the kitchen, under the sink,' Veronica Snowdon volunteered cheerily. 'I'll go and get it.' She got to her feet. 'And I'll need to make sure that Silvio hasn't done his business on the floor again.'

'Get me some paracetamol while you're at it, please,' Sir Michael mumbled.

'Yes, dear.' As she headed for the door, Carlyle was mildly surprised that she didn't offer to make everyone a cup of tea, on top of everything else. Stepping round both Miller and Spanner, she disappeared towards the rear of the house. Belatedly getting to his feet, the inspector gave Gideon a nod.

'Thanks for your help on this.'

'No problem.' Gideon sounded detached bordering on uninterested.

'Dom asked you to keep an eye on me?'

The merest of nods. 'I've been on it for the last couple of days.'

'I didn't realize.'

Gideon shot him a look that said *That was the idea*. After a few moments, Veronica Snowdon returned from the kitchen and handed Gideon a length of green and white plastic cable. Sticking the Browning into the belt of his jeans, Gideon pulled Miller's hands behind his back and expertly tied them together.

'Nice to see that the old Army training still comes in handy,' Carlyle observed.

Retrieving his Browning, Gideon said nothing.

'Here you are, Michael.' Moving over to the sofa, Veronica handed her husband a couple of tablets and a glass of water.

'Thank you,' Sir Michael grunted, dropping the tablets into his mouth and emptying the contents of the glass. 'So,' he said, turning to Carlyle, 'explain to me, just who is this man?'

Where to begin? The inspector gestured towards the Bladnoch. 'Mind if I have a drink first?'

'Of course, Inspector,' Veronica trilled. 'How remiss of us. Please, help yourself.'

'Thank you.' He glanced at Gideon, who shook his head.

'I'll have one,' Miller croaked, but Carlyle ignored him. Reaching for the bottle, he realized that his hand was shaking, badly. Pouring himself an extremely large measure, he drank deeply. Then, after refilling the glass almost to the brim, he turned to face the Snowdons and explained to them how Trevor Miller had killed their daughter.

Gideon patiently waited for him to finish before speaking up himself. 'I need to leave,' he said quietly.

Carlyle took another gulp of whisky. 'Yes.'

'And you need to get your story right.'

'Of course.'

Gideon eyed him doubtfully. 'Meaning I was never here.'

'No.' Carlyle stared at his almost empty glass. The Bladnoch was working a treat; his hands had almost stopped shaking and a warm glow had enveloped his insides. Under the circumstances, he had no embarrassment about reaching for the bottle for another refill.

'You're as bent as I am,' Miller scoffed. 'I'll tell them what really happened.'

318

'You'll tell them nothing.'

Turning, Carlyle was surprised to see that Veronica Snowdon had picked up the Glock and was now pointing it at Miller's chest. He shot Gideon a quizzical glance and both of them took a step away from the kneeling man.

Veronica's eyes narrowed. With the gun in her hand, she suddenly looked thirty years younger. 'Did you really kill my daughter?'

A nasty grin spread across Miller's sweaty face. 'Shit happens, love.'

'You complete and utter bastard!' she screamed, squeezing the trigger.

FORTY

Slowly letting out a breath, Carlyle contemplated the tableau in front of him. If anything, the look on Trevor Miller's face was one of disappointment. Gideon Spanner remained inscrutable. Still holding the gun at arm's length, Veronica Snowdon sobbed gently, her head bowed.

Struggling to his feet, Sir Michael put a comforting arm around his wife's shoulders. 'Come on, darling,' he whispered, carefully taking the gun from her trembling hand. 'This is not the way to do things. You can't just shoot a man standing in your living room, like that. Even if, well . . .' His voice trailed away as he composed himself. 'We've got what we wanted. Now that he's finally been caught, we have to let the courts do their job.' Planting a tender kiss on the crown of her head, he lowered her gently on to the sofa, before turning to Carlyle. 'We can manage to overlook that little moment, Inspector, don't you think?'

If it was me, I'd have just shot the bastard. Keeping his thoughts to himself, Carlyle nodded.

'Good,' the old man smiled. 'Thank you. Now, I think I need that drink. A large one, too.'

'Yes, sir.' Carlyle took another glass and half-filled it with whisky. 'Good job the safety was still on.'

'Indeed,' Sir Michael agreed. 'The Glock is an outstanding weapon, altogether a fantastic piece of craftsmanship. And it has multiple independent safety mechanisms in order to prevent accidental discharge.'

Carlyle turned back to face his host, holding a glass in each hand.

'I was in the Household Cavalry before I joined the Civil Service,' Sir Michael explained. 'And then, after that, I was in the Territorial Army for more than twenty years. As a result, I know my weaponry quite well.'

'Mm.'

'You have to pull the trigger properly or it won't fire.' The old man slowly brought the barrel of the Glock up to Trevor Miller's chest. 'Like this, in fact.' Squeezing off three rounds, he watched impassively as Miller keeled forward.

For a moment, there was silence. No one looked at each other as they all contemplated the body at their feet. Carlyle fleetingly wondered if he should check Miller for a pulse, but he knew it would be pointless. The man was dead. Taking another mouthful of whisky, his thoughts turned to what would happen next. Despite his alcohol intake, he felt reasonably alert; as long as he kept his account of Miller's death simple and broadly accurate, Forensics would join the dots and there should be no problem with Commander Simpson, or with the Met's internal investigators.

'As they say in America,' Sir Michael said airily, 'you have to keep your Glock cocked. Otherwise you won't be able to shoot it.' Sidestepping the advancing puddle of blood spreading across the carpet, he carefully placed the pistol on the dining-room table before accepting his drink from the inspector.

Gideon gestured towards the body. 'And what are you going to say about what happened here?'

'In situations like these, I find that it's always easiest to stick to the truth.' Sir Michael took a large mouthful of whisky and gave an appreciative sigh. 'At least some of the truth.' From the sofa, Veronica eyed him with wifely pride.

In situations like these? Carlyle wondered just what exactly the old boy had got up to during his cavalry days.

The old man gestured at Miller with his glass. 'He's not the first man I've killed, you know. Anyway, I want people to know that *I* killed that bastard. I'm not ashamed of it, not in the slightest.'

'Okay.' Carlyle placed his now empty glass back on the sideboard. 'We'll go with the truth, then.'

'Good.'

'Just not the whole truth.' The inspector gestured towards the kitchen. 'Is there a back way out of here?'

'So long as you don't mind jumping a few fences,' Sir Michael told him.

Gideon nodded. 'No problem.' Without another word, he turned and started off down the hallway.

'I'll wait five minutes, then call it in,' Carlyle shouted after him. Turning to Veronica, he smiled. 'If you don't mind, I'll just go and put the kettle on. It's going to be a long night and I think we will all need some strong coffee.'

Standing under a sickly-looking tree, Commander Carole Simpson sucked down a latte as she watched a couple of uniforms struggle to control the rapidly growing press pack behind the police tape twenty yards along the road. 'What am I going to tell that lot?' she asked, looking round for somewhere to toss her empty cup.

'Just tell them Miller was a total bastard who got what he deserved.'

'Helpful as always, John.' Unable to dispose of the cup satisfactorily, she stopped a passing WPC. 'Get rid of this for me, will you, please?'

'Yes, ma'am,' the WPC nodded, grabbing the cup and heading on towards the tape.

Carlyle watched in amusement as, little more than three yards further down the road, the WPC simply tossed the cup into the gutter. 'Kids today,' he laughed. 'I thought they were supposed to be into saving the environment.'

Simpson shook her head in disgust.

'Why don't you just tell them that a man in his fifties has been shot and killed,' Carlyle suggested, trying to bring things back to the matter in hand, 'and that the investigation is ongoing.'

'That's a bit bland, don't you think?'

'It's all they'll be expecting. Anyway, they probably already know more about what's going on than you do.'

'I suppose so,' said Simpson gloomily.

'Cheer up.' The adrenalin from the stand-off with Miller was still running round Carlyle's system. Mixed with the euphoria of Miller's execution, the whisky, and two cups of Veronica Snowdon's excellent Java Santos blend, it was enough to make him feel quite giddy.

'Christ!' Simpson's face fell even further. 'John Carlyle is telling me to cheer up. Things must be bad.'

'This is going to clear up a lot of mess.'

'Oh?'

'For a start,' Carlyle explained, 'I expect that they'll find that Miller's Glock was used to kill Simon Shelbourne. We already know that he killed both Hall and Snowdon. And he was also involved in the deaths of both Duncan Brown and Anton Fox. That's a lot of cases to clear off anyone's plate.'

'I suppose so.' But Simpson seemed strangely unenthusiastic.

'All in all, this is a major result.'

'How do you feel yourself?'

'Me? I'm buzzing.'

'You must be pleased, having finally got your man.'

Carlyle looked back towards the Snowdons' building and said savagely. 'Fuck him, he got what he deserved. Shame it took so long.'

'I spoke to Fulham, by the way. They're not happy about developments regarding Rosanna Snowdon. In fact, they're bloody furious.'

'Tough shit,' Carlyle growled. 'They shouldn't have been so keen to put that poor mug Simon Lovell in the frame.'

'We've all been there,' Simpson reminded him.

'Speak for yourself.' Along the road, a TV crew had now arrived, their lights illuminating the entire street. Carlyle jerked a thumb towards the growing throng. 'Your audience awaits.'

'What about Charlie Ross?' Simpson asked, clearly reluctant to move.

'Good question. I'm sure our friend Charlie is in it up to his neck. When it comes to Wickford Associates, he would be the brains of the operation. Although when it comes to working with Trevor Miller – RIP – an amoeba could be the brains behind the operation.' Carlyle stopped to chuckle at his own joke. 'Charlie Ross will no doubt have covered his tracks well. And even if we ever managed to get him into court, he would play the frail-old-man card, even though he's clearly as fit as a butcher's dog.'

'What about Sir Michael Snowdon? Won't he do basically the same thing? Claim some kind of diminished responsibility?'

'Maybe,' Carlyle said, 'maybe not.' He thought about it for a moment or two. 'But even if he did, why not?'

'Isn't that double standards?'

Carlyle grinned. 'I'm a pragmatist. The old bugger deserves a medal for what he did. He brought down a cop killer and saved the public a fortune in the process.'

Simpson shot him a sideways glance. 'And he did it all on his own, did he?'

'I did my bit,' said Carlyle defensively, 'as far as I could.'

'But you left it to a pensioner to rush an armed killer, grab his gun and shoot him dead?' The mixture of amusement and cynicism in her voice was unmistakable.

'Stranger things have happened.' Carlyle looked his boss straight in the eye. 'I didn't shoot Trevor Miller. But I would tell you if I had.'

'Okay,' the Commander nodded. 'I suppose I should just be grateful that Miller didn't end up shooting *himself* three times.'

'Are you taking the piss?' A look of mock consternation flitted across the inspector's face. 'After the traumatic experience I've just had? Maybe I should call my Rep. After all, shouldn't I be getting counselling or something?'

A broad grin spread across Simpson's face. 'You want counselling?'

'No, no,' said Carlyle quickly, 'I'm in a happy place. I've got all the closure I need.'

'Good for you.'

'Hopefully the Snowdons feel a bit better too.'

'Yes.' Simpson pointed along the road towards the media scrum. 'Whatever the law might think, Sir Michael will become a hero once the media get hold of him.'

An idea of how to gain further credit with Bernard Gilmore suddenly popped into Carlyle's head, and he chuckled. 'Think of how Bernie will write it up.'

'I'd rather not,' said Simpson tartly. 'And I don't want you leaking anything about this to him either.'

Carlyle looked down at his shoes. 'Not my style.'

'I'm not aware that you have a style,' Simpson quipped, pulling out a BlackBerry from her jacket pocket and hitting a few keys. 'And I don't suppose you know anything about this?' She handed him the machine. On its screen was a newspaper story headlined *TOP COP'S THIRTY GRAND FREEBIE.*

'News to me,' Carlyle mumbled, making a show of slowly scrolling down through the piece to read it carefully. 'That seems a lot of money for a couple of days in a health farm.'

'So you didn't give Bernie this information?'

Carlyle looked her in the eye as he handed back the smartphone. 'Nope.'

'Glad to hear it.'

'It would seem a bit of a risky thing for anyone to do, under the circumstances,' Carlyle mused. 'And anyway, being a whistleblower is a mug's game.'

Putting the BlackBerry away, Simpson started heading to-wards the police tape and the press waiting beyond it. 'Whoever the source was, let's hope that such irresponsible behaviour doesn't come back to haunt him.'

'Or her,' Carlyle added hastily.

Shaking her head, the Commander said nothing further as she stalked away.

While Carlyle watched his boss's press conference from a safe distance, Joe Szyszkowski appeared at his shoulder.

'I thought she didn't like dealing with the media any more; not since her old man – well, you know.'

'Not since her old man got done for massive fraud, you mean?'

'Quite.'

'You're right, she doesn't. But someone's got to feed the beast.'

'I suppose so. I hear you've been having a busy day?'

'Yes, I have. Thank you for asking,' Carlyle said sarcastically. 'By the way, where the hell have you been?'

'Monty Laws wrapped his car round a lamp-post near Hampstead Heath at six o'clock this morning,' Joe replied evenly, clearly not rising to the bait. 'He had Hannah Gillespie's ATM card in his pocket.'

Carlyle raised his eyes to the heavens. 'Jesus, it really is my lucky day.'

'Looks like it,' Joe agreed. 'By the time I got up to the Rosslyn Hill station, he'd already confessed to killing her.'

The inspector suddenly felt his energy levels plummet as he was gripped by a grim despair. 'And why did he do it?'

'No particular reason.'

'Great.' Sticking his hands in his pockets, Carlyle began walking along the road, heading away from the media scrum.

'You off, then?' Joe shouted after him. 'Seeing as I just got here?'

'That's right,' Carlyle replied, not bothering to look back. 'It's time to go home.'

* * *

'You fucking idiot!' Charlie Ross sipped at his tumbler of Scapa Orkney single malt as he watched Trevor Miller's face on the flickering TV screen. On the floor nearby was scattered a selection of travel brochures. It was time to take a trip. His bag was already packed. He had known for some time that this day would come, and he was ready for it. Reaching forward, he picked up the nearest brochure – Mexico. The strains of Frank Sinatra singing 'Come Fly With Me' briefly drifted through his head. As Frank ebbed away, Charlie frowned. Wasn't there some kind of civil war going on over there right now? The army fighting against the drug cartels; corpses hanging from motorway bridges, headless bodies dropped down wells? Things that made his adventures look like nothing more than silly games played by five year olds.

Maybe he should check out one of the alternative brochures?

Fuck it, it wasn't such a big deal. Mexico would do well enough.

'Ain't you gonna swallow?'

Ignoring her boyfriend, Melanie Henderson spat the majority of his juices into her coffee mug before wiping her chin on his jeans.

'Hey!' Ricky Haswell pushed her off and began folding himself away.

'Where's your mum anyway?'

'Out.'

'Urgh.' She pointed to the TV. On the screen, a body was being wheeled into an ambulance.

'Shooting . . . happened up the road.' Ricky gave her a sly glance. 'You gonna stay the night?'

'Nah, my mum would kill me,' Melanie said. 'After what happened to Hannah, she's really paranoid.'

'For someone who always thought she was so smart, that girl was dumb, dumb, dumb,' Ricky commented.

'Bloody police,' Melanie extended one leg and wiggled her toes at the TV. 'When it came to it, they weren't much use, were they?'

'John!' A knee in the small of his back forced Carlyle to open his eyes.'That's your bloody phone!'

'Okay, okay,' he said groggily, swinging his feet on to the carpet. The radio alarm on the bedside table said 3:06. He didn't even recognize the noise coming from his phone; obviously Alice had changed the damn ringtone again.

'Switch it off, for God's sake.'

'Go back to sleep,' he snapped. Picking his jeans from the floor, he pulled the mobile from a back pocket and stumbled out into the hallway. 'Yeah?'

'Are you asleep?' By comparison to his boss, Joe Szyszkowski sounded positively wide awake.

'Not any more, you fucking muppet. What do you want?'

'I'm at the station.'

'Good for you.' Reaching the living room, Carlyle fell straight on to the sofa, trying to ignore the aching tiredness that permeated his body. 'Why?'

'They've brought in Sonia Claesens,' Joe said cheerily. 'She beat up her boyfriend, apparently. The call came in a couple of hours ago. He's in A and E at St Thomas's; she's in a cell downstairs.'

'Who did you say?' Carlyle plumped up a cushion and placed it carefully behind his head.

'Sonia Claesens – the Managing Director of the Zenger Corporation,' Joe explained. 'She was Simon Shelbourne's boss, and also a mate of Edgar Carlton.'

'Good for her.'

'And she knew Trevor Miller.'

'Ah.' Now that Miller's dead, I couldn't really give a monkey's, Carlyle reflected. Closing his eyes, he swung his legs up on to the sofa. It was really quite comfortable here.

'Boss?'

'It's the middle of the fucking night,' he groaned, 'so why are you telling me all this?'

'She's screaming blue murder, and there's already press gathering outside. The powers-that-be want someone senior down here right away.'

'Well, go and find someone senior then.'

'They want *you* down here right away,' Joe persisted.

'Okay, okay,' Carlyle yawned. 'Fucking hell . . .'

'Thanks, boss.'

'I'll be there as quick as I can.' He switched off the phone and let the handset fall to the floor, adding to himself: 'After I've had a two-minute kip.'

'Where the hell have you been?' It was now almost eight o'clock and Joe's previous cheeriness was long gone.

Feeling more than a little sheepish, Carlyle held up a hand by way of apology. 'Sorry, sorry.'

'I left you loads of messages.'

'The battery died,' the inspector lied.

'It's now been five hours. I was going to call your home number.'

Carlyle gave him a surprised look. 'Just as well you didn't. Helen would have killed you – immediately after having killed me.'

'That's what I assumed.'

'Anyway, I fell asleep again. End of. Sorry.'

Grudgingly accepting his boss's apology, Joe gestured towards the police station entrance where a dozen or so reporters were milling about on the steps. 'They've been a pain in the arse all night.'

'Get the uniforms to handle them,' Carlyle said brusquely.

'It's been all over the TV news.'

'Why? She's hardly a fucking celebrity, is she?'

'You know what it's like,' Joe shrugged. 'The media loves the media.'

'I suppose.'

'And it's made the later editions of the papers.' Joe handed the inspector a copy of the *Daily Witness*, sister paper to the Sunday edition. 'Top of page four.'

Carlyle opened the tabloid and found himself staring at a picture of Edgar Carlton and Sonia Claesens deep in discussion at some charity reception. Briefly scanning the article, he burst out laughing. 'Fuck me, that was quick.'

'It's a dog-eat-dog world,' the sergeant shrugged. 'Do you want to go in and see her?'

'Not really.'

Joe shot him a look that indicated it wasn't really a question.

'Okay, in a minute. But first I need some caffeine.'

A double espresso had improved his mood somewhat by the time Sonia Claesens was brought into interview room seven. Dressed in black jeans and a pearl cashmere sweater over a grey T-shirt, she looked tired but composed.

'Why am I still here?' she demanded.

'There are various charges—' Carlyle began.

Claesens spoke over him. 'I have meetings.'

Good for you, Carlyle thought. 'Maybe when your lawyer gets here—'

Once again, she cut him off. 'The useless sod has switched his mobile off. So, God knows when he'll turn up.'

'In that case,' Carlyle smiled, 'I'm afraid that you'll have to wait.'

'That's impossible!' Irritated by this stupid policeman's refusal to comply with her demands, Claesens angrily slapped the palm of one hand on the table. 'I've got too many things to do.'

The inspector's grin widened.

Claesens's face darkened, and for a moment he thought she might jump up and hit him. 'What's so funny?'

Carlyle tossed Joe's copy of the *Daily Witness* on to the table. 'You're in your own newspaper today.'

'Not an uncommon occurrence,' she snapped, grabbing the tabloid and tearing it open.

'Top of page four.' Carlyle eyed her maliciously. 'Nice picture. The story says you've been sacked by the Zenger Corporation.'

'What?' Claesens shrieked. 'You've got to be fucking kidding!'

'It's there in black and white,' Carlyle deadpanned, 'so I guess that it must be true. After all, newspapers don't lie, do they?' Pushing back his chair, he got to his feet and turned towards the door.

Finding the article in question, Claesens began scanning the text with a bony finger. 'Fuck, fuck, fuck!'

'Looks like they've cut you loose.'

'The bastards!'

'I guess you just became too much of a liability for them,' Carlyle mused, happy to turn the knife while he had the chance.

Rereading the article, Claesens muttered something under her breath.

'Look on the bright side,' the inspector beamed. 'At least that frees up your day to help us here with our enquiries.'

'Fuck you!' she screamed, jumping to her feet and hurling the newspaper in the general direction of his head.

Laughing, Carlyle walked out of the room and headed down the corridor.

FORTY-ONE

Trying not to sound too cheery in front of the nurse, Carlyle pointed at the window. 'What happened?'

Yawning, the young man scratched at the stubble on his chin before folding his arms. 'He suffered a stroke. Quite a serious one too. It looks like he was lying on his living-room floor all night. No one found him until the cleaner came in the next morning. You never really know with these things, but I would expect a lot of the damage will be irreversible.'

Maybe there is a God, after all. Carlyle peered through the glass at Charlie Ross lying comatose in the hospital bed, tubes everywhere. It looked like there was enough technology to run a space shuttle being deployed to keep the old bastard alive. 'Can I talk to him?'

The nurse shook his head. 'Family only.' Exhausted, he hopped from foot to foot, desperate to get off shift.

Shit, Carlyle thought, I shouldn't have shown this little jobsworth my bloody warrant card. 'I understand.'

'Sorry,' the nurse mumbled unconvincingly.

'To be honest though, I'm the nearest thing he has to family,' he pleaded, hoping that he looked suitably concerned about the sick man. 'We worked together on the Force for more than twenty years. He taught me a hell of a lot.'

'Mm.'

Carlyle gestured towards the private room. 'He saved my life once.' It was a blatant lie, but worth a go. When the nurse showed a flicker of interest, he added: 'Took out a guy who was just about to brain me with an axe.'

The nurse's eyes grew wide. 'Really?'

'Yeah,' Carlyle nodded, getting into it now. 'It was the bravest thing I've ever seen on The Job.'

'Wow.'

'Obviously, it was a long time ago now.'

'Obviously.'

'But still . . .'

'Yes.' The nurse glanced up and down the empty corridor. Unfolding his arms, he held up a finger. 'One minute. Just talk gently to him, and see if you can get a response.'

'Thank you.'

The nurse started off down the hallway. 'I'm going to get a coffee. Once I get back, you'll have to go.'

'Understood,' Carlyle said. 'Thank you.'

Stepping inside the room, he pulled up a chair and sat down, leaning forward until his face was barely eight inches from the ex-sergeant's head.

'Charlie . . .'

The old man's eyes slowly opened. As he focused on Carlyle's grinning mug, a palpable look of concern spread across his crumpled features.

Conscious of the CCTV camera high on the wall, focused on the bed, Carlyle kept a fixed smile. 'Don't worry,' he said quietly, 'I'm not going to put a pillow over your face – tempting though that may be.'

A bony hand appeared from under the covers. Carlyle reached out and grabbed it in his own before it could reach for the panic button. 'Relax, I'm not going to do you any harm. Unlike your boy, Trevor, you're not about to go down fighting.'

Ross eyed him anxiously.

'No,' Carlyle continued, 'I don't have to do a thing. You're a fucking vegetable now, and that's never going to change.' He gestured around the room. 'Even if you get out of here, the best you can hope for is some kind of hospice: a modern bedlam where they make you sit in your own shit while you're singing along to Cliff Richard records with all the other nutters.'

Charlie Ross let out the merest whimper. Maybe Cliff wasn't his thing.

'You know how we treat old people in this country. We fucking hate them. You become invisible, your human rights go straight out the window; you won't get washed, you won't get fed, you won't get your colostomy bag changed. Some bastard "carer" will steal your money and any possessions you have left, and give you a good slap if you complain.' The inspector let out a breath. 'In a lot of ways, I think Trevor got the better deal.'

The nurse reappeared outside, signalling through the window that it was time to go. Carlyle got to his feet. 'Good luck, Charlie,' he whispered, patting the old man on the head like he was a dog. 'I look forward to reading your obituary in the *Police Review* before too long.' Smiling broadly, he left the room, strolling past the bemused nurse without uttering another word.

As he returned to the station, there was a buzz of excitement on the third floor that made the inspector worry that some disaster was unfolding: maybe some bastard had just set off a bomb in the centre of the city, or the Mayor had been pelted with eggs by anarchists again.

'It's the Commissioner,' explained Joe Szyszkowski, after catching his eye. 'He resigned ten minutes ago.'

'Oh,' said Carlyle, relaxing again as he flopped into his chair.

'That story about his free thirty-grand visit to a health farm was what did for him.'

'Serves him right,' Carlyle said airily. 'People like that think they're entitled to everything they can grab.' As if on cue, his mobile started ringing. Pulling it from his pocket, he checked the number on the screen, laughing as he hit receive.

'The man himself.'

'Have you seen the news?'

'Yeah. Are you ringing me up so that I can congratulate you?'

'No, no,' Bernie Gilmore chuckled, 'I was just ringing up to say thank you.'

'For what?' Carlyle said, turning away from Joe and lowering his voice. 'I don't know where you get your stuff from and, more to the point, I don't want to know.'

'Sure, sure. Anyway, thanks for the tip. Things are really cooking at the moment; my agent is negotiating a deal for a book on this whole Trevor Miller stroke phone-hacking scandal, and there's talk of me presenting a new version of *London Crime*.'

'Be careful,' Carlyle said solemnly. 'Remember what happened to the last person to present that show.'

'Ah, yes, Rosanna Snowdon, RIP. What do you think about this rumour that she was one of Miller's victims?'

'No idea.'

'C'mon,' Bernie protested, 'it's me you're talking to.'

'You know that I never speak to the press,' Carlyle laughed, 'and I'm not going to start now.'

'Fair enough. I'll be in touch.'

'I'm sure you will,' the inspector replied, the smile fading from his face. But by then he was talking to himself because, moving on to his next source, his next story, his next *exclusive*, Bernie had already hung up. Tossing the handset on to the desk, Carlyle's thoughts turned to the various delights of the station canteen. Joe was hovering nearby, with a look of concern. 'We've got a problem,' he said.

Carlyle's heart sank.

'Gemma Millington.'

Suppressing a grin, the inspector thought back to Duncan Brown's déshabillée girlfriend in her pink wig. 'What about her?'

'That picture of her from the memory stick?' Making a show of trying to dredge a long-forgotten image from the depths of his memory bank, Carlyle nodded. 'Well, someone put it on the internet along with a few others. Apparently, it was viewed four hundred and seventeen thousand times before it got taken down.'

I'm not surprised, Carlyle thought.

'Her lawyer has been on the phone. She's going to sue.'

'Sue for what?'

'Dunno,' Joe shrugged. 'Breach of data-protection laws, maybe?'

The inspector stared at Joe. 'It wasn't you, was it?'

'No, no,' Joe said quickly. 'But I might have shown it to a few people.'

Listening to his stomach rumble, Carlyle told him, 'Well, it wasn't me.'

'What should we do?'

'No idea,' the inspector said honestly. 'Wait and see what happens, I suppose.'

'That's not much of a plan, is it?'

'Well,' said Carlyle with mock cheer, 'it's the only one we've got.'

FORTY-TWO

Striding forward, a stressed-looking Daniel Brabo was intercepted by a uniform before he could step through the door.

'Inspector!' His face was flushed and he looked like he'd been drinking.

'Not now,' Carlyle said sharply. 'You shouldn't be allowed in here.' He gestured to the uniform. 'Get him outside.'

'Who was that?' Simpson asked, as Brabo was unceremoniously hustled away.

'Dario Untersander's lawyer,' said Carlyle, as he carefully selected a shortbread finger from the plate on the art dealer's desk. Shortbread still wasn't his favourite but it would do; he could sense his sugar levels dropping and he needed something to eat before he turned irritable.

Or, rather, even more irritable.

'He doesn't look very happy.'

Carlyle nibbled at one corner of the biscuit and gave a nod of appreciation. *Not bad . . . for shortbread.* 'Neither does his client.'

Stifling a grin, the Commander gazed at the inert body of Dario Untersander, slumped in his chair with a bemused expression on his bloodied face.

'Ivor Mosman smashed in his skull with an antique silver candlestick,' Carlyle explained.

'How quaint.'

'I guess Dario shagging his wife was one thing, but having her and their son killed was quite another.'

337

'Mm. And where is Mr Mosman now?'

'They've taken him to the Savile Row station, along with the candlestick in question.'

'Very efficient of them.'

'It was all rather straightforward,' said Carlyle, ignoring her sarcasm. 'After offing Untersander, Mosman called 999 and waited patiently for the police to arrive. When they got here, he was enjoying a cup of coffee and a shortbread finger. He explained precisely what had happened, and they arrested him on the spot.'

'That was considerate of him,' Simpson mused.

'Yes,' Carlyle agreed. 'If only everyone who committed a violent crime could be as accommodating towards the forces of law and order, our lives would be a lot easier.'

'I trust that the judge will take such exemplary behaviour into account when it comes to his sentencing.'

'Who knows?' Carlyle popped the rest of the shortbread into his mouth, chewing happily.

Simpson checked her watch. 'I would be surprised if he hasn't signed his confession by now.'

Top man, the inspector thought.

'We still have to find the paintings though.'

'That's the Arts Unit's job,' Carlyle observed.

'Don't you want to see it through?'

'I *have* seen it through,' Carlyle said firmly. 'The paintings are incidental.'

'That's an interesting point of view for a policeman to take,' the Commander said archly.

'Isn't the stuff insured?'

'No idea.'

'Anyway,' Carlyle continued, 'from what I hear, it's all fairly second-rate stuff. There's nothing involved likely to make much of a dent in the national debt.'

'So now you're an art critic?'

'Isn't everyone?' Carlyle shrugged.

338

'I suppose,' Simpson moved on, 'it looks like you did call it correctly, broadly speaking.'

Carlyle gave a modest bow. 'It happens now and again.'

'It would have been much better though, if there had been rather less mess involved.' A patronizing smile skipped across her face and for a moment he caught a glimpse of the old, bitch-from-hell Commander Simpson. 'It's nice to actually *prevent* the odd crime, you know, rather than just wait for them to happen and then bang up the perpetrator.'

'Yes,' he said, not rising to the bait.

'We were never in control of this situation.'

'No.' To Carlyle, she sounded just like a football manager trying to find fault with his team after they had just won a game.

'And then this happens.' She fixed him with a grim stare. 'You know that I had to be called away from Maude Hall's funeral?'

'Sorry.'

'At least Joe Szyszkowski was there,' the Commander sniffed.

'We decided that one of us should go.' Carlyle didn't really want to discuss WPC Hall. 'What do you make of Sir Chester's resignation?' he asked, trying to change the subject.

'He was the author of his own misfortune,' she said simply. 'I can't say that I have much sympathy.'

'Any idea who'll get his job?'

She shook her head. 'No idea. These days I'm as out of the loop as you are – well, almost.'

'Not our problem, eh?'

'No.' Simpson gave him a thin smile. 'By the way, I spoke to Maude's father at the funeral.'

Carlyle thought back to his own conversation with Mervyn Hall on the street outside his daughter's flat, and he nodded.

'He asked me,' said Simpson, lowering her voice as if the dead man might be listening in to their conversation, 'to thank you.'

The inspector tried to look bemused. 'For what?'

'You tell me. Maybe he thought you had more of a hand in Trevor Miller's death than you are letting on.'

339

Carlyle stared at his shoes. 'And why would he think that?'

'You tell me,' Simpson repeated.

'I explained to you what happened.'

'The whole story?'

'The whole story.'

The Commander eyed him carefully, the look on her face a mixture of annoyance and affection. 'You never change, do you, John?' Without waiting for a reply, she walked away, slipping through the door, before heading for the blessed relief of the street outside.

FORTY-THREE

'*I know you've been meaning to thank me, but don't worry. It was my pleasure – Gideon's too for that matter. Anyway, I wondered if you might be able to do a little something for me. Not a big deal, but . . .*'

Cutting off Dominic Silver's voicemail in mid-flow, Carlyle dropped the phone back into his pocket. Whatever Dom wanted could wait for a little while. Right now, Carlyle just wanted to enjoy his breakfast.

Sitting by the window in the Smithfield café, on the south side of the meat market, he watched Alice munching on her *pain au chocolat*, her head stuck in a young adult novel. Few things in life gave him as much pleasure as watching his daughter read a book, even if it was a story about lovelorn teenage vampires.

Finishing his coffee, he checked out a pretty girl sitting at the next table, who was reading an Italian edition of Roberto Saviano's *Gomorra*. As she looked up, he let his gaze drift towards the flat-screen TV fixed high up on the back wall. Sky News was reporting that the Zenger Corporation had admitted responsibility for hacking Hannah Gillespie's phone. This was far worse than listening to the phone messages of a few witless celebrities; so the scandal was growing.

In the TV studio, a couple of talking heads were discussing speculation about the media company having to pay the Gillespie family compensation of several million pounds.

Blood money, Carlyle thought. It's like we're reverting back to the Middle Ages.

Shifting in his seat, he turned his back on the screen and looked through the window at the azure blue sky. Once he had dropped Alice off at school, he would head to the gym; afterwards, he might meet Helen for lunch if she wasn't too busy. Off the clock, he didn't want to be thinking about Hannah Gillespie – or Duncan Brown or Horatio Mosman or Rosanna Snowdon either. It would take time, however, for all the details to seep away from his brain, and for the small triumphs and the larger failures to be forgotten.

Alice glanced up from her book and gave him a concerned look. 'What's wrong?'

'Um . . . nothing.'

'You were scowling. Your face was all scrunched up. What were you thinking about?'

'Nothing important. Doesn't matter,' Carlyle smiled, gesturing to the crumbs around her mouth.

Picking up a paper napkin, Alice roughly wiped away the remains of her pastry. 'I've got a joke for you.'

His smile grew wider. 'Okay.'

'Where does Dracula keep his money?'

Carlyle made a show of thinking about the possible answer for a few moments, before saying, 'Dunno.'

'In a blood bank,' she cackled. 'Geddit? A *blood* bank.'

'That's terrible,' Carlyle groaned.

She shot him a look that said *Let's see if you can come up with anything better.* 'Your turn.'

The inspector thought about it for a moment. Jokes were not his strong point. Whenever he heard one he liked, he would try and store it away in his brain for future use, but they never seemed to stick. Right now, there was only one he could recall. 'What do you call an exploding monkey?'

'I told you that one myself,' Alice objected. 'It's rubbish.'

'I thought you liked it,' Carlyle protested.

Laughing, she shook her head. 'Rubbish.'

'C'mon,' Carlyle teased, waving his hands in the air, 'it's the best joke ever. What do you call an exploding monkey?'

'Dunno,' she said, humouring her father.
'A baboom!'
'Da-ad!'
'Ba-*boom*!'